MW01256166

A CROWN OF CRUEL LIES

LANA PECHERCZYK

Copyright © 2022 Lana Pecherczyk
All rights reserved.

A Crown of Cruel Lies
Ebook ASIN: B0BBZV3RST
Print ISBN: 978-1-922989-01-7

This is a work of fiction. Names, characters, businesses, places, events and incidents are either the products of the author's imagination or used in a fictitious manner. Any resemblance to actual persons, living or dead, or actual events is purely coincidental.

Text copyright © Lana Pecherczyk 2022
Cover design © Lana Pecherczyk 2022
Structural Editor: Ann Harth

www.lanapecherczyk.com

A CROWN OF CRUEL LIES

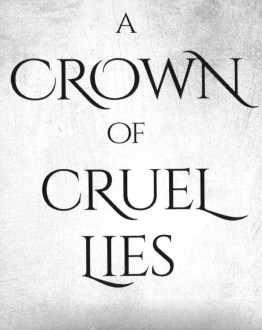

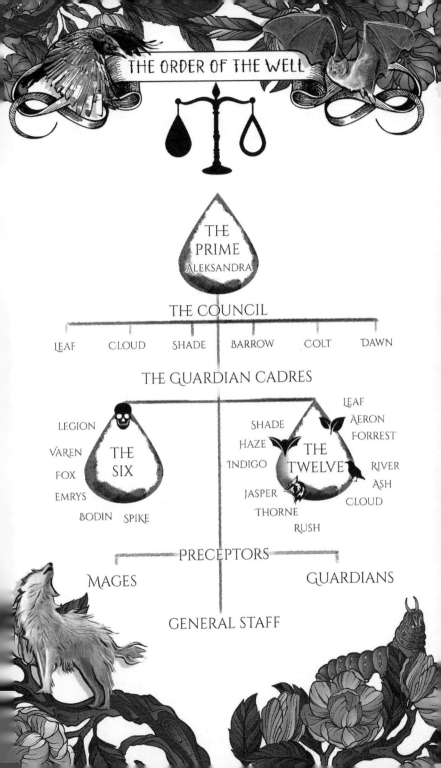

THE ORDER OF THE WELL

THE PRIME
Aleksandra

THE COUNCIL

LEAF   CLOUD   SHADE   BARROW   COLT   DAWN

THE GUARDIAN CADRES

LEGION

VAREN

FOX

EMRYS

BODIN   SPIKE

THE SIX

SHADE

HAZE

INDIGO

JASPER

THORNE

RUSH

LEAF

AERON

FORREST

RIVER

ASH

CLOUD

THE TWELVE

PRECEPTORS

MAGES   GUARDIANS

GENERAL STAFF

EL

WINTER COUR
ACONITE CITY

ACONITE SEA

ICE WITCH

THE ICE FOREST

UNSEELIE KINGDOM

SEELIE KINGDOM

HUMAN TERRITORY

CRYSTAL
CITY

RUSH'S
CABIN

MEANDER
WOOD

WHISPERING
WOODS

CRESCENT
HOLLOW

BLURB

Fae can't lie.

That's the golden rule woven into the people of Elphyne, but for deaf Elf Guardian Aeron, he knows this isn't true. Lies are told between the lines, in misdirection, and in false hope.

When he turns up at the Spring Court with his newfound, broken human mate in his arms, he learns the most cruelest lie of all. He is not who he thought he was. His whole life has been orchestrated... even this moment... even this new love burgeoning in his heart for a human enemy with more secrets than his own.

Learning to trust and accept is hard for both of them, but with civil war on their doorstep, fae plotting to take them down, and the taint on the Well growing more dangerous, they have no choice but to try. Trust can only be found if they start from within.

Only then will they know where their true enemies lie...

PROLOGUE

"You shouldn't do that," Maebh said to Jackson as he dipped his fingers into the warm lake. Whispers in their sleep had coaxed them across the icy landscape that was once a desert.

The strange lake was full of glowing bioluminescent life and atmospheric energy that virtually crawled across the water to brush their faces with a lover's caress. It made their stomachs dip, their hearts pitter-patter, and their minds thrill. No one could deny the powerful force of nature when standing on the shore of this icy lake.

"Why not?" Jackson grumbled. "What is the point if we're not taking risks?"

"The point is you might die," Aleksandra pointed out dryly before taking Maebh's hand and squeezing it tight. Maebh was still unnerved by Aleksandra's new icy hair color and lashes, but she loved her all the same. Would never stop loving her.

Maebh said, "You know as well as any of us that life here has changed. There are nightmares out there."

"And there are miracles," he claimed, his eyes turning distant as he no doubt recalled the one he'd lost.

Aleksandra continued, "If something happens to you, then it will be just Maebh and myself left."

"Careful what you're insinuating, Sandy," Maebh teased with a pout. "Unless you want to sleep alone tonight."

Aleksandra's eyes softened on Maebh. "You know how I feel. So long as there's breath in my body—"

"And blood in my veins," Maebh finished and then kissed Aleksandra.

As usual, Jackson ignored their relationship as though it didn't exist. It wasn't as though he disapproved of females together but that his heart ached for the one he lost to the Fallout. Many regrets kept him awake at night. They might be almost immortal in these new bodies, but that meant so were their memories. Some faded, but most —the worst—haunted them like lingering ghosts in their dreams.

Closure was impossible when memory could not be caught or defined. Completely forgetting was not an option. Maebh let go of Aleksandra's hand. She felt bad flaunting their love before a man so damaged.

Aleksandra said to Jackson, "We need to be careful. We

are responsible for returning to the other survivors intact and armed with the knowledge of this new world."

Maebh turned on her. "We owe them nothing. They vilified us for our love."

Jackson's arched brow almost disappeared beneath his fur hood. "You're being a bit melodramatic, don't you think?"

"Says the entitled man."

His eyes narrowed at them, and Maebh knew she'd hit a nerve.

"We no longer deal in the prejudice of sex or color, but with fae versus humanity. They think we're abominations."

"Exactly," Maebh snapped. "Same story, different book."

"Enough, you two," Aleksandra interjected. "We can't fight amongst ourselves. The world has changed. It's up to us to write the new story."

It took all the self-control Maebh had to stop herself from clocking the arrogant elf's ass, but she knew his mouth spurted off like this when he was lonely and bitter. She tried to have patience, but it was wearing as thin as the cold air around them.

She scowled at the tall, male counterpart of their group as Aleksandra said, "Ninety-nine percent of humanity is gone, Jack. Half of what's left is like us—changed. They're crying out for understanding. So no, I don't think it's melodramatic to want to return to them with answers."

They'd been trekking in the wilderness for days, surviving by following their new baser instincts. If it hadn't been for Aleksandra's ruthless hunting in owl form, none of them would be alive. Jackson had barely changed from his human appearance apart from his new pointed ears and strong connection to the magic energy source.

Maebh, on the other hand, was completely changed. Her brown skin and afro hair might look the same, but her new sanguineous diet was mind-boggling and still hard to stomach. She could barely walk during the day because of the bone-deep lethargy the sun caused. There were others like her at the settlement who'd branched off and left the group, quite happy to claim the identity of a vampire. But Maebh didn't want to leave Aleksandra behind. She refused to be ostracized from a relationship she'd fought hard to keep. They finally had a chance to be free.

They'd decided to follow Jackson on his suicidal expedition to get answers from this magical source that called to them during sleep. Into the snowy, desolate wild they'd gone... called by some unnamed and invisible entity that whispered enticing promises in their heads.

Find me and find home, it said. *Find peace. Find paradise.*

A warm breeze flew off the lake and brought whispering endearments and platitudes, telling them they were in the right place. This was where they belonged. Here they would find answers, and everything would be right.

"It is like a well, is it not?" Aleksandra murmured, her

eyes on the water. "It fills us up and we are restored. It gives us life, and it is plentiful."

"The Well. I like that." Jackson pulled his journal from his fur cloak and scribbled notes. He glanced at the two of them and handed over his journal. "Keep that safe."

"What are you doing?" Maebh asked as he began stripping.

"I'm taking a risk."

"It's not worth it." Aleksandra grabbed his shoulder. "Whatever you're thinking, it's not worth it."

But he shucked her off.

"We need to know why it's calling to us." He frowned and removed his boots. "If one of you goes in and dies, the other will be an insufferable pain in my ass. So, this is me being selfish if you think about it."

"Jackson!"

PRESENT DAY

Maebh slammed her book on Celtic mythology shut, hoping to dispel the memory of her crying as her friend entered the lake. And then the foolish shame that came after because Jackson had proved her wrong. He'd emerged from that lake that day a Guardian—the first of his kind. He'd returned to shore after being judged worthy by the

Well Worms and was armed with knowledge about their new world. The three of them started a new life for the fae.

Everything had gone well.

Until Maebh had wanted more.

Until she'd wanted a child—a legacy—and everything fell to dust.

Her lips twisted bitterly. All she'd wanted was to *talk* about it, but Aleksandra had shut down. Closed herself off. She blamed prophecy. Maebh blamed her cold heart. They fought. They separated. And then, eventually, even their friendship with Jackson hadn't been enough to keep them united.

The three of them drifted apart until, one day, Jackson decided he'd had enough and entered the lake a second time. Maebh still wasn't sure why he'd done that. Maybe to seek guidance again from the Well like he had that first time. But it never came. And he never returned. He didn't even float.

The Well Worms must have eaten him.

Maebh looked at the wrinkled skin on the back of her hand. With the taint leaking into the universal mana supply, and Maebh's own sacrifice of her permanent mana stores to create the demogorgon, her own life was unraveling. Her infinite time was running out. And she refused to let Aleksandra have free reign.

Not while she had breath in her body, or blood in her veins.

That bitch ruined everything.

Aeron heard not a sound as the satyr circled him on the main training field at the Order. The sparring match had only just begun, but Aeron knew how to take down the rookie Guardian—his horns were dull when they should have been sharpened to points. His cloven hooves were clumsy when they should be precise and lethal like the metal sword gripped incorrectly in his hands. His leather breeches were unevenly fastened, which meant his fingers were probably clumsy too... or he was lazy. He would go for the easiest way to attack Aeron.

Hand-to-hand combat was essential now that the taint on the Well warped the outcome of mana use. Aeron might not be cleared for field work, but he could teach these ingrates a lesson on humility and improve their chances of survival.

Just look at him, Aeron thought as his eyes scanned the rookie. Hair all disheveled, eyes darting, clothes filthy, and giving off a stink that would attract animals. If they were in the wild, and Aeron was a mana-warped monster, the rookie would be eaten before he could scream.

The satyr's thigh twitched, telegraphing he was about to strike. Aeron ducked and punched the thick torso with his fist. The rookie was mid-swing and still aiming for the space Aeron's head had vacated. Combined with Aeron's punch, he lost balance and stumbled. If Aeron was another fae, like River or Cloud, he might toy with the rookie—to prove he was still one of the Twelve and better. But he finished him off with a swift uppercut to the jaw.

The ground vibrated as the heavy fae fell in a dead weight. Aeron shook out his smarting fist and stood over the knocked-out satyr. That was too easy. Almost as if... he glanced at the small crowd of Guardians by the hedges surrounding the field. They averted their gazes. A crowd wasn't unusual when one of the Twelve displayed his elite talents—but there was something off about their curiosity. They had the same look about them as bystanders did when Aeron was paraded through the Rubrum City streets as a child by his bully tormentors—his half-siblings.

Aeron checked the satyr at his feet again and noticed he wasn't unconscious like Aeron had initially assumed. His chest lifted and fell too erratically for him to be passed out, and his facial expression wasn't lax enough. Before Aeron's injury, he might have missed those tiny details, which made this situation even more infuriating. Pretending to be unconscious was worse than if the satyr had exploited Aeron's hearing loss. That, Aeron could rally against.

But this... this was insulting.

Hot prickles washed over Aeron, and his elf ears burned as the truth became clear: the satyr had thrown the match. Aeron now understood that look in the bystanders' eyes. He remembered why it felt so familiar. It was *pity*.

Aeron had intended to teach the rookie a lesson in humiliation, but it was he who'd been schooled. His degradation turned to defiance as he was sent back to his childhood. He would *not* be treated differently because of his hearing loss. He was at a disadvantage, yes. He understood that. But he was not useless.

For Crimson's sake, a rookie was taking it easy on him—one of the Twelve.

Aeron grabbed the satyr by the horns, lifted his thick neck clear off the ground until the fae opened his eyes, and swung with his sword. But Aeron had been ready. He twisted them so the sword went wide. Then Aeron dropped the satyr face-first into the dirt.

It took every ounce of his composure to turn his back and resist watching the satyr spluttering. But bottled fury forced him to stalk back to where he'd dumped his sword, *Honor,* and jacket. There was no point trying to communicate with the satyr. These ignorant fools weren't worth his time.

He scoffed. *Going easy on him... as if he was Lesser.*

Aeron barely slipped his arms into his jacket when a flash of wind and kingfisher blue, brown, and white hit his periphery. Without looking, he knew who it was. The Prime with her smooth brown skin, blue dress, white hair, and feather owl shifter wings.

He ignored her too.

Unlike the Guardians, who'd picked up on Aeron's foul mood and scrammed, the Prime strode confidently to meet Aeron as he started down a path that led to the house of the Twelve. As usual, her timeless face had an impenetrable expression plastered on it.

She handed Aeron a sealed letter. He glanced at Leaf's name penned in the Prime's impeccable script. She signed her gratitude to Aeron, then spun on her heels and left.

Gratitude for what?

Since it had been weeks, if not turns-of-the-moon, since Aeron's injury from the demogorogon's screech, he had spent time grieving his loss. The world wasn't just a little dimmer for Aeron. It was silent. He'd also spent time denying his fate and seeking out healers in the Order—and Ada, Jasper's mate—only to be told the taint risked worse things than hearing loss, like death. He'd also collected samples of said taint on power sources around Elphyne. Now... he glanced at the letter... now it seemed he was only good enough to be the Prime's errand boy.

On the walk through the Order campus to his house, Aeron clenched his jaw so hard that his tendons ached. The large communal house had barely come into Aeron's line of sight when he lost his battle with tolerance and ripped open the letter.

The ground tilted beneath his feet as he read the first scrawled line—*List of Potential Replacements for D'arn Aeron*.

Aeron's heart palpitated. His breathing stopped. He existed out of time in deafening silence. She'd had the gall to hand this letter to him. Under normal circumstances, he would never have opened a letter addressed to someone else. But something about this had itched at him.

All emotion cleared from his body as his system prepared subconsciously for a battle he couldn't fight. But that didn't mean he'd go down voluntarily. With his cheeks still flaming, he crumpled the letter in his fist and walked with quick, sure strides to the house of the Twelve. He needed his hearing restored, and only one way was possible. Since he'd collected tainted biosamples for the Order, he'd percolated a few theories. The taint was largely invisible when drawing from one's personal well, but it sometimes left an oily black residue after use. It reminded him of the inky side of the Well—the dark, chaotic place no one should access mana, but some did anyway.

Cloud, River, Ash, and Haze's power-enhancing tattoos used mana from this part of the Well and were perilously close to blasphemy as far as the Council was concerned. But since Cloud was on the council, they'd not imposed sanctions on the tattoos. Aeron, for one, was glad because it had allowed him to study how the substance was locked in place by the tattoo's barrier. It was like curse marks—which were illegal.

The problem with the taint as it stood now was that no boundaries or confinement kept it from bleeding and infecting everything else. Aeron wondered if a containment spell could be crafted to hold the taint in the Cosmic Well at bay, just as it did with a curse or tattoo. He was still lost in thought when he strode up the wooden steps to the house and almost bumped into Clarke, Rush's redheaded and psychic mate.

Unlike the others who still redundantly communicated with speech, she placed a palm on his shoulder and smiled pleasantly until she had his attention. Then she handed him a letter and bade him read it as she pulled a pencil from her top knot.

Feeling the hot burn of the crumpled letter in his hand, he didn't want to read hers. He was starting to think he was better off without communication. Ignorance could be bliss.

The truth was that Aeron needed his hearing. It was how he'd done anything of importance in his life. Eavesdropping at doors and windows had taught him to read and move on silent feet. To *not* be heard he had to hear. The irony was not lost on him.

Steeling himself for more bad news, he shoved Leaf's letter into a pocket and opened Clarke's.

It is time for you to collect your mate. She is known as the Tinker, but I don't believe that's her true name. She's currently located on the west side of the forest outside Delphinium City. In my visions, I see a tree with purple leaves and then one with mushrooms growing at the bottom like this—

A crude sketch of spotted mushrooms followed the words.

I'm not an artist, but you get the picture.
I also see a crown of antlers, so I'm thinking you'll need to head to the Spring Court. The Tinker has dark, curly hair and is pale like me. She's British, but I don't suppose you know what that means, only that she has a different accent. Which I guess won't matter to you either. Forget I said it.
You must leave immediately. I don't know how long she will be at that location.

Aeron calmly folded the paper and gave Clarke his best polite smile, but he had no intention of tracking down a human mate. One benefit to not talking was that people

13

made up their own minds about his intentions. He could get away with more than he used to.

For instance, heading out on this mission to clean the taint from the Well by himself without telling anyone. He could even use Clarke's letter as a red herring. He briefly considered telling Forrest but he was consumed with his new relationship with his mate Melody. She seemed nice but was a stranger to Aeron.

He would do this alone.

He was about to push past Clarke when she took his wrist and flattened her lips. One look from the blue-eyed beauty was enough to unnerve him. She had a spark in her eye, a clever and shrewd way about her that said she saw straight through his polite, accommodating charade. She knew exactly that he'd intended to ignore her instructions.

Perhaps she'd even seen it in a vision.

She wrote at the bottom of her letter:

If you don't leave within the next turn of the sun, events will unfold that will leave your mate back in the hands of the enemy. You will lose her.

His gaze flicked back to Clarke's. He tried to find answers in her eyes. Would the Tinker accept him the way he was? Or was he just doomed to burden her as he was with the Prime?

⚖

SITTING ALONE IN HIS ROOM, Aeron signed his name on the letter he'd penned to his future mate. His uniform handwriting had been crafted from countless hours of self-imposed practice as a child.

As an unwanted bastard son to the Rubrum King, Aeron had been refused the right of education despite the rest of his royal siblings receiving every entitlement.

Aeron's half-brother Forrest was only a few years older than him but also a victim of a horrific childhood at the whims of the Unseelie Autumn Court. Forrest had existed purely to satisfy the family's sacrifice to the Well. United in shared pain, the two had been thick as thieves, but where Forrest found his peace with his mind-to-mind link with animals, Aeron found it between the pages of books.

He'd learned what honor meant, not from his father, but from stories of ancient heroes and quests to save fair maidens from inevitable doom. When Forrest had been sacrificed to the Well at the ceremonial lake, Aeron knew there would only be one future for him—becoming a Guardian too.

He sighed and folded the letter. If Clarke's visions were to be trusted—and with the taint, no one could be sure—then bringing his mate back to the Order safely was imperative.

If the Tinker was alone and lost in this world, then she would need to be with friends here... even if Aeron wasn't planning on returning until he had found a way to restore his hearing. In all those books, the knight was a perfect specimen. Perfect. No defects.

He smoothed his calloused fingers against the parchment crease three more times and then stared at it until he scowled, applied the seal, and shoved it into his travel satchel.

The princess wouldn't be expecting a broken knight.

He could be like this forever, and forever was a long time for fae.

That's why he left like a coward in the night.

AERON

CHAPTER
TWO

An elf sat beneath Trix's tree.

Not just any elf, but one dressed in hardcore leather clothes. His big sword rested across his knees as he leaned against the trunk. And when she said big, she meant *big*. She bet the hilt would be as high as her head if he placed it next to her, point touching the ground.

Maybe he was a soldier from the Autumn Court here to return her to prison.

They will never take me alive.

Sun glinted off his sword as he twisted to survey the forest. Glyphs inscribed across the blade glowed blue. *Metal...* But wasn't metal outlawed in Elphyne? Nero always told her fae weren't allowed to touch the substance.

But she'd since learned he was a Grade A liar.

Now that she thought about it, there *was* a group of fae allowed to use metal. She should know. After all, she'd created a machine fueled by their mana. So, if this elf was a Guardian, and he waited beneath her tree, it meant only one thing. Her heart rate spiked. Her ears heated. She rolled back from the treehouse platform edge, hyperventilating, and trying not to make a sound.

Oh fuck. He was probably here to make her pay for her Guardian-killing invention. To seek revenge. *Oh, God. Can't breathe.* Someone had tied a piece of string around her lungs. *Can't breathe.* She hiccuped and stared at the green leaves rustling above her, using their soft repetition to focus and compose.

Wait.

Wait.

The Guardian would have shaken the tree down if he knew she was here. He'd have done something to get to her; if he hadn't, perhaps he was simply resting after a long journey.

She calmed enough to crawl back to the platform edge and studied the elf again.

Long brown hair braided at the sides ensured his sharp elven ears were obvious. Fae tended to keep their ears out in the open for easy fae identification. His leather armor was scuffed but had been oiled and cared for. She imagined his painstaking efforts to keep it conditioned, despite the scratches and gouges marring the surface.

Trix had heard stories about Guardians. They were brutal, unforgiving warriors who cut down anything endangering their power source—including humans. Like all fanatics, they were convinced their way was the right way. She hated to be the one who told them others could use their power source too. And it wasn't called magic but science.

When Nero came to her a few years ago, asking her to devise a way to allow them to travel through portals with metal, she'd accepted the challenge and excelled. Nero had supplied the fuel. She'd studied it with colleagues—including Justin, her ex. And together, they'd come up with an incredible solution. To be honest, she wasn't exactly sure how it worked, but it did, and that was all that mattered.

Maybe it wasn't science.

She frowned.

Returning to the elf, she noticed he scrutinized the woods around them, always vigilant, always ready. The more she studied, the more she was certain he had no idea she was up here—he would have looked up by now. Surely. She'd not exactly been nimble when she woke. Her mother used to say she had the steps of a rhino but the temperament of a butterfly. Trix used to think this was her mother calling her fat, but then she grew up and realized she meant something about how Trix went through life. She was impulsive and emotional.

This elf ruined everything by being here. Her berry and nut cache was empty. How was she supposed to get down and find food? She might have to wait hours. If he took longer than that, she would have to resort to the magical ability that had saved her in the Autumn Court dungeon. She closed her eyes against the horrific memories, but the visual of soldiers being stabbed by vines lurching from the ground flashed in her mind. The vines had twisted *through* the soldiers and around until they looked like morbid Christs on a cross.

She opened her eyes and focused on the trees ahead until the screams in her memory dimmed.

She refused to do that to another living creature. Nero was right. This power was dangerous. She hadn't known she was the cause of the stabby vines until it was too late. All she remembered was the power surge in her veins—the delayed understanding—then the horror and subsequent escape.

Trix had snuck out of the Autumn Court, which seemed to be in an uproar after the king died. The confused crowd was easy to get lost in. She followed a couple through a portal and ended up here, where she'd built the treehouse with that same dangerous power. It had a platform of solid wood, leaves and vines enshrouding her at night. And a working toilet. Sort of. She'd made a little pipeline out of woven vines, and any time she needed to go, she did her business, shut the wooden lid, and then used her power to push all the waste down into the soil beneath the tree.

Science.

Magic.

Gah, she didn't know anymore. But she knew it made

her feel warm and fuzzy to see something good come from the power within her. After she'd killed those soldiers and escaped, she'd lived up here for weeks, hiding from the enemy, studying Elphyne and her power. Nero had always said humans were incapable of carrying mana. He said it tainted and corrupted them from within.

Lies.

Everywhere she turned, she found dishonesty. She grabbed a notebook she'd stolen from the local markets and quietly flicked through the pages of gathered evidence of his lies. It was almost full. Already. She shook her head, disparaging. This was why the elf had to go. When her notebooks filled, she became restless. Her ideas had to go somewhere, and if not between the pages, they blurted out of her mouth. Some people didn't like her lack of filter. Or the restlessness transferred to her body, and if she couldn't keep still, she got into trouble.

Continuing through her notebook, she stopped at a sketch of a strange cat that had stolen her food the previous night. The tail needed fixing. It wasn't right. There were also drawings of other creatures in Elphyne she'd been studying. This elf would be another entry in her book. A book she should call *Trix's Arc*. No—she crossed that out. *The Bestiary*. Boring. That wasn't good, either. There were more than beasts in here. She'd have to come up with something better when she wasn't so wired.

What had she been doing?

Oh, yeah. The elf. That's right. Finding a clean page,

she put her charcoal stick to paper and sketched him, starting with his long brown hair and pointed ears. Her fingers stole the busyness from her mind and allowed her to think clearly.

She didn't trust fae. Didn't trust humans, either. She'd been lied to the entire time she'd been awake in this time. The only person she could trust was herself.

This elf looked particularly untrustworthy with his stiff and serious demeanor—she flattened herself on the slatted wooden platform, carefully staying quiet as she peeked over the edge, but it creaked beneath her. She winced and stilled, hoping he hadn't heard. When he didn't look up, she tested the wood beneath her. Definitely a weak spot in there. She'd have to give it a—suddenly remembering why she was looking over the edge, she went back to studying the elf. All right, sure. He was handsome... in a weird blend of aristocratic barbarian sort of way. But weren't all fae good-looking?

All the better to entrap her.

He kind of reminded her of a student she went to MIT with. Whenever she had a wrong answer, he would find her after class and do his best to passive-aggressively mansplain. It was as though his kink was degrading her.

Nope. *Don't like elves.*

His pointed ears twitched as though he'd heard her move... or a fly landed on them. Her eyes narrowed. She didn't know elf ears twitched. She wrote a quick note next to his sketch to remind herself to investigate the lineage of elves. Every fae race stemmed from a blend of humanity and animal or insect. It fascinated her to no end. When she returned to studying him, his head turned methodically as though he patrolled the woods with the sweep of his eyes. Left to right, then right to left.

She tapped her lip with a charcoal-stained finger. Pointed ears... easy to see the link to other animals like wolves or vampire bats. But an elf? Maybe the ears were just the tiny bit of animal DNA, and they were as close to humans as any fae could get.

Interesting.

A warning prickle went off again as Trix fidgeted with her charcoal stick.

Why *was* he here?

What if she couldn't just wait him out?

What if she starved to death?

Every day since she'd made the treehouse with her power, she'd hidden here to gather her bearings. One of her own kind had sold her to the fae. It made sense for her to work out a few truths before making a rash decision to return to a bunch of liars and betrayers. She only meant to stay for a few days, but, well, Elphyne *fascinated* her.

From its lush greenery to dangerous inhabitants to the magic-maybe-science pumping new life into her veins. If it wasn't for her undercurrent of fear, she felt terrific... like she'd just downed ten coffees, but they were filled with pure energy and offered no caffeine hangover.

Hmm. She tapped her lip again and noted: *Figure out why I feel like I have so much more energy.*

She wanted to know how it all ticked.

President Nero had capitalized on her thirst for knowledge. He'd handed her things to make, things to pull apart, things to invent, machines to resurrect. It wasn't only the president telling her lies about Elphyne. It had been her ex, Justin. Or rather, the Professor, they'd called him. She was the Tinker, and he was the Professor. They'd been a fitting couple—two clever, elite inhabitants of the Tower in Crystal City.

He used to call Trix clever... said that she was remarkable. But her brain obviously wasn't enough to keep him stimulated. Not long before she was sold to the fae, she found Justin in bed with a much prettier, less "clever" version of herself.

Sliding back from the ledge, she crawled to a haphazard stack of notebooks. Further into the treehouse, cocooned by wooden roots and foxglove flowers, her bedding was made of fresh leaves.

Apart from a few lonely nights, she'd been okay here. She grew her berries and nuts with her power. She found water in the leaves. She was reluctant to sneak into the city market unless it was to grab supplies. Okay, steal them. She stole them when no one looked.

She didn't even think of Justin until those nights when the forest sounds were loudest, and it was only because she'd close her eyes and imagine his arms around her as she drifted to sleep.

Ugh. There she went again, giving him more time in her brain than that twat deserved. She only wished for him because she didn't want to be lonely. And maybe... maybe because she didn't think she deserved anyone better.

Trix lost her place in her book, then flipped through it again with a scowl. The cat-like creature whose tail she was supposed to fix stole her attention again. She tidied the drawing and remembered how it had snuffled around the toadstools beneath her tree. Trix smiled as she recalled it purring and rolling in the mushrooms. It had triggered some kind of glowing phosphorescence and stumbled away drunk.

She must remember to gather a sample of that substance. It might come in handy. She wondered what the fae called it and jotted down a few suggestions. Once she'd done that, she continued writing other observations and sketches. Before she knew it, the natural sunlight in the treehouse dimmed to a point where she found it hard to see.

Alarmed, she sat upright and looked around.

Bollocks.

Night was here. Biting her lip, panicked, she stood so suddenly she hit her head on a bough. Ouch. She'd done it again! Lost track of time and... what had she been doing before? Oh, yeah. The elf. *Bloody hell.* She peeked over the edge but wasn't looking where she put her foot. A weak spot in the platform broke. The wood dropped from beneath her, and suddenly, she was weightless.

A scream tore from her lungs. Her notebook flew from her hand. Branches whizzed past. Leaves and twigs hit her face. It all happened so fast. She reached within to access her power, to grow vines, to maybe catch herself, but—her feet hit the ground, and her knees buckled. Her teeth clacked. Everything went black.

She regained consciousness slowly. Leaves rustled with a gentle wind. The smell of forest eased into her lungs. A shuffle of boots—her eyes shot open. The handsome elf was frowning down at her legs.

Her wobbly gaze shifted to her left leg sticking out at an odd angle. She cocked her head, confused. Why did it look like that—*Oh fuck*—the pain hit.

White-hot agony scorched her like a chemical injection. Everything hurt. The air hurt. Her lips parted. She wanted to scream but was too afraid to inhale. She did. It *hurt*. The scream started deep in her chest. It rose and exploded. She could only exist in pain. Vaguely she registered the elf moving before her.

She lashed out. He was the enemy. He would take her away and put her back in a dungeon. But with each thrash of her arms, the pain worsened. The next time she blacked out, she didn't wake up.

CHAPTER
THREE

Aeron's jaw dropped. A woman had fallen from the sky and now lay broken on the ground. *Curly black hair. Pale. Human.* This must be his mate.

She needed a healer—fast. He reached to lift her, but his hands froze.

A dark Unseelie part of him knew this was an opportunity he'd never see again. If he left her now before the Well-blessed bond triggered, he would be free from the shame of not being the knight she'd probably expected. And she would be dead before the impenetrable pain of losing a mate burdened her. Usually, when one half of a mated pair died, the other joined not long after from a broken heart. So if they avoided all of that now, then he could carry out his plan to purge the taint on the Well and prove to all those fuckers he still had what it took to be a

Guardian. He would prove to the Prime she couldn't get rid of him that easily.

He stared until guilt kicked in. His lips gave a bitter twist as he clenched his sword and studied her injuries. Broken legs, that much was clear. But if her spine, neck, or head was damaged, any attempt at moving her would be dangerous.

He'd not heard her scream. He'd not heard the leaves rustle or the branches break. The first sign something was wrong had been the prickle on the back of his neck seconds before she landed.

He'd thought the earth had quaked. Or perhaps a mana-warped monster was charging. Or, inexplicably, the satyr Guardian had come back for round two. He'd even had *Honor* out and ready to shred. But it had been his mate crashing to the ground like a fallen princess from one of his old novels.

As a child, he'd found peace and freedom between the pages of books. He still did because when he read, he was not an unwanted bastard son, nor a deaf Guardian, but thousands of others. Reading was a freedom of the mind.

Sometimes he wished for those cruel early days of his life purely because of that innocent comfort. It was all bitterly tainted now. He hadn't been able to pick up a novel without feeling envy at the perfect characters, so he'd stuck to non-fiction.

Despite Aeron's lifelong thirst for knowledge, he was forbidden to braid his hair at the Autumn Court, as was the right for educated royals. Instead, they'd shaved and cut it with blunt clipping shears, so it had been patchy and in clumps. He ran his hand down the bumpy length of a braid, remembering how he'd hidden once in the vast royal library to avoid facing anyone with his new embarrassing hairstyle.

"Rats don't have long hair," his eldest brother had said as he'd cut all but a small strip of hair at Aeron's nape. *"They have tails."*

As Aeron glanced up to the platform twenty feet high, his self-made braids knocked against his shoulders. No wonder he'd missed the treehouse. It was covered in cleverly camouflaged leaves and branches. The platform looked naturally formed with the tree's growth. It must have been magically created. Fae around here were adept in woodland magic. Fae like Elves, Oak Men, and the Stag shifters. Maybe the human did it. These Well-blessed women had all been gifted incredible powers by the Well.

Movement at his feet drew his attention. Her thick dark eyelashes fluttered. She might have moaned, going by the movement of her lips. He checked her vitals by pressing two fingers to the pulse at her neck. The moment they touched, blue light sprung from the ground around them. His stomach lurched, and he shielded his eyes from the intensity. *No. No no no.* He knew what this light meant and wasn't ready for it. Bitter dread filled him. When the light dimmed, a matching web of bioluminescent blue lines had settled along his arm and hers. *No denying it now.* They were Well-blessed mates, forever linked by mana and emotion.

He wanted to stay annoyed. He wanted to wallow in his irritation because he'd hoped to have his hearing back before they made this connection. Now she would sense every ounce of self-hatred in his soul just as he was about to feel hers.

Her helplessness coursed through their bond. It staggered him. It beat against his silent heart, causing it to thud in his chest.

He wasn't ready for this. *Fuck.*

Her eyes opened, tried to focus, then rolled to the back of her head. *Unconscious again.* He calmed and reminded himself that he chose to come here for her. Some part of him had accepted this fate. Just... not yet.

He assessed her injuries more acutely this time. Her knees and ankles were most likely shattered. Maybe her lower left leg. He felt along her thin body, along the curve of her skull beneath her silky curls. No swelling on her head. No blood. Good. Hopefully, that meant her blackout was not from a trauma to her brain.

The good news was that if their bond triggered, she was connected to the Well. She would heal faster than the average human. Her lifespan was now as infinite as the fae. Still, the sooner he took her to a healer, the cleaner those injuries would mend, unlike his hearing.

Forcing himself to exhale, he glanced at his sword. The shining blade glinted with Elven glyphs and taunted him with the name he'd given it—*Honor*. He wanted to be reminded of those knights and legends in the books. That even if the world was often malevolent, he didn't have to be.

Even in the darkest pit of his despair, he knew he couldn't leave this woman to a cruel fate, so he shoved his weapon into his baldric sheath and collected his mate's fallen items—a notebook and charcoal sticks—then tucked them into his leather travel satchel and slung it over his shoulder.

The only portal stones he had were keyed to the Order, Delphinium City, or Cornucopia. The latter would be useless for this kind of injury. The former, too many people watching and judging. Fuck that.

Clarke had mentioned purple or magenta leaves on a tree in her visions. It sounded like The Great Elder Tree in Delphinium. So, it had to be Delphinium City—home of the Seelie Spring Court. Having a solid distaste for royal courts, Aeron wasn't a regular there but knew his way around.

He activated his portal stone in a clearing. The scent of ozone filled the air. He knew from experience there should be an electric buzzing, but it was silent. Hope still lurched in his heart, anyway. Stupid of him to think his hearing would magically come back, but he also knew one day he might forget sound altogether, so letting himself hope was a way of keeping it alive. Or torturing himself.

He slid his hands beneath the Tinker's legs and shoulders, lifted her gently, then stepped through the portal.

THEY ARRIVED at the front of the wrought-root gates of Delphinium—a city nestled within a green valley crowded by trees. The palace was built into the Great Elder Tree's trunk and root system.

Aeron was disappointed at the response to their arrival. Only two guards manned the gate. It could be because the city's highly magical forest acted as protection. Only a few roads were safe into Delphinium. Any deviation from them was filled with mana-warped monsters or duplicitous fae creatures. But two?

That was ridiculously underwhelming for a city like this.

Whoever oversaw security wasn't doing their job.

A glance at his Guardian uniform was all the currency Aeron needed for the gates to open. Seeing the unconscious woman in his arms, one of the guards brought him to the palace infirmary, where little to no security kept the general public out of the royal residence.

Was everyone here so trustworthy, or were they just relaxed? Or did the king have his people wrapped in a city-wide geas of good behavior? Aeron had seen Queen Maebh do worse to her people. Magically enforcing conduct wouldn't be unheard of.

The infirmary had high ceilings with wooden beams crisscrossing in an ornate pattern. Aeron moved past three rows of empty beds toward a yellow-haired healer with wooden striations on her face. She was restocking porcelain surgical instruments into a jar. Tiny leaves had sprouted from her eyebrows. She must have Oak Man in her ancestry, but she also wore the blue robe of a Mage of the Order. Those with this lineage were known for being adept with mana. The glowing teardrop stamped on the middle of her bottom lip also confirmed her Order status. She frowned as she saw Aeron and his bundle. Her lips moved rapidly, most likely asking him what had happened to the unconscious woman in his arms.

Frustration scored through him. His hands were occupied, so it wasn't exactly like he could take that pencil knotting her hair to write out his answer.

His lips flattened. He gave a pointed look at his mate. *Just check her.*

She glared at him.

He didn't have time for this.

Since his injury, he hated talking. All he felt was a vibration in his throat. He had no idea if his words or tongue had forgotten to form words. What if it came out wrong?

"I'm deaf," he said gruffly, trying to suppress the way his skin prickled with humiliation. "She fell from a tree."

The Mage's eyes darted to his ears, his long elven braids, and then to his Guardian teardrop glowing beneath his left eye. Her eyes widened as she finally put the puzzle together. There weren't any other Guardians living with his injury. Word about him must have traveled here.

He took a step toward the Mage. His mate needed care *now*. Over the short journey, she'd barely regained consciousness. The only emotion he'd sensed from her down their bond was a small, steady thread of angst, and he guessed that was from her pain. The Mage didn't balk at his anger, and her own had dissipated. She waved him further into the palace infirmary and ordered him to place the Tinker on an empty bed.

Aeron did, gently, and then stepped back. He retreated further into the room, away from the bed, and rubbed his aching shoulders as he watched the Mage assess his woman. *His?* He blinked at his train of thought. It was way too soon for him to think of her like that... but... she was.

He frowned at himself and focused on the Mage. How much mana would she risk, and how much of what happened next relied on beneficial herbs and methods because of the taint? Would it be enough?

A tickle of regret slithered through him, winding its way up to squeeze around his chest. He should have spent less time wallowing.

He wiped dirty sweat from his face and found himself slinking into a corner of the room to avoid the flurry of activity as more healers entered the infirmary. None of these wore the blue robe of a Mage. One was an elf. One was a shifter with fur-tipped ears. Brown twists of jute rope tied long green robes at their waists.

They cut the Tinker's clothes with a ceramic knife. He watched to make sure they were decent as they poked and prodded. A few glares slid his way. They probably weren't used to a Guardian in uniform supervising. Eventually, they forgot about him as they worked, which made his guilt grow. She must be more severely injured than he'd realized.

At some point, they covered his mate's mouth and nose with a cloth, and he smelled something acidic. His pulse escalated when the angst throbbing down their bond faded to fuzziness and then nothing. That small ounce of emotion had kept him company. Now that it was gone. It was quiet again. Empty.

Why wasn't she moving?

He shoved a healer out of the way. She crashed side-long into a table with instruments, but Aeron didn't care. He checked his mate's pulse by pushing two brutish fingers against her delicate wrist. Alive. Just asleep. It must be a chemical anesthetic. He'd read about their use in the old world.

Elves loved their elixirs. Coming here was the right choice. Out of any fae in Elphyne equipped to resort to old-world methods, it would be these here.... Or those at the Autumn Court, and that was the last place he would visit willingly again.

The Mage plucked that pencil out of her hair and scribbled something on a hastily grabbed parchment before holding it out for him to read.

My name is Thistle. I'm a consulting healer from the Order.

He gathered as much but nodded his understanding. Mages, like Guardians, operated outside the usual laws of fae courts. She was invited here by the grace of the king and queen to learn and teach. Most likely because of the taint. She had no real power unless it came to maintaining the integrity of the Well, but she would do what she could. She wrote:

Bones are broken in multiple places. No spinal injury. We will set the bones the old-fashioned way and recommend she bathe in the healing waters of the Well-Fed Great Elder Tree.

So... she won't die. At least he hadn't messed up too badly. Thistle continued:

She will need help moving around until she's healed.

Aeron frowned and took her pencil to reply.

For how long?

She pointed to her new sentence:

Do you have somewhere better to be?

He bristled at the insinuation, but yes, he did. The sooner he left, the sooner he could fix the taint, the sooner he could come back and resume... he glanced at his mate. Resume being the mate she deserved.

She might never forgive him if he left her alone in this state. He didn't feel good about abandoning her now, but he also felt worse about introducing himself like this. The need to prove his worth to the Prime burned beneath his skin. He also took his job very seriously. If he delayed getting out there and doing what he could to fix the taint, he put more space between his injury and having it heal successfully.

But if these Spring Court fae realized the Tinker wasn't just from Crystal City but that she had worked with the human leader—the enemy of Elphyne—then being a Guardian's Well-blessed mate would not be enough to grant her amnesty. They would vilify her and possibly execute her. Protecting her would also be part of a Guardian's job. Each of these women from the old world had awoken with incredible power. That the Tinker was here after being in the hands of the enemy was too important to dismiss.

I'll stay, he wrote, ignoring the anxiety building in his body. He would remain until the Tinker could travel back to the Order and be with Melody. It might be a little awkward for him, but leaving her would be irresponsible, and that he was not.

Thistle replied,

Good, I'll check you next.

He nodded. Wait. What?

She bustled him across the room and shoved a sharp finger at his chest. He fell onto a bed on his ass and had to balance with his hands. Hard items connected with his clumsy fingers. Something dropped. It must have been loud because Thistle flinched. She went for his ears, and out of habit, he slapped her away.

Big-eared freak!

The childhood taunt crashed into his head, as loud as the first day he'd heard it. He tensed. His ears had always been a touch bigger than usual for elves.

You got those ears from your whore mother, they'd said.

But she was an elf, just like the Autumn Court King. Or so Aeron had been told. He was too young to remember the king executing her on the steps of his palace. A few years older than Aeron, Forrest was the only one who told Aeron any details about his mother.

She had dark hair and sad eyes but a determined face. Quiet. Silent. Like a thief. No one had known she was there, creeping toward the king's dais until she was upon it and out in the open, spouting her truth for all to hear.

"This is your son."

Aeron signed his apology to Thistle by rubbing his fist over his heart in a circular motion. She waved him off and returned to inspecting his ears.

The shame heating his cheeks kept him immobile. It also made him a little irritated. Everyone kept looking at his injury, but nobody could fix him. Despite this logic, a traitorous lurch of hope moved in his chest. All he'd wanted since the accident was his hearing back. Learning to function without it had been the singular most difficult thing in his life... no, that was false. It was learning to accept that he might never get it back.

Sure enough, after peering inside his ears and checking about his head with her fingers, she returned to his front with a pensive look. Not resigned. Not a look of defeat. *Interesting.*

That stirring of hope lifted again.

She briefly called over the blond elf healer who had been tying the Tinker's leg splints. She then, in turn, checked his ears too. The two healers conversed for a moment before the elf returned to Aeron's mate.

Thistle wrote down.:

Where are you originally from?

He replied:

Rubrum.

Her eyes narrowed further.

Royal lineage?

He ground his teeth but nodded. It had been decades since he'd left the Autumn Court. Aeron and Forrest had kept their blood relation quiet from even the Twelve. It was no one's business.

Thistle tapped the paper to grab his attention.

I will request that you stay at the palace.

He tried shaking his head. They wouldn't be here long enough to bother the royals. But she took her note and returned to Aeron's mate. He joined her with a frown. There was no point staying at the palace. Usually, a Guardian was seen about only for monsters and tax. No one liked the idea of having one sleeping in close quarters.

But the healer patted him patronizingly and then pointed to his mate, meaning she would need the added protection of being within palace grounds. Thistle was right. This wasn't about Aeron. So he wrote down a few more requests and handed over coin to make sure his orders would be followed through.

They left him alone with his sleeping mate. Aeron sat heavily on a seat beside her bed and looked at the woman who'd derailed his plans. Her curly dark hair had more life than her skin had color. He gently touched her pallid cheek. Smooth. She flinched, and he wrenched his fingers away.

He watched intently to see if she would wake, but the movement of her chest—now clothed in simple, linen— rose and fell rhythmically. Back asleep.

That sliver of her angst petered out.

With nothing else to do, he opened his satchel and retrieved her notebook. It was filled with clever observations about fae... and her special gift. With each turn of the page, his eyebrows lifted. These notes were detailed and studious. Her skill at capturing the likeness of her subject was talented and far better than Clarke's chicken-scratch scrawl.

There were also pages with names in the margins and funny words he'd not heard before: Justin is a *twat*. Justin is a *numpty*. Justin can suck a bag of dicks—his brows lifted again and he smirked. Those words he knew. He guessed the others weren't all that positive either. Whoever this Justin person was, they must have hurt her. Aeron's frown deepened when he found another name in her scribbles. Nero.

President Nero my arse. Nero the Zero is no Hero.

She wanted a hero...

He glanced at her peaceful sleeping form. Freckles dusted her nose. Slightly parted, her lips looked full and soft. Dark loose curls framed a beautiful, heart-shaped face. She was exactly the kind of female he'd imagined as a princess in his old adventure novels. But she probably had a sharp tongue and even sharper wit to back it up. She probably didn't need rescuing but would do it herself. He couldn't help the smile tugging his lips.

It was a pity he would leave her soon. If he'd been whole, he'd have immersed himself in getting to know her before setting off to clear the taint. Proving his worth to the Prime would be a non-factor. But seeing the Tinker's talent, knowing she'd be clever, proved his point that she needed a hero—a knight.

And that he was not.

KELVHAN

FOUR

Like swimming through hot jelly, Trix rose to the surface of consciousness. Her eyelids were lead. Her body felt weird. She hadn't been this groggy since she'd accidentally eaten one of her brother's special brownies.

Trevor had been two years younger than her, but where she'd managed to funnel her never-ending curiosity into academics, he'd gone in the opposite direction. Like, one-eighty opposite. When the Nuclear Winter hit, freezing the world, he'd been passed out in the back of a Combi van, pulled over on a highway somewhere.

The Nuclear Winter hit so fast that most people were frozen in the middle of going about their day. Trix had no idea if he'd died alone. That thought plagued her on many sleepless nights. When nights were particularly rough, when Trix missed her family most, she liked to pretend

LANA PECHERCZYK

that Trevor made it into this world with her. That his addictions weren't controlling him. That he prospered somewhere.

Knowing she was awake, knowing this was not a dream, she opened her eyes and blinked at the handsome elf warrior coming into focus beside her bed. It was the same one who'd sat beneath her tree. He looked so much like the elves who had kept her prisoner. Sharp cheekbones, long braids dangling between silken hair, and smooth bronze skin. As he pored over her notebook, his angular face seemed frozen in a brooding state. Her notebook!

Not bloody likely.

Panic like she'd never known hit. That was private. It was like looking into her mind, which was a messy, embarrassing place, and *he was her enemy!*

"No," she croaked in disbelief.

She yanked off her blanket. *Had to get out. Had to escape.* Her legs slid across the bed and—

Agony pierced the fuzziness of her mind. She screamed and seized in pain. Someone had put razors inside her legs. What the fuck.

The elf calmly set aside the book and pressed her down on the bed, but she gritted her teeth and swore at him before pushing back. The fuzziness in her head wouldn't clear, but she had enough sense to know when she was in danger. Enemy. Dungeon. Bad elf.

"No," she shouted... slurred. "You'll never take me."

Bloody hell. Drugged. She tried to reach for the ability that had saved her once before, but like grasping quicksand, it slipped through her fingers. She lashed out as the elf's hands took control of her shoulders.

So easy!

He'd pushed her down like a grain of sand, and just like that, she was pinned. She was a fly beating its wings against a storm. How could she possibly win a battle against him?

Didn't matter. She would *not* go back to that stinking prison. She would fight until the end. Bracing herself to face more excruciating pain, she tensed, ready to battle, but the elf caught her flailing wrists and pinned them over her head. Those copper eyes erupted into flames. His dark brows pinched together, and Trix feared this was the end of the line for her.

Heartbeat pounding in her chest, she was ready to scratch his eyes out. She was not ready for the wave of calm that crashed into her. It was as though someone had drugged her again. But with air. With something... invisible. Was this real?

The foreign sensation watered her system, and she was helpless against it. Her head fell back and landed on the pillow. Her lungs slowed. She became lost in his eyes—so vibrant inside those thick dark lashes. Copper colored with patina flecks like the old pipes outside her dad's garage. And that sparkling blue teardrop beneath the left eye. The elves keeping her prisoner didn't have anything like that.

Pretty. Her gaze darted down to his battle leathers, and she remembered he was a Guardian. Still her enemy. Just not the ones that kept her captive.

But like the ones her invention had violated. Guilt slammed into her.

These drugs confused her. She stopped struggling and let the pain ebb away. He was a Guardian, but he didn't seem to want to hurt her. For now.

"What the bloody hell is going on?" she mumbled.

His gaze dipped to her lips, his frown deepened, and he let go of her hand to point at his ears.

"You're an elf?"

Was that what he was trying to tell her, or was her muddled mind seeing things? Why point to his ears? Her gaze wandered as she recalled who'd held her captive in the Autumn Court. They had pointed ears, but lots of fae had pointed ears. Elves. Shifters. Except theirs often had fur on the tips. Not all of them, though, she supposed. She'd seen owl shifters with round ears, stag and deer shifters with big floppy pointed ears. They were the cutest. She wanted to pinch their noses and ruffle their hair which she assumed was a huge no-no.

One time, while in her treehouse, a family of deer shifters had ambled past—

His fingers on her jaw brought her attention back to him. Heat burned her cheeks, and she readied herself for a berating.

Pay attention.

That's what they all said. Especially the stuffy professors she usually worked with. Her ex hated it when her mind wandered as he spoke to her. He hated it more when she interrupted him because he was so slow sometimes at getting his point across. So had President Nero. But the elf didn't speak. He patiently pointed to his ears before holding his fists together and gesturing like he was snapping a pencil.

Broken.

Ears.

"You're deaf?"

His gaze darted to her lips, then back up again, but he just stared.

She guessed that was a yes, then.

So... he wasn't here to hurt her. Yet. Feeling a little more comfortable, she braved a look at their surroundings. They were in an infirmary with a high arched ceiling made from intricately carved wood. Sterile porcelain and glass equipment sat neatly organized on benches by a wall. Plants and herbs dangled in bouquets from ropes on the ceiling. Two empty beds were in the room. The smell of antiseptic. Peppermint. Her legs were in splints. *Oh, God.*

She couldn't walk.

Trying not to hyperventilate, Trix closed her eyes, exhaled slowly, and then forced herself to look at this situation again. Memories floated back into her muddy mind. She'd fallen out of her tree—her fault. The glowering elf didn't know her from a bar of soap, but he'd helped her.

49

He'd probably carried her all the way here! How embarrassing.

Her stupid misstep had caused the most grievous accident. At least she hadn't landed on him. He looked in good health.

Her mind flicked over to the other information she'd just learned. He was deaf. She knew a little sign language. At MIT, a student in her advanced chemistry class had been deaf. Even among nerds, Trix hadn't been popular. And with her inquisitive mind, she'd approached learning the language with vigor so she could converse with him. She particularly loved how facial expressions and body language were a form of grammar.

Gathering her resolve, she met the elf's eyes and signed with raised brows and a shrug as she said, "Where am I?"

Well, she hoped she'd signed. She was a little rusty. He gave her gesturing hands a confused look. She tried another few words, thinking perhaps, there was a new version of sign language in this time. Or maybe ASL wasn't the preferred type. But he returned the same confused look.

"Don't understand?" she asked, shrugging. She pointed to her lips and raised her brows. "I suppose you can't lipread?"

How did he communicate?

No response except a growing feeling of frustration and annoyance but, again, the feeling felt foreign. Like it pulsed at her from the outside, not from within. Maybe she'd hit her head.

He scowled and folded his arms. Biceps popped beneath his leather Guardian jacket, stretching the seams with a creak. That's where all that strength had come from when he'd pinned her down. No wonder it had been so easy. She was skinny as a rake compared to him.

She tossed in one last hand sign—a thank you for helping her—and was about to collapse exhausted on the pillow when his copper eyes lit up. He echoed her action by putting his fingers to his lips and then pushing them down and toward her.

"Thank you," she confirmed, smiling and nodding.

His excitement turned to alarm. He covered her mouth before checking around the room. It was the dumbest thing—his hand on her mouth was nice. Warm, calloused contact. It had been so long since she'd touched another person that the effect on her body was glaringly obvious. Every cell tingled. But once satisfied no one watched, he let go and then waggled his finger at her with a frown. To see this oxymoron of an elf—both distinguished yet dangerous —wagging a finger at her was so comical that she laughed.

And then immediately regretted the movement.

Her body jolted. Pain shot through her limbs. Arching her back, she squeezed her eyes shut and tried to breathe. The drugs had worn off. The pain was too much. She cried out.

He stood to leave. She tugged him back by the wrist.

"Stay."

She had no idea why she grabbed him, but the thought of him going was like ice down her spine. He was the first kind-eyed fae she'd met. The first who had helped her, not imprisoned her. Through eye-watering pain, she registered a glowing blue pattern on her arm—he had something similar on his—then another calming wave bled into her, making her feel like jelly.

He pried her hand off him and walked out of the room. She barely had enough time to register her crushing disappointment before he stormed back in behind a tall, frightened female elf wearing a green monk-like robe. She walked like the devil was on her heels and poured liquid from a vial onto a cloth before pushing it against Trix's mouth and nose.

Chemical burn.

Her vision blurred. Everything dulled. She only had a moment to think... this is what she got for trusting this warrior elf... and then darkness claimed her.

WHEN TRIX WOKE, the elf was still by her bedside. Only he wasn't reading her notebook. He had a new stack of books beside him and was deeply engrossed with one on his lap. Not her notebook this time, but leather-bound tomes. It looked like it had diagrams inside.

She patted herself softly. *Still alive.* Not in prison. In one piece. Same infirmary as before.

The elf noticed her immediately as if he was attuned to her. Concern etched over his striking features, and he shut the book. She tried to say something but could hardly move her mouth. In her haste, that healer might have given Trix the wrong dose.

Voices came from somewhere close. With heavy movements, Trix dragged her gaze around the room. Two fae argued and gesticulated—one female, one male. They stood hunched and heads together near the open wooden exit doors.

"Shh," the male said. "He'll hear you."

"He's deaf," scoffed the elf. It was the same blond who'd dosed the drug. Trix's mental warning signals went off. She listened harder. "I overheard Thistle tell the Queen he's got the mark."

"You mean the Guardian mark?"

"Idiot. That's obvious. I mean, he's got *the* mark."

"*The* mark? You mean—" He hushed his voice and whispered something.

"Yes. There's no mistaking it." She gestured to her ear. "It's *inside* his ear. No one else in Delphinium history has had the mark there."

"But... how can that be? He's supposed to be dead."

"They didn't do a good job of it."

"Are you sure? I mean... once Kelvhan finds out about this... we'd better be sure."

"As I said, only one has ever had that mark inside their ear except for you-know-who. It can't be a coincidence."

"Then there's only one thing to do."

The Guardian was oblivious to the conversation going on behind him. Instead, his full attention was on Trix. This didn't feel right. She opened her mouth to speak, but the blond healer caught Trix's movement. The Guardian chose that moment to click his fingers at the healer and point at a glass of water by a bowl, then at Trix.

"Yes, D'arn Aeron. Of course. She must be thirsty." The healer bobbed her head and rushed to collect the water.

The Guardian elf—D'arn Aeron, by the sound of it—grabbed the cup and gently handed it to Trix. She drank greedily, trying not to look the healer in the eye.

"How long have you been awake?" the healer asked with a false smile.

CHAPTER
FIVE

Aeron knew something was wrong from the moment his mate woke. Trepidation simmered below her angst and confusion. At first, he thought her distrust was aimed at him—he'd called for the healer earlier, and she'd drugged his mate unexpectedly. He'd only hoped for something to help with the pain.

He caught the nervous flick of his mate's gaze over his shoulder and followed her attention just as the healer's gaze skated away from him.

He narrowed his eyes.

That was a guilty avoidance of eye contact. Since his accident, he'd paid close attention to body language. This was the grey in the lies of fae. The area where pure truth lived. Whether tensing or a tic, if he watched carefully, the real truth was usually revealed through a tell.

His palm itched for Honor, but he'd placed his baldric

and other weapons behind the door thinking they were safe. Only Guardians were allowed into the infirmary with their weapons, so he'd not felt any danger. Thistle was a Mage planted in the Spring Court for decades to help educate others on the correct ways to access the Well. He thought he was among friends.

But Thistle was gone, and a second person he'd not met stood with his arms folded, watching Aeron and the Tinker warily from the doorway. Aeron straightened his posture and stared hard at the male. He was rewarded with a lowering of the eyes. Not a concession, but a biding of time.

Thistle bustled in as the male left. Two well-dressed fae followed Thistle. One was tall, with long silken blond hair braided into an intricate half-updo that displayed his elven ears. His green velvet and patterned leather suit had been custom-made to fit his lithe form. A hand-stitched insignia of antlers, leaves, and flowing water stood out boldly on the breast pocket. The stag shifter following the elf wasn't so slick. His broad shoulders stretched the seams of his leather jacket. His antlers were shifted out, each fork pointed and ready to stab. His hair was piled and tied into a messy knot at his nape. But it was the mana-fortified wooden sword at his hip that drew Aeron's concern.

So he was a Royal Guard, then. And the elf was the Steward. Great, Aeron thought. Two pompous floaters were just what he needed.

Aeron had been inside the palace infirmary for almost

two days, and since he'd not personally announced himself to the royal family, he imagined they would feel slighted. They'd probably waited in their throne room for hours for him to turn up, but since Aeron had only left his mate's side to piss and shave at the basin, they would have to keep waiting. He'd even had his food brought here.

The steward's lips flattened at Aeron's indifference. His body language stiffened, his chin lifted, his expression became haughty, and he made limp gestures with his hands as though proudly decreeing some kuturi-shit. Flashes of his mate's disdain and dislike hit Aeron now and then, which meant the speech was not something he'd want to listen to even if he could.

So he turned back to his mate. He knew what was being said, anyway. Guardians weren't well-liked at the best of times, but one who'd avoided palace protocol was the dirt beneath a fee-lion's claws.

The steward also probably knew Aeron was friends with the current Seelie High King, Jasper Darkfoot. Jasper had been one of the Twelve before he took the Glass Crown from King Mithras and left the Order with Ada. From what Aeron had garnered about that harrowing time, the Spring Court King and Queen had been at the Darkfoot pack's Lupercalia rite to support Jasper in taking the Summer Court throne. But then half the party had been massacred by Mithras. The Spring Court Royals escaped with their lives, but some of their Lords and Nobles had not.

At the time, Jasper had been ignoring his calling. Some

would say the massacre might not have happened if he'd taken up arms sooner against his father. But to be fair to Jasper, he'd been abused for ten years. He had also been under the influence of a curse and suffering from amnesia. Give the wolf a break. Whether there was bad blood from this history, Aeron guessed he would soon find out.

The war between the Seelie and Unseelie had remained a threat, and until recently, Maebh's attacks had been nothing but a thorn in Jasper's side. She'd picked at the edges of his tapestry only enough to remind him of her might. To pester and poke him as Unseelie were known to do. But since Forrest had failed to bring back Maebh's halfling granddaughter from Crystal City, the war was about to get serious. The tapestry was about to unravel.

But a Guardian stayed out of the politics of everyday fae in Elphyne. It wasn't up to them to get involved or pick sides. However, it was up to them to clear the taint on the Well and protect it from desolation their Seers had predicted would come from the human city.

...and the steward was still up on his soap box. He strode toward Aeron, his lips moving rapidly. Aeron's mate tried to tell him something—probably that Aeron couldn't hear—but the steward snapped at her.

Every muscle in Aeron's body tensed. His fingers curled into fists. There was a way to bring Honor to his palm by using a transference spell. He considered doing it, despite the risk the spell would warp from the taint. Instead, he slowly rose to his full height and stared down the steward, daring him with a look to speak like that to his mate again. As it turned out, the steward wasn't a complete dimwit. He balked and shrank under Aeron's scrutiny. When he was sure the male had learned his place, Aeron returned to his seat and focused on his mate's face.

She tried to hide it, but he felt her disdain toward the steward's superfluous demeanor. He echoed her scornful look, and she smirked. That she found Aeron humorous made his stomach flutter. She'd only just met him, but she was siding with him.

He guessed *floaters* were the same whether human or fae. The Well Worms wouldn't discriminate in their judgment. All unworthy, no matter what their skin looked like or their mana capacity, would float and bloat on the waters of the ceremonial lake.

Thistle bustled in and stopped, clearly feeling the tension in the air. The steward mumbled something to her. She pursed her lips, took a letter from the steward, and handed it to Aeron. It reminded him that he'd penned a letter for his mate. When the time was right, he'd give it to her. But first, he broke the Spring Court wax seal and read it.

D'arn Aeron,
Your presence is cordially requested in the Spring Court for the inaugural Delphinium

Spring Festival in one turn of the moon. As you're aware, with growing unrest between Seelie and Unseelie, a show of support from the Order will be well received.

In the meantime, please accept our hospitality and resources for healing your wounded.

Signed,

Your Generous Spring King Tian and Queen Oleana.

A show of Order support? Aeron crumpled the letter in his fist. He couldn't give a rat's ass about the war. It had nothing to do with him or his purpose. He would be out of here as soon as he could. The steward handed him another letter, a tiny smirk on his lips.

This one read:

Your guest suite has been prepared for your stay as requested. Mage Thistle will be at your service. Please follow us.

Aeron stared at the guard. In other words, in return for the healing services his Well-blessed mate received, Aeron must pay by volunteering his time at the festival. He reached to take Thistle's pencil and write a response, but the steward plopped another letter onto Aeron's lap, then rocked haughtily on his heels and waited with a smug look.

The image of Aeron's fist meeting the steward's nose was tempting.

With a forced exhale, he opened the last letter. If he'd been wise, he'd have paid attention to the seal before snapping it open. His temper flared as he read.

I approve the request of the Spring Court for D'arn Aeron's and his Well-blessed Mate, Beatrix Beckford's presence at the Delphinium Spring Festival, and for the duration from the date on this letter until then.

In these dark times where the Order is losing Guardians at an alarming rate, it is important to present a strong front and to encourage new recruits to replenish our ranks.

Signed,

Aleksandra, Prime of the Order of the Well.

The Prime *approved*. His fist swallowed the letter as he crumpled it. At first, he was stunned. This wasn't a job for a Guardian in the Twelve. But then, of course, Aeron thought bitterly. He was useless to her. She already wanted him replaced. The sooner, the better it seemed. This meant his time to find a cure for the taint was wearing thin. Even more reason he had to be out of there fast.

Fuck.

After his anger eased, he smoothed out the letter and read his mate's name—Beatrix. She took the letter from him, beckoned for Thistle's pencil, and then scratched out the first half of her name. She pointed at her chest and smiled sheepishly at him.

Trix.

That suited her better than Tinker. He couldn't explain why. There was something trickster-like in her eyes. Something mischievous he wanted to peel back and investigate. Later, when he had time.

She tapped the paper. It took him a moment to wrench his gaze from hers, and then he noticed where she tapped. At his name. He nodded and pointed at himself, then crossed out the D'arn part. That was the official part. Only the Prime and a certain blond team leader with a carrot stuck up his elf ass used it.

Feeling his ears warm, he cleared his throat and stood. He would have to find a way to work on the taint from here. He could use this time to raid the Spring Court libraries for any other recorded observations about physical manifestations of the inky side of the Well. He could test out his theories here just as he could elsewhere, and he'd intended to do it without the help of the Order, anyway.

This small sidestep would be temporary. He could still deposit Trix back at the Order and then head off to the ceremonial lake to work on his theories. That was the strongest power source in Elphyne. It made sense the inky taint would be easier to track there.

Aeron caught Trix reading the rest of the Prime's letter with a frown and wide eyes. He followed her attention and noted the second part where the Prime worried about losing Guardians. It was true. They'd lost more than usual lately. Whether to the monsters they fought, the humans who raided, or some that went missing in action.

Maybe he should skip this festival. Conflicted, he grabbed the note and crumpled it.

CHAPTER
SIX

A split second had the power to make or break futures, decide life or death, set fire or douse the flames. As Kelvhan waited by the Great Elder Tree, he stewed over the constant stream of fires he'd had to put out during his life as High Lord and brother to the Queen Consort. It seemed once one fire was out, another was lit.

When his sister had mated with King Tian, Kelvhan had eyes on the throne. He'd always known the king was sterile. It was Kelvhan who'd secretly made him that way, after all. And it was Kelvhan who'd ensured the king's sister conveniently died during childbirth. With so much tragedy in the king's bloodline, legend of their ties to the Horned God Eulios shifted from bountiful and godly to cursed and feared.

Once, invoking Eulios's name ensured rain fell, crops

grew, and fertility peaked. After centuries of frozen famine, this had been revered as necessary for a prospering kingdom. But now the Great Elder Tree Eulios planted with his seed no longer stood tall and virile at the center of their woodland city. Its magenta leaves fell into a crusty and tainted carpet for the first time in centuries. Its bark was dry and cracked. Its roots were poisoned.

Some said the Horned God was displeased with them. Others said he was dead. But the ones who said it was time for a change made Kelvhan proud and excited, and he'd not even suggested the rebellion in their minds. They'd come to a conclusion all on their own.

This spring festival was their last attempt to please the Horned God, but Kelvhan knew it would fall short. He would make sure of it. Tian was old, sickly, and had no heir, so the rituals were weak without a blood tie to run them. Soon Eulios would be a figment of imagination, as would the people's loyalty toward that royal bloodline.

Leaves rustled to Kelvhan's right. The steward emerged from the path between two hedges. He dusted leaves from his hair.

"And?" Kelvhan asked, impatient.

"And they both said the same thing. He bears Eulios's mark."

"How is that possible?" Kelvhan kicked the Great Elder Tree. Leaves dropped on his head, and he cursed, brushing them off. "Not now. Not when everything is coming together."

The steward flicked leaves from his shoulders and raised his brows. "I don't know why you're so upset. He is one fae without his hearing. He knows not of what he is."

"The king and queen requested his presence at the festival," Kelvhan grumbled. "He's a Well-blessed *Guardian* and one of the Twelve, no less. I have no doubt he is still a formidable foe."

"One who is more concerned with healing his human mate than anything else."

"You're right." Kelvhan tapped his lips. "She is human. All we need to do is ensure her healing is painful and slow. Hopefully, he'll leave before the festival."

"Shouldn't be a problem with how mana is corrupted at the moment." The steward's eyes flared with cruel mischief. "All we need is for something to go wrong."

"The Guardian won't leave her side."

"He has to at some point."

"If he doesn't, then we'll have to be more direct. Get Selly on it."

The steward shook his head. "She's too reckless. She might kill them. All we need is—"

"I said, send her in. The mate is human, for Crimson's sake. Who cares if she dies? His death will attract attention from the Order, and we don't want that. But without her, he will simply leave. As long as it's before the festival but not too close, then everything will move forward as planned." Kelvhan glared at the steward. *Of all the gall.* Since when did he make decisions? "This war will be on our doorstep any day. Do you really want that sap in charge or someone who will make the hard choices?"

The steward stared hard for a moment. Kelvhan thought he'd say no. But the steward dropped his chin and bowed.

"As you wish."

CHAPTER
SEVEN

Sometimes it was hard for Trix to tell the difference between anxiety and excitement. Like now, for instance, when the handsome and brooding warrior elf slipped one hand beneath her broken thighs. He braced the other around her back, looked deeply into her eyes, and paused.

He was inches away. Atoms clashed in her body. It was a storm and inferno all at once. Already woozy from the drugs and pain, her head swam as she became trapped in his coppery gaze. She shouldn't feel like this about her enemy, but he'd not acted like one. The intimacy confused her. It took her a moment to understand that he waited for her to do something... why was he... *oh*.

His dark brows pinched together as he guided her hands to his neck for extra support before repositioning himself. *Oh no*. Her heart positively galloped now. It must be nerves. Nerves because he was about to move her, and the pain would slice her legs into ribbons. It certainly wasn't how he looked right into her soul as though he knew every little dark secret about her... and accepted it all with patience.

Patience: that's all she'd ever wanted from a partner. Someone who understood her stupid, flibbertigibbet ways. Someone who smiled at her fondly when she did it and loved her for it. But it was impossible to know that about someone so soon after meeting him. She screwed up her face. Why was she thinking of this elf like that?

Wishful thinking, she told herself. Always with her head in the clouds instead of looking where her feet were moving. Exhibit A, her broken legs.

A wash of self-deprecation and shame cleared her nerves. Those kinds of thoughts were dangerous around an enemy. She stiffly wrapped her hands around the elf's neck and tried not to look at his face in case he sensed her quickening pulse. This was so embarrassing. Who was he to her? Why was he helping?

He'd been doing nothing but sitting under her tree, watching the world go by, and she'd all but fallen on top of him. She was human—his enemy. He should have tossed her into a dungeon as the other elf had.

Maybe it had something to do with the blue pattern on her arm. She poked it. Weird. It didn't rub off and didn't hurt. How did her skin even make that color?

The moment he lifted her, nausea rolled with the pain

stabbing her legs. Darkness closed in. She fainted. When her eyes fluttered open again, warm leather pressed against her cheek. It was his chest. His heartbeat was steady. She couldn't say she was upset about leaning against him like this. The rhythm was oh-so calming as it interplayed with his footsteps echoing down a hollow hall.

Stop it, she mentally scolded. *Stay alert. Don't trust him. Look what happened with the last guy you trusted.*

"Where are we?" she tried to say but drooled instead. Whoops. She wiped her mouth, guessing the sleeping draught wasn't entirely out of her system.

Aeron sensed her wakefulness. His grip on her tightened, and peace suddenly rolled over her again. She braced against the stabs of pain from jostling. The muffled heartbeat beneath her ear was a soothing lullaby. He might not have words, but he spoke in other ways. Earlier, he was as confused and angry as she was. But now he was calm, steady, and unworried. It was weird she knew that. But despite her nervous caution, knowing how he felt made her feel good, which was also weird.

Think about it tomorrow, she thought drowsily. For now, she was going with the dopamine hit.

The palace hallway was vast in both width and height. Made from twisted wood that had been coaxed to grow organically in great architectural designs. Open windows let in a breeze of fresh air. When Trix's pain ebbed, she shifted her gaze to the light and gasped at the beautiful landscape blossoming with roses, a cut lawn, and manicured trees. She was in some kind of natural wonderland and half-expected a giant smoking caterpillar or a well-dressed white rabbit running about.

Every so often, Elven runes glowed softly on panels in the wooden walls. She'd seen those runes around a few places—often carved into some natural substance to magically strengthen it. It was the fae answer to metal. Ingenious, really. She should write that down. The Well took, but it gave a substitute. She wondered how long the reinforcement lasted. She'd always built things out of metal because it made sense. It was long-lasting, conducive to electricity, and primarily impenetrable.

It wasn't until Aeron shifted his grip and angled her that Trix realized she'd craned her neck, trying to read runes on a support beam they passed. Feeling foolish, she forced her eyes back to the front, but he didn't seem to mind.

Again, weird that she knew that. It was more than reading his body language. Before she could dwell on it, they arrived at a door.

"Here is your room," Thistle said as a palace worker opened the large carved wooden doors.

Trix gaped at the decor as they went inside. Room was an understatement. Perhaps a luxurious nature suite was better. A grand four-poster bed sat at the end of the quaint room. The wooden posts were twisted ornately as though the bed had been grown, not made. A sprinkling of lush-leafed vines made the canopy. The pillows were plush and bountiful. An arched doorway led to a bathing suite with a free-standing porcelain bath on clawed feet.

A table for two sat near an arched open window overlooking a magnificent tree. Oh no, it was only a part of the tree. The rest of it grew roots that traveled over the lawn and caged the palace. The enormous tree reached over a hundred feet and had deep purplish wood and magenta leaves. It seemed deciduous like it was shedding. Everything smelled green—like nature. Trix inhaled and smiled. It reminded her of her treehouse.

She turned her gaze to the rest of the room. Shelves with a sprinkling of books lined a wall. They seemed like the same sort Aeron had been reading earlier. Probably non-fiction. She itched to open them and see if any had information she could compare with her notes.

A dormant stone fireplace was ready for the colder months. Somewhere behind, another open archway looked like a dressing room... filled with clothes, a chaise, and a hand-blown black looking glass.

When Aeron placed her on the bed, she sank into the mattress. It was soft, yet not too soft. Goldilocks perfect. She ran her hand over the fuzzy blanket and tried to place the material—not wool. Too soft for that. Maybe another fae animal, then? She pulled the cover aside to test the sheets.

"Bloody hell," she breathed. "This is so good, isn't it?"

Crystal City had raw, rough, colorless bedding. Only a few of the elite had better colors inside their rooms. But she was the Tinker, too preoccupied with her nose in an invention to worry about luxury like this. Maybe she should have been a little more demanding.

She was still staring at the bedding, wondering what it was made from, when she realized Aeron paced the room, doing something with his hands at certain intervals, particularly at the windows and door.

"What's he doing?" Trix asked Thistle, who busied herself with writing care instructions with a pencil and paper.

"Presumably setting privacy wards so no one can hear us."

What?

"Oh." Trix paused. Swallowed a lump. As in... no one can hear her scream? Panic started to squeeze her lungs. "Who would be listening in? Why would they care?"

"He's a Guardian." Thistle shrugged as if Guardians did weird shit like this all the time.

Trix's mind went a thousand miles an hour, trying to figure out if she was in danger.

She had the sudden urge to be back in her tree. At least there, all she had to worry about was herself and her notebooks. Sometimes being alone with her thoughts was all she needed. Thoughts, a notebook, and a nice cup of tea. And the brilliant toilet she'd made. She sighed and rested her head on the pillow, staring up at the pretty, delicate leafy canopy.

How was her treehouse doing? Would it fall into

disarray without her to run maintenance? If she learned how to cast some of those reinforcing runes, she might have—

"Trix?"

"Whoops, Thistle. Were you saying something?"

Thistle continued to talk over Trix. "... so for that reason, any work using mana to heal your broken bones might end up doing more harm than good. It's one thing for Aeron to cast wards, but another to work on a body that feels and reacts. My recommendation is that we take the long route for your healing plan—"

"How do I get this blue stuff off?"

"—I've written it all down for your mate to read over."

"I'm sorry, did you say mate?"

Trix had suffered many disapproving looks in her time, but the one Thistle blinked at her was the worst. It was like —*Duh, you know the answer, and you're pretending to be dumb.* It was the same look that Justin used to give Trix after he'd been explaining something and she interrupted or hadn't been paying attention.

Thistle's demeanor softened upon seeing Trix shrink into herself. She took Trix's hand and squeezed gently.

"Trix, do you not know what these blue marks mean?"

Nerves prickled in Trix's chest. "That's why I asked."

Thistle's lips twisted. She frowned and glanced at Aeron, who still worked.

"Bloody hell, don't keep me in suspense," Trix blurted. "What does it mean?"

"It's a—"

Aeron waved his letter at the Mage, stealing her attention. A storm brewed in his eyes as he pointed at a particular paragraph on the paper. Thistle patted Trix, pulled a pencil out of her hair, and beckoned for the letter. She wrote something else down. Trix couldn't see, but Aeron's nostrils flared, and he nodded.

"What?" Trix barked. "What aren't you telling me? Am I dying?"

They didn't answer. Oh, God. She wouldn't be able to walk again. Her head hit the pillow, and she blinked tears from her eyes. "I survived an apocalypse, and now I'm dying because I got distracted and fell out of my tree. And I have weird blue marks. Probably infected him, and that's why we're both here. I'm a twat. A class-A numpty."

Aeron's palm flattened against her sternum. Shocked at his touch, her gaze flicked to his. Defiant words were on the tip of her tongue, but he did that stare thing—he held her eyes captive until her heartbeat steadied. Calm settled on her like a blanket, and then he lifted his hand. She wanted to snatch it back and keep it there but forced herself to hand sign her gratitude instead.

His lips twitched.

They were sensual, and she couldn't put her finger on why. There was a slight curve or a pout that wasn't a pout. Was that twitch the start of a reluctant smile?

Then he returned to Thistle, pointed to a section on the letter, and jerked his chin toward Trix.

Thistle said to her with a sigh, "I have permission to tell you some of it but not all of it."

"It's my body. I want to know it all."

"You're not dying."

"Thank fuck." She covered her mouth and mumbled through her fingers. "I can't control my mouth sometimes. And for the record, I thanked fuck. Not you. Please don't trap me into a fae bargain."

Trix knew a little about fae bargains. Don't say sorry or thank you, or they'll claim a debt enforced by the Well. There were other, more subtle ways fae could claim a debt, but since she'd hidden away in her tree for most of her time in Elphyne, she was still to learn the ins and outs of the custom.

Thistle's laugh was like tinkling bells. She gave a dismissive shake of the head, so the tiny leaves sprouting in her hair rustled.

Trix pointed at her. "If you're laughing, then it must be good news."

"Well, that's up for debate. The short of it is there's no way for you to heal speedily, as I mentioned. But if you're connected to the Well— which means don't revert to your human ways and use forbidden substances—then your healing will be faster than usual. I've recommended bedrest, daily baths in the sacred healing waters of the Great Elder Tree, and for your mate to make sure you stay off your feet."

"You said mate again. You mean mate, right? Like he's my good mate, yeah?"

"I'll let him explain that. I'm expecting your full recovery to take two weeks."

"Two weeks! Is that all?" Injuries like this took months in Crystal City.

"I'll be back in a week and see if you're ready to start walking. Here is some elixir that will help you sleep at night. Only take it under supervision."

She placed a small vial of liquid on the bedside table next to a lamp glowing with manabeeze inside and said, "I'll make sure three meals a day are delivered for the both of you. If you could find a way to pass that on to your mate, it would save me writing it down."

Before Trix could ask questions, Aeron hand signed his gratitude, and Thistle left the room.

He closed the door, stripped off his baldric, unsheathed his sword, and stabbed the length of it through the door's bolt casings. Once satisfied it held firm, he cracked his neck, sighed, and busied himself by removing his leather jacket. Beneath, he wore a simple linen shirt that stretched across broad shoulders, defined musculature, and a narrow waist. He carefully draped the jacket over the back of a plush armchair and then thoroughly tested the security on the blown glass windows.

Trix stared dumbfounded as he moved about the room, doing benign duties such as washing his face, placing furniture the way he liked, and dropping a pillow and extra blankets on the couch by the window. He completely ignored her as he sat and pulled a sealed letter out of his satchel. He turned it over, studied it, then stared out the window. Then his shoulders dropped as he exhaled. He tucked the letter back into his bag.

EIGHT

Aeron had spent much of the journey from the infirmary contemplating his next move. He was stuck here with his mate. At least until the Festival.

It grated on him that he was forced to spend time with her like this... half a fae. He was already frustrated at not being able to communicate. It wouldn't be long before he became a burden to her.

"You're a rat," said his brother decades ago. *"You're a sniveling little rat."*

"You should have a tail," agreed his sister as she plucked his long hair. *"Let's make him a tail to go with those big rat ears."*

She sliced and sheared off his hair. Helpless, he watched it fall in streams on the floor, not understanding, not knowing what he could do to help himself.

"Yes, let's make him wear it to court."

"Father won't like that."

"Father will love having something to laugh at. What better than an object dumped on his steps by a whore mother who didn't want him."

Aeron stuffed the memory deep down where all his dark ones lived. He glanced at his sword shoved into the bolt casings and reminded himself who he was. Not the reality, but the ones in the books—the heroes. The knights. The ones who'd gotten him through his darkest days as he read their stories in books.

Honor.

He stared at his letter to Trix, and his stomach squirmed. Since he'd had his accident, his childhood memories returned with a vengeance. He might not be enough for Trix in this state. It was better that he was cruel to be kind and told her he didn't want them to be together in the state he was in. But something made him shove the letter back into his satchel.

Later. He was too tired to deal with more drama right now. Trix had looked tired too. With any luck, she would fall asleep, and they could work out a plan in the morning.

He briefly considered making a blood connection through the water to Forrest. Even if he couldn't talk, Trix could speak with Melody and set her mind at ease. But the moment anyone found out where he was, they would come running, and the chance of him proving himself capable went out the window.

No. He punched a pillow on the couch and readied

himself to nap. It had been a long night and day. In the morning, he would deal with helping Trix heal enough to take her back to the Order, then leave her and find a way to clear the taint.

His job and self-respect depended on it.

CHAPTER
NINE

Trix sat on her bed, fuming and glaring as the elf settled into sleep.

"What am I supposed to do?" she shouted at him.

He hadn't asked if she needed anything. He'd barely looked at her after Thistle left. What the hell was going on?

He couldn't hear her, which was why she unleashed all her angst and frustration on him with words. It was a cop-out, but to be honest, he was also acting like a right—*gah!*

It wasn't like she chose this. It wasn't like she had other options. Her emotions threatened to get the better of her, and tears stung her eyes. She was so confused. Thistle said he was there to help her and would give her answers about the blue marks. This *mate* business. Was he really that tired, or was he ignoring her?

And what was with the ignoring of her hand signs?

Sure, he might not understand... but he gave no alternative besides hastily scribbled notes. Even when Thistle wrote, he looked frustrated as hell. But at least he could walk, and —realization hit her like a ton of bricks—she won't be able to walk to the toilet. Or to dress herself. Maybe. Will she be able to wipe her ass?

She gasped. "Oh my god. My life is over."

I feel sick.

She took a pillow and smashed her face into it, and screamed. It felt good. Maybe the elf should try it sometimes. He seemed to have a lot of pent-up frustration bubbling beneath the surface. Releasing some of that stress would be good for him.

Still panting from her scream, she glared over at the couch and bit her lip. Was he genuinely sleeping? She waved her hands, trying to get his attention, but no luck.

"Oi!" she shouted.

Naturally, he didn't respond, so she looked for something to throw. A pillow. That's all she had. She tossed it at him, hurt herself, and cried out. Tears burned her eyes as pain throbbed down her legs. And the bloody pillow didn't even get far.

Bastard.

When the pain died down, she was losing her grip on reality. She was a fidgeter at the best of times, but being contained in this bed sent her fingers scrunching fabric, tapping her thighs, tugging hair, eyes darting about.

She used to have an Irish worry stone back at the

Crystal City lab. It was one of the rare gifts from her brother Trevor. The green marble had a groove worn out from rubbing her thumb to relieve anxiety. A surge of melancholy washed through her, and she squeezed her eyes to prevent it from worsening.

This elf had rescued her but now seemingly ignored her. What the fuck was going on?

She pushed up on her elbows and scowled his way.

"Oi!" she shouted again. "Don't ignore me, wanker!"

There was one thing she hadn't tried yet to get his attention—using her special gift. As soon as the thought hit, she imagined conjuring vines that wrapped all around him and smothered him. Then she felt guilty and laid back down. Hadn't she already done enough bad things to Guardians with her invention?

Maybe his lack of response was because he was a typical male and hadn't considered her needs. And without his hearing, he didn't realize she was there shouting.

He could have checked first, though. She scowled.

She might have laid there for an hour before finally giving in to the knowledge that she needed to go to the bathroom.

This was humiliating. She squeezed her eyes shut and willed herself not to cry. He didn't deserve her tears.

"Come on, Trix," she said. "You're used to dealing with butt-faced men. Suck it up and show him you're better. You don't need him."

Taking a deep breath, she searched around the bed and found notepaper on a side table. Thistle had used it earlier. Trix wrote a message for the elf and scrunched it into a tight little ball. Then she squinted, stuck her tongue out a little, then tossed it across the room.

CHAPTER TEN

Aeron tried to sleep. He'd thought without his hearing, that simple feat would have been easy. But, no. Every time Trix's emotions swirled and eddied like water, he felt them brush up against his own.

She went through a full range of emotions, from anger to sadness and despair. He refused to get up and try to talk with her. It would be tedious and a burden, and Aeron would not be that. Never again.

Besides, if either of them became attached to each other now, then the chances he'd leave her and head off to clean the taint would be low. He'd seen how Melody and Forrest looked at each other. Forrest had given up his mission to extract Willow for Melody. Aeron couldn't afford to give up his mission.

It was better they kept distance between them. Probably better she didn't know about the blue marks, despite her asking Thistle. His body already wanted to go to her. His mind told him to stay. Don't interact too much. Keep her at arm's length. Just for now. Just until he had completed his mission.

But with each passing second, that internal argument lost its legs. Especially when he sensed her emotions turn to feeling neglected. Then anger.

It reminded him too much of his youth. He would never forget feeling unwanted when he was a child. Whether it was from his siblings, the people of the Autumn Court, or his stepmother, the queen who had barely acknowledged his existence. It was as though he'd not existed.

But the king made sure Aeron knew every minute that he was unwanted.

"You have the scraps," the king had said one mealtime. "It's not like we planned to have you here. Otherwise, we would have ordered more food."

But the table had been overflowing with food. A starving boy with a feast before his eyes, Aeron had waited in his broken chair with a wobbly leg. His mouth watered as his family ate. As the designated Sacrifice, Forrest was ignored completely. There was no place for him at the table, and he often ate in his room. But he was given food. The Sacrifice had to stay alive to serve his purpose, after all. He had to stay educated, or at least appear it so that the public assumed he was cared for.

Aeron was forced to sit and watch as they ate until their bellies bloated. He couldn't reach for anything until the family had left the table. There was *always* food left. It had confounded his child mind.

Until he understood why: misdirected truth was the cruelest lie, and fae were the masters of it. They might not lie with their tongues, but they did so with expectations. They intentionally manipulated emotion. They made him *hope* and then squashed it beneath their boots.

After his family was finished at the table, the king would signal for his Well Hounds to eat. Aeron had to fight them off with his hands to get his portion.

False hope was a dangerous thing. He couldn't work out if he gave Trix false hope by being here or if his own false hope blinded him to reality.

Something small and crinkly bounced off his head. He sat up, his pulse racing. Eyes darting about, he located the projectile. A scrunched piece of paper rested on his legs. He picked it up, frowning, and glanced over to Trix, who scowled at him.

He opened the paper and smoothed it out.

I need to go to the bathroom. Please.

He glanced at her. This time, her scowl took on a different meaning. Shame, awkwardness, and an underlying sense of despair trickled down their bond. She folded her arms and looked away with glistening eyes.

This must be hard for her. He'd been insensitive and wrapped up in his own needs. This was not how a knight would behave, regardless of whether his mission had been derailed. Honor always came first.

She was in pain. Probably hungry. He put the paper aside and got to his feet.

She kept her eyes studiously averted when he arrived at her bedside. Her jaw clenched. Her lips pursed. But he slid his hand beneath her thighs and waited for her to put her arm around his neck. As he walked her to the bathroom and placed her on the porcelain latrine, her anxiety thickened.

He paused and stared at her in case she needed something.

She gaped and pointed out the door. He hesitated. Her legs stuck out like matchsticks from her thighs. Wooden splints were strapped to each leg by silk rope. It would be difficult for her to remove her pants—even the flowing ones the healers had dressed her in. He didn't want her to hurt herself, so he reached out to help, but she slapped him away—fire in her eyes.

Humiliation hammered him from down their bond.

She made rapid hand signals and then pointed harshly to the door. *Go*, her lips read. He supposed he deserved that. Aeron showed his palms in surrender. He understood how she felt. He hated being treated like an invalid, so he walked casually to the door, left it open but waited just outside.

It was one thing to avoid getting close to her now. It was another to be complicit in her misfortune. He'd already failed to hear her scream once. He wouldn't miss her distress again.

He focused on the bookshelf on the far wall. He counted the books and noted a few were novels. His eyes kept tracking back to them. It had been decades since he'd fallen into fiction.

A smile tipped his lips as he remembered the fun of staying up all night, exhausted, and hiding out in the stables with Forrest. They used to hide together. Aeron did this for fear of being brutally ridiculed or humiliated, and Forrest just wanted company.

"*You be the pirate,*" *Aeron had said, pointing a wooden sword at his older brother.*

"*I don't want to be the pirate.*" *Forrest scowled and then pointed at one of the Well Hound puppies he spoke to in his mind.* "*Rabbit will be the pirate, won't you?*"

The dog yipped, but its acidic eye fluid splashed the straw and sizzled.

"*Maybe you should be the pirate,*" *Forrest mumbled.*

"*I don't want to be a pirate. I want to be a knight. Or a king.*" *Then no one could tell him what to do. He pointed at the Well Hounds and squinted, imagining them his subjects and him giving them orders.*

"*Fine. You be the knight,*" *Forrest conceded.*

"*I need a princess to rescue.*"

"*Rabbit.*" *Forrest pointed very fast.*

"So... you don't want to be the princess? But you have the long hair, and I don't!"

Forrest's eyes softened on Aeron. "One day, you can grow your hair as long as you want, and no one can say anything."

Aeron curled his braid around his fist, then let the length bump through his fingers. He'd come a long way from those stolen nights. So had Forrest, who rescued his very own princess from a tower. Melody might not be royalty in this world, but she was as good as one in the old world. She sang to hundreds of thousands, if not millions, of adoring fans.

Aeron was happy for his brother.

He touched his ears and frowned. He might have needed his hearing to learn to read and to fight and defend, but much of that knowledge was still there in his head. It didn't go anywhere. It just needed a different perspective.

It wasn't until he sensed Trix's frustration boil into infuriation that he angled his head slightly to see if she was done. A projectile flew at him. He ducked. He was about to laugh at the absurdity of her throwing things still, but then he startled when Trix's alarm and utter helplessness sliced into him deeply.

Concerned, he braved another look. She was on the tiled ground, hunched over, her face in her hands, sobbing. Her pants were half around her creamy thighs and gathered where the splints ended. She saw him coming and tried frantically to lift them, but she was hurting herself.

While he couldn't exactly feel bodily sensations

through their bond, he felt her distress. This was his fault. When he'd first turned to see if she was okay, she must have panicked and grabbed the closest item to toss at his head. And in doing so, she fell.

His cheeks heated. How did he keep messing things up?

He raced to her side and dropped to his knees. She batted him away and then focused on hastily lifting her pants and covering herself. He tried to help. She lashed out, despite her obvious pain. He captured her hands and held them until she stopped struggling. Tears ran down her cheeks. Her chest lifted in stilted sobs. The tip of her nose was stained pink. She refused to meet his eyes.

He forced himself to feel calm, to think of the waves in the ocean on a warm day, and then pushed that feeling into her with all the compassion he could think of. He'd done this a few times before when she was in the infirmary, and it seemed to work. When her sobs lessened, he wiped a tear from her cheek with a thumb and then guided her arms around his neck. He ensured her pants were held firm and lifted her off the ground. She refused to meet his eyes, even as he laid her down on her bed and offered her a drink. She just closed her eyes and turned away.

He might not be able to hear a monster coming, might not hear her scream or fall, but he could do this. He could make sure she never shed another tear caused by his actions again.

CHAPTER ELEVEN

Trix refused to look at Aeron. The worst part was that he seemed to blame himself. He thought what had happened was his fault, and while part of her blamed him, it wasn't entirely true.

It was the lie she told so she didn't have to blame herself.

Some kind of switch had flipped when she was on that toilet seat, that was all. She didn't realize how fragile her state of mind had been. She thought she was fine. In control. That she was taking everything in her stride, but she couldn't *move*.

She couldn't do things for herself, and she needed to do things. Trix was a woman who always did things. Whether tinkering on a new project, pulling apart something, or wandering the halls thinking. The trapped feeling didn't hit her until she was on the toilet, desperately trying to pull her pants up so the stupid brooding elf wouldn't see her bottom.

And then he'd turned. That imperious profile of his angled her way. She'd freaked, grabbed a bottle of bath salts, and tossed them at his head. In doing so, she'd wrenched her body painfully, twisted her legs, and fell from the seat.

The weight of every emotion she'd stifled since she'd woken in the dungeon fell on top of her. Just like that. She was lonely, humiliated, and stuck. And the stupid brooding elf rushed over to help her like she was a broken thing.

Maybe she was.

Maybe it was more than the broken legs. The simple fact of it was Trix had no idea what to do with herself. Sometimes life tossed curve balls. Sometimes those balls piled on each other and became boulders. Sometimes she didn't want to lift them off.

Now all she could think about was the heavy weight of the blanket as she tugged it over her body. One minute she had it on her, liking the pressure. The next, she shoved the stifling thing off.

What would Trevor think of her if he saw her now? Her black sheep brother also had a view of life that astounded her. He never cared for the opinions of other people. He did what he wanted, what made him feel good.

For someone who reacted so viscerally sometimes at others' opinions, Trix had been in awe of him. She'd learned to temper those reactions as she grew older, but sometimes, they still had a way of overwhelming her.

Back then, it had seemed like such a waste of a life. Why sit and while away endless hours to feel good? Boring. Of course, now she understood perfectly. Feeling good was everything. Feeling loved. Safe. Cherished. Accepted. If she could put that on a T-shirt and wear it, she would. But at least she'd given Trevor acceptance. She brought him gifts and groceries.

She knew he had a disease, and the addiction could have easily been hers, so she'd always done her best to support him any way she could. She missed him.

Trix rolled into her pillow, feeling sorry for herself, and sniffed. She stared at the bedside table vacantly and plucked at the blanket. Aeron's shadow came into view, then a bottle—the elixir Thistle had left. It was meant to help with the pain.

He was still trying to help her in his weird half-hearted way. It was almost like he wanted to help her, but something held him back. Maybe it was that she was human. She'd thought about Thistle saying they were mates and remembered a few things about fae culture. Mating was like a marriage. If that's what this was, it made no sense. It confused the hell out of her... but maybe it also confused him.

"I need answers," she mumbled and slid watery eyes his way.

His brows lifted in the middle. It made her throat thicken. He looked confused.

Maybe he was figuring out things too, and they'd just been thrown together. He got stuck with a woman with broken legs who kept talking to him when he couldn't hear. She hand signed her apology. His eyes widened, and he captured her fist as it made a round motion on her chest. He shook his head. When she didn't quite understand, he kissed her knuckles.

Speechless.

Trix was... the soft touch of his lips against her skin. The heat of his breath. The gentle, hesitant lifting of his gaze to meet hers. He didn't want her to feel sorry for what had happened.

"It goes both ways, mate," she said. "Don't feel like it was your fault."

He watched her lips move, but the recognition wasn't in his eyes, so she boldly pulled his rough, warrior's hand to her lips and kissed his knuckles. His audible escape of air made her smile. If only for a short while.

"Tomorrow," she announced, not caring if he understood. "I'm just going to teach you a few signs whether you like it or not. No need to get your knickers in a twist. Deal with it."

He measured a dose of the elixir and handed it to her. As she drank it down, she knew something profound had changed between them. The reluctance and unease were still there, simmering beneath the surface. But they both recognized they were two people in the same situation. This mating situation must be new to him, too. For all of her reasons to distrust him, he had his own to be wary of her. Tomorrow they could figure it out together.

Already feeling the warmth of the liquid take hold of her body, Trix laid her head down on the pillow and watched the twinkling on her blue arm marks until they blurred. Not long after, the weight of a warm hand landed on her head and stroked deftly down her hair.

Now, this weight... this weight she liked.

TWELVE

Maebh dragged her sorry ass along her private terrace in the Obsidian Palace. Every step she took hurt. Not even she was brave enough to tap into her depleted mana stores now to keep the glamour up that hid her aging face and body. She'd taken to wearing masks and gloves. She stayed in her private chambers. She lived for these views across the Aconite Sea in the direction of Crystal City, where her only living heir resided.

And she dared to dream of revenge.

Those Fae Guardians had promised her Aurora, but they were dragging their feet.

The bargain she made with them was useless without a time limit. They had known that when they made it with her. They'd deliberately capitalized on her desperation and vulnerability.

But if the bargain was useless, holding up her end was

null. Maebh had fought so long and hard for the existence of that heir. She'd sacrificed everything. She became a monster and created monsters. She tickled her pet demogorgon beneath his split, drooling maw and enjoyed its strange clicking language as she contemplated her next steps.

"My queen," Dimitri said from behind her, but she refused to turn her head, and the mask blocked her peripheral view as he continued pushing her with his demands. "Come inside and feed. It's cold out here."

He knew.

He knew she could not keep the ice from the air like she used to. He knew she was aged—he'd seen it despite her best efforts. He knew this war was her last-ditch effort at claiming a meaningful legacy.

She could march her soldiers and demogorgon down to Crystal City. She could hammer their gates and forcibly remove her granddaughter and bring her home, but Maebh was no fool. She knew what lies had been told about her to her flesh and blood. She knew that an act of aggression now would only push Aurora away. With the taint on the Well, there was also a slim chance that some of her best warriors would lose their advantage. The only reliable tool Maebh had was the demogorgon, and even he sometimes ignored directives and did as he pleased. The only living person in this world the demogorgon would not kill was Maebh.

The best hope Maebh had of reclaiming Aurora was to

take back control of this Well-forsaken land. Make it whole under her rule. But Aleksandra and her Order stood in the way when they could have had everything together—especially with Jackson gone.

Sometimes Maebh wondered if those two had had an affair, despite his pining over his lost love. Did Aleksandra somehow blame Maebh for his death? But for all of her searching for excuses, there were none.

Only after Maebh united Elphyne would she have two options to reclaim her granddaughter—bargain with the humans for her. Two, send a united army in to decimate and retrieve.

Or...

"Maebh."

She hissed at her first in command for daring to press. She reached for him and plunged her fangs into his neck.

Or she could just lay waste to it all.

CHAPTER
THIRTEEN

Aeron had stewed all night while Trix slept. He was angry at himself, mostly. The anger had increased with each stroke of her hair as she drifted off.

This felt so good, and that was why he simmered. Being here, caring for her, putting her before anything else. He shouldn't be feeling these things. They were exactly why he wanted to keep himself at a distance from her. Leaving would be hard enough, but now...

Maybe he could take her with him to the ceremonial lake as he worked out the taint. She would be an asset to the investigation. But, no. It was dangerous in Elphyne. He needed to hear monsters and creatures to hunt; as it turned out, everyone training with him at the Order had gone easy on him. He had no idea if his skills were up to scratch.

He might fail. Trix would die, and then he'd never forgive himself.

But he was here, in the bed, stroking her hair anyway.

Trix knew of his impairment, and she didn't seem to care. It was his own stubbornness and bitterness messing things up. He hadn't even explained what the mating bond meant. She'd asked a few times but had subsequently been distracted, and he'd let it go.

Instead of laying on that couch pretending to sleep while she had been alone and adjusting to her new circumstances, he should have sat by her side and communicated answers to her questions.

He also should have given her his letter. That would explain his reluctance to get to know her. It also sounded stupid now that he'd realized keeping himself at bay wasn't an option because it kept hurting her. He might have seen that earlier if he hadn't been so wrapped up in his own needs.

The moment he remembered his letter, he remembered the others—the Prime's list to Leaf. The Prime instructed him to stay here and wave genially like some token member of the Order. If Trix didn't need Aeron, he'd have already ignored the Prime's letter and headed off on his mission.

But, it seemed Trix kept changing his plans, drawing him back to her like the moon pulled the tides.

He may have smoothed her hair long after she fell asleep because it calmed him as much as it soothed her.

Finally, as he braved a hand on Trix's softly rising and falling sternum, his anger dissipated altogether.

She was alive. Breathing. Solid heartbeat beneath his touch. A tiny push of her angst tried to weasel its way in beneath the drugging effects of the elixir. She would probably wake in the night, and if he wanted to be there for her, he had to sleep by her side to sense when she woke.

If she complained, he'd move.

So, he rested next to her and closed his eyes. Sometime after midnight, she woke in pain and panicked, shouting things he couldn't hear. But he was there by her side, calmly taking her hands. He administered another dose of elixir and calmed her back to sleep. She took his hand this time and held it fiercely, facing him as she drifted off again.

As they touched, sprouts of tiny leaves grew from the canopy of vines above them. Awed and a little cautious, Aeron watched as lush vines bloomed around them and curled along the bed toward her. But they didn't hurt or strangle. They caressed and pillowed.

It wasn't Aeron using magic; unless someone else was nearby, it must have been caused by her. Was this her gift?

Mana was often expended through emotions. Even being connected to her down their bond had not revealed this truth—she was lonely and needed companionship.

It was that small vulnerability that did him in, for he knew in times like this—when all else seemed hopeless and stark—one's true need shone through.

Forrest had been on the other end of Aeron's need as a

106

child. That time Aeron's hair was shorn off in chunks, Forrest had found him hiding beneath a desk. He'd offered his hand in kindness, and Aeron had taken it, squeezing it tight as Forrest guided him outside and into the light. He took Aeron down to the stables and showed Aeron how to feed a kuturi without having his fingers pecked off.

Aeron wondered if humans in Trix's city were as cruel as Aeron's own family had been to him. Was it stamped into every living soul on this earth? Was it inevitable?

Only a thought of his brother now, living in harmony with his mate, proved that thought wrong before it set roots and grew. Every one of the Twelve who'd found their mates had proven it wrong. He had to trust that the Well had a plan for him. But was deafness and fixing the taint part of the plan? Or was it Trix? Because right now, he couldn't see how it could be both.

CHAPTER
FOURTEEN

Aeron reclined and tried to make out Trix's face in the dark. The leaves surrounding her made way for him, as though already accepting him as something linked to her. He wanted to reach out again, but he'd run out of excuses to touch her. Her soft, sweet breath tickled his face, telling him she was alive. The ambient blue glow from their matching marks pulsed gently in tandem as if it came from a vein of the same heart. Her lips parted, she frowned, and then her lips moved.

Talking in her sleep?

He lost the battle to keep his hand at his side and slid his fingers over the soft curve of her neck. His thumb pressed carefully against her throat until the small vibrations of her voice box tingled against his skin. Yes, she was sleep-talking. He wished he knew what she said, but as she covered his hand with hers and snuggled into him, he lost

108

the will to care. He was too busy thinking about other tingles she caused low in his belly.

When the sun came up, Aeron knew he was done for. Trix had become the light in his dimming world, and her happiness came before anything else. Even his own selfish desires. Even the taint he had to fix.

He rose before her and tugged on the bell cord to the room. When the palace attendant arrived, he confirmed Thistle's food order by note and asked for a few items to be delivered so that when Trix woke, he was ready with a plan.

An hour later, she caught him setting out the gifts he'd requested by her bedside. Sleepily, she rubbed her eyes and frowned. He pointed at the food tray, the water, a pile of freshly laundered clothes, new notebooks, and writing instruments.

She gave him a confused look, so he gathered her old notebook from his bag, handed it to her, and then pointed at the new one. She could use it for whatever she wanted. When her eyes lit up, and a rush of warmth radiated in his chest, he knew it was worth it.

Trix shoved a piece of fruit in her mouth and beckoned him over. When he arrived, she wrote in her book and pointed to it.

I'm going to fill this with everything I know about sign language. So we can communicate better.

He borrowed the pencil and replied:

I hope to get my hearing back soon. The time is better served on different pursuits. Like concentrating on healing.

She pursed her lips and then wrote:

Healing will happen anyway. And until you get your hearing back, we will have a way to communicate. It can be our own secret language.

Secret language.

Those two words appealed to the young boy who used to read under his blanket and play out his adventurous fantasies in the stables. Trix was right. What was the harm in learning? Even if the Well shone down on him, and he found a way to clear the taint *and* fix his hearing while keeping her safe, then he'd have a special language only he and his mate understood. He liked that idea. So, he gave her a nod, to which she grinned and popped another morsel of fruit in her mouth as she wriggled with barely contained excitement.

While she was in a good mood, he thought he should probably talk about the Well-blessed bond. He'd stopped Thistle from revealing it before because... he supposed he wasn't ready to admit it himself. But there was no going back. He borrowed her pencil and wrote:

> The marks on our hands are a sign of a
> Well-blessed mating. We don't choose them. The
> Well does. The bond also allows us to share
> emotions.

Her brows lifted sky high. He was sure she said, *What?* He didn't know how to reply, so he pointed back to his original note.

He sensed her confusion, uncertainty, and defiance. They were all natural responses. He'd had more than enough defiance when he'd first learned he'd be mated to someone he'd never met.

She took the pencil from him and wrote:

> So I have no choice?

He shook his head and pointed to himself. Neither did he. She seemed to get lost in her thoughts, so he wrote one last thing before leaving her to it.

> If you want me to leave or answer ques-
> tions at any point, just let me know.

She nodded, then went back to drawing pictures of

hands, arrows, and words. He supposed this was how she sorted through her emotions and thoughts. He wanted to give her space, but another part of him was hoping for more of a reaction. More excitement about their union. It was a foolish notion because it was unnatural to jump into a relationship so fast.

He wasn't sure he was there himself. But at least all their cards were on the table.

While she worked, he went about the room preparing their belongings to take with them down to the healing waters for her bathing ritual. Thistle had said to do it daily, and they didn't go yesterday, so he would start today.

He would start everything anew today.

He was nothing if not thorough, so he went through every item of guest clothing in the closet and ensured she had the right size to fit her smaller frame before packing it. He wrote a note to order more items she might need and set aside coin to pay the attendant. He packed his travel satchel and considered whether to bring *Honor*, but since the sacred waterhole was on the palace grounds, he didn't think there would be a danger.

The king and queen had officially invited them to the festival, and so far, he knew there was no danger of attack from Maebh here. Her quarrel was with Jasper first, potentially the Order second. The Spring Court should be the last place she attacked.

On a last thought, he penned a quick note to the royals

saying that he would like more time before accepting their standing invitation to dinner.

When he was done, he waited for Trix to finish filling her book with diagrams and explanations. He honestly thought she wouldn't have stopped had he not tapped her page to remind her to finish her meal. She glanced up guiltily, but he just smiled back. He liked her passion. He liked it even more that she focused on helping them communicate... like she already cared.

He rubbed his chest. If she approached most things in life as she did with filling that notebook, he would have a fascinating life ahead of him.

So long as she knew when it was time to stop.

He tapped her page again when she inadvertently went back to drawing. This time, she came away from her notes with a better look. He took the pencil from her hand and then went to write her a message in her notebook, but she gasped and blocked her page from his offense.

"No," she said with her mouth and hand. She repeated it until he understood and echoed it back.

No? he signed and lifted his brows.

She grinned, then pointed to some of her pages. Each showed a diagram of a hand sign demonstrating a word. All the basics were covered. No, yes, maybe, okay, wait, stop, go, good, bad. She wanted to show more, but her healing was more important, so he wrote,

Show me later. It's time to go to the healing waters to bathe.

She sniffed beneath her arms and wrote,

I smell fine.

Holding in a laugh, he arched a single brow. She rolled her eyes with a smirk before showing him her fist, making it nod, and saying, "*Yes.*"

He blinked at that tiny action, shocked that he'd quickly understood the shape her mouth made together with her body language and hand signal. The potential for more understanding gave him a rush, and he tugged on his braid, his mind already churning at the possibilities.

Trix made him repeat the sign, and he did so eagerly, chest inflating at her smile of approval. He slipped the bag over his shoulder and helped her into a jacket. He reached for her, but she nabbed her notebook and gave him a sheepish look as she held it protectively against her chest.

Yes, he signed, earning himself another one of her smiles.

He was virtually preening with satisfaction as he carried her out of the room and down the hall, and he couldn't help drawing the contrast between his worries and reality. He'd thought she would hate an elf with his disability. He thought she'd want the perfect knight. But she was behaving the furthest from it. She wanted to know more about him. To communicate. And she was energized by it. He was almost sure it wasn't because she used him as a project to keep occupied. *Almost.* His steps faltered, and he shook his head to dispel the thought. She wasn't angry like he had been with himself.

She also didn't object to him carrying her or holding her luscious body against him. A body that now smelled like the leaves she'd slept in. They must have felt so natural to her that she'd not even mentioned them upon waking. When they had more time and could communicate better, he would find out how much of her gift she'd learned to control. She might not even know about the taint.

Aeron was so caught up in his thoughts that he almost missed the blond elf from the infirmary watching them as they passed. At first, he thought she had just noticed Aeron and Trix walk down the hall and had been caught unawares. He was about to nod in greeting, but the moment she met his eyes, she turned and went the other way.

FIFTEEN

Anxiety followed Trix as Aeron carried her through the ornately carved hallways of the palace. She still processed all the emotions she'd been having since she met Aeron might not be hers. And her legs were stuck out at an odd angle due to the splints. Passersby had to give them a wide berth to avoid hitting her. The idea that anyone could crash into her and trigger indescribable pain was almost too much to ignore.

But all it took was a single look at Aeron's Guardian teardrop, and people scattered fast. They were afraid of him, and it wasn't his battle uniform—he'd left that in the room in favor of a linen shirt and soft brown breeches. It was more than his warrior's physique and intelligent gaze. More than his confident, no-nonsense demeanor or glowing marks.

It must be the stigma that came with being a Guardian.

If the most badass soldiers Trix knew, the Reapers of Crystal City, were afraid of Guardians then they must be powerful. Then again, it wasn't always fear Trix saw in their eyes as people rushed out of the way. It was contempt.

In Trix's time, and in this one with humanity, no one liked a party pooper. If Aeron had to police behavior, if he had the right to do that to kings and queens, then he wasn't just powerful himself. He was a *threat* to power.

She remembered the hazy conversation she'd over-heard when she first woke in the infirmary. She'd almost forgotten it. The blond elf healer had been talking in a tone that made Trix think Aeron was in danger... but what had she been saying exactly?

Before Trix could ruminate, two giant carved exit doors nabbed her attention as they approached. Aeron angled his shoulder to push through, but a picture on the door stopped her. She grabbed his shirt and then signed, "*Look.*"

She wasn't sure if he understood, but he stopped and allowed her time to study it. She even reached out and traced her fingers along the smooth, beautifully carved artwork and the inscription above it: *From Eulios to the Well and Back.*

A handsome man's face covered the doors, but he had leaves in his hair and antlers sprouting from his head. Water flowed between his hair, antlers, and droopy pointed ears. His muscular body took up most of the door... all the way down to his—oh goodness. Her eyes widened. The character was completely naked, his virile manhood there for all to see. Oh, now she felt like a fool asking Aeron to stop... but...

She narrowed her eyes and focused inward on her emotions. No scorn or contempt came from Aeron. The more she focused, the more she could isolate his versus hers—definitely time for a new page in her notebook.

Emotion transference. It was unheard of in her time.

The door opened from the outside, and a palace staffer walked through, saving Trix further awkwardness. The staffer's eyes widened, and he stepped back to allow Aeron and Trix through.

Outside, a gloriously luscious landscape existed within the enormous, sprawling roots of the Great Elder Tree. She could see now that the palace was built into the tree. They went down a path through the garden that she had glimpsed from her window. All around them, from the palace to the main trunk of the Great Elder Tree, fae of all kinds busied themselves with setting up decorations for what Trix guessed was for the festival.

Rolling hills carpeted with green lawns led from the palace to a forest that crowded around them. The leaves from the forest and the big purple tree partly swallowed the blue sky. This was the first time Trix had been inside the palace grounds at Delphinium. She'd snuck into the city a few times to steal supplies from the markets but had always seen the Great Tree from outside the palace gates.

She had not realized the palace was half inside the tree's enormous roots.

Voices hushed as they approached the tree trunk, where an open archway led beneath the roots. The rustling leaves quietened, making Aeron's footsteps echo like thunder as they passed through a tunnel of roots and went deeper into the tree's hollow.

The shadowed path turned damp and sweet with dropped berries and moss.

It should be cold under this tree, but it was oddly humid. More than once, a little buzzing thing flew at her face, and she swatted it away. As they drew close to the sound of dripping water, two enormous, muscular guards came into view and dropped their halberd axes to cross and block the path. Trix couldn't see their mouths through their ornate wooden helmets with antlers. Their bodies were covered with the same carved wooden armor, leather, and green velvet she'd seen on the Spring Court staff.

Trix opened her mouth to tell them the healer's instructions, but again, they took one look at Aeron's Guardian mark and opened entry. Trix's brows lifted. Okay then.

Aeron took Trix through dark tunnels made from giant roots until they ended in a great cavern filled with pools of sparkling water. Trix gasped at the beauty. To think this was all here while she'd been locked in the Sky Tower, hiding out in her workshop, her nose in a book or invention.

An attendant greeted them near the water with towels and a basket of supplies. She beckoned for them to follow her down a tunnel. Trix's heart rate increased as they passed other root columns and alcoves covered with dangling vines and creepers. Hushed murmurs filtered out of each, making her wonder who these people were and why it needed to be private unless... unless this wasn't just a swimming hole but a bath. As in... she'd have to get naked. With Aeron.

She couldn't believe it took her so long to put two-and-two together. Thistle had even said it was bathing. And now she was double mortified because Aeron could sense her reaction. She patted her cheeks and tried to cool them down.

The attendant pulled back the vine curtain and ushered them into their assigned lot. She put their supplies down on the silty floor and then left. Inside, the air was moist and warm. Illumination came from twinkling bioluminescent moss and peat creeping up the root walls. The pool of water glowed softly and looked clear to the bottom. It filtered out to a darkening confluence that most likely fed other canals and alcoves.

Looking up, she only saw the twisted roots of the tree and a smattering of glowing moss.

While this spot was private from passersby on foot, it was open to anyone swimming out there. Aeron didn't seem bothered and placed Trix carefully on the silt ground next to a curved root that acted like a backrest.

She tried not to feel awkward. After all, he'd seen her vulnerable, lying on the bathroom floor with her pants down. He bustled about, looking through their supplies, and then undressed. Trix glanced away, tapped her fingers on her thighs, and waited. The jury was out on whether she liked this emotion-sharing thing. He seemed to have his under control, but regulating hers had always been hard.

She supposed there was nothing she could do about it now, so she took a deep breath and then focused on her splinted legs. They covered her pants. Was she supposed to submerge with them on?

Aeron waved at her face to get her attention. He wasn't naked. Just shirtless. She wasn't sure whether to be relieved or disappointed. As he crouched before her, she couldn't stop staring at the smooth expanse of bronze skin. There was so much definition in his abs that they looked hewn by a razor blade. It should be illegal. Like, seriously. Who looked like that?

A hit of approval shot down their bond from him, and Trix realized what she was doing—staring and appreciating all the masculinity that was her apparent life-long partner. And he liked it. He liked that she liked it.

His lips curved on one side but he didn't further her embarrassment by lingering. He showed her a linen blouse and a change of pants he'd brought her to dress into afterward. She guessed that meant she would submerge with her clothes on.

Thank God.

Because she was most definitely *not* carved by a razor blade. Maybe a donut blade, if such a thing was possible. Although, she glanced down at her stomach. It had flattened a little on a diet of berries, nuts, and stolen food over the past few weeks. But it certainly wasn't carved.

Two fingers on her jaw lifted her gaze to meet Aeron's. His eyes crinkled, and he slid his legs over the lagoon's side and slipped into the water. It came up to his waist, but the space was narrow, like a long bath. If she sat in there, her legs would have to point toward the opening where the canals continued to have enough room. These spots were definitely for a limited number of occupants.

It took Trix a while before she realized Aeron was trying to tell her something with gestures and facial expressions. He pointed to her legs and made the breaking action again, then squished up his face. When she shrugged, she felt his frustration through their link, and he tried a few other movements. This time, he counted out one finger and made a smiling face. Then he counted ten and made a crying face.

"Oh!" she gasped, clapping because she knew the answer. "You mean, how bad do my legs hurt?"

She knew the hand sign for pain, so she demonstrated and made him repeat it. He was asking, from a scale of one to ten—one being good, ten being agony—how much did her legs hurt? She bit her lip and thought about it. Her legs

LANA PECHERCZYK

were better than yesterday but sore if she jolted or flexed. Painful if knocked. Just not agony.

"Five," she held up one splayed hand.

His eyes lit up. He nodded, and then he patted her shoulder.

Good girl, his gaze seemed to say along with his emotions. The praise warmed her in all the right places. When he started unlacing the splints, she knew why he'd asked. Too much pain, and he'd probably have left them on, be damned with wetting them.

He seemed to know his way around the splints. No nervous energy came from their bond, so she assumed he knew what he was doing. When he was done, he shifted the wooden lengths to the side and then directed her to hold onto him as he slipped his hands beneath her legs.

He raised his brows.

Ready? his eyes seemed to say.

She nodded, and he hoisted her effortlessly into the water with him. That's when it got weird for two reasons. One, the warm water immediately had a rejuvenating feeling as it met her skin. It was like sitting in an effervescent bubble bath, only there were no bubbles, and the effervescence was in her blood. Two, Aeron sat and placed her on his lap.

"You're just gonna—whoop. Yep. You are. Right." Trix went through a full gamut of reactions. Surprise. Acceptance. Sensation. Embarrassment. "Brilliant," she mumbled awkwardly. "Just brilliant."

124

She didn't know what to do with her hands, but he directed them to his neck. Their faces were inches apart. Heat came off his skin more than the water up to their sternums.

"So... what now?" she mumbled.

He frowned at her lips and slid his hand up her arm to collect her hand on his neck. The simple action, combined with lubrication from the water, sent goosebumps rippling over her skin. An uncontrollable shiver rattled through her.

She swallowed and braved a look at his face. His lashes were lowered, his cheeks were turning a rosy pink, and his touch on her waist tensed. She glanced down to where he looked. Her linen shirt had turned see-through from the water. The dark shadow of her nipples behind the white had hardened to apparent peaks.

Something else hardened obviously beneath her bottom.

Their gazes clashed, his own widened, and a surge of nervousness cascaded between them. But it was good nervous. Like new butterflies breaking out of their cocoon for the first time. She would have kissed him right there and then, but he had other ideas. He cleared his throat and adjusted her to sit with her back against his chest and her legs resting along his so they stayed straight. Then he banded his arm around her middle and used the other to move her head back to rest against his chest. He closed her eyes with two fingers. She giggled.

"Yeah, yeah. Relax. I get it."

Still filled with joy, she smiled. Couldn't believe she was here, giggling like this with an elf's arms around her. Everything she knew was getting mixed up. He definitely didn't feel like an enemy anymore. And when he started massaging her neck, she groaned and fully submitted to the experience.

He was a god with his hands.

She dropped her head back to the crook in his shoulder and moaned as his clever touch kneaded and rubbed all the aching parts in her arms, neck, and jawline. It felt so natural to have his hands on her. So right. Never had she felt like this with Justin. That tosser had not once touched her with care unless she forced him to cuddle late at night. And then he was asleep in seconds.

When Aeron removed his hands from her, she realized he must have felt her sharp bitterness at the thought of her ex.

"No," she blurted and snatched his hands to place them back on her sternum. "That wasn't directed at you."

Of course, he couldn't hear her, so she moved his finger on her shoulders, emulating the massage. A soft chuckle came out of him, and he nuzzled into her ear playfully. Those butterflies in her stomach migrated to the rest of her body as he resumed his massage.

"Oh, God." She flung her head back again to rest on him. "I'm in heaven. Can I keep you?"

She was only brave enough to say it aloud because she

knew he couldn't hear. It felt liberating and unreal all at once.

Eyes closed. Warm water. Soft trickling came from somewhere.

How did she get here? A few weeks ago, she'd been lamenting about her ex cheating on her, arguing with a megalomaniac captain, fearing for her life in a dungeon, freaking out about sprouts and vines she grew with her mind, hiding out in a treehouse... falling... and then... Then there was Aeron. Her mate, who seemed never to feel anything negative about her.

Maybe this emotion-sharing thing was okay. Maybe being mated to an elf was okay.

No one could be this brilliant, could they? The last person she thought was this good ended up breaking her heart.

CHAPTER
SIXTEEN

The following week passed in a strange haze for Aeron. The more time he spent with his mate, the more he grew helplessly attracted to her, and the further he moved from his urgent need to clear the taint and prove his worth to the Prime.

His mind was occupied elsewhere. From the way Trix attacked her nightly meals with frenzy, to her fervent instructions on how to sign, to her passion for reading every book he found in the Spring Court library. He wanted to spend every hour by her side.

Her favorite books were the technical kind and the ones describing the biology of Elphyne animals and plants.

She'd been particularly enthralled with the plant books, and they'd fumbled through some communication regarding her power. She didn't know how it worked but was fascinated to learn. Most of her notebook space was taken up with the hand sign language she'd recalled from her old world.

Many people in her time were in his position. It was odd to see her so at ease with it. Odd, but in a good way because she looked up at him with eyes of wonder when he dropped books into her lap.

The way she looked up at him in those moments was everything. Eyes full of joy. Fervor. Spark. And she always babbled afterward. Those pretty lips constantly confounded him, but at the same time, he wasn't worried he was missing out. Anything she wished him to understand, she taught him how to sign, or wrote it down.

She took notes on everything.

Once, he'd caught her stopping mid-note, then turning a page and starting a new note. Her facial expression had been so animated and excited that he had to peek over her shoulder. She wrote something about cornstarch being a good substitute for plastic, and he growled at her as he wrote:

Plastic is forbidden.

She snatched his pencil and smugly replied:

Aah, but cornstarch can work like plastic but it is natural.

Curious, he'd wanted to know more, but she was already writing about something else, and he was already entranced with the pink tip of her tongue sticking out from between her lips.

They'd attended the healing waters every day, and on this particular afternoon, her legs felt good. He knew not only because there was less angst trickling down their connection but because she sat in the pool with her body twisted as she studied a snail crawling along a twisted root. It left a bioluminescent trail she swiped her finger through and marveled at, then swiped some on the blue marks on her body and compared.

He could bottle her curiosity and become a rich man. Watching her face light up made his blood sing. She'd surprised him by refraining from using her gift, and he didn't think it was her wariness of the taint. Any time he brought it up by tapping at one of her notes or pointing out that, subconsciously, she'd grown a few plants in her sleep, she only shrugged and changed the subject. He'd let the topic lie because it was still hard to communicate for long periods, but also he felt flashes of her guilt and anxiety any time he mentioned it.

Something bad had happened, and her gift was at the center of it. He would let her heal first, but then his gut told him she needed tutelage. Or at least understanding.

Aeron let his gaze rake down her body from top to where the water lapped at her shoulders. Dark, curly hair plastered to her skin and stood out starkly on her wet, white linen shirt. Each morning he laid out two blouses— one darker colored and one light. She always picked the light.

She would dress and smirk at him with a coy glance from beneath her lashes. She knew full well how she looked while bathing. Knew exactly how hard it made his cock, but she chose the white shirt, and he gave her the option for both.

Trix's head canted as she studied the snail. Her lips pressed together randomly, and he was sure she hummed a tune. Every drop of his blood was in a frenzy wanting to feel her again. Especially the vibrations her voice made at her throat. He obsessively fantasized about how touching her there would keep his memories of a female voice alive.

He couldn't stop staring at her delicate neck when she swallowed. When she sighed. Laughed. Her décolletage called to his base male instincts. He needed to feel her soft skin under his rough touch like a guilty pleasure reserved for savagely guarded moments. He would store moments in his memory and open them like a treasure whenever he felt dull.

Arousal spiked low and hot in his belly for the tenth time since they'd arrived. He mentally cursed because this attraction wasn't going away. His initial desire to keep them at bay was a long, distant memory. But his need to clean the taint and prove his worth wasn't. Frowning, he pushed that logic away as she glanced at him demurely. She knew exactly what he felt and why. Enough with this tension between them.

It was time to kiss his mate.

He crooked his finger at her.

She pushed off the side of the private lagoon and paddled the short distance to him. Her legs must feel better for her to move without flinching, so he dragged her onto his lap, but this time kept her facing him. She straddled him effortlessly and speared fingers into his hair, digging along his scalp. His eyes wanted to roll in bliss, but he held them firm on her moisture-dappled face. He didn't braid his hair when he learned she liked to comb her fingers through the long lengths.

Touching.

So much touching between them.

Every trace sent zings through his body. Without sound, it was easier to focus on how her wet body made him feel as it pressed against him. They stared into each other's eyes. *Crimson*, she was so beautiful like this. Flushed cheeks. Dewy drops on her skin. Bright eyes.

Need burned beneath his skin, building in pressure. He wanted to kiss her so badly but didn't know how to ask. She'd not taught him how to sign the gesture for kiss, but he knew the sign for "What is?"

He opened both his palms, faced them up, moved them in and out, and shrugged, then pointed to her and hesitated... Can't go straight for the lips. It's too obvious.

He pointed to her nose, meaning... *What is the sign for nose?*

Her lips squished to the side, and then she pointed to her nose and raised her brows.

Fair enough. *All right, here's one for you, mate.* His lips twitched. He signed *what is* again but, this time pointed to her lips. Her smirk widened, and she swiped around her lips, but he shook his head and captured her finger. Holding her gaze, enjoying how her pupils dilated, he slowly drew her finger into his mouth and sucked on the tip. He swirled his tongue around it, then pulled it out and repeated the sign for *what*.

Trix's lips parted.

Yes, that's right. Lips. Kiss.

Aeron sucked in a ragged gasp. He wasn't the only one breathless. Trix's chest rose and fell rapidly, which drew his attention to her drenched blouse. He wanted to kiss there, too, but he still needed to know the sign.

What is, he signed, then hooked his finger under her chin and pressed his lips against hers. The visceral reaction in his body was instant. Lightning rolled through him, and thunder crashed... a surge in desire clashing down their bond—all from a single chaste press of lips. He should have stopped and asked again, to be clear that he wanted to know the sign for kiss, but he couldn't stop. He swiped his tongue along her seam, enjoyed how she parted hesitantly for him and loved how her full body squirmed against him.

And then she gripped his face, tugged him hard against her, and moaned—she must have. What else would cause the heat of her breath and tingle against his lips? He needed to know. Needed to taste her sound. His restraint snapped, and he cupped her neck with two hands, placing each thumb at the hollow, and then he deepened their kiss, giving her everything until that moan vibrated into his thumbs, zipping up his arms, wrapping itself around his heart before heading south.

Hot, wet, salty. She was his whole world. She was all he needed. Every rock of her hips was turning him into a primal beast. He wouldn't be able to hold back if she didn't stop, and she still needed to heal.

Fuck.

Thistle wasn't due to clear her for walking until tomorrow, and he had her straddling him like a wanton Rosebud Courtesan.

He pulled back suddenly, swiftly, and without mercy. A rumble of approval slipped out of his lips as she pouted and chased his lips with hers. The way she looked at him, so full of unapologetic want and desire, astounded him. Fuck it. He went in for seconds, just a small taste. A dip of his tongue. A delve into her mouth. A small savoring.

But then she touched his ears.

She fondled and rubbed them. She stroked the tips and caressed. An eruption of hot, liquid desire filled his body. A low, shuddering groan tore from his lips. *Do that again.* He nudged his ears into her and signed, *Good.*

She licked his lobe, and he damned near spilled his seed right there at the fucking bathing hole. He wasn't sure if every sensation was acute because of his hearing loss, because these waters infused energy, or because she was his mate, but he'd never felt like this.

This was only meant to be a kiss—to find out the sign —but it had become something else. A door opening. A dam breaking. A truth forming.

Swallowing hard, he forced himself to rein it in. Back in their room, they could explore more. Not here in relative public. He wanted her to himself. He wanted to take the time to get to know her intimately.

Many of his fellow Guardians in the Twelve hadn't had this opportunity when they'd met their mate. He should relish it while he could because the moment she was healed, they had to leave and clean the taint from the Well. He still wanted to do that.

Being a Guardian was his identity.

He refused to let the Prime take this from him.

But why-oh-why wasn't he holding onto that resolve so tightly anymore? That realization scared him. He'd lost contact with his identity; he was moving too far from his original need. This had to slow down.

Aeron signed the word *Go* and pointed to them both and then out the door.

Trix smiled and nodded, but before she moved off him, she took his fingers and touched them to her lips, then swiped up her cheek and kissed the air.

Kiss.

They needed to get to their room quick-smart. Slowing down just became redundant as his mind repeated that one sexy hand sign she'd demonstrated using his fingers.

Before lifting her out of the water, he had to get into dry clothes.

Her bottom lip popped out when he motioned for her to stay put while he dressed. She simpered and started signing excuses for why it was time to let her get out of the pool on her own. For some of it, he understood and sympathized. The rest he was yet to learn, so he just gave her a patient smile and waved her down.

He'd kept her relegated to the rooms and this lagoon. It was enough to drive him mad, too. Perhaps tomorrow, he would take her further out into the gardens if Thistle allowed her to get on her feet. They also had a standing invitation to join the king and queen for dinner but had been reluctant to go. Even with the new basic hand signs he'd learned, the thought of keeping up with a conversation gave him a headache. His lack of attendance bordered on offense, and he wasn't sure why they kept letting him stay here. He expected guards at his door every morning to drag him to an audience with the royals. But none came.

Trix signed at him with a scowl, *I walk good.*

Thistle's orders were not to walk until she said so. Rules were rules. *Wait.*

He laid out a towel to place Trix on. He removed the dry clothes from the bag and hung them over a curved exposed root. Then he began the same tension-filled dance they'd been doing every day when it was time to leave.

Facing the wall, he undressed.

Trix's emotions fluttered down their bond, and he smiled. He must be vain because his chest puffed out whenever he sensed her approval. When he was back in dry clothes, and he turned, she averted her gaze and stared studiously at the water as if she hadn't just been ogling his naked rear end.

He went about flattening the towel and pulling her clothes from his pack. He moved with languid actions, feeling like these past few days had been the vacation he'd not had the time nor desire to have. Tonight he would—

Alarm stabbed him from down their bond.

He jolted and checked on Trix, but she was gone. All that was left were bubbles and the soft glow of her Well-blessed mating marks receding into the depths of the water. Panic pulsed adrenaline into his veins. He dove into the water, aiming directly for the blue of their connection. There were no thoughts, only the inescapable urge to find her. To save her from whatever dragged her under. Wide eyes found him in the gloom, but they weren't Trix's.

A water nymph grinned mockingly as though what happened next was inevitable. As though she held some deep personal desire to ruin his life by stealing his mate. It didn't make sense. Nymphs were annoying but not usually dangerous. They flirted and sometimes dragged males into the waters to mate, but they always returned them to shore satisfied, if not a little shell-shocked.

They shouldn't be in these guarded and protected healing waters.

Why would a nymph be after Trix?

Kicking his legs harder, he reached for his mate and connected with her upper arm. An instant later, he felt as calm as the water around him. His panic left. She would be safe now that he had her. He knew it in his bones. The Well wouldn't give her to him and then take her away so soon.

He hooked his arm around her torso and turned the full force of his strength into reversing their trajectory. Blue nymph hair fanned out as she jerked back with him. He booted her face, appreciated the snap of her jaw, and then once he was certain Trix was not in danger, he called on his mana—be damned with the taint—and unleashed it at the nymph in the form of an underwater tornado. Satisfaction bloomed when she blasted away.

He didn't waste time checking to see if the nymph was dead. He swam Trix to the surface and then back to shore. She was still gasping for air and blinking in shock when he hoisted her onto the silty ledge between two purple roots. He pushed her backward, signaling her to escape the water. And just as well.

The nymph came back, only this time, she launched at Aeron. Cold fingers wrapped around his ankle and pulled. Unprepared, he lost his balance. He hesitated before gathering his bearings. A glance showed Trix safely shuffling on her bottom toward the exit, eyes wide with alarm, dark hair plastered to her face, her collarbone bleeding.

Bleeding.

The sight of her injury flipped a dark, primal switch in Aeron. That cool, calm place he'd visited while under the water expanded and took over.

CHAPTER
SEVENTEEN

For the first time since Trix had met Aeron, she experienced what it truly meant for him to have earned the lethal moniker of Guardian.

His change wasn't something obvious to the naked eye. It was a stillness, an emptiness down their bond—no emotion. His copper eyes dimmed as though his consciousness left his body, but it was him taking in all the details with more than one sense. It was him feeling the ripples in the water, seeing the shadows move, tasting the magic in the air. She could tell by the calculating dart of his eyes as they landed on places.

Then he exploded in retaliation against the blue, buxom nymph. With methodical kill strikes, he punched and jabbed. It wasn't like something Trix had seen in the movies. It wasn't choreographed like a pretty dance.

It was death.

Swift, ruthless, aggressive action with purpose.

Fingers to the eyes took out the nymph's sight. A box to her ears put her at the same level as Aeron. He shoved her against a root wall with a hand around her throat. Then he plunged fingers into the gills at her neck, digging. The nymph gasped and begged, but it was too late. Half of Aeron's hand disappeared and came out with something white and bloody. Parts of her spine.

The nymph dropped dead into the water.

Aeron flicked his carnage with a snarl on his upper lip. His gaze slid to Trix, and she sensed his trepidation, his worry at her having seen him like this. He pushed the nymph's body away with disgust, watching until manabeeze popped out of it, signaling the nymph was dead and its mana released into nature.

Trix knew about manabeeze because she'd helped Justin with a harvesting gadget that eventually fed the portal machine. But the horror of seeing it in the flesh was jarring. Knowing it was someone's life force seemed so different in person. Shame pierced her heart. Her mind took her to dark, dangerous places that hurt her brain trying to comprehend. Nothing cognitive came out of it. Just feelings. Horrible feelings that she couldn't connect.

Sensing her turmoil, Aeron left the floating corpse behind and waded to Trix. She wrenched her gaze from the manabeeze, but, too late, noticed the second blue head rising slowly out of the water like a crocodile stalking its prey.

Trix screamed a warning, but the nymph flew out of the water faster than humanly possible. Aeron looked at Trix, perhaps sensing her alarm again, but he failed to sense the thing hurtling toward him from behind, her sharp teeth gnashing, her fingers clawed and primed to gouge.

Like Trix's soul was being ripped from her body, her instinct to protect Aeron reached into her core and drew on her mana to manipulate nature. Purple vines and roots burst upward from the silty waterbed, skewering the nymph mid-leap. Water sprayed like a geyser. Vines multiplied, threading through the slick-blue-skinned woman like a piece of embroidery until finally lashing out and latching onto the walls and high in the cavern.

By now, Aeron had sensed the disturbance and watched in shock at what Trix wrought with her power. The glowing balls of light popping out of its body were a wistful contrast to the savage imagery. The second dead nymph hung suspended like some kind of macabre art installation reminiscent of a spider web and its prey. Aeron went to it to inspect. Dark oozing liquid bled from the vines and dripped into the water. He frowned, wiped a smear from his skin, and then inspected it by rubbing it between his forefinger and thumb.

It wasn't red. It was black tar. He scowled at it.

Guilt, shame, and a letdown of adrenaline fell on Trix like a shuddering veil. Had they overreacted? It had all happened so fast. What actually happened? She couldn't meet Aeron's eyes as he levered himself out of the water and came to her side, water dripping from his long hair and sluicing down his scratched body. She thought he'd be horrified at what she'd done, but he wasn't.

He pinched her chattering chin with his forefinger and thumb and pointed to the silt in the dirt as he wrote the words: Self-Defense. Then he smoothed water from her face.

She shook her head. Maybe if she'd been paying attention, she could have warned him sooner. A sick feeling grew in her stomach when she recalled another time she'd not paid attention. A few years ago, she had burned her fingers on a soldering iron because she'd become immersed in trying to solve a problem that had come up with wiring not connecting. She wished she could say she forgot the soldering iron was in her hand but knew it was there on some level. She simply hadn't been paying attention to it. Then she'd placed her hand down and knocked the hot poker, burning her palm before realizing what she'd done. Justin had scolded her. *"How can you forget something so vital? What is wrong with you?"*

She rubbed the raised skin on her palm, still there from the old injury.

But Aeron never berated. He dropped his lips reverently to her collarbone and pressed gently over her injury. His touch was a switch on bottled emotion. She squeezed her eyes shut, then wrapped her arms around him and held him tight. A sigh escaped his lips.

On the surface, an embrace was so simple: two people wrapping their arms around each other and squeezing. But the reaction inside Trix's body was as confounding as an exploding constellation. Her heart swelled as he held her tight. He'd saved her life, and she'd saved his.

They pulled apart for a second before coming back with lips clashing in a brutal, needy, hot kiss. This was nothing like the slow, torturous game they'd played in the water. This kind of hunger came from a deep, animalistic place. She wasn't sure whose need was feeding whose, only that both were desperate for this connection. Wanted more.

Aeron pulled away and turned to inspect the carnage. He was right to look. There could be more danger. He took a step forward but, unable to help herself, Trix tugged him back.

"Don't go in there," she begged. "Please."

The scowl disappeared from his face. He bent and lifted her into his arms like a fireman. He only had eyes for her as they walked out. But out in the entrance foyer, his frown returned, and he jerked his head back angrily to where they'd come from.

When the attendant deadpanned, Trix took it upon herself to explain.

"We were attacked," she said, voice a little shaky. "By these blue women who came from the water."

"Nymphs? But that's impossible."

Aeron growled and jerked his head there again. Frustrated with the lack of understanding, he placed Trix down and grabbed the attendant by the scruff of her shirt before shoving her into their nook. When he returned, he disappeared through the main exit where the two armored guards were.

Trix gaped as he returned and shoved them too. Her mate was smaller, but they followed his lead like recalcitrant children. Left alone, Trix's nerves twanged. Aeron would want her to stay here and avoid walking, but she couldn't be alone. He might need her help translating. She stepped after them, testing her weight on her healing legs. They ached a little, but she summoned her courage and pressed on.

She didn't realize how lonely she'd been in her tree-house and Crystal City until Aeron stepped out of sight, and she feared she'd lose him. She limped back to their spot to see him fearlessly jump back into the water and collect the floating corpse. He weaved through the vine web holding the second nymph and returned to shore.

"Shit," mumbled a guard in a deep voice.

"Fuck," said the other. "We're going to get fired."

"He probably invited them here. Well-damn Guardians attract trouble wherever they go."

"Yeah. Fucker probably started it. I mean, they're *nymphs*."

Trix didn't like that tone. Warning bells went off. They didn't know she was behind them until the attendant whimpered and pressed herself against the wall. Aeron climbed out of the water and dragged the corpse onto the ledge. The attendant looked terrified. Trix limped over to her.

"Are you okay?"

She glanced at Trix and mumbled, "It's so gross."

Trix flinched, immediately throwing up her guard. "Yeah, well, they attacked us first. It was self-defense."

She took special care to increase the volume of her voice. One guard glanced over but held his tongue.

Alarmed, the attendant reached for Trix. "Oh, I don't mean... it's just... I've worked here for six years and never seen a nymph attack."

Trix frowned at her, trying to figure out if she was also calling them a liar in her own way, but the honest shock on her face said otherwise.

"So, this is out of the ordinary?" Trix asked. "Do they usually swim in these waters?"

"No one is allowed here unless they pass through the guards at the front. The waterways are also guarded. The tree must be protected." Her gaze tracked up the vines Trix had grown... all the way to the splayed and speared corpse in the web. Then she turned and vomited.

"Oh, dear." Trix rubbed the attendant's back.

Aeron noticed Trix standing and glowered before clicking his fingers, pointing to her face, and then down to the ground. Right. Sit. Don't stand.

"Yes, boss." Trix saluted him.

His lips twitched with humor but grew flat as he directed the guards to inspect the corpse.

Trix tugged the attendant away from her vomit and slid them both down to sit and watch as Aeron went about the business of being a Guardian—well, she assumed this was what he did because he was so good at it. She marveled at his confidence in checking the area, directing the guards, and pointing at the evidence. Apart from some frustration on the communication front, he didn't let his lack of hearing hold him back.

There was so much about Aeron she was attracted to, but that was the biggest part. His eyes were bright. He looked in his element as he investigated the scene beneath her ugly horror web. It was such a gruesome thing. She was ashamed it came out of her.

Within moments of her feeling so down, Aeron waded back to shore and checked on her. He pressed his hands to her legs and signed, *Pain?*

She shrugged and held up a single finger. He touched her cheek gently, then went back to the guards.

"Wow," the attendant sighed, wiping her lip with the back of her hand. "He's really something."

"What do you mean?" Trix tensed, ready to clock the elf if she was talking shit about Aeron. She was surprised at her protective instinct being so vehement.

"I mean, I've never met a Guardian like this. Never seen what they can do." She pointed at the nymphs. "If they attacked, then he saved your life."

"They attacked." She glared. "Believe me."

"He cares for you." The elf sniffed, looking at Trix's web. "You're lucky he did that."

"He's a good fae." Trix bit her lip. She didn't want to correct her and say the vines were her fault. She chose instead to focus on the rest of that statement. Aeron was amazing. She was lucky to have him in her life.

Aeron was the type of fae hurt by Trix's portal invention.

Would he feel the same way about her once he discovered what she'd built for Nero? If she didn't confess to him soon, it would become less about finding the right time and more about lying.

CHAPTER EIGHTEEN

N ow that Aeron had distance from the attack and wasn't obsessing about Trix's safety, he was furious. Why here? Why now? The nymphs appeared normal, not warped by tainted mana as some of the creatures he'd hunted for the Order. The nymphs had attacked to kill. That mocking smirk from one of them haunted him. Neither gave him the impression they'd intended to pull their punches. Nevertheless, after shoving the incompetent guard's face in their failure, he did his due diligence to see if they were at further risk of attack. He checked their surrounding areas and then went to study the vines.

A black oozy substance dripped from them. In some instances, the inky taint seemed to manifest physically or warped the intent of the mana being called upon. He'd seen portals open to the wrong sections of Elphyne and into strange lands. He'd seen things explode. He'd seen the wrong object conjured. He'd seen death.

He looked up at the web of vines covered in the nymph's blood and oily sludge. He would ask Trix questions when they had privacy. Her reluctance to talk about her gift made sense. There was a dark side to it. For her gift to manifest so viciously, she was either inexperienced, malicious at heart, or it was the taint. He hoped it was the first. At least that he could fix.

Aeron swiped sludge off the vines intending to study it in his fingers, but the vine disintegrated. Black necrosis grew until it spread across the length of the vine, eventually becoming dust crumbling into the water. Aeron jerked back to miss the possible contagious substance. He'd seen Shade's mate's gift pour out of her chest like a black cloud. Every object it touched turned necrotic. Silver had avoided accepting her gift at first, but through training, she'd learned to harness it and draw the darkness back into her body.

Aeron straightened with a thought. Silver's gift came from the inky side of the Well. When collecting samples with rookie Guardians, he'd theorized the sludge was a manifestation of the taint. Now, he was sure it was all linked.

If Silver could somehow draw this into her, would it perhaps cleanse the source?

Back on shore, Aeron instructed the guards to set up a boundary to protect the integrity of the scene. He needed to return his mate to their rooms, dressed and calmed after the ordeal. She'd been reserved since the attack, and he worried she was in shock. He also needed her to rest. She'd been on her feet for too long.

He might even call for Thistle.

Crouching beside her, he touched her face gently to politely steal her attention from the attendant she spoke with.

Let's go, he signed.

She smiled tightly and then said something to the attendant. Trix attempted to stand on her own, but he slid his hands beneath her and lifted her into a carry position. The attendant tried to follow, but Aeron jerked his head back down to the ground where she'd been. *Stay,* he mouthed and glared. She should be here to answer questions from the palace authorities should Aeron delay returning.

Trix's unease prickled through their bond as they walked back to the palace. If he allowed himself to dwell on it, he'd realize how close he came to losing her before they'd even begun to—he shook his head and grumbled. He wouldn't let his mind go there. Especially not after having spent every waking hour, every day, for a week free from destructive thoughts that had kept him company after his injury. Trix's fingers flexed on his arm, and he kissed the top of her head to assure her his anger wasn't directed at her.

It just was.

And he needed to send it somewhere. He would see her safe first, and then he would come back down here and find a way to reprimand these incompetent ingrates. Allowing such a malicious attack in their innermost sanctum was abhorrent.

What was King Tian thinking to leave it so unguarded? Aeron realized he would know if he'd taken the time to visit the royals when he'd arrived. More shame hit him when he realized he'd allowed his hearing loss to keep him from his duty for too long.

Palace guards strolled toward the bathing waters as Aeron carried Trix away from it. The guards weren't in a hurry, and he wanted to shout at them to hurry up and do their job. It took a few deep breaths to calm his raging impulses. They all saw the look on his face and swiftly deviated from the path. He would deal with that later. When he arrived at their room, he deposited Trix on a chair next to the bed and went to get her dry clothes from the closet.

He didn't realize how much his bad mood affected her until he handed her the new set, and she flinched. Alarmed, he crouched before her and put a hand on her damp knees.

You good? he signed.

She didn't respond. He placed his palm on her sternum and pressed to show her he worried about her heart and feelings. She covered his hand and started talking rapidly. With anyone else, he would walk away from their ignorance, but with her, he knew her impulses weren't always easy to control. She seemed to have the predisposition to jump in headfirst before thinking. It didn't mean she wasn't smart.

In fact, sometimes he liked those impulses... like when she'd chased his lips for more kisses.

He covered her moving lips with his hand and lifted a questioning brow. She jolted. Blinked. He smiled gently and then went to find note paper and a pencil. She took them gratefully and scribbled,

> I didn't mean to do that to the nymph. It just happened. You must think I'm the worst person, that I hate fae and, and I don't. I don't know what I felt. I just hid away from the world and thought that avoiding questions was okay because I was given free rein to make whatever tickled my fancy. I should have seen the big picture instead of focusing on what was in front of me. I should have asked more questions!

She was going in circles and not making much sense. He stopped her from continuing and shook his head.

No, he signed and then pointed at her and signed, *Good*.

She wrote,

But how am I supposed to know what you think? I don't know anything about you apart from that you're a Guardian and my mate. You don't know anything about me.

Knowing how we each feel isn't enough.

Guilt hit him hard. Guilt and self-loathing and all sorts of inadequacy. If he could hear, then they would already have had these sorts of getting-to-know-you conversations. If he talked and heard, then they could ask any questions and answer them immediately. She could simply ask him if she had concerns. There would be no communication breakdown. He'd been foolish to think they were getting along fine, that their kiss was a step forward, but this whole time their relationship had been simmering below the borderline of what they needed for this to work.

With each passing day, the letter he'd penned before he met her became more redundant. But that need for information and to know where she stood still existed. He wanted to be able to devote himself to her. To be with her. To solidify their bond and commitment. But he still needed to prove himself to his peers.

Trix pointed at her next words:

I need to tell you things about myself too.

Later. I'll be back soon, he signed and stood, ready to leave, but she stood too.

No, she signed and lifted her chin. *I'm coming with you.*

He sensed her determination and knew he'd be up for a fight if he left her behind. Part of him liked her close, to know she was safe, so he gently pushed her onto the bed so she got off her feet. She resisted and clasped his wrists. Fire blazed in her eyes.

Aeron tugged her shirt up. Clever girl must have known she'd won the argument and raised her arms with a small smile curving her lips. He smirked and tossed her shirt in her face before heading back to the closet, peeling off his clothes and dressing into his Guardian leathers.

This time, when they returned to the alcove, he would do it with the full force of his position behind him. Not once did he doubt himself. He should have at least been cautious because when he arrived, the queen's brother waited for him with a group of soldiers.

CHAPTER
NINETEEN

Aeron might not have given Trix the baring of his soul she'd hoped for, but she couldn't really blame him. Her feelings had been raw and overloaded after the attack. She wanted to be closer to him, to take any path to get to a place where they could whole-heartedly trust each other, but the timing wasn't right.

She liked that about him. He was dutiful and reliable and so unlike Justin. Somehow, she didn't think Aeron would ever hop into bed with another woman while they were officially together. This mating thing was serious. She guessed the sharing of emotions had a way of protecting them from hurting each other.

Aeron insisted on carrying her back to the pools, even though she felt better. The pain was almost gone in her legs. Thistle had said about two weeks to heal, and even though she was due to clear Trix for walking, it didn't mean she was healed. There was still a full week to go before that happened, so Trix understood why Aeron was cautious.

The daily trips to the waters had made her feel so good. It didn't make the desire to get down and walk herself easy to ignore.

Aeron also liked his orders and rules. She felt so good with his strong arms around her. She could be the rhino and butterfly at once and wouldn't fall into danger.

A small angry crowd gathered at the tunnel entrance beneath the tree.

"This is a sacred place!" one person shouted.

"I need to get in and decorate for the festival ritual," said another.

"This is exactly why Eulios has forsaken us."

The ground rumbled beneath their feet, shaking leaves off the tree. Purple and blue dropped and showered everyone's heads. The shock was palpable. Not a single person said a word.

Then they started arguing again. Most blamed the sudden loss of leaves on their horned god's wrath. But another faction blamed Aeron for the dying tree.

"What did you do?" shouted a portly male fae with fur-tipped ears. "You must have done something!"

Trix's protective mode kicked in. She opened her lips to give the fae a 'What for' but Aeron pushed through the crowd with a gritted jaw until he made it to the front where the guards stood.

They were different than the ones from earlier. Aeron went straight inside and put Trix on her feet at the main foyer entrance. Further down the tunnel toward where they'd been attacked, voices grew louder as someone approached.

The two enormous guards with antlered helmets entered the room and paused, eyes warily on Aeron in his new battle gear. The royal steward and another elf dressed in elite attire arrived next. This new elf had long, dirty blond hair and a mustache. He wore tailored clothes with the royal crest on the breast pocket. From the way he set his shoulders to the lift of his chin, Trix immediately developed a disliking for him.

She shouldn't judge someone by their looks, but she couldn't help it. There was something off about him. She could feel the contempt in his eyes as he scanned Trix and Aeron. His lip curled upon seeing her round, human ears, and then he dismissed her as not worth his time. His gaze landed on Aeron, and he snapped, "You murdered two of our subjects in cold blood."

Trix gaped.

Aeron ignored him and searched the area. He signed to her, *Girl?*

It took Trix a moment to realize he was talking about the attendant, so she asked anyone who would listen, "Where is the attendant who worked here?"

"She was sent home to recover from her ordeal," replied the steward sharply.

Trix translated to Aeron as best she could. His brow furrowed. She knew he wanted to ask her more questions.

The important-looking elf with a mustache stepped before Aeron. "Explain yourself, Guardian. Or face criminal charges."

Whoa, whoa. Trix held up her hands. "Let's not get carried away. We were *attacked*. This was self-defense."

As she replied, she continued to sign as best she could so Aeron could keep up. She knew he wouldn't understand all of it, but he seemed to follow enough.

His expression darkened. His jaw clenched, and he pointed at the elf, then signed, *Who?*

Trix translated, "Who are you?"

Offended that Aeron had the gall not to recognize him, the elf's nostrils flared. He stared long and hard before finally answering. "I am High Lord Kelvhan, the queen's brother and head of the royal guard. I am the one you should be afraid of."

Trix spelled out his name using sign language to Aeron.

"Can't you talk?" Kelvhan sneered at Aeron. "Is something wrong with you?"

Trix's brows went sky-high, and anger punched her in the gut. She glowered and stepped toward him so hard that her knees buckled, but she gathered herself and pointed at his smug face.

"There's nothing wrong with him," she answered. "He's deaf. But you, on the other hand... that question remains to be answered."

"A deaf Guardian." Kelvhan laughed. "Who ever heard of a deaf Guardian?"

She took another step, fury turning her muscles rigid. She was going to kill him. End him for talking about her mate like this. Just as a snarl ripped from her lips, she felt Aeron's hands slot around her waist and tug her back to him. She winced at a sudden pain in her legs and limped, something this High Lord Wanker found even more hilarious.

He caught the eye of his guards and pointed to his ears and then her legs. "A deaf Guardian and a disabled human. I doubt they had the skills to murder two nymphs."

One of the guards looked down on Trix and scoffed, "She probably got jealous of him getting some because of her—"

Trix broke free of Aeron and punched him in the face. The helmet clashed with her fist, but before she got another hit in, Aeron dragged her back to him and wrapped her in his arms while he shushed calmly into her ear.

The atmosphere suddenly turned thick with tension. Kelvhan's eyes narrowed on Trix, and he flicked his fingers at the guards. They stopped laughing and stepped toward her.

"Nobody attacks my guards and gets away with it," Kelvhan declared.

Aeron stepped before Trix, blocking her from the guards. That's all he did, and guards bigger and burlier than him hesitated. If she had any doubt this warrior was meant for her, it vanished at that moment. In a single step, Aeron had proven his loyalty to her.

"She insulted me," Kelvhan said to Aeron, knowing full well he couldn't hear. "This will not be accepted."

Fuck. Trix had no idea how to talk her way out of this, but Aeron pointed down the path to the alcove and lifted his brows. He gestured using his Well-blessed marked hand for Kelvhan to move down. The High Lord straightened defensively when his eyes landed on the glow. Trix had no idea why that simple action was enough to make the High Lord do as Aeron asked, but he did. She knew the mating was special, but why did it make him afraid?

For now, the High Lord and the guards reluctantly walked to where Aeron directed. But Trix didn't for one second believe the danger was over. She could virtually see the cogs turning in the evil elf's head.

Trix hesitated before passing through the draping vines covering the doorway to their alcove. The nymph's cold dead eyes flashed in her mind, and she shuddered. She was probably going to have nightmares tonight. At least Aeron would be there. He'd slept beside her on the bed, but she wanted more tonight. She wanted the full comfort this relationship could bring.

Forcing herself to be brave, she followed Aeron and balked once inside. The vines were gone. The corpses were gone. Aeron was also shocked.

"Where is everything?" Trix asked.

"We have an important festival coming up," the steward replied. "We simply cannot have this sort of mess down here."

Trix translated, and Aeron's eyes narrowed. Anger pelted her through their bond. He wanted to unleash on them, but he held back. She wasn't so patient but wasn't sure what was happening here.

Kelvhan looked smugly at Aeron. "You see, it's your word against ours, so you will explain why you murdered two harmless subjects of this court." He looked at Trix briefly before continuing. "And if you can't explain yourself, you will be forced to accept the punishment. Even your Prime will not be able to stop us from demanding compensation."

"It was self-defense," she repeated.

"Liar. Nymphs aren't the attacking type." His lips twisted as he gave her another scathing once-over. "As it was said before, perhaps you were jealous of the attention your mate received and took it out on the innocent. After all, there's nothing like a scorned female... unless you include a scorned *human* female."

Trix's anger was swift to rally. She quickly signed the situation to Aeron, who didn't react as she'd expected. For a moment, she thought he didn't understand her and was about to write it out on the dirt, but Aeron beat her to it. He snapped off a dry root and scratched in the dirt:

We will discuss this with the king and queen over dinner tonight.

Kelvhan blinked. Trix did too. Surely Aeron wasn't giving this tale credence, but then she remembered there had been a standing invitation to have dinner with the king and queen. And an expectation of being at the festival. This High Lord probably had no idea of the nature of their invitation.

"You dare to think you can simply invite yourself into the royal household?"

Nope. He didn't. Trix smiled tightly and said, "We have an invitation."

Kelvhan turned on Trix and whispered harshly, "I know what you are, human. I know what you've done. Mark my words, you might get away with murdering my kind, but your true colors will show soon. And then we'll be waiting."

CHAPTER
TWENTY

Trix was still fuming when they arrived back at their room. That elf had insulted her and Aeron. He'd laughed at her mate like a schoolyard bully. She'd felt so small in Aeron's arms on the walk back. He placed her on the bed and then locked the bedroom door with his sword through the bolt casings.

When Aeron returned to her, his eyes were bright and full of sharp fury. He found her notebook and scribbled something down before showing it to her.

What did he say to you at the end?

Trix shook her head. Confessing to Aeron had been all she'd wanted to do before heading back down to those pools, but suddenly now, after seeing Kelvhan's response, she was ashamed. And adding this to his worries just added to her shame.

He held his note before her and demanded with his eyes. *Tell me.*

"No," she said stubbornly, signing.

He dropped the book and stormed to the window, where he checked the privacy wards he'd set on their first day were in place. He went about his actions with stilted movements, and she felt bad she'd added to his already simmering frustration. But if she told him what Kelvhan said, there was still nothing Aeron could do to diffuse the situation. Trix wasn't that person building things without seeing the big picture anymore. It might have been her true colors back in Crystal City, but her eyes were wide open now.

It was just words. Words Aeron was lucky he didn't have to hear.

She could fix this for them. Keep the worst of it from him.

She curled up on the bed and hugged a pillow. Helplessness overwhelmed her. There were two things wrong with that thought—one, was it really her right to censor the world from him? Two, she didn't know enough about this world or where she fit into it.

Maybe Kelvhan was right. Maybe her being human was a destiny to fail. She closed her eyes and blinked away the tears, hating how one cruel elf's vicious words could make her feel so empty.

A tender touch on her cheek had her opening her eyes. Aeron crouched next to the bed. His gaze had softened. Frustration was replaced with concern. He held up a paper, this time begging her with his eyes to write what Kelvhan had said.

God, he was hot when he looked at her like that, all caring and compassionate.

She hesitated. Bit her lip.

He lowered his lips to press against each of her eyes as though he wanted to kiss her pain away. It was such a tender moment that she caved and wrote down what Kelvhan had accused her of.

I made bad things when I was in Crystal City. He said, he knows what I've done, that I murdered his kind, and when my true colors show, he'll be waiting.

Aeron didn't get angry. He went silent—like he did just before he'd attacked the nymph.

Trix's skin prickled at the sense of danger. Was it aimed at her? She hadn't even confessed the part she was most ashamed of, that the portal machine used Guardian mana. Sensing miscommunication, Trix went for the note, but Aeron crumpled it and stood.

When his cold eyes slid to the door and his sword, Trix knew he would go after Kelvhan. He wanted to protect her just like she had tried to protect him when Kelvhan hurled nasty words. Maybe this passionate reaction was a side effect of this bond, this sharing of vulnerable emotions. Because of this understanding, she panicked and launched off the bed toward him. She caught his wrist.

"No," she said. "He's not worth it."

He tugged out of her touch and stormed to the door, pointing for her to get back to bed. Trix's panic magnified. She ran after him. Her feet hit the floor hard, and pain spiked in her knees. She limped after him, heedless of the burn growing in her legs. Uncaring about the way they weakened with every step. Her bloody rhino steps had no finesse.

"No," she repeated, cringing at her pain.

His eyes widened at her limp. He set his jaw and scooped her into his arms. By the time he returned to the bed, she was desperate to keep him with her. She needed to feel close to him. To feel something other than the despair creeping in. She plucked at the bone studs holding his jacket together. She kissed his lips, dug her fingers beneath the hem of his jacket, and felt the rock-hard and smooth abdomen bunching as he lowered her.

A needy groan escaped her lips.

More.

She needed more.

Don't leave.

She had plucked most of the studs on his jacket by the time he straightened. When he met her eyes, she saw an echo of her need in his—it went beyond sexual, beyond physical. But he shook his head firmly and pointed at her legs.

"I don't care," she said and reached for him. "I'm fine."

He stepped out of her reach, and she wanted to scream at him. They stared at each other, their breaths laboring, their stubborn wills at odds. And he looked damn fine. His long hair was still unbraided from the soak earlier. His jacket was open, flashing a perfectly bronzed torso with a tiny smattering of hair trailing from his belly button to his pants. Seeing his erection strain at the leather of his battle breeches undid her.

He wanted her, needed her, but shook his head firmly and signed, *No. Rest.*

Trix had always been a stubborn girl. And she hated feeling like crap. If there was one thing she liked to fix more than a broken gadget, it was her feelings. Right now, she needed to feel good.

Boldly holding his gaze, she slid her hand down her stomach and dipped beneath the waistband of her flowing pants. She pressed her fingers to her aching sex and groaned as pleasure rolled through her body. Her vision blurred, but she kept her attention on him as she felt her slick arousal. Another groan slipped out as she started to twirl her finger around her sensitive nub to feel better.

She knew it was a quick fix, but she didn't care. Sometimes a quick fix worked just as well.

He watched her with dark, smoldering eyes that were

so fucking hot she almost came just from holding his gaze. He stubbornly wouldn't let go of her gaze, and she wouldn't stop. She needed this. Needed him.

His raw desire clashed down their bond with hers until she existed in a pool of bliss swirling and sparking. As he watched, Aeron's breath grew ragged, but his feet were rooted to the spot. She didn't want to feel alone.

Help, she signed.

"Help me." *Please.*

Her mate was at the bedside in seconds. He captured her wrist and pulled her hand from her pants. Gasping and a little furious, she tugged her hand back down. If she wanted to touch herself, she bloody well would. But the cheeky sod's brows slammed together, and he used his strength to control her hand. He forced her hand out of her pants again.

"You wanker," she swore. "Don't you dare—oh."

He sucked on her fingers.

"Ooh."

He twirled his tongue around. He lapped and suckled until she forgot what she'd been saying. Her mind latched onto the expert feel of his slippery and hot mouth until he dragged her fingers out and stared at her, his eyelids half-mast, his pupils blown with desire.

The air was heady with the smell of her arousal, a fact he noted and craved—his eyes shuttered, he inhaled deeply, and then he held her hand between them as he exhaled over her fingers. Air tickled the wetness he'd left, and she shivered. As they stared, stunned by his actions, heat gathered low in her body, begging for release. She tugged on her hand, desperate to relieve her need, but he still held it firm.

His brows lifted as if to say, *Is this what you really want?*

"What?" she breathed, confused. "What do you want?"

A battle passed over his expression. She knew he wanted her, needed her as much as she did him, but he didn't want to hurt her. That must be it. She was fine. A little sore, but fine. She dared him by using her other hand to squeeze her breast through her thin shirt. A bolt of pleasure rocked straight down to her core. She arched back, moaning.

Aeron snapped. He ripped off his jacket and then climbed over her to fit himself behind. Using his brute strength, he positioned her on her side so she fit into the curve of his body like they were about to settle for sleep. She whimpered defiantly, but he didn't spoon her to relax. He put his fingers in her mouth and growled in her ear, "Suck."

Hearing his voice, so rough and thick with desire, turned her into a puddle of obedience. She sucked his fingers and twirled her tongue around them.

"Spit on it," he demanded, voice ragged. "More."

God, she was a mess for him. That he spoke for her, to instruct her when he felt self-conscious about his voice, caused a low, needy groan to slip from her lips. She gathered lubrication in her mouth and coated his fingers.

He grunted in approval. "Good girl."

Then his hand dove beneath the waistband of her pants. He slid wet fingers between her thighs and folds, notching at her sensitive clit. He didn't mess about. He didn't play. He fingered her until she writhed and arched into him, until she pawed at him for release.

"Oh, fuck," she blurted as he hit the spot. "Yes. Yes. There. Like that. Don't stop."

A moment of panic hit her when she realized he couldn't hear her. How would he know when she liked it the most... the way she liked it. Would sensing her emotions be enough? Should she arch more into him? Touch him more? Direct him?

But Aeron surprised her. While his right hand was deep in her pants, his left burrowed beneath her neck and wrapped around her throat. He pressed his fingers against her voice box and nuzzled into her hair. It was a pleading movement. A request. He licked and kissed her hesitantly. He pressed her neck. He held back.

"Aeron." She covered his hand and pushed it against her throat. He'd done that in the pools—felt her moans. The pressure of his hand stifled her airway, but she didn't feel unsafe. It turned her on, and she groaned loudly through the resistance—giving him something to feel.

His erection grew to a painful dig against her rear end. He eased his fingers when she needed to breathe—perhaps he sensed her panic rising—but then he pressed when she moaned, catching her pleasure with his touch. And he worked her between the thighs with his fingers.

"You're so wet for me," he rasped. "So fucking hot."

"Yes," she repeatedly muttered until the sensations were too much. Until her words defied her.

"I want to feel you come on my fingers." He slid his finger into her core while stimulating her nub with his thumb. "Fuck, you're tight. Come for me, my mate. Let me feel you."

She climaxed with stars exploding behind her eyes, making her cry out and arch into him. Aeron captured her lips with his own, swallowing her desire with as much enthusiasm as his fingers had shown. When she finally came down from her high, she smiled... melted... and touched her fingers to her lips before pushing them down and out toward him in the hand sign for gratitude.

"Thank you," she smirked. "And when can we do that again."

A bashful smile flittered over his lips, and he tried to tuck her against his front so she would relax, but she rolled to face him with a frown and swiped a lock of hair that had fallen on his face. His eyes were two bright sparks of satisfaction as he looked at her, but only for a moment. A flash of embarrassment came over him and he glanced away.

She put a finger to his chin and brought his face back to her.

She signed and said, "What? Was it me?"

His eyes widened in alarm, and he shook his head.

"Then what?"

He blushed and took her hand and put it on his throat.

"My voice," he said, but without the same gusto as before. With more shyness and fear.

"It was sexy," she said, grinning. He frowned at her lips, and she struggled to think of a sign that would match her words. She'd never signed that with her friend from MIT. They were friends, not lovers. It would have been inappropriate. She only knew the word kiss because they'd been joking about two dumplings sitting so close they looked like they were kissing.

So how could she let Aeron know how she felt about it?

"Sexy," she said and pointed at his lips, then made various lewd gestures, including grabbing herself between the legs.

Aeron barked a laugh and nodded.

"I'm serious. I like it when you talk dirty. I want more." A rush of warmth flooded her chest, and she brushed his stubbled jaw. "I like that it's something you did for me."

He didn't understand her, but he sighed, seemingly appeased. He stared at the ceiling and tapped his chest in thought. Okay. Now, what did that mean?

She swiped her fingers from her lips to her cheek and back again. *Kiss?*

His eyes crinkled, and he drew closer to press his lips against hers, but she put her hand over his mouth and shook her head. When his brows lifted, confused, she smirked and pointed to his erection still straining against his leather breeches.

He thought about her offer. She could tell by the fluctuating desire in his emotions and the way his eyes lit up—but then he shut it down and shook his head.

No, he signed.

"What?" she gasped. "No?"

He laughed at her outrage, but it was a good laugh. It wasn't to make fun of her, and it confused the heck out of her. She went for his pants, and he slapped her away, his mood turning serious. He pointed at her legs and signed, *Pain. Later.*

"We can do this without me on my knees," she insisted.

But he bundled her in his arms and rolled her to face the door while he tucked himself in behind her. Then he kissed her nape and sighed again. It was too deep and satisfying for her to complain. He was pleased with what had just happened between them.

She huffed a little, and he tugged her close. This time, she allowed herself to relax. There was no use fighting him over it. There were other ways to entice him... later.

On a whim, Trix took his hand at her chest and kissed his knuckles before resting her head on the pillow and sighing too. They had a few hours before they were due at dinner with the king and queen. She should use the time to relax.

Truly, her legs were sore. She'd overdone it. Despite that, contentment rolled through her like a warm drink spreading outward. Aeron had trusted her with his voice. She felt honored and... loved. *In* love.

Wow.

She just went there, and it didn't feel creepy or weird. It felt right.

Tonight, after dinner, she would sit him down and tell him all the things she'd done for Nero in Crystal City. Hopefully, Aeron felt just as strongly toward Trix. Hopefully, he wouldn't feel the same as the High Lord did. Hopefully, he'd forgive her.

TWENTY-ONE

Aeron stood before the black mirror at the bathroom basin and braided his hair. It was the last thing he had to do to prepare for dinner with the King and Queen. He'd considered turning up in his Guardian uniform but decided to dress casually. Guardian business was often dangerous and deadly. He wanted to build a good impression with them, to be allies so that Kelvhan's threats stayed nullified.

He'd already pushed the extent of their goodwill by ignoring the invitation to dinner all week.

He wore a tailored shirt, linen breeches, and a simple tan leather jacket. Understated and, he hoped, friendly.

In the mirror's reflection, Trix limped up behind him. He scowled, dropped his braid, and turned to her. She shouldn't be walking after hurting her legs earlier. It was his fault for going off half-cocked after hearing Kelvhan had insulted her.

He had every intention of picking her up and carrying her back to bed, but the sight of her in a skin-tight dress arrested him. *Beautiful*. She was a vision in white. The dress cinched her waist but flared at the hips to cascade down to the ground. A single split gave him a tantalizing view of shapely legs. His mouth watered at the thought of sliding his hands up her thighs and pushing aside the fabric, his fingertips probing and reaching for the same hot, wet place he'd had a taste of earlier.

His scowl returned when he remembered she was on her feet. He put his hands around her waist, noted how small and delicate she was, then lifted her and placed her on the bathroom vanity counter. His lips flattened at her smirk. He sensed that even after she was healed, she would always enjoy pushing him. Teasing him. And if the little thrill in his stomach was anything to go by, he'd love every minute of it.

She opened her legs so he could slot in as she tugged his collar to bring him closer. Then, with appreciative eyes, she ran her hands down his shirt to flatten any creases. When her eyes dipped to his pants, she kept her eyes glued there and signed, *Kiss later*.

His cock jerked at the attention. Crimson, help him now. In just a few more days, he could be as rough, needy, and indulgent with her as he wanted. Going by how she'd responded to him earlier, she'd be enthused about it every step of the way. She'd even encouraged him to feel the vibrations her voice had made.

His cock jerked again.

Fuck.

He scrubbed his face and went back to braiding his hair. He had a pattern, a routine. It eased something inside him. The braids were usually styled off his forehead and loose down the back. It was common in Rubrum City.

But tonight, he couldn't say no to the soft, tender touch of Trix's deft fingers as she plucked out random sections of his hair and plaited them. He stopped doing his own and instead threw himself into the sheer pleasure of studying his mate's tics of concentration. Her little pink tongue pressed against the corner of her lips. She scrunched up her nose when she made a mistake. Her eyes crinkled when she was pleased with her efforts.

"Why the braids?" she asked.

He'd been so lost in the tiny joys of her face that he'd not noticed her sign the words at first. She had to repeat herself.

Why the braids?

His instant reaction was to tense. The answer lay in a past he'd rather forget, but one he supposed had shaped his identity. She would learn sooner or later. She might have already overheard some of it.

He retrieved paper and a pencil from the bedroom and wrote his answer.

Braids mean you're educated in the Autumn Court. Despite reading every book I could get my hands on, I was not allowed to claim the right of education. I was the bastard son of the King. They used to cut my hair as a joke.

So when I became a Guardian, I braided my hair to claim that right for myself.

From how her expression dropped as she read it, he didn't think she expected his honest answer, but he wouldn't hide his past from her. Not this incredible woman who seemed to fill the very depths of his bitter soul with hope again.

She wrote beneath his words,

I think you look sexy with or without braids. You're everything to me.

His throat closed, his cheeks heated, and he swallowed hard. He lifted his gaze to hers and was met with a burning curiosity. Then a strange shattering of good intentions, a dip in her desire. It was as though she struggled with something. She opened her mouth a few times but closed her lips and instead started to write more.

I have to tell you something...

But he knew if they continued this baring of the souls, he'd be quite happy to stand up a king and queen.

Later, he signed with a questioning shrug. *We're late to eat.*

She thought about it, then nodded her agreement. He picked her up and carried her out. He wanted nothing between them, but for that, they needed complete and utter privacy and not to be rushed. Dinner with the queen and king would be over before they knew it.

AERON'S MATE insisted he put her feet on the ground before they entered the royal quarters of the palace. It was against his judgment, especially after she'd hurt herself earlier. He understood why she wanted to be independent, but when she leaned on him heavily and winced, he almost scooped her back up. Apprehension churned in his gut. She was in pain—more pain than this morning. She should let him carry her into the chair. He was sure the king and queen wouldn't mind.

But he didn't want to make a scene, so he steadied her until she smiled at him. She was brave, and he suspected that didn't even scratch the surface of who she was. He brushed long, curly hair off her shoulders, and the urge to kiss the hollow next to her neck was too much.

She blushed.

Despite avoiding this inevitable dinner from the

moment they'd arrived in Delphinium, there was no place he'd rather be than by his mate's side. All that angst over communication had been lessened, not just because she could translate and carry a conversation for him, but because he also knew if she couldn't, he was now confident enough to figure ways around it. He couldn't believe a week ago, he'd wanted to leave her behind to pursue purifying the taint on the Well alone.

He put his arm around her shoulder and looked at the steward to let him know they were ready. It was the same steward who'd stood by the High Lord Kelvhan in the tunnels beneath the Great Elder Tree. Aeron already didn't trust the fae, but he wasn't prepared for the strange look on the male's face. It was so brief that he almost missed it. Hate? Surprise? Trepidation? It was too brief for Aeron to decipher, but it left a wary feeling behind when they were guided through the large carved doors.

Those kinds of false facial expressions were another way fae lied. Aeron might not have caught it before his loss of hearing. He studied body language more now and had found more truth in actions than words... even those from fae. He stored the steward's impression away for later examination and followed him through the doors.

Aeron and Trix stopped just inside the doors and blinked at their sudden change in surroundings. He'd expected to see a room but found open sprawling gardens alit with manabeeze trapped in glass lanterns. Ripe fruit and blooming flowers gave the air a pleasant scent. It wasn't stagnant, but in true spring flavor, it brought the zest of new life to the atmosphere.

Aeron breathed deeply and cupped Trix's nape when he sensed her doing the same thing.

The air here was invigorating... and enticing. Like the very essence of mana coated his tongue. Once the idea hit, his instincts immediately went on the defensive. If he could taste magic in the air, things might not be as they seemed.

The steward led them down a cobblestone path toward an oblong table beneath a Weeping Willow decorated with garlands and lanterns. Small walled frescos depicted scenes from Spring Court history at regular intervals along the path. Aeron recognized Eulios in his virile glory, standing over what he guessed was the purple sapling of the Great Elder Tree.

Another panel showed Jackson Crimson, the blond elf who discovered the link between the Well, mana, and forbidden substances. He was the same fae who worked with Aleksandra, the current Prime, to create the Order of the Well. Similar storytelling art was in the Academy at the Order.

Another fresco showed Crimson being swallowed by the ceremonial lake. And a third showed Eulios and Crimson, their heads bowed as though discussing secrets.

As he expected, Trix was so enamored with the paintings that she lost all focus on the two lavishly dressed royals waiting for them at the table. He gently nudged her and guided her toward the head of the grand table.

King Tian sat next to Queen Oleana. His crown of antlers, flowers, and leaves appeared abnormally vibrant on his pallid, frail head. She looked radiant and young. Technically, they were the same age, but something had happened to age him. Their mating was a love match. She touched him gently and fawned over him. Her gaze softened every time it landed on his wrinkled face. For a fae to age thus, their mana had to be permanently removed. Why the king would have done so was a mystery Aeron hoped to have answered.

The longer he spent in this city, the more he felt things weren't quite right.

Something was amiss.

As a Guardian, he should keep his nose out of politics... but the king's aging could point to abuse of mana. And that was definitely a place a Guardian should put his nose.

Aeron took Trix's hand and stepped up to the royal couple, she leaned more heavily on him than she had when they'd arrived.

Don't pick her up.

She'll not like it.

The king and queen's lips moved as Aeron and Trix arrived at the table. Trix explained that he couldn't hear. He liked that she continued to sign for his benefit as she spoke. He'd never asked her to, but that she'd done it from the start of their relationship was a testament to her character.

Royal jaws dropped at Trix's explanation of his hearing loss, but the queen rallied first. She smiled politely at Aeron and gestured for them to sit opposite her and next to the king. He first pulled out the chair for Trix, but the queen waved Trix to her side of the table. Trix gave him a nervous look, but he nodded that it was suitable for her to do so.

Somehow, he thought she would do just fine talking to a queen as she would a pauper.

In all his time alive, he'd barely heard a bad word about this royal Seelie couple. Despite that lick of magic in the evening air, he didn't think they would cause harm tonight. The more Aeron thought about it, the more he felt that sense came from the garden. It was as if the Well itself fed into the soil. It could be a power source where mana replenishes faster than usual.

It might well do, and possibly why the royals spent time out here. Often the pull of being close to a power source was hard to resist.

The king tried to stand and called the steward over, but his frail body didn't let him get far. The queen asked in his stead and directed her mate to sit back down. Moments later, the steward returned with paper and a pencil. The moment the steward's back turned, his mask of pleasantry dropped. He caught Aeron watching and put it back in place before scurrying back to his post near the entrance.

Interesting.

Aeron wondered if he'd planned to listen in on the conversation; now that half of it would be written down, he was unhappy. Only one other person hadn't been happy about this dinner—the queen's brother.

There was no use avoiding the topic. Aeron had always been a straight talker. He supposed that shouldn't matter now that he chose not to use his voice. He picked up the pencil and wrote:

Nymphs attacked us in the healing waters.

CHAPTER
TWENTY-TWO

This kind of formal event usually made Trix feel out of place. She hated visiting the grand dining hall full of the lavishly dressed elite in the Sky Tower back at Crystal City. Even when Miss Melody had played, Trix preferred to watch from the recess of the stage and stayed hidden in the shadows. She liked grease beneath her fingernails and coveralls hiding her frame.

So when she'd put on the sexy white dress hanging in the closet, she was surprised at how comfortable she felt sitting next to a queen who looked like a million diamonds. Seriously, Trix couldn't stop staring at her flawless skin and long silken hair, partly braided into majestical patterns, partially woven. Her dress sparkled with jewels that matched the earrings dangling from her elfin ears. The light they cast reminded Trix of the reflections on the water.

She could be intimidating, that much was true, but Trix felt entirely at ease.

Maybe it was the friendly way she had beckoned Trix over.

"How wonderful to meet you," she said to Trix with a gentle smile. "Please sit. I'd love to speak with you more closely. Let the males have boring conversations about the state of the world."

Trix limped around the table, hating how attention was drawn to her gait. She sensed Aeron's need to come to her aid, but she straightened her spine and curtseyed when she arrived at Queen Oleana's side. To her credit, the queen didn't mention the limp, nor had she balked at Aeron's deafness.

Trix supposed having a mate in the king's unusual condition would change how she viewed the world. Trix had fast learned over the past week that fae weren't tolerant of those with disabilities when they were rarely present in the near-immortal race.

"Congratulations on a rare Well-blessed mating." The queen pointed to Trix's blue arm markings. "How wonderful to have the Well approving your union."

Trix remembered her manners to hand sign her gratitude as she sat.

"It took me some time to understand," she replied, her gaze skating to Aeron. "But now I see we're quite a good match."

Trix had never thought she'd say that about an

arranged marriage-type situation but couldn't deny that sharing emotions had a way of deepening a relationship on a different level.

"How long have you been in Elphyne, dear?" the queen asked.

"A few years in Crystal City and a few months in Elphyne," she said, and when Oleana gave her a confused look, Trix's first reaction was to guard her emotions because she'd gone and blurted something she hadn't thought through. Drawing attention to her humanity probably wasn't a good thing here in Elphyne. And the queen had only asked about Elphyne... not Crystal City. Goodness. Heat flushed Trix's cheeks, and she wanted to hide under a rock. Sometimes consequences came from her impulsive moments that she wasn't prepared for. But the queen didn't dwell on Trix's humanity.

"And how are you finding Elphyne?"

"Well, I guess I was kidnapped and sold to the Autumn Court King. So there's that." Trix had to mentally slap herself in the face. Two impulsive comments in a row. What was she thinking? Someone needed to put a zip on her lips.

Seeking comfort, Trix's gaze went to Aeron. Seeing him made her exhale and remember that she should stop trying to be someone she wasn't. Aeron liked her just fine.

"Kidnapped?" Oleana's pretty eyes widened. "Oh. How unfortunate. Are you well?"

"I am." No use hiding the elephant in the room. "My leg

injury was all my fault, I'm afraid. Wasn't watching where I was going."

Trix noticed Aeron and the king scribbling on paper. The queen caught the direction of her gaze, leaned over, read something the king wrote down, and then asked Trix, "Nymphs attacked you *here*?"

Trix should have realized Aeron would get straight to the point. Where she was ashamed of her impulsivity, he owned his choices. She liked that about him. Trix turned to Oleana and said, "Yes. One tried to drown me, and another tried to kill Aeron."

"Well, I hope they got what was coming to them." The queen scoffed. "Attacking a Guardian *and* his Well-blessed mate. We believe there's no higher calling than protecting one's mate."

Sadness flickered in her eyes and, on instinct, Trix reached out and squeezed her hand. The queen's shocked gaze snapped to Trix as they touched. Trix sensed that true acts of compassion would be few and far between in the queen's life.

Like in Trix's time, anyone in this kind of role would have little in the way of friendships without strings attached.

Oleana's expression turned grim, and she cast a worried glance at her king, who wrote more down to Aeron with a shaky hand. Then he wrote on a second paper and called the steward over.

The king tried to stand but hobbled on his leg and

ended up sitting back down. Trix had noticed he'd done the same before. But unlike her injury, which would heal, his was most likely due to age. And she didn't see a cane or walking apparatus.

That gave her an idea.

"Would you like me to build the king an aid to help him walk?" she asked Oleana.

"An aid?"

"Yes. I know you're probably unfamiliar with them since the fae are usually all so fit and healthy, but where I come from, age is common, as is the decline of full motor function. We make walking frames or a cane—" She gestured a yard length with her hand. "It's a long walking stick you use to balance on."

"Oh. That would help dear Tian an awful lot." Oleana smiled. "First, you help us with the festival, and now this. We would owe you a great debt of gratitude."

"Don't be silly," Trix said. "Your healers have helped me immensely."

"As I understand, it's a healer from the Order who has worked with you. We only supplied the room."

"And this lovely dress."

Oleana leaned in. "That, my dear, was paid and bought for in coin from your mate. He spared no expense to keep you comfortable."

Trix's gaze snapped to where Aeron was deep in conversation with the king. Had he paid for all the extravagance in their room?

Even before he knew he liked her.

The blue twinkling on Trix's arm stole her attention. This bond must be special for him to have given so much to her at first sight. Hadn't the queen said they were rare?

"Will you indulge an old queen and tell me about your mate?" Oleana asked. "I hope it's not too forward of me, but I do love a mystery and a good love story."

"Oh. I guess I don't know too much about him yet. He came from the Autumn Court to the Order and likes braiding his hair because he's smart."

Oleana laughed. "He does seem the quiet, clever type, and you know what they say about those."

"Um... I'm not sure I do."

The queen winked at her. "They're a dynamite between the sheets."

Trix tried not to blush. "I guess I can't refute that."

"I know because Tian used to be the same sort. So I'm allowed to say things like that." Oleana smirked as she took a sip of her drink.

They shared a giggle. Trix liked this elf queen.

Oleana asked, "But the Autumn Court, you say. Do you know Aeron's age?"

Trix shook her head. This line of questioning seemed to get personal rather fast, and she had the sneaking suspicion that there was more to this dinner than met the eye. Trix glanced over at Aeron in time to catch the oddest occurrence.

The king's hand lashed out and nabbed Aeron's ear. He yanked Aeron closer and peered inside.

"Tian!" Oleana exclaimed. "Just what do you think you're doing?"

She bolted out of her seat and helped Aeron pry his ear back from the king, who was already sitting back as if nothing had happened. Oleana smiled apologetically to Aeron.

"You'll have to forgive him. He's not himself." She signed an apology to Aeron and then tutted over her mate. "He probably got excited to see another elf with ears like his."

Oleana acted like this was the act of an old senile elf but Trix caught a shrewdness in the king's eyes. Aeron glanced at Trix and rubbed his ear absently.

Are you okay? Trix signed. She was ready to get up and launch herself at a king. These overprotective urges were getting stronger the more she grew attached to Aeron.

He nodded and gave her the barest waving down of his hand. Trix realized she had, indeed, leaped to her feet and was poised to attack.

Movement in the garden brought her attention to royal guards with antlered helmets. She'd not seen them there upon entry but guessed they were there all along—part of the scenery.

The king's cloudy blue eyes widened as though he'd just had a thought, and he scribbled down something in excitement for Aeron to read. Strange happening forgotten,

Oleana returned to her seat with a small, placating smile sent Trix's way.

"I wish I could say this behavior was new, but since his only sister died during childbirth, he's been steadily declining."

Trix shifted awkwardly in her seat. Should she be hearing about this? But the queen seemed to trust her and continued to speak as she straightened the dinnerware she'd messed up in her haste to get to her mate.

"I'm not sure how much longer I can be the stoic one. I've tried. For decades I've tried, but I—" She swallowed.

"It must be hard," Trix said. "And lonely. I know what it's like to feel separated from everyone else. If you ever want someone to talk to, please know you can call on me."

"You feel like that because you're human?"

"Well..." Trix shrugged. "I think I've felt like that my entire life. I'm not exactly what people call normal."

"Pah," she said. "Normal is overrated. Come. The food is about to be served. Let's have a drink and forget about normal. Just for one night."

It turned out to be more than one drink. Maybe three. Or four. Trix lost count, but she stumbled on clouds by the time the plates were scraped clean, and a blue glow in the queen's drink nabbed her attention.

"Kelvhan," Oleana slurred, squinting at her cup. "What do you want? I'm in the middle of something." She dramatically rolled her eyes at Trix and mouthed *Brothers* before returning her focus to the cup.

But Trix was blown away. What the hell was happening here? Why was there a picture of a man in her drink? Not man—elf. Kelvhan.

"Oh my god, Aeron. Are you seeing this?" she said to him, signing.

Unlike her, Aeron was not drunk. As severe and stalwart as usual, his brow lifted at her uncoordinated hand signs, but he picked up the gist. Neither he nor the king was full of the same wonder Trix was. Leaning toward the queen on a wobbly elbow, almost knocking her drink, Trix poked the water in the queen's cup. Kelvhan's face wobbled as he spoke with a glare at his sister.

"You are entertaining two murderers," he said.

"Murderers!" Oleana fanned her face with mock surprise. "My goodness. Whatever will we do?"

"This is serious, sister."

Oleana's humor died, and she straightened. Gone was the playful female. In was the queen.

"Speak carefully, Kelvhan. You are too familiar."

"They murdered two of your subjects in cold blood in the sacred healing waters of the Great Elder Tree. And you have nothing to say about it?"

She pursed her lips. "He is fae. He is a Guardian. So when he speaks, he tells the truth. You're the one who told us the word of high fae must be taken as truth, or our society will break down. The taint is doing strange things to everyone. That two nymphs attacked is why we need

197

Guardians in our midst. Now, if that is all, you are rudely interrupting."

Kelvhan said nothing but glared, and the queen cut the connection by dashing her finger through the liquid. After a shared look with her mate, she smiled politely at Trix and Aeron.

"He is a little overzealous in protecting this kingdom, but rest assured, we do not share the same views."

"My queen is right about that," said the king. "In fact, I was hoping you would spend time down in the barracks with my soldiers."

"Me?" Trix blurted.

"D'arn Aeron." The king forgot he'd not written down his request, but once he had, Aeron nodded respectfully.

The queen beamed and placed her hand on Trix. "I would love you to spend time with me. It's ever so dull around here sometimes." She lowered her voice. "Especially when Tian naps."

"Of course!" Trix replied. "I could make that walking cane I spoke about. Oh. And I'd love to hear more about this communication method you have. Why is it through water? How does it work?"

"We will have a full week ahead of us to talk about such matters." Oleana's gaze slid to her king, whose eyelids drooped with fatigue. "I think it is time for us to end this meal and retire."

Trix got to her feet as the queen did and felt a stab of

pain slice her legs like fire, but she covered by squealing and hugging the elf queen.

"I'm so grateful to have met you," she said and then hand signed her thanks.

She was proud that she stayed on her feet until the royal couple left. Then she collapsed back on the chair with tears in her eyes. Even through the haze of alcohol, the pain was glaring. Aeron used his mana to burn the papers used to converse with the king, then he rushed over and kneeled before her.

Pain on a scale of one to ten, he signed.

She could lie.

She'd only just made her first friend, and he might insist she stay in their rooms. But the thought of adding more secrets to the big one already between them was too much. She held up eight fingers with a wince.

Aeron cupped her face and nodded. Then he scooped her up and carried her home.

TWENTY-THREE

The look Thistle gave Aeron the following morning was dark enough to reach inside his chest and squeeze his heart. He knew it. He should have protected Trix from her need to get moving, but when you loved someone, sometimes it was hard to balance what you thought was best for them versus what made them happy.

He loved her.

He hardly knew her, but it didn't matter. Their souls spoke to each other in a way he'd never had with another person before. She needed him, and he needed her.

Shame heated his cheeks as he paced around the bed, watching while Thistle examined Trix. His perpetually optimistic mate tried to laugh off the seriousness of her condition, but he felt her guilt inside. They'd both leaped in headfirst without a single thought of consequences.

Aeron couldn't even blame the nymph attack. Trix's pain had worsened when he'd wanted to storm out of the room by himself and attack Kelvhan and then when he'd let her walk to dinner. He blamed himself.

He should have waited for confirmation from an expert.

He was not a leap-first person. He planned. And he was ready to do whatever he could to help Trix heal. If her legs were ruined... if he'd allowed them to heal wrong...

Thistle handed him a note and then waited as he read. While there was no tone of voice in the written word, he could feel her disapproval vibrate through the air. He deserved it.

Thistle wrote:

> *She has taken a step backward in her healing. There is new swelling around the knees and ankles. Without permission to use mana, I'm afraid there may be permanent damage. Even mortal consequences if the infection doesn't rectify itself.*

Aeron closed his eyes and exhaled. How could he have let this happen? A million thoughts whirled in his head, stopping him from opening his eyes and facing reality, but Thistle touched his arm gently. He met her stare as she pointed to another line of her written word:

Is the taint still dangerous?

He nodded, but as he did, he recalled the black ooze on the vines. He had theorized this was of similar substance to Silver's dark gift. If he could get Silver to purge the taint while Thistle worked, Trix might still be okay.

He wrote:

I might have a way to purge the taint while you work. But I will need some time. How much do we have?

Thistle took the pencil and replied,

Hard to say. Best case scenario, perhaps a few days before the damage becomes the new normal for her body, just like your hearing.

Aeron nodded grimly. His eardrums had healed wrong. His body healed the wound, not repaired the sense.

He scrubbed his face.

New plan. He would find a way to get in touch with Shade and Silver, beg them to come here, and then beg Silver to fill herself with a toxic taint so Trix could walk. He would contact Jasper and Ada and beg them to help too. And he'd have to do it all within a day because he wouldn't take any chances this time.

He wrote:

Give me two days.

Thistle nodded and replied,

More soaking in the waters until then.

Aeron touched his fingers to his lips and pushed them down and out. Thistle smiled, said something to Trix, and then collected her healer's basket and left. When Aeron met his mate at her bed, she looked up at him sullenly.

She pointed to herself and signed, *Trouble?*

He kissed her and shook his head. Not if he could help it. Using more notes, he explained to her what needed to happen and was surprised to find out Trix didn't know about the taint on the Well. She'd assumed what occurred with the vines was her fault. She said the same thing had happened to her before. He cautioned her not to use mana unless it was an emergency and then went to the bathroom to make a blood connection through the water.

The risk was worth it. There was no other option besides leaving this place and journeying back to the Order. Even then, he wasn't certain Shade and Silver would be there. They'd spent much of their time living at Rush's cabin, closer to Crystal City than the Order.

Aeron prepared himself for the taint to blow back in his face, but he wasn't prepared for it to connect him to another blood tie instead of Forrest—the face of his tormentor from his youth, one of his half-brothers from the Autumn Court.

Niall was a sturdy elf. He had a body made for bullying and liked to hold Aeron's head underwater while telling him they were playing a game called *How Not To Die*. So when Aeron saw his face, his block jaw, and cruel eyes all warped in the water, it took him straight back to his youth decades—a century—ago. Aeron was there, not here. His lungs were burning. His ability to voice his scream was swallowed by viscous liquid around him.

Are you dead yet?

Aeron spluttered and gasped for air. He had no control of his young lungs. They barely pumped with life before his brother said, "No? Let's try it again."

Something hard hit Aeron on the head, snapping him out of his memories. Sensing his turmoil, Trix had tossed another item at him. He glanced down to see a wooden cup on the floor.

Thank you, he signed, which confused her even more. She beckoned him over.

Stepping away from his past and toward his future had never been so easy. Aeron dashed his hand through the water, obliterating his brother's cruel face, and then he went to his mate, took her face between his hands, and kissed her passionately.

She froze at first but swiftly conceded. Her guard came

down the second his tongue slipped passed her soft lips and delved deeply inside. In a simultaneous move, his hands dug into her hair, clenched, and held her in place while he devoured her like she was the air he'd needed when his brother had held him down.

If she wasn't injured, if she'd let him, he'd have taken her right there and then to seek comfort. From the eager way she kissed him back and how her hands roamed over his body, he knew she'd let him. But he'd allowed himself to forget how serious her injury was before. He wouldn't do it again.

He pulled away and rested his forehead on hers until his breathing was under control. She tried to tug him back, but he shook his head and signed, *Later*.

That earned him a pout, but he distracted her with the letter he was meant to send to Forrest. As she read it, her demeanor became serious, and she nodded, understanding the gravity of her situation. She swallowed, folded the letter, and handed it back to him. Then she asked him what had happened earlier.

He wrote that down too. He told her that seeing his brother had brought back old, dark memories he'd rather forget. How his family treated him as a child. How Forrest had been his only friend. But also how he'd turned his life around when he became a Guardian. As Trix read, her sense of justice barreled toward him from down their bond, and he wanted to kiss her all over again, for he knew she was thinking of protecting him. All his life, he'd never dreamed of having someone trust him so implicitly. There was nothing between them but this injury—not even his lack of hearing.

She wrote:

Bring some water here. Make the connection with me by your side.

Aeron wasn't a coward. He would make the connection again on his own, but the thought of having his mate, his female, and his lover by his side in the same way the queen supported the king was as tempting as a drug. Wasn't that what every soul craved? To have someone they loved sitting by their side until the end?

He emptied the fruit bowl on the table, filled it with water, and then set it down on the bedside table. He had to shift the recently grown vines from Trix's gift. After she healed, he would need to find a way to teach her to control it without actually using it.

For now, he cut his palm and sent his blood into the Well. He watched it swirl, blend with the water, and bade it to hunt for the only blood tie he cared for—Forrest. Maybe it was the soothing presence of Aeron's mate, or perhaps the taint went easy on them, but this time he connected with the right person.

Forrest's relieved face appeared in the luminous water,

and Aeron tensed. He hadn't been prepared for his body's reaction upon seeing his brother. Two factions of emotion warred inside him. One was linked to his love for his brother, the only fae who'd accepted and protected him as a child. The other was related to his bitterness at what Forrest in his Guardian uniform now represented—the inevitable future of Aeron being replaced.

He wondered if Forrest knew.

They all probably knew.

In the seconds his paranoia overwhelmed him, Trix took his hand and squeezed. He breathed a little easier and held up the letter to Forrest. It would be easier to get his mate to read the words aloud, but this had to come from Aeron. He was asking a lot.

Transference runes were scratched onto the outer surface of the letter. Aeron figured if this connection went to Forrest as intended, then the taint was minimal, so he dropped the letter into the water and activated the runes with his mana. Instead of hitting the bottom of the bowl as it sank, the letter went straight through. When the water's surface ripples settled, Aeron saw Forrest already reading the dripping letter. Within moments, Forrest caught Aeron's eyes and nodded. He said something, to which Trix leaned over and replied, smiled and waved, then sat back on the bed with a bashful glance Aeron's way.

Forrest must have introduced himself to Trix and vice versa.

The knowing look in Forrest's eyes brought heat to Aeron's face, but also a kinship—solidarity. He knew his brother would understand Aeron's need to protect his mate. He knew Forrest would do everything he could to get Shade and Silver here.

CHAPTER
TWENTY-FOUR

Two days later, Trix was well and truly at the edge of her patience. Bedridden since her healing had taken a step backward, she drove herself insane trying to keep occupied. But for someone like her, it was torture to do so from a bed. She filled another notebook with hand signs and asked Aeron to practice with her. He embraced everything she had to give, plus they'd even come up with a few signs they'd made up to fill the void of things she'd either not known or had forgotten.

She liked that this became more of a secret language just for the two of them.

Trix also wrote out schematics for at least four different walking canes for the king and three ideas for creating a portable handheld device fae could use to communicate with each other. The best was two pieces of glass with trapped water inside. The only hurdle she'd encountered was the ability to drop blood into the water to activate the communication spell.

She hadn't given up.

She was just antsy.

Queen Oleana visited. And left.

Thistle visited. And left. Three times. Each time the expression on Thistle's face grew grimmer until, on the third day, when she pressed the back of her hand to Trix's feverish forehead, she walked out briskly and took Aeron with her.

Apart from visiting the barracks for an hour on both days, he'd barely left her bedside.

The pain wouldn't lessen this time, even after each visit to the healing waters. She knew what that meant, even if they weren't honest with her. They tried to remain hopeful, but the fact was that Trix felt wrong inside. She slept more than she should.

When a knock came at the door, Aeron sat at the table by the window, poring over her notebook about hand signs. He didn't hear, so she tossed an apple core at his head. He sensed it coming and snatched it out of the air with a smirk.

It had become a game between them.

She would find something to toss. She would try to surprise him. And he would sense it coming. So far, he'd beaten her every time except once.

He strode over and placed his notebook on the bed

before answering the door. It wasn't her ASL notebook like she'd thought, but an ancient-looking book. She flicked through the pages. It was on the theory of how mana and the Well were connected and how forbidden items made this power stop flowing. It was written by someone called Jackson Crimson. She became so entranced in the account that she forgot about the new arrivals until a familiar voice with a southern twang grew loud.

"Well, aren't you a sight for sore eyes?"

Trix looked up, but her mind was still in the book, and she looked back at the paper before her brain processed who she'd just seen. She slammed the book shut and gasped.

"Miss Melody?"

The ghost from Trix's past pushed Aeron out of the way and made a beeline for the bed. She looked the same as Trix remembered... A little thinner but a whole lot happier. Her platinum hair was out and carefree. Her cheeks were stained pink. And she also had a blue, glowing mark down her arm.

"You're—" Trix pointed. "Like me."

Melody blinked, then scowled at Aeron before returning to Trix. "Now, don't tell me your tall drink of water hasn't mentioned I'm here in Elphyne? Or that I'm mated to his brother?"

Trix was too dumbfounded to answer. She just shook her head. Aeron's guilt flashed down their bond as he wrote notes to his brother and clearly picked up the conversation.

"You look amazing," Trix said as Melody sat on the edge of the bed.

"Not having food forced on me has done wonders."

"What?" Trix gaped. "Who forced... oh. Oh, no. He did? What a bastard."

Melody bit her lip, and the life in her drained before she rallied and patted the bed next to Trix. "That's all behind me now. I feel the best I've ever felt. My mate is amazing. I love the body I'm in, and I'm also in love."

"I'm so happy for you. I... gosh, I'm still so gobsmacked. I had no idea." Melody shot another scowl at Aeron, but Trix came to his defense. "I don't think he did it on purpose. We've had a lot going on. There are also things I still haven't told him."

"You're right. I can only imagine how difficult it's been. I'm sure we have a lot to catch up on. But you—tell me about you. Is he treating you well? What happened to your legs?"

"I can only blame myself for this," Trix mumbled. "I fell out of a tree. I wasn't looking. Aeron has been by my side, helping me ever since."

Melody smiled at Aeron and Forrest before returning her gaze to Trix. "Forrest speaks very highly of Aeron."

There was much Trix was still to learn about Aeron's past and family, both chosen and old, but all she needed was one glance at them to know they cared deeply for each other. The look in Forrest's eyes as he watched his brother write was something Trix could only describe as compassion and respect. And Aeron, when he handed his note to Forrest, had a similar look. He cared about his brother's opinion. When Forrest nodded, clapped a hand on Aeron's shoulder, and squeezed, Trix felt Aeron's relief through their bond.

She sighed and rested her heavy, hot head on the pillow. "At least I know he has a family."

"Now, that sounds pessimistic." Melody's brow puckered.

"I don't feel well," Trix replied softly, hating the train of her thoughts but unable to stop the flood of them pushing at her mind. From the fever-filled memories of being admonished for making stupid mistakes when she was back at Crystal City and then further back in the old world. To the fresh mistakes in this world. She always had the best intentions. She never wanted to hurt or offend anyone.

But sometimes she didn't *think*.

Sometimes she focused on what was in front of her because seeing the big picture was frightening.

"You don't think," Justin had said, poking her temple with his finger. *"For someone so clever, it astounds me."*

The tear leaking from her eye burned.

Aeron was there instantly, taking her hand and swiping

hair from her sweaty forehead. She tried to smile for him, but the will to put on a brave face evaporated.

"Honey," Melody said. "Don't lose hope. We're all here to help."

TWENTY-FIVE

T rix woke to an unfamiliar female voice. *Must have dozed off.*

"You know what to do," the woman said.

"Darling, you know I do." The smooth male voice was also unfamiliar.

Trix fought the sleepiness dragging her down, and peeled open her eyes. On the couches by the window, a beautiful woman with a long silver braid sat with a very handsome man... his ears were pointed, and he had leathery bat wings sprouting from his back. So he was fae, not man. And he was in a Guardian uniform.

Aeron squeezed Trix's hand to let her know he was at her bedside. She licked her lips, feeling so thirsty. Before she could sign what she needed, he had a cup of water ready.

She drank greedily.

When she was done, she noticed more people in the room—most of them stood watching the first couple. Forrest was still there with Melody, as was a tall blond elf in his Guardian uniform. And a well-dressed blond woman... next to a brown-haired shifter wearing a regal outfit he hated wearing because he tugged at the collar continuously. He had a Guardian teardrop beneath his left eye but wasn't in the leather uniform.

"Who are these people?" Trix rasped and signed to Aeron.

He replied, *Friends.*

Aeron waved Melody over.

"How are you feeling, hun?" she asked.

"Tired." Trix frowned. "Aeron said these are friends, but who?"

"The women have all thawed out from our time and are now mated to a Guardian." Melody pointed them out. "That's Silver with Shade on the couch. They're about to test Aeron's theory about purging the inky taint from the Well with her gift." She swung her finger to point at the rest. "That's High Queen Ada and High King Jasper—he was one of the Twelve before he took the Summer Court throne. Ada's gift is healing. If it's okay with you, she will assess you."

Trix nodded.

Melody continued, "And that glowering elf supervising it all is Leaf. He's the team leader for the Twelve."

A spike of bitterness hit Aeron as Melody pointed at

Leaf. Trix guessed her mate had some issues with him. But she'd also felt his mood change when he'd communicated with his brother.

Melody beckoned Ada, who came with a gentle smile and wave. "Hello, Trix. Your mate and Thistle have asked me to look at your injuries. I'm going to do that now if that's okay?"

Like Melody, Ada also had an American accent. This further solidified Trix's theory that they were still in America somewhere... only thousands of years after the Fallout. The museum at the Sky Tower was American-centric, but it was always good to gather more evidence—

"Trix?" Ada asked, bringing Trix's attention back to her.

"My bad. Go ahead," Trix said, expecting Ada to lift the blankets and look at her legs, but she placed her hands on Trix's ankles over the blanket and then closed her eyes. A look of concentration came over her. It lasted for a good minute, and then she opened her eyes and said loudly, "I'm done."

Silver suddenly jumped out of her seat and raced to the bathroom. Shade dashed in after her, fear and worry all over his features. Hushed murmurs rose over the group. Some looked at Trix, and some wandered over to the bathroom and peeked inside.

The sound of her vomiting was glaring in the silence.
Oh, no.

"Are you okay, Silver?" Ada asked from the doorway.

"Fine." Her voice filtered out. "Nausea took me by surprise, that's all."

"Maybe he knocked her up," Jasper mumbled, eyes wide to Ada.

Ada replied, "Somehow, I don't think those two are keen to rush into the family life. No, this is the effect of the taint."

Shade's low murmurs came through, then the sound of running water. A few minutes later, Silver walked out of the bathroom, patting her face with a wet cloth. Shade followed nervously, but Silver looked confident.

"It worked," she said to Ada. "I feel the wrongness inside me. I think I'm processing it, but I'll find out soon enough. Did you do your assessment?"

Ada nodded and grinned. "I did."

Shade's eyes narrowed on Silver. "But it made you sick."

In all the commotion, Trix took a moment to realize Aeron sat watching, his eyes narrowed as he tried to follow the conversation. She translated for him—*It worked. But she's sick.*

His jaw set. He nodded.

Leaf asked, "Is this what always happens when you reverse your gift?"

"No. That's a little different. This is drawing from the Cosmic Well, not a specific small patch of necrosis." She walked over to Trix and braved a smile. "I'm Silver. This is Shade. I lived in Crystal City for a few years working on the docks. Heard a lot about you from Rory. She called you the Tinker, so I didn't know your real name. Nice to meet you."

Ada smiled as she added, "We're all happy to meet you."

"Hi. It's Trix. Beatrix. Wait... Silver, you know Rory?"

Silver nodded. "I was a Reaper. I also worked on the airship prototype."

"Oh wow." Trix tensed. This woman was as deadly as the fae warriors around her. Silver could know every dark secret about Trix's inventions. But she said nothing. Instead, she turned to Thistle and Ada, who'd come closer.

"I feel the inky taint curdling inside me. I honestly don't know if I will have to purge it somewhere, and things will die on contact, or if I can metabolize."

Thistle asked Ada, "What did you find in your assessment?"

"Her bones are shattered in all the wrong places," Ada confirmed. "The infection is too great even for your new Well-connected body to fight. I've started to see this kind of thing in the Summer Court. It can only be linked to the taint. You need surgery, Trix. We must remove the splintered bones. But without X-ray machines, like we used to have, there's no way of finding where the bones are unless I use my mana. Explorative surgery without the right tools could be dangerous." She glanced at Silver, who gave a curt nod. "If Silver can purify the Well while I work with mana, it's the safest bet."

Shade stepped forward, his expression grim. "There's

no telling if what Silver is doing will permanently damage her. You saw how sick she became after one small try. I won't allow it."

"Hey," Silver shot. "I make my own choices."

"Admit it, darling." His voice turned soft when he looked at her. "You know this is true. You cannot take on the taint for two of them."

Silver's shoulders dropped, and her head dipped as she said, "I know."

Only enough for one go. Who else would need healing? Trix's eyes widened as they settled on Aeron. Shade meant it was either get Aeron's hearing back or save Trix's legs.

"No," Trix said flat out. "I choose Aeron."

"I think he would have something different to say," Shade retorted.

"So don't tell him. This is my body, my choice."

Something like respect flickered in Shade's eyes, and it caught her attention. It triggered a warning bell deep inside her. If Shade liked that she wanted to sacrifice herself, then maybe it was because he would do the same for his mate.... then maybe... it would mean Aeron would. Her thoughts distracted her long enough to miss the fact that Forrest had already written down the ultimatum and showed Aeron.

Aeron didn't hesitate after reading it. He gestured at Trix, and then nodded to Ada.

"No." Trix's throat closed up. Her eyes burned. "Not me."

Aeron frowned at her and signed, *Why?*

Her mouth opened. Closed. She couldn't say it while everyone watched. She couldn't tell him she was worse than the scum on his boots to all these people. She was as bad as Kelvhan claimed she was. But here, in this room, there were at least four. *Five Guardians!* When she couldn't answer, Aeron took her hand and squeezed.

"Why?" Trix asked.

I want to take care of you, he signed.

"But I don't deserve this devotion. When you find out —" He captured her hands, stopping her from signing, and shook his head.

I don't care, he mouthed. He'd made his choice. He was choosing her over his hearing.

When he saw the alarm in her eyes, the unfathomable doubt, he lowered his lips to her ears and spoke for her in his private, deep, unused voice. "Losing you will hurt more."

He pressed his lips to the spot beneath her ear, and tears spilled down her eyes. Her throat closed. He said that now... but as soon as he knew the true depths of what she'd done. She tried one last time to write down her confession, but he took the pencil and signed, *Later.*

Trix cursed the day she'd ever taught him that hand sign!

Aeron signaled for Silver and Ada to start work on her legs.

"Don't," she sobbed to him. "Don't put that pressure on me."

"Can we leave the room?" Melody stood up and shooed everyone watching. "Give them a moment."

One by one, each person in the room filed out. The instant they were alone, Trix signed to Aeron. "I'm responsible for the death of many of you."

He shrugged, frowning. Her eyes darted about, lost. Then her gaze landed on a pile of letters on the nightstand. One was from the Spring Court King and Queen. Another was that first one from the Prime he'd received in the infirmary. Trix opened it and showed him the line where the Prime spoke about Guardian deaths.

"That's my fault," Trix said, pointing to herself and then scribbling down,

I created a portal machine fueled on Guardian mana.

TWENTY-SIX

Aeron let Trix's confession settle on him, and many devastating puzzle pieces fell into place. The lifespan for a Guardian was always low, considering the dangerous life they led. But lately, they'd been losing more than usual in mysterious ways. That, coupled with the fact that the Order hadn't figured out how humans were appearing in strange places around Elphyne and raiding for forbidden resources, made no sense.

Now it made sense.

They'd been portaling. And by using Guardian mana approved by the Well to carry metals and plastic, they'd skirted the caveats the Well had set in place.

Horrifying. Overwhelming. Clever.

His gaze snapped to his mate and searched her face for signs that she still felt this portal machine she'd built was the moral thing to do. Fever-bright eyes watered as she looked back at him.

I tried to tell you, she signed. *But the time was never right.*

Just like it had never been right for him to show her the letter he'd written before meeting her. It still sat in a dusty corner of his travel satchel because he'd changed. His motivations had changed.

Trying not to let his heart speak of betrayal, he forced himself to use his head.

Like Melody, like Silver, like many of the women from the old world, Trix had worked for Nero—an evil man. Whether it was out of manipulation, desperation, or a misguided sense of justice, Aeron didn't think Trix truly meant to harm Guardians. Or fae. She'd been horrified when her gift had killed that nymph, even after it had attacked her. It took Aeron a moment to realize Trix was writing a note. She handed it to him with hopeful, glistening eyes.

I blame myself for not paying attention to what I built. They started off by giving me tiny problems to solve. But as my interest grew, I became so focused on this machine that I didn't stop to think about what it was used for or who it harmed in its creation.

And when I found out... I buried my head in the sand and found something else to distract me, so what was out of sight was out of mind.

I'm ashamed and I'm so sorry.

He re-read the letter a few times to ensure he understood. It fit with his understanding of who she was and how her brilliant mind could get lost in the details and not see what else was happening. Someone like Nero would take advantage of that. And someone like Trix wouldn't see how she'd been manipulated.

He scrubbed his face, coming to terms with it, and realizing that no matter what had happened in the past—in either of their histories—he knew what he felt in his soul. She wasn't malicious. She cared for him deeply.

Only a Well-blessed bond would show him that.

So the choice to have her legs healed over his ears was easy.

It wasn't a choice between who was wrong or good. It wasn't a choice between his hearing or her legs. It was life or death.

And every time, he would choose her.

Okay, he signed, nodding to her confession.

What? she signed back.

I understand.

So... you'll have Ada heal your hearing?

No.

Immediate panic gripped Trix again, and it broke his

heart. He tried to hug and console her, but she pushed him away. She flailed against him.

No, she signed, gulping in air. *Not me.*

His chest felt like a band constricted around it. He held her tight and spoke close to her ear, hoping his words came out right but also knowing this was how he had to deliver the message. Only she could make him feel this way. Only she made him want to use his voice, despite knowing it would sound different.

"I want a future with you," he said soundlessly. "I want you more than I want to hear."

She clutched him. Her chest shuddered, and she sobbed beneath him. She still wasn't convinced. So, he said one last thing.

"Before you, I didn't know who I was. With you—" He choked up. He tightened his grip on her as he recalled those boyish fantasies of being a knight and saving a princess. It had never been about the adventure or validation and praise but rather the acceptance, the purpose. Being with someone who wanted him. "With you, I belong."

She stilled beneath him. He eased off and met her waterlogged eyes. Neither of them had been given a choice about this relationship. Like all the Well-blessed mates, it was thrust upon them. There had to be a reason, but even if there wasn't, he was hard-pressed to find anything about her he didn't like.

Belong to me, he signed, begging. *Be with me.*

She sniffed. And then signed back, *Yes*.

A grin split across his face. His heart, already raw, burst with joy. With jubilant energy, he kissed her on the head and raced outside to retrieve the others. He avoided looking at Shade, who was unhappy about his mate putting herself in harm's way, but Aeron trusted Silver knew her limits. She was a brave woman.

And Aeron was desperate.

After everyone filed back in, Thistle gave Trix a sleeping draught, and Aeron sat by her side. He held her hand against his mouth to smell her as she fell asleep. There was something so comforting about her warmth and feminine scent that it soothed him. Without sound, he wasn't focused on the healers bustling about and preparing to cut into her. His world was her scent, softness, and pulse at her wrist. If he was calm, then she would be too.

His brows pinched slightly as he realized how vital touch had become to him since his injury. Touch, taste, sight, and smell. Knowing that he might never get his hearing back, he experienced her more intensely using those other senses. He took more of her in, and he captured every detail.

Then the real work started. Silver sat on the couch with Shade, meditating and focusing on keeping the Well taint-free so Ada and Thistle could work. Ada used her gift to work out where the bone shards resided in Trix's body, and between the two of them, they worked out the pieces from Trix's flesh. The whole process only took fifteen minutes.

And it was just as well. Not long after they'd cleaned up and healed the open wounds, Silver started retching.

Shade called a halt to the process, but within seconds, black ooze bubbled from Silver's mouth, and she doubled over vomiting. Aeron lost sight of her as Ada ran to her side. Moments later, Shade rose with Silver in his arms, and her head lolled against his chest.

She said something and wiped her lips, to which Shade glowered and barked something back. He shot Aeron a dark look loaded with anger, but then his mate stole his attention, and he softened.

Aeron turned to Trix, holding his breath. Even though she slept, she looked better. The color was back in her skin. The sweat was gone. She breathed evenly.

Aeron hand signed his gratitude to Shade, who nodded curtly and then kicked open the window to the terrace. He stepped out into the sunset and said one last thing before snapping his vampiric wings out and launching them into the sky.

Aeron didn't need to hear to know what Shade said.

Never again.

CHAPTER
TWENTY-SEVEN

"She lives," the steward said.

Kelvhan cursed and tossed his stein into the bonfire, setting off an explosion of sparks. He braced himself on the stone mantle and glared at the flames. The nymph attack didn't work. Letting the human's flawed immune system kill her didn't work. The king and queen had invited the couple to participate in the spring festival in a few days. Knowing what he knew about Aeron's ancestry, Kelvhan couldn't let that happen.

Maybe he should suck it up and kill the elf Guardian.

He already had a sneaking suspicion the king recognized his kin.

"There's something else," the steward said, and Kelvhan braced for more bad news, more fuel for the fire, but the steward surprised Kelvhan. "The Guardian forgot to reset his privacy wards when the Seelie High Queen and King visited."

"Meaning?"

"I overheard something interesting."

Kelvhan's elf ears pricked. He turned to face his ally. "If it can help us, spit it out."

"Trix confessed to making a portal device for the humans. It is fueled on Guardian mana."

"How will that help us?"

"I'm sure the humans will be missing their special inventor."

Kelvhan smiled. "Reach out to our contacts in Crystal City. Tell them we're ready to make a trade."

CHAPTER
TWENTY-EIGHT

It had been three days since Trix had her life-changing healing experience. She'd slept for one day and recovered in bed for the next. It turned out advanced healing could make you quite tired. And hungry. She felt like she ate a horse over the period. But by the third —today—she virtually bounced out of bed in the morning. Plants and vines had grown again overnight, but she ripped them out of the way and stumbled out of bed.

Aeron wasn't there, but a note at her bedside said he would return from the library soon. Perfect. She wanted to wash up on her own and make herself presentable. Sitting on the toilet, doing her business, she thought about how her life had changed. And more remarkably, how much better she felt, both emotionally and physically.

She'd made more friends. She'd been welcomed. Silver had made herself sick to help Trix, and while she knew this was all out of friendship for Aeron, she was a part of that circle. The thought of returning to the cold concrete laboratory filled with metal and oil made her shudder.

The contrast between that place and here was so stark that she could clearly see what the fae were fighting to protect—what the Guardians were fighting for. It was admirable that they continued to do so, even when faced with continuous pushback from those that didn't understand.

And while she knew no civilization was perfect, she also understood that her experience with the Autumn Court wasn't something she should base her opinions of Elphyne and fae on. Melody and Forrest had come to help her too. Ada and Jasper—a High Queen and King. Even Leaf, the elf Guardian who'd watched over proceedings like a hawk, had been there to help her. She didn't know half of them, but they knew Aeron.

The only thing about the past few days that confused her was the tension and bitterness she sensed in Aeron when he'd been around his cadre.

Why did they come to help her if he felt that way?

It wasn't until Trix finished on the toilet that it hit her —she could walk. She was *healed*. Days ago, she was on death's door. A week ago, she could not pull her pants up by herself!

This was the big picture she should have been looking at. This magic was a blessing. So much suffering could be eradicated so long as the Well still flowed its magic through the land. She had to help Aeron with his fight to protect this incredible power.

But first, she had a quick bath and then dressed into comfortable flowing pants and a blouse with a strange arrangement of straps across her body. What she wouldn't give for her simple overalls that buttoned up. There was a set in the drawer, but keeping her mind in the big-picture mentality, she knew she had to embrace more of what Elphyne had to offer. From the fashion to the food to the people and customs. The blouse straps took some time to work out. She might have spent a little too long staring at herself in the black looking glass, testing different formations for tying. Then she spent a little too long staring at the mirror itself, marveling at how fae had replaced metal in mirrors by using black glass to create a life-like reflection.

She ran her fingers over the surface. The glass was handblown, so not exactly crisp. There was a slight wobble in her reflection.

She wondered if there were any other substances found in nature she could use to sharpen a reflection in a mirror. Or make the handblown glass more uniform. She'd have to put her thinking cap on and see if she could remember any techniques. In the meantime, she should write it down and start a list of big-picture things she could bring back without affecting the integrity of the Well.

In the end, Trix's stomach growling reminded her she'd

been at the mirror for too long, getting lost in her thoughts as usual.

Quickly finishing her blouse ties, she secured her unruly hair into a knot and then padded out to the main room for food. A platter of fruit sat on the table near the window and couches. She plucked an apple-type thing and bit into it. The fruit tasted different. Tart and sweet. Maybe with a mango vibe.

"Yum," she mumbled.

As she chewed, her eyes roamed over the table and the paperwork Aeron had left behind. He'd been researching something, she realized. It probably brought him to the library while she'd slept all those times. She plucked paper out of a pile and laughed when she saw it was a hand-written note to Aeron. From the bossy tone, she guessed it was from Leaf. He was Aeron's team leader, as she recalled.

Your mate needs training.

My mate is of no concern to the Order.

Trix virtually felt the tension vibrate off the page.

You know that's not the case. Either train here or take her back to the Order and I'll train her myself.

She belongs to me.

I'm not disputing that.

The Prime has requested I stay here until the spring festival. She made no mention of training Trix.

Then teach her to control her gift from here. I don't give a fuck where.

How can I do that when the taint stops us from using mana?

Be inventive.

Trix snorted and flipped the page, intending to read the second half, but a wax seal on an unopened letter was stuck at the bottom. She peeled it off. It was addressed in Aeron's handwriting: *The Tinker.*

That's odd. No one had called her that since Crystal City.

The door opened, startling her. She cast a guilty glance over her shoulder, expecting Aeron.

"I swear, I wasn't snooping."

But it wasn't Aeron. It was the High Lord Kelvhan and his steward. The door swung open, and they stepped in uninvited. Both glanced about the room. Kelvhan's eyes landed on the vines creeping around the bed, narrowed briefly, and settled on Trix.

"I see you're all healed."

Ice ran down her spine. Why were they here?

And they'd let themselves in. Usually, Aeron stabbed his sword through the locking bolt casings, but his note said he'd only be gone for a few minutes. He obviously hadn't expected anyone to waltz in like they owned the place.

Trix squinted. She guessed that as the queen's brother, Kelvhan did own the place.

She straightened her spine and said, "You were not invited inside."

"I won't be long." Kelvhan's brief smile didn't reach his eyes. "I just wanted to ensure you will be fit for guest duties at the festival."

Somehow, Trix didn't believe a word he said. He rubbed his mustache and surveyed her up and down. It made her shudder internally. She was about to demand he leave when a sharp, peppery prick of fury crashed into her from down their bond. Seconds later, Aeron turned up behind Kelvhan in the doorway, and Trix exhaled.

A part of her knew it was unlikely he had come to do her real harm, but another part still remembered how cold those dungeon tiles were. So, when Aeron used his broad shoulders to push past Kelvhan and the steward, then stand in front of her protectively, she reached out and grasped the loose fabric of his shirt at the small of his back.

Although Kelvhan didn't sneer with his face, Trix felt it in every ounce of his stare.

"I guess we will see you in three days, then," Kelvhan said and gestured for the steward to follow him out.

Aeron closed the door after them and picked up his sword from where it sat by the doorframe. He shoved the sharp length through the bolt casings and then signed to her, *What did he want?*

Trix picked up an extra hand sign in his communication and was silently impressed. It meant he had kept studying her notes while she'd been out.

"To make sure I was—"

He put his fingers to his lips. She stopped talking and continued with sign only.

To make sure I was healed so I could attend the festival.

Aeron scowled and rubbed his chin. *I will refresh the wards.*

I don't trust them either, she signed.

He went about the room, waving his hands and making finger actions in strange places. When done, he returned to the workstation he'd set up by the couches and put down the new books he'd collected. He saw the notes there had been moved and signed to her, *You read this?*

She nodded. *Sorry.*

He shrugged and sat down.

Trix bit her lip, not knowing what to do. They hadn't

had a chance to discuss what had happened—the sacrifice he'd made for her. It felt like a big elephant staring at her from the corner of the room. She approached him and stood there momentarily, thinking of something to say. In the end, she pointed at the conversation and signed as she said, "He wasn't in a very good mood."

Aeron's eyes followed her hands and lips, and then he replied, *He's never in a good mood.*

"And the others?"

Aeron's shoulders bunched, and Trix knew she'd hit a nerve. There was no point skirting the subject, so she clarified, "You felt bitter when they were around. Is everything okay?"

He scrubbed his face, and she saw he wrestled with the topic. The same bitterness swirled in his emotions. She sank onto the couch next to him. He sat back, sighed, and then wrote:

They want to replace me. I can't be a Guardian if I can't hear.

"They said that?" she gaped, then quickly signed. His jaw worked, and he shook his head.

I saw a list of replacements.

This bothered him. A lot. It was not only in the emotions she sensed but in his body language. He wouldn't look her in the eyes. He fidgeted with the papers and books. He didn't want to feel this way, but he did.

And if she'd not been in the picture, he'd likely have had the chance to have his hearing fixed.

"I'm sorry," she said. "This is my fault."

No! he signed, suddenly turning his attention to her. *I'll choose you in a heartbeat.*

She guessed that was what he said. He signed himself, then *choose*, and then placed his palm on his heart. Trix got stuck on his signing.

"You've been practicing."

He blushed, nodded, then pointed to her notebooks beneath the ones he'd been reading on Jackson Crimson. Trix shuffled closer to him. She put her fingers on his freshly shaven jaw and turned his face her way. Inches apart, she suddenly felt so full of emotion. So much feeling wanted to burst from her chest.

She placed his hand on her heart so he would feel it thudding for him. He pressed harder, getting as close as he could. His eyes darkened as he stared at his hand on her chest. His long lashes lifted, and their gazes clashed.

How was it possible that one look could turn her into a melting puddle of hormones?

Every ounce of skin on her body tingled and tightened. That smoldering gaze of his followed his hand working itself around her throat. He pressed gently with his thumb into her voice box and cocked his head. A thrill dipped in her stomach, and she moaned loudly. She could only

241

describe the look that came over him as male appreciation
—*want, desire, lust*—and she knew he was remembering
the last time he'd felt her little moans.

His hand eased off her throat, and he signed, *Pain?*

On a scale of one to ten? She made a zero with her forefinger and thumb and smiled.

He swept books and papers from the coffee table,
picked her up by the waist, and deposited her facing him.
She gasped as he opened her thighs and kneeled between
them. His fingers slid up the underside of her blouse. His
thumbs toyed with the bottom of her naked breasts.

"Aeron," she murmured, begged, but he wasn't looking
at her face. He was focused solely on where his hands
roamed beneath her shirt.

He finally dragged his fingers out and swiped them up
and down his cheek. *Kiss?*

CHAPTER
TWENTY-NINE

K*iss?*

Every muscle in Aeron's body pulled taut like a bow string, ready to fire. One word from her, one action, one response, was all he needed. He watched, studied, and felt every tiny change in the atmosphere tell him her answer. It came as a punch of her desire through their bond.

His lips curved. Oh yes, his mate liked the idea of that very much.

Kiss her, but where? On her neck, where he loved to feel her voice. On her breasts, which he'd only just begun to appreciate. Between her legs—no, that was a joy he would savor at the end, right before he sank his aching cock into her.

His eyelids fluttered, and he released a breath at the thought.

Trix bit her lip as she unraveled his hair. With every touch of her fingers, lightning sparked in his body. He could do this forever, this touching in tiny places, this learning of his mate, this submission for her to do the same.

A touching war began between them. He gripped her nape and tasted her there. She hooked her heel onto his back and tugged him closer, but he was already slamming her into him by the small of her back. His erection hit the soft, willing groove between her thighs.

He exhaled.

She gasped.

He pushed her down on the table, hunched over her, and buried his face into her neck.

She pulled his braids. Unraveled more of his hair. He nipped her jaw.

And then it became not a war of wills but of concession, submission. Both parties giving in. Both doing as the other wanted.

Trix started tugging his shirt over his head. He finished pulling it off.

He tried to loosen the ties of her blouse. She yanked on one, and the whole thing unraveled.

She sat forward and chased his lips, hunting for a kiss, but he pushed her back and took his fill.

There would never be another moment like this. The first time was to be treasured. She was pale and pink. Her breasts were two aroused and perfect mounds. Hard nipples jutted out, begging for his tongue. His mouth watered. Goosebumps erupted over her flesh as she saw the admiration come over him. Desperation washed into him from down their bond. He flashed her a knowing grin.

She wanted to take this fast. He wanted slow.

And so they were at war again. A battle he would gladly fight so long as she was the one true victor in the end. Aeron picked her up and carried her to the bed. He dropped her on the soft mattress and enjoyed the bobble of her breasts. He enjoyed her scowl of impatience even more. But when she started pulling off her pants, he remembered what happened the last time he tried to go slow.

Vixen.

She'd impatiently demanded to go fast and pleasured herself. A rumble tore out of him, and he took over. He slid her pants completely off and then stood back, once again needing to soak her up, to remember this moment forever. She held his gaze and spread her thighs, beckoning him forward.

He thought he was a patient male. But—

Aeron dove between her legs, slotted his hands beneath her bottom and tugged her sex to his lips. Her divine taste hit him like an elixir, and he was gone, lost forever as he feasted and probed with his tongue. The heady smell of her drove into his lungs and made a home. He lost all sense of time until he felt her body arch, felt her tense. When he plunged his fingers into her tight, wet sheath, she pulsed and clenched around him, her inner walls milking his fingers most deliciously.

His pants were off in an instant, and then he notched the head of his cock into that blissful spot. He wanted to fuck her and feel her clench around his cock. He wanted to feel it all. He thrust in and held deep, chasing more pulsing of her inner walls, but they had faded. He looked at her face, and she was smiling, biting her lips, eyes closed, writhing and melting languidly.

He found a new treasure to worship—her facial expressions. He dragged out of her and then thrust in small, sharp fluctuations. She rewarded him by turning her lips into a round O-shape as she received the new sensations he gave. When her face smoothed out again, he switched up his style. He rotated his hips, grinding the ridge of his cock into her clit. He wasn't satisfied until he got her O-lips back. And when that, too, eventually smoothed out, he slid out and flicked the tip of his cock over her little sensitive nub.

Eventually, his clever little mate figured out his game.

You're playing with me, she signed, scowling, blushing, panting.

He smirked and signed, *Problem?*

She rolled them until he was on the bottom, and she was on top, straddling him. This time, it was Trix who worshiped him. He laid there, hands on her hips, bracing her while she explored his abdomen, massaging and appreciating his musculature as he flexed his hips and gently slid into her.

He would swing swords all day if it awarded him the look of pure, sensual appreciation in her eyes.

She ground her hips against his, and a frown of concentration graced her face. She swiped her hair from her sweaty forehead, and he paused. Was this position bad for her newly healed legs?

He quickly signed, *Pain?*

Zero.

Go harder. He sat up and embraced her. She rocked, and he thrust. She kissed and moaned, and then his lips were pressed against her throat again, this time biting gently as he tried to hold back his rising climax. He didn't want this to end. But his mate, his little vixen, was having none of it. She palmed his chest and pushed him down to his back. Then she rode his cock hard. One dip of his eyes to where they joined, to see his glistening length slide in and out of her soft, pink center, and he erupted. His vision darkened. His fingers dug into her waist. And then she collapsed on top of him, breathing hard.

Aeron ran his hands down Trix's thighs and squeezed, loving the good solid muscle he found.

Pain? he signed.

She hesitated. He rolled them in a panic, thinking he'd gone and undone all the good healing. But she only smiled at him in a daze, her curling dark hair framing her face. He couldn't believe how lucky he was to have her in his life.

And because of this feeling, because he had never been allowed to have anything of value—ever—he couldn't help worrying something was about to go wrong.

AERON DIDN'T WANT to leave Trix. He wanted to stay in bed all afternoon, but the more he thought about that unsettled feeling, the more he knew something was wrong. A few things played on his mind. The first was the Prime's replacement list. The second was Trix's untrained gift. The third was that his Autumn Court brother had been wearing war armor when Aeron had accidentally communicated with him.

The latter concern had only just occurred to him. He'd been lying there in bed, running his finger down Trix's shoulder, when his mind had traveled back to the times he was never allowed to be happy. To the moments he'd been fed scraps from the table with the dogs. To when they'd force-cut his hair. Further... to when he'd been dumped on the steps of a king who didn't want him but had been powerless to refuse him in public.

Something his mother said must have backed the king into a corner. It didn't make sense. The Autumn Court had the Sacrifice—Forrest—to endear the public to their rule.

Why did the king need to look magnanimous? He was Unseelie. He could have just as quickly killed Aeron and his mother, despite being told he was the father.

He'd accepted Aeron as a bastard and then publicly ridiculed him.

Why was Aeron thinking about this now?

A grating feeling churned in his stomach. He'd left that life behind him decades ago. He'd not spoken to the Autumn Court King in decades. When Forrest told Aeron that his mother had killed him, Aeron barely batted an eyelid. But since Aeron had seen that replacement list, his mind turned back in time.

His fingers thrummed against his stomach as he stared at the ceiling and turned his mind to more concerns on his list. Number four: High Lord Kelvhan sticking his nose where it wasn't wanted. Number five: the taint. Number six: Trix's confession about the device she'd built. While he didn't think it posed a threat—what was in the past had a way of resurfacing—he couldn't help but worry the humans would want her back.

The Void—or President Nero as Melody had called him —coveted Melody's skills as a harbinger songstress. And that was before she'd had use of her Well-blessed gift.

Trix's smiling face appeared above Aeron's.

What are you thinking? she signed and then caressed his ear.

He shuddered as sensation tingled down his body,

coaxing his cock back to life. He was hard again; all she'd needed to do was touch his ears. He captured her hand and kissed it, hoping she'd let go of her question, but his mate was relentless.

He imagined this trait soared her to great heights—once she fixated on something she was interested in, she would keep going.

She raised her brow at him. He didn't know which of his concerns to focus on, so he went with the one he knew.

Unless I fix my hearing, I will no longer be a Guardian, he signed.

She repeated the hand sign for fix, as if she didn't understand it. But when he nodded, she frowned and signed *Heal. Not fix.*

No, he meant fix.

This sent her into a spiral of defiance. She pursed her lips, pushed off his body, and searched for paper and a pencil. He sensed that what she was about to tell him was too long for the basic hand signs he'd learned. Was this what arguing would look like for them in the future? Would he know when a scolding was coming because she searched for paper?

He realized he was smiling because he looked forward to that with her. He could push her buttons and hide all the paper in the house. She'd probably start writing on his body, the walls, or anything to get her point across.

She found paper, came back to the bed, and sat cross-legged. Naked. He knew he should probably be watching her face or how she stuck out her tongue as she concentrated, but that was impossible. He tickled her thigh with his finger.

She swatted him.

He tickled more.

She scratched where he tickled.

He—

"Stop it!" she shouted, or something to that manner. He was getting better at reading lips and picking up on the mood.

His lips curved, but he stopped smiling when she shoved her note before his eyes.

I understand you want to be healed, but you do not need to be fixed. That implies that you are broken, and you're not.

When he didn't reply, she continued to write.

I am an expert in knowing when and how to fix things. I should know.

Aeron's heart thudded in his chest. He lifted his gaze to hers and saw only concern echoing back at him. He nodded, agreeing. He didn't need to be fixed.

She smiled and signed something he'd only ever seen in her books.

I love you.

He could sign it back, but he preferred to show her in a way that meant something more. He pushed her down on the bed, fit the tip of his cock between her thighs, and thrust in as he whispered in a silent voice he saved only for her, "I love you too."

THIRTY

"Dearest Tian wanted me to show you this," Queen Oleana said. She guided Trix and Aeron through a hallway that led to the private royal library. "He regrets being unable to do so himself, but he is so very tired."

She had surprised them with a visit not long after Trix and Aeron put their bed to good use. If she noticed they were a little disheveled upon opening the door, she didn't mention it. It was lucky they'd managed to clothe themselves at all.

Knowing the queen's trouble with her relationship, Trix did her best to contain her every urge to jump Aeron's bones... and from the secret looks filled with longing he cast her way, he felt the same.

King Tian probably had trouble walking down such lengthy halls. Trix's plans to make him a walking aid were even more relevant. He might want something to help him attend the festival. He might even want something he could hide beneath robes, like a walking brace strapped to his legs. It was a pity that there was no robotics to help him move. Before the nuclear fallout, Trix had been looking into studying in the field... she'd been graduated for years, and yet couldn't find a field to focus on.

They passed palace staff putting up decorations for the spring festival. From green garlands across doorways to glass icicles and jewels at windows, the outcome was breathtaking. Trix stopped at an open window to inspect dangling glass on strings. A breeze gently pushed the blue jeweled decorations. When the sun hit just right, reflections cast patterns on the hallway, reminding Trix of being underwater.

She had a flash of the nymphs dragging her under and shuddered. Aeron was by her side instantly, his hand running across her back.

I'm fine, she signed, but signed gratefully. *Bad memory.*

He wasn't convinced she was fine, so she changed the subject and pointed to the decorations. *These are beautiful.*

She admired the craftsmanship. Much thought had gone into the kinds of reflections each piece cast.

Movement outside the window stole Trix's attention. Three dark, angelic crow shifters were perched on a bough and staring intently at Trix. Well, she assumed they were crows from their black feathered wings. She'd never met any in person, but they fascinated her, like everything in

Elphyne. Her fingers itched for one of her notebooks, wanting to sketch them. Their tattered clothes were held together with colored scraps. Trinkets were woven into their hair. Colorful war paint around their eyes accentuated the bright weapons strapped to their belts, thighs, and arms. It was almost a warning sign glaring at anyone who walked past—*see my weapons and know I'll use them.*

They reminded Trix of commune hippies she'd rescued her wayward brother from once. Trevor had told her the party started the usual—singing, dancing, drinking, and smoking weed. They were all happy people, but as soon as Trevor had woken, he found them and his personal belongings gone.

These crow shifters looked like a more dangerous version of that. Like they would steal everything Trix had when her back was turned, they wouldn't pretend it never happened like the ones at the commune. These shifters proudly pinned their treasure to their outfits for all to see.

"*Eulios* save us," Oleana mumbled as she saw what waited outside. "Don't mind them. The crows have started to arrive for the spring festival. It's their favorite time of year. They're not looking at you but at the decorations in your hands."

Trix let go and watched them swing. She wasn't quite following. "They like this festival because of the decorations?"

"Among other things. In particular, they like the coins sacrificed to the holy well right before the Great Elder

Tree's seeding ritual." Oleana pursed her lips. "Every year, we train guards to protect the donations people make, but they get smarter and continue to outwit us."

Trix's hand clapped over her gasp. "They steal your donations?"

She sighed. "We often put more treasure in to appease them and ward them off. But this year, with Maebh's threat to turn up at our borders, we don't have much to spare. The crows don't usually cause harm, so we've learned to tolerate them. I just hope they don't cause too much mischief at the festival."

She glanced at Aeron, whose eyes narrowed. He shifted the reflective glass baubles out of the way and watched the crows intensely. Two seconds later, the shifters cawed and shouted curse words before flapping their wings and taking off.

Trix wanted to laugh. They were exactly how she'd imagined crows to be if they were human. She wondered if pure crows that didn't shift still existed. She also wondered if they held grudges like crows had been known to do. Once all feathered watchers were gone, palace staffers wandered onto the lawn and placed little glass jars at random intervals.

"What are they doing now?" Trix asked.

"Setting about the dew catchers." Oleana traced her finger on the window wistfully. "I remember the first time Tian and I sampled holy dew for the festival."

"Holy dew?"

A CROWN OF CRUEL LIES

"Oh, yes." Oleana smiled. "Dew collected from nights near the festival is said to be rich in mana and straight from the Cosmic Well itself. There are many uses for it, especially after it has been purified. Pain relief, bringing on labor for a struggling mother, ridding one of bad breath. If painted on the face, it makes a female sexually attractive to a potential mate. A male will grow longer whiskers if he paints it on his face. A child might have their ailments cured. Right now, all around Delphinium, fae are putting out their glass canisters."

"Is that how you met the king?" Trix asked, grinning as she felt a meet-cute story coming on. She was a sucker for a good romance. "You used it on yourself? Or he used it? Tell me he did it."

Oleana blushed. She opened her mouth and closed it. "I shouldn't."

"Aw, come on. It's only us." Trix glanced around to make sure all the staff were gone, and they were. "See?"

In the past few days that Trix had known Oleana, she felt they were more than royal and subject. She checked to see if Aeron had followed her hand signs as she spoke, and he also nodded eagerly.

Tell us, he signed, looking at the queen.

God, Trix loved his mind. He was as curious as Trix. He also had a bit of a romantic streak in him. She couldn't wait to start a new life with him.

"Well, all right then," Oleana mumbled. "It was on the eve of the festival, and the king's sister encouraged me to use it. But it wasn't as though I did it to entrap him, I'll have you know."

"I didn't know he has a sister," Trix blurted.

Oleana's smile faded. "He did. Long ago. She died in childbirth."

"I'm so—" Trix rubbed her fist in a circle over her heart.

The queen nodded gratefully and then continued her story. "But this was a little before that. Tian's sister dragged me to the festival as her companion because she had plans to attract a mate. She had a special jar of holy dew gifted by the Prime." She paused, her brow crinkling as she reached deep into her memories. "The dew only works if feelings are already brewing in the other person. So, when she painted it on herself, she didn't expect to attract the attention of the Autumn Court King, who was visiting with some of his court. I also never expected to attract the attention of King Tian."

Trix's brows winged up. The jovial atmosphere that had started the story seemed to fizzle out. Trix tried translating as best as she could for Aeron, but he'd also lost his excitement. He stared hard at the queen and scratched his ear. Her gaze met his for a brief moment before dropping. Trix felt she was missing something here. Something important.

"I blame myself," Oleana said. "The potency of that dew was extreme. I encouraged her to use more on both of us, not knowing how fast it would work. The Autumn

Court was here to join in the celebrations and for a long overdue parlay. We're both the sub-courts of the greater Summer and Winter. So sometimes we act as a go-between for High Royals…"

Her voice trailed off. Purple leaves from the Great Elder Tree floated onto the lawn. The queen's breath hitched. She splayed her hand on the window.

"The tree is dying, along with my mate. They say it is because I have not given him an heir. But we have completed the seeding ritual every festival. We have always done what was asked of us since that first time. This festival may very well be the last we ever hold."

She cleared her throat and straightened herself to a stiff queenly posture.

"We're grateful D'arn Aeron has spent time at the barracks, but we fear it hasn't been enough to prepare for what's coming."

"What's coming?" Trix said, signing.

"We fear once the tree is dead, once Eulios has completely forsaken us, then the protection this valley provides will be gone." She glanced at Aeron, who watched intently with a frown. "I'm afraid that being a Guardian means your presence at the festival is all that will be afforded to us in terms of protection. If Maebh turns up with her regular armies and not her new beast, then it is a political maneuver and as such has nothing to do with the integrity of the Well. We will have no help from the Order."

Aeron signed, *What about the Seelie High King?*

"They were just here helping me heal," Trix added after translating for Aeron.

"Their forces are already occupied with protecting their own territory. I'm afraid, High King Darkfoot's reinforcements will not be of much use as most are occupied with protecting Helianthus. Maebh knows what she's doing. She's pecking the sides of all Seelie flanks. She's ensuring we don't know where she will strike first."

"Aeron and I are willing to help in any way we can. It's the least we can do after the hospitality you've shown us."

Oleana squeezed Trix's hand, pressed her fingers to her lips, and pushed them down and out. "My brother was supposed to help, but... well... he's been rather preoccupied of late. And he grates on my nerves. Let's move on, shall we?"

She gestured for them to continue following her to an enormous double door. "Tian noticed D'arn Aeron was frequenting the public library, and, well, it's been a while since we've trusted someone enough to open these doors. Here you go."

The door swung open to a vast room filled with books from floor to ornately carved and painted ceiling. Trix's jaw dropped as she followed them in. It smelled like ink, cedar oil, and dust. Bright flowers in vases added a pleasant smell. She felt like Belle walking into the Beast's library. Everywhere she looked was books.

Some were ancient—like *from-Trix's-time* ancient. Some were new. Some were carved with glowing elven glyphs that pulsed gently with a blue light. She ran her fingers over the leather-bound spines. As the books went from old to new, she noticed an evolution of linguistics. One end was written in Korean Hangul. As she moved on, reading the spines, she noticed the lines shift into the elven glyphs commonly used today. Perhaps the first elven settlers here had been Korean Americans. She wanted to pull out each edition and study it. To follow that evolution.

She realized she'd gone and invited herself to the books without a second thought about her original purpose. She even sat on a stool with a book in her lap. How did that happen? She must have been moving automatically while her mind was stuck in a book.

Initially, she'd wanted to use this time to work on a walking aid for the king and to pick Oleana's brains about what he needed.

Shaking her head, she closed the book and slid it back onto a shelf before locating the other two.

Queen Oleana showed Aeron a section of shelves, to which he immediately became deeply engrossed.

Oleana turned to Trix with a wink. "Now he's suitably busy, we can talk."

Oh good. Trix could ask about the walking aid.

But Oleana continued, "Let's talk about the festival expectations and more about that oath you made to do anything you could to help."

Oath? As in... binding fae oath?

TRIX

THIRTY-ONE

Apart of Aeron wanted to spy on his mate's conversation with the queen. Another part was glad he couldn't hear it. Much of what he'd tried to follow in the hallway was confusing. He wasn't sure he understood Trix's hand signs correctly and thought, while his comprehension was still growing, he didn't want to get in the way. Not when the wealth of knowledge before him was so enticing.

There were more Jackson Crimson journals here than in the lower library. It struck him as odd that the Prime hadn't confiscated these journals and kept them in the Order's Academy library or her private collection. He plucked out two and thumbed through the pages. This one was dated close to the elf's untimely death, and Aeron couldn't help himself reading.

Spring Equinox, Year Fourteen-Ten ANF.

Aeron had no idea what that dating system meant but kept reading for clues on how to. The handwriting looked messy, unlike the other journal he'd read.

> *Having exhausted options for our search for the artifact, I am now exhausted myself.*
> *I am tired.*
> *So tired.*
> *How many times must I allow my hopes to soar, only for them to be crushed. It has been centuries. Aleksandra says I must not give up. A new Seer has been born who she hopes will restore our guidance after the last one perished. But Maebh is changing. She stopped searching long ago and now has learned to bargain with the Well. To give and to receive. And she is not sharing her secrets. Only that*

Aeron turned the page only to find it missing. It had been torn out. He flicked through more which seemed to be mindful notes about theological reasons the Well enforced a no-lying caveat on fae in exchange for mana access. Something about keeping them honest and stopping them from falling into old, deceitful patterns. But Aeron wanted to know more about the relationship between Maebh, Jackson, and Aleksandra—the Prime.

Aeron had always suspected the Prime was alive at the

same time as Jackson Crimson, but he never knew all three of them had worked together on finding some artifact. The final journal entry was incomplete, and there was no date.

Memories weigh me down.
I have waited for eons. Artifact or not, she is gone.
Even if she returned, she would see my failings and be ashamed.
I am not the man she once knew.
The Well calls to me a second time, teasing me with absolution.

A palace attendant appeared at Aeron's side. He slammed the journal shut, not knowing why, but those last words felt private. The staffer started fitting flowers and other decorations in his hair. He frowned and swatted her away. *What in the Well's name?*

She jumped away like a frightened lamb and looked to the queen for help. Aeron scowled at Trix, who signed back with an apologetic explanation, *It's for the festival.*

She gestured to her own hair, which another attendant currently decorated.

He had to wear flowers in his hair?

His scowl deepened, but both Trix and the queen looked at him hopefully, so he gave a reluctant nod and motioned the staffer back. Fine. For his mate, he would wear flowers in his hair. At least none of the Twelve would be here to see it.

He endured the tugging, plucking, and teasing... wondering why they decorated now instead of tomorrow when the festival was. He tried to continue reading but was hesitant to open the journal again with someone looking over his shoulder. So he searched the shelf closest to him. The title on one of the spines caught his eye: A Family History of the Spring Court.

Earlier, Oleana had said a few curious things. She'd said the king and queen didn't let people into this room often, but they trusted Trix and Aeron. Why? Who were they to them?

It led him to another thought that had bothered him— the story of Oleana and the King's sister. The one who'd died in childbirth... right after a visit from the Autumn Court King during a spring festival renowned for its fertility celebrations, and right after applying a hefty dose of holy dew that the Prime gifted. That's what Aeron had thought Trix translated. But he might be wrong. He tapped his thigh as he stared at the spine on the volume, wondering why every cell in his body was urging him to pull it from the shelf. Was it just his curiosity, or was it instinct?

Either way, he lost the battle, and, between tugs on his hair, he reached forward and slid the book out. Inside were many pages of family history detailing Tian's family tree... supposedly dating back centuries to when the Great

Elder Tree was first seeded by Eulios. There were even etchings depicting how he united with a Goddess of the Woods to make it happen. Aeron raised his brows at the graphic detail, but this kind of sexual liberty wasn't unusual with the elves. It certainly wouldn't be hidden for these beings who worshipped new life and spring waters.

Aeron had always known about Tian's familial link to the great mythical Horned God, but seeing it documented here made it even more real. It wasn't a myth. Not if these papers were to be trusted. But as Aeron had learned in his youth, lying for fae could occur in other formats than the spoken word.

A sharp tug at his hair made him huff and glare at the attendant. She hastily signed her apology, then returned to whatever monstrosity she created.

When he looked at the book again, he found he'd accidentally turned to another page. Two painted portraits, one of Tian and one of his sister. They were twins. And while the Tian of today was old and grayed, here he was young and with long dark hair. His sister was the same— an echo of each other. Aeron squinted at the cameo portraits and drew them closer to study better. What he found made his stomach drop out.

The young king and his sister looked familiar. Very familiar. It was like Aeron was looking into a mirror. And the sister had the same birthmark on her shoulder as Aeron had inside his ear—antlers. Their ears were more prominent than the average elf... larger than their horned god ancestor. Like Aeron's ears.

He stood swiftly, knocking the attendant out of the way. She gaped at him, shocked. He removed what she'd been building on his head. It was a floral wreath with antlers. He glowered at the queen, then stalked over and shoved the book in her face. He tapped at the portrait of the king's sister, then pointed in his ear—the same ear King Tian had stretched to peek inside at dinner the other night. The same ear Thistle had looked at. Aeron jabbed his finger at the picture of Tian in his youth—now Aeron saw the similarities in their features. Tian was his uncle. He had to be. But where was his birthmark?

The queen gave him a guilty look. She pointed at her ribs.

So Tian's antler birthmark was hidden by clothes, but he had it, which meant *she knew*. So did Tian. They both knew who Aeron was before he did. No wonder they'd trusted him so willingly. No wonder they'd opened their palace infirmary so swiftly. No wonder Kelvhan had taken a disliking to him. Aeron's presence challenged his sister's claim to the throne after Tian died.

And then there was the fact that any kingdom in Elphyne could be taken by force. It didn't happen often, but when it did, there was always an established pattern of the current monarch failing to protect and lead the people. Often the coup occurred from within the pre-existing familial ranks, just like Jasper had done to his father. This is probably what Kelvhan had been planning for.

Aeron recalled the passage he'd read in Jackson's journal about a new Seer coming to guide them. He'd bet that was Preceptress Dawn. She was on the Council, and she'd been alive for centuries. It's possible Aeron's brain was leaping to conclusions to fit his narrative, but why couldn't he stop thinking about it?

Was it possible they'd been meddling from the start? Moving about Guardians in the Twelve like pawns on a giant chess board. It couldn't be a coincidence that Jasper was now on the Summer Court Throne. Forrest had ties to the Autumn Court throne. He'd not taken it as he probably could have, as the Prime had perhaps wanted him to. But Forrest and Melody had helped his mother kill her tyrant mate—Aeron's biological father.

Aeron's head hurt at all the possibilities.

The list—the Prime's replacement list for Aeron may very well have had nothing to do with his loss of hearing but everything to do with his arrival here and how she'd moved all the pieces around for decades for him to be the next king.

After his injury, a small part of him had always wondered why they'd tolerated him staying at the Order when he contributed nothing.

He desperately wanted to get his hands on the so-called prophecy that had led them to the Chosen One. The one who would lead them to everlasting peace. The Prime had said it was Clarke—that she would lead them to all the Well-blessed humans waking from the old world. But perhaps this prophecy held more information in it. Maybe it led to all the meddling done in the past and all that would be done in the future. There were still four Guardians in the Twelve yet to be mated, after all.

Four chess pieces were yet to be moved to their final resting place.

Aeron knew Rush had felt worse when he realized his life had been toyed with to get Clarke on their side. He'd been manipulated into having a child when there had been a law against it. He'd been separated from his son for decades and cursed to be lonely, untouchable.

Was it entirely obscene to think the Prime had done the same to Aeron? That she'd found a way to separate him from his birth mother—perhaps taken him from a court where he'd have been a target from birth and put in another where he might have been treated poorly, but as an anonymous bastard, he had been alive with his identity hidden. He had been on a path to becoming one of the Twelve. One of the few who would mate with a Well-blessed human, tipping the power scale in the fae's favor in this endless war against humanity.

So who was the female who'd brought him to the Autumn Court King's footsteps? Who sacrificed her life for the Prime's plan? Because it wasn't his birth mother. She'd died in childbirth. He supposed it didn't matter whoever she was. She was dead.

These lies were cruel. Aeron wanted no more part in them. He signed to Trix that they were leaving. The queen tried to stop him, but he held her back and mouthed as he signed, *You lied.*

She shook her head. Tears had formed in her eyes. Why did she care? Why would she want him—a bastard son, possibly one of rape—on the throne instead of her brother?

He repeated his accusation, this time adding, *Withholding the truth is another form of lying.*

A helpless look came about her as Trix translated. Her glistening gaze darted about the room, searching for a solution when there was none. For all Aeron knew, this could all still be a lie—fake books. A fake portrait. Fake everything.

He knew one way to prove whether he had a blood tie to the king.

Bring me water, he signed to Trix. *Please.*

She translated for him, and the queen's brow raised cautiously.

"Why?" the queen asked.

Aeron read her lips and intention through body language. He was already signing to Trix before she translated the queen's question.

I will attempt a blood connection. If I am related to the king, I will connect with him.

She shook her head and spoke. Frustrated, Aeron looked to his mate, who signed the queen's words for him.

He has no mana. He is mortal. Kelvhan poisoned him. Kelvhan wants the throne for himself.

More untruths. Aeron shook his head. Who in their right mind would allow treason of that level, even from a blood relative, to stand? Who would let this person be head of her royal guard? When he signed his rebuttal and Trix translated the queen's answer, he felt a pang of pity for her.

"We have no proof," the queen had said.

THIRTY-TWO

When Trix followed Aeron into their room, he signed *I'm sorry* after closing the door.

"What? Why?" she asked and signed.

But he didn't answer. His eyes were locked onto the bed. Trix swiveled to see why and found the two ceremonial headdresses. Made from flowers, leaves, and antlers, they were beautiful.

Aeron's nostrils flared with his anger. He took a menacing step toward the bed, but she stopped him by the hand.

"Don't," she said.

Why?

"Let's talk about it before you do something you'll regret."

He exhaled slowly and scrubbed his face. He looked

tired. Deflated. Lost. She hated seeing him like this. She took his hand and guided him to the couch by the window.

"Tell me about it," she said, signing.

Aeron explained to her, both by note and in sign, how he felt the Twelve had been manipulated since they were born. How he felt like his destiny wasn't his own. How they were all being moved about in a grand master plan to fulfill a prophecy he'd not seen. How they hoped to thwart the Void's—President Nero's—plans to destroy everything the fae had built.

When he was done, Trix sat back on the couch and rested her head on her fist. She glanced over at the head-dresses and sighed. Oleana had said Kelvhan had poisoned the king, but she couldn't prove it. Kelvhan had denied all involvement, and since fae couldn't lie, his words had to be taken as gospel. Oleana wanted Aeron to be king because he would be better than her brother.

Trix didn't think the Prime meddling would have changed the circumstances here at the court. Even if the king's sister lived, Tian and Oleana would still be in danger from Kelvhan's machinations.

She conveyed this to Aeron, and he nodded. He sank onto the couch and stared at the ceiling.

"You know what I do when I'm stuck?" she said, signing.

He shook his head.

"I find something to fix. Or pull apart. But I do some-thing." She searched and picked up some of the vines she'd

274

accidentally grown on the bed. "I want to grow the pieces I need for a walking aid for the king."

Aeron shook his head. *Too dangerous. Taint.*

"Then show me where to find supplies."

His gaze flicked to hers. Held. Then he signed, *I know somewhere.*

Grinning, Trix jumped to her feet and held out her hand. He put his in hers, and she thought he'd use her to lever himself up, but he tugged her onto his lap. She landed with a thump, and he tucked her in close. Then he threaded his fingers into her hair and kissed her softly on the lips before resting his forehead on hers.

No words were needed.

They felt each other's love down their bond.

AN HOUR LATER, Aeron took Trix down to the soldier's barracks. He'd visited a few times while she was ill but had only taken advantage of the training field and weapons. The armory and blacksmiths were full of tools and supplies she could use to craft her walking aid. The blacksmiths had no metal, but all manner of other resources fae used to replace it. She was unsettled to see some of it was bone, but there was plenty of wood and sandpaper.

It was also empty.

Dust collected on items. The fireplace was cold. The workbench was bare.

"Where is everyone?" Trix asked, signing.

Aeron shrugged. *It's been like this every time I've visited.*

"Do you think it's because of..." *Kelvhan?*

His jaw clenched, and he nodded. His disapproval washed into Trix. She supposed he saw, as she did, that the lack of defenses and running of the place was even more glaringly obvious. When Kelvhan finally staged his coup, he would use this lack of organization and activity for his gain.

I'm going to find the blacksmith. Determination steeled Aeron's eyes, and he strode out with a clear goal in mind.

"Oh well," Trix mumbled to herself. "I guess I'll get to work."

Aeron returned an hour later with sweat tracks down the dust on his flushed face. His linen shirt clung to his sweaty chest. His long hair was tied at his nape, so his elf ears stuck out.

"You've been working out?" she asked, signing.

Training, he replied, wiping his forehead with the back of his hand before continuing to sign. *I found lazy guards.*

She grinned. "I'll bet you whipped them into shape."

His copper eyes crinkled. He gave her work a curious look—it was a long stick she'd sanded to use as a walking cane. She also had found slabs of glass she hoped to cut and make a hand-held communication device. Then he signed, *You good for longer?*

She smiled as she looked around the workshop. It felt like home. "I'll be good for hours."

He kissed her briefly and then patted the workbench before jogging out. Trix hadn't seen him so happy. He'd been full of joy when she agreed to let Ada work on her, not him. But this happiness was more of the self-satisfaction kind. Like he felt confident and purposeful. The distraction had done him good. In fact, she quickly tidied up her mess. It wasn't a good clean, but she wanted to follow Aeron and see what he'd been up to. She collected the walking cane and jogged after him.

Aeron wasn't far.

He stood at the center of a dirty courtyard surrounded by racks of rune-enforced wooden weapons. Some looked sharp, but some were blunt. A tall, lithe elf with a practice sword walked up to Aeron from a rack. On Aeron's three o'clock and nine were two more guards. He must be fighting three at once.

This should be interesting.

Trix walked up to the yard and leaned on a rack. Next to her were two sweaty and dirty fae spectating. She guessed they were Aeron's round one from the welts on their faces and arms. The closest guard smiled at Trix and nodded toward Aeron.

"For a deaf elf, he's not half bad."

Her brows raised, silently offended for Aeron. But the guard signed his apology and added, "I meant no offense. He's put us all to shame with his skills."

"He told me he found lazy guards," she joked, teasing them back.

The guard shrugged. "It's been a while since someone has taken an interest in us."

"Two oak coins say he takes them out in under a minute," said the second guard.

"Two coins says he does it in less," returned the first.

"No mana, though."

"Good point." He rubbed his chin. "Those Well-blessed marks won't help him in this bout. No offense, m'lady."

Trix scoffed. She was not a lady—clearly, he could see that from the overalls she wore. But she took it as a sign of respect, for her and for Aeron. It meant even more because the public often didn't treat Guardians well. Maybe it was because Aeron wasn't in his Guardian uniform... or maybe it was because he'd forgone the braids that set him apart as educated and, thus, a status above others. But these fae respected him.

He would need it if he chose to claim his birthright here. Trix didn't care where she stayed. As long as she was with him, and he was happy, she would be too. There was nothing for her back at Crystal City. And to be honest, she wasn't a fan of living at the Order. It sounded like they'd have her doing all sorts of things, and the last thing she wanted to do was to become another person's puppet.

Aeron might have forgiven her for her invention that used Guardian mana, but others might not.

"Three coins say he disarms them in under thirty seconds, yeah?" she announced. She'd seen Aeron in action. He was a no-nonsense sort of warrior. He wouldn't mess about it.

The guard said, "You're on."

"Brilliant." She rubbed her hands together.

Aeron proved her right. The second his opponents advanced, he had their wooden swords twisted or knocked out of their hands, one after the other. It was like he knew exactly where they'd strike or how they'd move. His eyes had darted down to strange places she would never have thought to look first. Like the guard who twitched his left leg, the one who glanced at the other. They all telegraphed their movements in tiny ways and she wondered if, like him sensing the projectiles she'd tossed at him, he was doing something similar.

After Aeron disarmed them, he showed them what they'd done wrong. He only glanced over once for her to translate. The rest he taught by moving, by showing.

When they returned to their rooms that evening to clean up and sit down for a meal, Trix reached across the table and squeezed Aeron's hand. He'd been silent—more so than usual with her—on the walk back.

Trix had half expected Oleana or Kelvhan to approach them at some point during the day, but they'd been left alone. It was probably a good thing.

"What are you thinking?" she asked, signing.

I don't know.

He dug into his stew with a fork and chewed hard,

shaking his head. Probably thinking about what had made him so angry in the first place.

"What are your options?" she asked him.

Take the crown or leave, he signed. *We can go and live elsewhere.*

"Where?"

He shrugged and took another bite.

What do you want to do? he signed.

"I don't want to return to Crystal City," she replied, signing. "Not after what I know. But I'm not as brave as Silver. I can't fight."

His brows joined in the middle. *I would never ask you to.*

"You have the advantage of what none of them have," she said, signing. "We know the lies they told, so they can't be used against you anymore." She lifted the headdress with antlers off the bed and held it before her face, thinking it looked like a pretty crown. "I say... I say claim the lies. Own them."

How? he signed. *They manipulated me—us—with them.*

"Wear them like a crown." She put the headdress on his head. "Show them you know what they've been doing. Take your destiny back. Do it your way."

His eyes sparkled with hope as he looked at her. *You would be my queen?*

"I would be your anything."

Aeron took her hips, brought her close to him, and kissed between her breasts. She put her hands on his shoulders and tickled his hair. He hugged her tighter.

Again, she was left wondering how she got here. How did she get to be so lucky?

Was it really the hand of some mysterious, meddling Prime? Or was it something much larger? She'd always thought the Well was just a power source. It made sense to her science-loving brain. But after being in Elphyne, and learning more of its history, she started to wonder.

"Oh no," she gasped, remembering what she'd been speaking to Oleana about at the library.

Aeron looked up. *What?*

She made an awkward face. "I accidentally made a bargain with the queen."

His eyes narrowed as she signed.

"I said we would do anything to help her. She's asked us to complete the seeding ritual at the festival. She said as the Horned God's heir, you'll bring the tree back to life. Now I realize this ritual will probably be a way to declare you as Tian's heir... and the new Spring Court King."

CHAPTER
THIRTY-THREE

Aeron woke on the day of the festival, knowing tonight Delphinium would learn about this kingdom being his birthright. He wasn't happy that they'd been manipulated to this point—both by the Prime and the royals—but Trix was right. Events had already passed. He knew now. The next time he faced the Prime, he could wear the lies proudly. Being a king came with a certain amount of power.

When Trix had asked him what their options were, he could only find two—accept the crown or leave. He knew there was no real choice to make. He did not run and stick his head in the sand. He wouldn't hide from this. That Trix was willing to do whatever he needed made him love her more.

But before the night's festivities started, he knew he couldn't proceed until he told one person how his future would change tonight. Forrest had been by Aeron's side since the start. He deserved to know. Perhaps even to be here. If he wanted.

Aeron stood at the basin in the bathroom and filled it with water, but before he could make a connection, Trix rushed in, waving a glass rectangle about the size of his palm.

What's that? he signed.

I made it, she signed, grinning proudly.

She tucked the object between her chin and chest so she could continue to speak and sign. He had no idea what her last words were, but they meant something to her, so he watched patiently until she found a way to explain. In between her writing notes and demonstrating, he figured out the glass rectangle was a portable communication object. So instead of waiting to be nearby water for either party, he could contact Forrest anywhere with this device. And if Forrest had one of these on him, he could answer from anywhere.

You're smart, he signed to Trix.

Her cheeks turned rosy. *Just remember that tonight when we have to do the ritual.*

His lashes lowered, and he tugged her close before whispering near her ear, "That's the only part of tonight I'm looking forward to."

She slapped him on the chest and giggled coquettishly. He loved how she reacted to his voice. He knew by now that it sounded different. Toneless. Perhaps not quite annunciating. But she melted. She became a puddle of want and need for him.

He might have forgotten how to use it if it wasn't for her. And as he saw when he first walked into the infirmary with her in his arms, sometimes he'd have to use his voice in an emergency.

So... if he thought about it, talking dirty to her was a safe way for him to practice that skill.

While he entertained all the dark and delicious ways he could make her squirm with his words, she held the small glass device and pulled out a small wooden stopper from the top. She gestured for him to drop his blood into the hole and make the connection.

He hesitated. The last time he'd tried this, the connection went to a family member he wanted nothing to do with. But this time, he had Trix. He had the knowledge of those lies. He was made for greater things than cowering under those Unseelie elves. Aeron nodded, poked his finger with his knife, and then dropped the blood into the device hole. Trix stoppered it again and handed it to Aeron.

He sat on the bed and urged his mana to make the connection. Blue light glittered on the surface of the glass, and then an image slowly came into focus. Trix jumped and clapped her hands, excited. But Aeron would save his joy for later. Right now, he watched the scene play out before him.

He looked at an armored horse spattered with blood and watery mud. While Forrest had an affinity with animals, he usually preferred to travel by kuturi. This wasn't Forrest. This was one of Forrest's siblings... one of Aeron's other half-siblings. A dark shadow passed in the storm clouds above the rider's head.

His gut rolled, and he looked closer—the shadow had tentacles. The demogorgon.

And if the Autumn Court rode with it, they were doing so on Maebh's orders. It mattered not if Forrest's mother owed him. The Autumn Court answered to Maebh, just like the Spring Court would eventually have to do as Jasper bid.

Aeron cut the connection before the rider they spied on looked down and noticed the blue glow beneath him. Alarmed, Aeron met Trix's eyes and signed, *Did you hear anything?*

She signed back, *A screech. Maybe an animal?*

As it turned out, Aeron couldn't stop being a Guardian. He cursed. This was precisely what the Prime had wanted—those in the Twelve had been indoctrinated into the Order's ways. She knew if she manipulated them enough, they would come crawling home when there was danger. The presence of the mana-warped demogorgon meant this was a matter for the Order to get involved.

Fuck.

He had too many friends at the Order. With the taint warping Clarke's and Dawn's psychic visions, they might not see this coming. For all Aeron knew, Maebh used the Autumn Court to attack the Order. Or Helianthus. Or if

Maebh was coming here, then he had to start acting like a king.

Aeron wrote a note for Trix to read out. Then he tried Forrest again. If the connection went to the wrong family member, he'd have to keep trying. It took him three attempts before he connected rightly. Forrest was somewhere dark—perhaps in the stables. He had straw in his auburn hair. He saw the floral, antlered wreath on Aeron's head and did a double take, but Aeron had no time to explain.

Trix read the letter aloud. "The demogorgon is riding with the Autumn Court army. Someone is about to be attacked."

DRESSED in a green robe covering his naked torso and breeches, Aeron held Trix's hand as they walked to meet the king and queen out by the Great Elder Tree's trunk. After discovering the marching army, they alerted the royal couple and helped them prepare as much as possible for an attack. Tian and Oleana insisted they continue with the festival and not alert the public. Aeron would have preferred everything to be canceled, but he could see the benefit in not arousing panic or suspicion. His intel wasn't solid on who Maebh was attacking.

Since the point of the spring festival was to honor the wild Horned God, Aeron's hair was unbraided and out. Trix looked resplendent in her free-flowing curly hair and green, goddess-like robe. The barest hint of a white strap beneath drew Aeron's attention. He couldn't stop looking at the thin strap peeking out from beneath the robe collar at her shoulder.

What was she wearing beneath that?

She refused to let him see her dress. Any time he tried to peek beneath the robe, she'd rapped him over the head with the walking cane she'd made for the king. It made the anticipation of unwrapping her even more enticing. It gave him something to look forward to in all this madness.

Twilight had fallen. Bonfires were lit. Sprites danced with fireflies through the leaves of surrounding trees. Fresh air left a tang of magic on his tongue.

The May Pole had been covered with flowers and ribbon. The maidens were spent, having already danced around for most of the day. The evening was for other, darker shades of celebration.

But before sunset, it was time for the sacrificial ceremony at the holy well—the well being a long, natural pool a few feet from the Great Tree. Bonfires surrounding the pool caused jewels and coins in the water to sparkle like stars.

Aeron frowned and glanced around, letting his eyes take in every person, every movement, every scent. If Maebh were to attack, would he see any warning signs? Trix squeezed his hand to nab his attention and then signed, *Relax. Nothing we can do about Maebh now.*

He smiled tightly and nodded. She was right. Unless he wanted to join the Spring Court scouts that had left to search their lands for signs of Maebh's army, he had to sit back and wait. He had to remind himself that these weren't his people yet. Nothing had been proven. It could all be some wild manipulation or lie. Another thought occurred to him—the taint could have shown him a mirage or a false image. It had never happened before, but it was entirely possible. And Aeron couldn't risk connecting again with his brother through the water. The blue light would give away that he watched, and so long as that connection remained open, an attack could be sent through the water via transference runes.

King Mithras had once sent a ponaturi through a connection to Jasper. The poisonous creature would have ended Jasper's life if it wasn't for Ada's burgeoning healing powers saving him.

Aeron's Autumn Court family were ruthless *floaters*. They wouldn't hesitate to do something worse. He wouldn't risk Trix to the same fate.

Movement up high drew Aeron's gaze. Crow shifters had perched in the boughs of the Great Elder Tree. Their dark-winged silhouettes were everywhere. Waiting. Watching. Not creepy at all.

Crows were an ambiguous, strange sort. Nobody knew whether they were Seelie or Unseelie. One would be forgiven for believing they held no loyalty as they switched sides according to who gave them value, but they were always loyal to their own. Even if they appeared to hate each other, there was an unwritten code of vengeance if one of their own was grievously offended.

Aeron would keep his eyes on them in case they caused a stir.

Earlier today, before he'd prepared for the festival, he'd taken Trix down with him to the barracks, and they prepared the guards for the possibility of attack. Kelvhan was nowhere to be seen, and the king was frail. Queen Oleana had passed on Aeron's warnings to him. The guards were sorely underprepared for any attack.

He'd never met a more ill-equipped army. They were more like a ragtag crew of fae who liked to fight.

Many still believed the Great Elder Tree would afford them protection the way it always had. Aeron wasn't convinced the fact this city had gone uncontested for so many centuries was due to the tree. It was probably blind luck or perhaps the thick, dangerous forest surrounding them.

He had information packets sent to all the appropriate high-ranking soldiers, and he planned to talk more with the king as soon as they met. As one of the Twelve, everyone in Elphyne had to follow his orders so long as he believed the integrity of the Well was threatened.

Sensing his fluctuating turmoil, Trix squeezed Aeron's hand as they walked across the decorated lawns. Every time she did that, he felt grounded. He wondered if she knew the effect she had on him. She must. His emotions would settle. The thought made one side of his lips curve, and briefly, he forgot about searching the crowd for anything suspicious.

It didn't last long. His gaze darted back to all the people watching them walk. Some curious. Some grinning. Some, not so much.

Many fae had floral headdresses, like them, but none had antlers unless they were stag shifters themselves. So when Trix and Aeron passed, they were noticed.

A human and a Guardian, each wearing a ceremonial headdress. *Of all the nerve.*

Aeron smirked at imagined retorts they would be thinking. He was used to it, and since his accident, he had to admit that not hearing the muttered taunts made it easier for him to ignore. But perhaps Aeron should have prepared his mate for the animosity. Her defiance and outrage prickled at him down their bond. It grew as they walked toward the holy well until a few feet out, a fully bloomed head of a peony smacked him in the face.

He stopped. Blinked.

Did that happen?

Aeron had always prided himself on being a tolerant fae, but at that moment, facing humiliation in front of his mate was a rage-inducing experience. He clenched his fists and angled his head in the direction the peony had come from. Did malicious intent cause the hit or was it something else? He scanned the crowd. In the low twilight, his vision was unreliable. Things weren't as they seemed.

He glanced up at the crows and narrowed his eyes, but he didn't think it was them. He tugged Trix toward the holy well where the king and queen stood on a decorated dais overlooking the water.

Before Aeron could target his rage at someone, the crowd turned their attention to three winged fae descending from the turquoise and orange sky. Aeron knew who they were before their silhouettes came into focus. He recognized the way they moved. Had studied them as opponents in training at the Order.

Cloud, River, and Ash. The three crow shifters in the Cadre of Twelve.

AERON

CHAPTER
THIRTY-FOUR

Trix watched as three dark angels in Guardian leather uniforms descended on the celebration without care for decorum. She was already furious after the reception these fae had given Aeron. As they'd walked from the palace, she heard multiple people spit out vitriol at him. She knew Guardians weren't liked around Elphyne, but when she'd heard someone shout that a deaf elf shouldn't be wearing the headdress, that Eulios was virile, that he was perfect and not lesser, she'd been ready to clock him in the face.

And then Aeron got hit by a peony.

Her only saving grace was that the animosity didn't come from all of them, just a select few. She'd seen smiling faces, shouts of encouragement, and hopeful excitement that they were trying something different this year. The peony might have been a mistake—petals were also being strewn around. Someone might have grabbed an entire flower instead of a fist full of petals.

It was just a shame that she focused on the mean words. They were the hardest to forget.

Now, these other Guardians were taking the spotlight. Aeron took advantage of the distraction and tugged her toward the king and queen. He wasn't concerned with the new arrivals, so she followed his lead. But even as they moved quickly, her eyes kept skating back to the excessively showy newcomers.

People scattered as they landed. They all had dark hair, black feathered wings, and tattoos that glimmered like a colorful oil slick. Metal weapons ranged from swords to daggers to wire with barbs. All had the blue twinkling Guardian teardrop beneath their left eye and an attitude that said they were god's gift to fae. Trix wondered if Forrest had sent backup.

"My, isn't this a bit of excitement for the evening?" Queen Oleana squeezed her mate. "Aren't we lucky to have such attention for this year's festivities?"

The hunched king gave the crow Guardians a wry look but then turned his attention to Aeron and clapped him on the shoulder.

"I am overjoyed to have you here, nephew."

A hushed silence immediately fell on anyone within earshot as the gravity of his words sank in. This was the first time anyone had publicly mentioned Aeron's ties to the crown. Queen Oleana had told them they would make an official announcement before the ceremony, and the headdresses were a fair clue to anyone that something was different this year. Only Eulios's descendants could complete the ritual.

Trix translated the king's words for Aeron in the aftermath of the shock. However, nephew wasn't a word they'd covered, so she'd put family.

"Oh dear," Oleana said quietly to her king. "Darling, you weren't supposed to say anything until later."

"Bah." He waved her down. "I'm too old to wait."

"We're the same age, honey."

The sparkle in his eyes as he looked at his queen made Trix smile.

Shouting in the crowd drew their attention. One of the Guardians had recognized a friend in the visiting crow shifters, and they were having a loud reunion. It broke the tension and allowed Aeron a moment to remind her of the gift she had in her hands.

She startled. Oh, right. She'd completely forgotten she held it.

Trix stepped up to the king and presented the cane.

"Your Highness, I made you something to help with your walking."

His eyes widened. He swished his green and brown embroidered robes out of the way and took it from her hands with a frown.

"It's a stick," he mumbled.

"Yes," she replied. "You put it down like so and use it to

hold your weight as you walk. I've also drawn up blue-prints for more complicated leg braces that we can fit to your legs beneath your robes."

He cocked his head at her. "Are you a builder?"

"Well, I quite fancy myself an engineer. Actually, I'm a bit more than that, I—"

"Who are you, dear?"

Oleana's facial expression dropped. "That's Trix, Tian. She's Aeron's mate."

The king's eyes glazed, and he shook his head. He was about to ask who Aeron was, she was sure, but Oleana took his arm and turned him to the holy well.

"Darling, it's time to begin the ceremony. The sun is going down."

"Yes," he said, and they turned to the crowd. They cheered as he stepped up to the railing at the dais. He raised his hands, smiled, and waved them down.

The crow shifters in the trees shuffled and fidgeted, their eyes on the well.

"It is that time of year," the king announced. "When we sacrifice that which is most precious to us in the hope of new life, rebirth, and growth in return."

The speech sounded rehearsed. He'd probably given it over many years. He spoke more about how the Spring Court people stood out from the rest in Elphyne. How, like the Great Tree, they held firm to their roots and remem-bered where they came from. How they provided shade for each other when it was too hot, shelter when it rained, and food when others were hungry. How they stood proud of their actions. How they'd built a community of integrity and reaped what they sowed.

Trix's gaze wandered over the crowd, and it was clear they adored their king and queen. They smiled and nodded at his sermon. And Trix was sure even some of them looked bashful as she guessed they pondered over the times they'd not been so benevolent—like those who had shouted insults at Aeron as they'd passed.

The king announced it was time to throw sacrifices into the well. To give and to grow. Then he tossed in Trix's cane. She tried not to be offended. Oleana's eyes widened, and she hastily signed her apology to Trix before returning to her mate and helping him back from the railing. He turned back to them, a little dazed. The commotion that erupted behind him didn't help proceedings.

Crow shifters launched off the boughs, their wings flapping madly in the air. Leaves and feathers rained down on them as coins and treasures were dropped into the water. One by one, the fae on the ground also dropped items into the water. It surprised Trix that it wasn't all coins and jewels but strange objects—often wooden carvings.

"He dropped the cane in because he wished for health," a deep male voice said next to Trix. Startling, she twisted to see one of the crow-shifter Guardians. This one had longish black hair tied at his forehead by a leather band.

The blue teardrop beneath his eye twinkled extra brightly in the low light.

"I'm Ash," he said softly, his expression unreadable. "I work with Aeron."

Trix virtually felt the presence vibrate off him. He seemed quiet, but she'd seen a quiet Guardian in action. Aeron was ruthless when it came to fighting.

"Hello," she smiled hesitantly and glanced at her mate, whose eyes narrowed on the crows hovering in the air.

"Tell him to relax," Ash said, nodding to Aeron. "They won't cause trouble tonight."

"Why not?"

His leather jacket creaked as he folded his arms and replied cryptically, "There is enough change on the wind."

Trix tapped Aeron on the shoulder and translated. When she turned back around, Ash was gone.

"Fancy yourself a bit of a Houdini then, do you?" she mumbled.

Once the sacrificial ceremony was over, most of the crows who'd watched from the tree took off into the sky. Their dark silhouettes blended as one black mass against the turquoise and orange backdrop before they grew smaller and disappeared. With their exit, the mood turned a little more comfortable. Someone started playing the flute. Then drums. The bonfires sparked and exploded. When Trix's gaze flew to see the sparks, she caught some people tossing in something that must have been like gunpowder.

The mini explosions drew a hush all around.

Trix's skin prickled, and she shared a glance with Aeron. The fire reflected in his copper eyes gave him an otherworldly look. Maybe it was the antlers on his head casting flickering shadows behind them. Or the robes. But her breath caught at the impact of seeing him like this.

Her heart beat louder in her chest. She placed her palm there to calm herself. It didn't help when Aeron's lips curved as he registered her quickening emotions from looking at him.

It was time for the seeding ritual. It was time for the king to officially announce Aeron's destiny.

With his queen's help, Tian ambled back to the railing overlooking the holy well. He placed his hands on the smooth wooden banister and looked hard at his subjects. A leaf from the Great Elder Tree chose that moment to waft lazily down over the water in front of him. Some of them gasped. Some put their hands to their chest. It was as if a collective sigh of sadness rippled over them all.

"Beloved citizens of Delphinium," the king said. "It is with great sorrow that I announce my time to return to the Cosmic Well draws close."

Murmurs of anguish rose. Trix's gaze snagged on a particular fae stepping forward in the crowd at the front near the water. Kelvhan's eyes were stark in the low light, but he didn't appear volatile. He watched the king's speech with calm, collected eyes.

If there was ever a person who gave her the creeps, it

was this elf with his yellow hair and caterpillar mustache. It was in the way his eyelids weren't always open, as if they weren't strong enough to hold up his disdain for the people he looked down upon.

"You may have noticed," Tian said, "That we have had a Well-blessed Guardian and his mate staying with us these past few weeks."

"Eat shit, Guardian!" someone shouted and tossed another peony.

Aeron snatched it out of the air and dropped it into the water without a hair out of place. Trix didn't want to translate, and he didn't look to her for it, but it didn't stop the simmering annoyance in her gut.

She wasn't the only one.

One of the crow Guardians—she couldn't tell which in the low light—slipped like a shadow through the crowd, and suddenly the fae who'd tossed the peony dropped. One second, Trix saw his startled face above the crowd; the next, he was gone. Two minutes later, the Guardian reappeared at the shore of the holy well, his arms folded and with murder in his eyes. But not a drop of blood on him.

The people next to him stepped awkwardly away, and firelight spilled onto his face, illuminating a cold smile. He was the heavily tattooed Guardian with shaggy black hair. And his dagger was missing from his belt. She knew because she'd marked the dagger upon their descent. His blue eyes flicked to Trix, she jolted, and then hastily averted her gaze back to the king as he continued his speech.

"The Great Eulios has given us hope in our darkest hour," the king said, "by returning a lost son of Delphinium to us. My sister's child, once thought lost, is returned. Where I have failed to seed our sacred tree, he will not."

Hesitant murmurs of approval rose over the crowd like a wave, gathering force the further it went until finally some shouted their excitement.

"We are saved!"

"But he's a Guardian!" a rogue voice called out.

"And he is blessed by the Well," Queen Oleana replied loudly, as her mate was out of breath and leaning heavily on the rail. "As is his mate. What better chance to have our good fortune restored to us than to have someone who is both a descendant of the Horned God and Well-blessed at the same time."

Kelvhan finally stepped forward and projected his voice. "And if he fails? If the tree continues to die, what then?"

"It won't," the king said, glaring at his brother-in-law. "When his seed is spilled, it will prove his bloodline, and you will all see. The Horned God has not forsaken us." He paused, his eyes turning liquid and shifting to his queen. "Only me."

"If he does not, then perhaps it is time to give up worshiping a god who no longer respects us. Perhaps it is time to take our destiny into our own hands." Kelvhan's treasonous proclamation was met with silence. Then he smiled abruptly and faced his peers. "But for tonight, let us forget our sorrows and celebrate."

Young fae dressed like flower girls at a wedding came forward and showered Trix and Aeron with petals. The queen and king clapped their hands and gestured for Trix and Aeron to head toward the Great Elder Tree where a curtain of vines and blossoming jasmine dangled from a doorway. Like the one they entered for the healing waters, Trix assumed this would lead to a chamber for their ritual.

The showering petals thickened the air too much. It became hard to see. They landed on Trix's lashes and cheeks. God, this felt like they were a married couple heading off on a honeymoon. It kind of was. She wasn't sure if she was happy about what had to happen next or weirded out. When Oleana had explained their duties, Trix hadn't really been listening. She hadn't let it sink in.

Aeron grabbed her hand and guided her through the petal cloud. Just before she reached the doorway, another person clutched her free hand and tugged her arm sharply. Trix glanced down, alarmed.

The attendant that had served them when the nymph attacked looked up from beneath the cowl of a hooded robe. With pleading eyes, she whispered loudly, "He's poisoning the tree."

Then she let go of Trix's hand, and the petals swallowed her whole. Aeron glanced over at Trix and signed, *You okay?*

She nodded. Then she smoothed the frown from her face and followed him into the chamber beneath a giant, dying tree.

CHAPTER
THIRTY-FIVE

Like the healing waters chamber, this ceiling was made of enormous roots twined into arches. But there was no water. No open tunnels. Just a small room with an altar covered in flowers and lush greenery at the center. Light glittered from manabeeze floating inside jar lanterns spaced around the floor. Other jars were scattered on a table next to the altar. Trix could only assume they were aids for the ritual. She blushed and turned the way they'd entered but could no longer see anything through the doorway.

The vines and roots had closed up.

They were trapped inside this little cave.

But she wasn't alone.

She turned to Aeron and, keeping her voice to herself for privacy, she signed, *I spoke to the attendant from the attack.*

His eyes narrowed. He repeated the word attendant, and she wrote it down for him in the dirt.

What did she say? he signed.

Kelvhan is poisoning the tree.

Aeron's jaw clenched, and he shook his head in disgust. For a moment, Trix thought Aeron would forget about this ritual and dive back into the fray, find Kelvhan, and break his spine.

This is good news, she signed. *We can find out how he's doing it, stop it, and then save the tree.* She glanced at the altar. *We don't have to do this ritual.*

As usual, Trix wasn't sure how much Aeron understood of her word vomit, but his shoulders deflated, and his bottom lip stuck out briefly in a pout. Then his nose wrinkled, and he signed, *I like kissing you.*

Oh.

So he wanted to do the ritual. She hadn't been sure if he was on board with all it had entailed. That there would be no turning back after this. But... okay. She guessed that was her own insecurities shining through. She could get down with a little ritualistic shagging.

His feet scuffed as he braced himself on the altar. Trix felt more confusing emotions coming from him. Angst. Longing. Disappointment. Duty. It made her heart clench in compassion. Some of those people out there were so rude to him. He would have picked up the vibe even if he couldn't hear them. He had faced bullying his entire life. It started in his youth and then when he was a Guardian.

And—Trix looked at the altar—only now realizing how important this would be to him.

If it succeeded, there would be irrefutable evidence of who he was.

Until now, he had been an isolated elf. His only real family was Forrest, who was now mated and would probably start his own family soon. These people presented a chance for him to claim another side of his lineage. Back when she was about to have surgery, he'd asked Trix to belong to him with such longing in his eyes.

He craved this.

Not so much the ritual—okay, maybe a little bit about the ritual, he did say he was looking forward to it—but also what it represented. Once successfully completed, once he spilled his seed, the tree should come back to life. This power only came from a descendent of Eulios and, coupled with his antler birthmark, would cement him as Delphinium's new leader. Aeron would belong not only to her but to the people. And they would have no recourse to deny him that right. They would belong to him too.

And here was Trix, telling him he might not need to do the ritual.

She tugged on her ear, feeling like a right numpty who'd gone and put her foot in it. She'd jumped straight onto one path without considering the other still viable. Sometimes it hurt to know she'd never be rid of this part of herself. She'd always be jumping in headfirst, crashing like a rhino, and then fluttering about, floundering after realizing she'd fucked up something someone her age shouldn't be doing.

Her resistance to the ritual probably had something to do with the finality of it all. Once they did this, once Aeron was king and she was queen, then there was no turning back. For good.

She took a moment to collect herself and then went to him. She placed her palm on his back and rubbed gently before resting her head against his shoulder.

We can still do it, she signed. *I'll never say no to a good*—she inserted crude gestures as she still hadn't settled on a sign that she liked to represent a shag. It brought the smile she had hoped for to his eyes.

Bargain, he signed, smiling wryly. Meaning he knew they'd have to do it eventually. They were bound too. His disappointment was probably because he'd hoped for more enthusiasm from her. Maybe to prove that she meant it when she'd said she would be his queen. Not because some bargain made her do this. Now she felt even worse.

She replied and signed, "You're right. And if I am to be your queen, I must accept the customs and traditions."

Aeron pushed against the altar and tested how sturdy it was.

"I guess that's where we... um... you know," she mumbled. Then picked up a jar of oil or lubrication. Another jar looked like holy dew. "Wow, they've thought of everything."

Yesterday in the library, Oleana had explained what

was expected of them. Technically, Trix didn't need to get involved. It was Aeron's seed required, not hers. Oleana had made it sound so easy. Get in, get the job done, get out, and the tree should flourish again.

If the seeding ritual worked, flowers bloomed in the branches, and fruit blossomed amongst the leaves. The same fruit could be used in many ways, including healing salve, elixirs, and more.

Oleana had also explained how the Great Elder Tree kept evil spirits at bay. If the palace was attacked now, and the tree wasn't flowering, they would blame their demise on the tree's death. They would blame the current monarch. And they would allow Kelvhan to take the reign.

Okay, she signed, smirking. *Let's do it. But first, we find out how Kelvhan's poisoned the tree and fix it. Do you think I can use my gift?*

She placed a palm on the wall and pushed her mana into it, but as usual, she had little control over it.

Alarm flashed on Aeron's face, and he stopped her. *No.*

Why?

He shook his head again and signed, *Taint.*

Trix put her hands on her hips. Once she started something, it was physically painful to stop. She wasn't going to change her mind on this. Despite her nerves, what point was completing the seeding ritual if Kelvhan had a plan for it to fail? As usual, her conscious brain was half a step behind her actions.

She explained the need to stop the poisoning before they did the ritual and Aeron nodded thoughtfully.

His copper gaze darted about the small chamber as he calculated. Then he placed his palm on the root wall. He motioned for Trix to do the same. Had he changed his mind about the taint? Or maybe this was low risk. She copied him and then closed her eyes as he did. Nothing happened. She opened one eye, confused as to what they were supposed to be doing, and he was still closing his. But he sensed her movement and signed, *Focus. Talk to the tree.*

Okay. She guessed he didn't mean to talk with her voice but with her power. The same one that grew plants. Easier said than done. Using her power at her treehouse had often been a product of instinct or need. The cane she'd made for the king was from a found piece of wood. The only time she'd recently used magic was in her sleep, which had been subconscious.

She closed her eyes and focused inward. She took a deep breath and tried communicating with the tree. She recalled the feelings she had when she'd accessed her raw power. It had been like a building pressure. An overflowing of energy. Then an ebbing once the task was complete.

Her brow puckered as she deepened her thoughts. She'd called on her gift when she'd needed things. She'd been so desperate for a place to live that she'd built a tree-house. Then she'd been so desperate to eat that she conjured berries and nuts. Then the toilet she'd made. That was the best. Oh yeah! She almost jumped and clapped her hands with glee. That task had been something she'd done with purpose.

So she sent herself back to those moments. How did she feel? Calm. At peace. Hyper focusing. Oh yeah. She knew how to do that in spades. So long as she was interested in something, eventually, she would sink into the task. Anything not holding her fancy floated away.

So... let's be one with the tree.

Trix rested her ear and cheek against the wall, then added both palms to really get close to it. *Close your eyes. Listen.*

Slowly, sounds came into focus. Like a washing sound or flowing water. Was this the blood pumping in the veins of the sacred tree? She followed the sound and her awareness dived deeper. Like traveling on a train track, she made turns. Some tracks were faster than others. Icky feelings blocked some turns... she wondered if that was the taint.

She would go back to those spots later to investigate.

She should be writing this all down.

For now, her awareness kept traveling around the tree until finally, she landed in a painful spot and gasped. It hurt. It shouldn't hurt because the roots were feeding from water, but the water tasted like a chemical burn, and she couldn't move her roots out of it.

Trix opened her eyes and signed, *I found it.*

Well done. Aeron grinned and gripped her shoulder. *Where?*

She positively preened under his praise.

Where? he signed again.

She didn't know how to explain it, so she drew a map in the dirt with her finger. The thing with hyper-focusing was that her mind was usually still partly lost in those thoughts. It's why people called her flighty or distracted. She could fall so deep into thoughts about something that she lost track of reality.

So she was back at that painful spot in an instant, and she drew the tracks she'd traveled to get there easily. She placed an X in the painful spot.

Aeron rubbed his jaw, then signed. *We'll have to go through the tree.*

"Through the tree?" she asked, signing.

He nodded and then gestured, punching the wall, or what she guessed was actions for starting a fire? She was confused.

Her brows lifted, and she signed, *Maybe I can ask the tree to open up and let us through.*

He nodded, impressed.

She muttered, "Trust a man to think of destruction first."

What? he signed.

Nothing. She smiled sweetly, kissed him briefly, and then placed her palm back on the tree and reconnected. Well, she thought she had reconnected. But when she tried to will the tree to open up for her, it didn't respond.

"Pretty please let us through?" she begged.

Nothing.

Aeron sensed her frustration and removed her palm from the tree. He threaded his fingers with hers and held her stare before giving their joined hands a pointed look. Then he did it with their other hand.

He dipped his head close to her ears and spoke. "How does it feel to connect?"

She shivered as the rumbling base rattled down her body. How did it feel? Like she was turned on anytime he spoke. That's how it felt. But she didn't think that was what he meant. She reined in her hormones and focused on physical contact.

He swiped his thumb across hers, and she realized it took two to hold hands. One person pushing wasn't the same as two people interacting.

She had to open herself up to the tree. Or to the Well. Or whatever this life force was that pulsed inside her and it. She nodded to Aeron and tried again.

This time, she asked nicely, "Hello, Sacred Tree. We want to help you get better. Please take a look at me. We're made of the same stuff. If we work together, we can open a pathway for us to walk through to the sore spot. We can make the pain stop."

Trix didn't push her gift this time. She didn't make demands. She asked. She opened herself to inspection. And she was rewarded with a shifting in the root wall beneath her hand.

Take us here: she projected the image of the map she'd drawn and kept sending her power forward each time the path grew. A few times, she came to those cold yucky spots, but she avoided them as best she could.

The walls moved, but sometimes it felt like they moved through jelly. When it was done, she opened her eyes and told Aeron, *Some of it felt wrong.*

He searched the dark tunnel ahead of them and then signed back to her, *The taint. We'll be careful.*

He removed their headdresses and collected a jar of manabeeze. Then he took the lead. Trix rushed after him and clutched the robe at his back. She was glad she did because the walls closed behind her when they entered the tunnel.

THIRTY-SIX

Aeron's emotions had been in turmoil since that first peony was thrown at his head. It reminded him too much of the time his half-siblings had thrown shit at his face in the training yard when he'd asked to join in.

They'd given no excuse except that his presence irritated them. Walking in the dark brought the memory to the forefront of his mind.

Aeron wiped the steaming kuturi shit from his face and tried to stop his tears. They didn't deserve to see how they affected him.

"Why did you do that?" he asked, only to be rewarded with a multitude of unwanted answers.

"Bastard."

"You're a waste of air."

"No one wants you here!"

"You can't even be the sacrifice. That spot's already taken."

"You're not worth it."

"No, you're worth something." His eldest brother wiped more shit on Aeron's other cheek. *"Walk through the streets stinking like waste. Show everyone what you're worth."*

Aeron had suffered worse than a flower thrown at him. Maybe the memory had invaded because, this time, the humiliation was when he was with his mate. When he was close to feeling like he belonged. It made him doubt he had the right to be here.

Trix knew something was off with his emotions, but he didn't want to elaborate. So, he focused on following the tunnel beneath the tree. His hand flew behind his body and felt Trix. He needed to know she was safe before holding up the manabee jar for light and forging onward in the dark.

He briefly considered risking a transference spell to bring *Honor* to his hand but dismissed the idea. The taint could bring something else into his palm by mistake. It could cause more problems than it was worth. He would only call *Honor* if desperate.

It didn't take long before Trix tapped him on the shoulder and signed, *Here.*

He nodded and held the manabee jar ahead to light their path. But there was no water. Nothing but a wall of tree roots covered in moss. Trix placed her palm on the surface blocking their way. A few seconds later, it split to make a doorway, and he breathed a sigh of relief.

They'd been fortunate not to encounter problems with the taint. He wasn't sure how long their luck would hold out.

He walked through the doorway and hit a white, sticky wall. He tried to twist out of it, but one side from shoulder to thigh was stuck. What was this?

The sense of danger prickled over his skin.

Trix tried to pry him off, but he snarled for her to escape.

The flexible white wall twanged and vibrated as though someone had plucked it from further in the gloom. Two red lights blinked from the darkness, and suddenly Aeron knew what this was—a spider's web.

They'd found themselves in the lair of a *chigumo*. A predatory, mana-warped arachnid monster. It grew to ten feet high and lured victims with the song of their lute made from bones and spider silk. His heart leaped into his throat, and he barked, *"Run."*

Trix wouldn't leave him. She tried to tug him from the web. He shook his head. It was no good. The last time he'd faced one of these creatures, he was with a Guardian hunting party, and they lost one. These were trained professionals.

The chigumo was the cousin to the White Woman— the insectoid creature that lived in swamps and lured males with her siren song only to mate with them and feast on their head.

They were lured by sound.

But not him anymore, he realized with a start. He would be immune to the white woman, the chigumo, or any fae who relied on sound as a lure.

Trix stopped trying to free him. Her head cocked as though listening to something, and alarm prickled through him. The song of the lute. He needed his sword. He needed to be able to use mana without thought of consequences if it went awry. He needed Trix safe.

The directive came above all else. He did the only thing he could think of. He planted his foot at the center of her chest and pushed.

"Out," he shouted.

Trix's gaze locked with his, somewhat dazed. She must be fighting the bone lute's lure, but it wouldn't be for long. He shoved her again. She stumbled back, outraged. She shouted something at him, but he didn't care. He swallowed a lump and bellowed, hoping his words formed true: "You will get killed."

She ignored him and tried to pull him down. This time, he wasn't gentle when he kicked her. She stumbled and then fell back onto her bottom, clear into the tunnel they'd come from. He took advantage of her distance, and thinking only of his love for her, he summoned enough mana and fed it into the ground until the walls crumbled and crashed, blocking her from view.

ALONE WITH THE CHIGUMO, Aeron knew his time was limited. Soon it would figure out that he couldn't hear its siren tune and attack. Impending death drew closer like the beat of war drums in his blood.

Without Trix in immediate danger, his mind cleared enough to devise a plan. He still had a free hand, which was all he needed to carve transference runes into the palm of the stuck hand. He scratched the shapes with the nail of his forefinger, which was a difficult task, seeing as his nail wasn't long. But he drew enough blood, then sent his mana into the runes, and thanked Crimson he didn't have to speak to activate it.

He held his breath, hoping for the best as he felt power work through his hand and connect with his sword in his room at the palace. But it wasn't the sword that came.

It was the cane Trix had made for the king.

What the fuck?

He couldn't use this. Panic clawed at his chest, and he had to force himself to think. It would do no good to lose his cool. He glanced over his shoulder and peered into the darkness beyond the webbing. The red eyes were closer. *Shit.*

Calm down.

Assess the situation

What are the variables and options?

All he had was the jar of manabeeze, which he could break and use the glass to cut, but his light source would be gone. There was only one thing left to do... fire. Even if he risked burning himself, fire it was.

He checked to see if Trix was still behind the crumbled wall. He made sure to sense her existence down their bond —her fury at being left behind was palpable. But she would be safe for this next part. If he survived, hopefully, she forgave him. He gritted his teeth and summoned fire, then he sent it deep into the darkness, aiming straight for those red eyes blinking at him, praying to the Well that it would keep the taint away.

Flames burst from his hand like dragon's breath. In the firelight, he glimpsed the chigumo's true form: a hideous giant spider with multiple eyes and pincers for a mouth. The red eyes he'd seen were only two in hundreds. Its jaw pincers opened as if it screeched. He kept pushing his mana into his fire attack, fueling it to expand. Heat wafted his face. Spider silk around him melted. Aeron broke free. He barely caught the manabee jar before it crashed on the ground. The last thing he needed to contend with was buzzing manabeeze in the open air. Losing his wits now would be deadly. He placed the jar down gently and retreated until his back was against the wall.

He had to think strategically.

Chigumos were traditionally solitary creatures. But if the female had laid eggs... if anything else came for him now, he wouldn't be able to hear it. He waited, watching the creature thrash about in flames. He used the firelight to inspect the surrounding darkness. Just as the thrashing finished, and he sensed the animal dying, the wall moved behind him.

Heart leaping into his throat, he twisted but exhaled when Trix walked through. She must have asked the tree to split the wall for her again. But she wasn't as relieved to see him as he was to her. Face contorted in a fury, she palmed his chest and shoved.

"You left me!" she shouted, signing. "Bastard!"

Aeron didn't hear the last word. He read her lips, only knowing the formation because he'd seen that word spat at him a million times.

Bastard.

Shit landing on his face.

The humiliating walk he had to make through the castle stinking like a horse's stable.

Her word stabbed him in the heart. It sent him straight to the dark pits of despair. But he had no time to wallow. She came at him, punching his chest with her tiny fists— again and again. Tears glistened in her eyes as she gave her fear someplace to go.

Fear.

Trix wasn't the same as the people who'd hurt him during childhood. That word was nothing but an empty sound coming from her lips.

He captured her hands and tugged her close, banding his arms around her like steel. He crushed her to him and stepped away from the cavern, still burning in places and casting flickering shadows about the tunnel. He held her close and slid them to the ground, cradling her in his arms and stroking her hair. She trembled under his touch, so he tried to use every part of him to contain her, to wrap her.

"*Shh.*" For all he knew, the sound was nothing but hissed air, but he tried. He would always try for her. Only for her.

Soon she stopped fighting and started hugging him back. She clutched him fiercely and looked up at him. He brushed away the hair stuck to her tear-stained face. Fear still reflected in her eyes and down their bond. She peered into the chigumo's cavern, and he thought she might have said something but couldn't tell, so put his hand on her jaw. She was speaking but had forgotten to sign. Or maybe she was still angry and didn't want him to hear.

She hugged him and signed, *Are we safe?*

Can you hear? he signed and pointed into the gloom.

Her eyes narrowed, and she stared, cocked her head, then shook it.

I will look, he signed.

She stood with him; this time, he knew if he pushed her away, it would break her. He understood the need to be with someone who made her feel safe. He picked up the jar of manabeeze.

But before they went anywhere, he had to tell her one thing:

Don't call me a bastard. Pain— and then he rated his pain on a score of one to ten.

He had to use a combination of hand signs, spelling

and mouthing, but she got the gist. She felt the tension vibrate through him. Her eyes darted about as she realized what she'd said. How it might have hurt him.

Tears renewed in her eyes, and she signed her apology. She launched into his arms and buried her face in his chest. He felt her lips mumbling against him, felt her repeat her apology gesture, and hugged him again.

She pulled back to speak and sign, her face full of self-loathing and regret. Again, it was a conversation that took much interpretation and a variety of body language, hand signals, and some rudimentary lip reading. But from what he gathered, she said she has a disability like him. Only his stops him from hearing. Hers makes her brain impulsive and distracted. She used to take—elixirs, maybe she said? He wasn't sure—but since waking in this time, there were no elixirs for her brain. So she'd decided to make her difference her power because it also made her good at her work.

Something she said stopped him.

She made her difference her power, just like he'd chosen to focus on how his lack of hearing had helped him with the chigumo.

"Sometimes I hurt people without meaning it," she said, signing. "But I try to learn from my mistakes."

I know, he signed. It was why he loved her.

You belong to me, he reiterated.

She smiled through her tears and hugged him tightly. But despite his words, he still sensed her self-doubt and shame. From experience, he knew these thoughts were hard to change but would make it his life's mission to help her feel wanted just as she did for him. He sighed.

He placed his palm on the back of her head and kissed the top. Then he cupped her head and held her against his beating heart.

Trix untangled herself from him, collected the cane she'd made, and gaped, pointing at it with a shrug.

Don't ask. He rolled his eyes and then gestured for her to stay put.

He walked carefully into the gloom, dodging little fires still burning. It became sticky underfoot. A bitter, acrid smell filled the air and made breathing hard. They would have to get out of here soon. A few steps in, Trix tugged on his robe and signed, *Water ahead.*

Interesting. Aeron rubbed his jaw. He'd thought they'd come across the chigumo by mistake, but perhaps it was a sentinel Kelvhan had placed to guard the poison he'd fed the tree. Or maybe... maybe it was the reason the tree was sick. They could be in the right spot after all.

Taking a risk so that they could see further into the cavern, Aeron decided to release the manabeeze. He motioned for Trix to step behind him and then twisted the lid off the jar. The little balls of energy buzzed out drunkenly and swarmed around in lazy swirls.

Manabeeze are fae life-force, Aeron thought suddenly.

None had been released from the chigumo... meaning it was still alive. Aeron's adrenaline pumped back into his veins, and he crushed Trix to him, then faced the smoldering blob that was the chigumo's carcass. He pointed at it and signed to Trix: *Danger.*

Her jolt of fear bled through their bond, but she nodded and stayed behind him. He needed his sword. Holding his scratched palm before his face, he pressed his thumbs into the runes and made them bleed again. This time, he focused harder on *Honor*, hoping the spell would connect true. He kept his eyes on the smoldering carcass the entire time he waited for the transference spell to work.

Was that a leg moving? Or was it just the firelight flickering?

Seconds later, vibrations in the air signaled something was coming to him. He held his breath, praying to the Well. *Honor*'s hilt hit his palm and his fingers wrapped around it. Relief poured through him when it did.

He launched at the carcass, driving *Honor* straight through the center, cracking the exoskeleton. He twisted the blade to ensure efficacy and was about to pull it toward him to gut the monster.

But bright balls of energy started popping out of it.

He pulled his sword free and jogged backward. He put his hand on Trix's sternum. He pointed at the manabeeze and signed, *Danger.*

They'd never discussed the risk if these balls hit you. He knew she'd built a portal contraption that fed on mana, but her experience with mana was different from the raw material. She'd been frightened when seeing it leaving the nymphs.

She nodded and stayed still.

Together they watched manabeeze rise like floating stars, illuminating the web and roots surrounding them. Enough came out of the chigumo to brighten the entire cavern, allowing them to see into the far corners.

As far as he could see, there were no more creatures. Not even eggs in a sac. It gave more credence to the theory that this chigumo was placed here by Kelvhan. If it was in its natural habitat, there would have been an escape tunnel and silk cocoons stuffed with prey waiting to be eaten. With the manabeeze floating further from the carcass—and them—Acron stepped closer to inspect it.

The chigumos he'd battled in the past hadn't gone down so easily. But upon closer inspection, he could see it was already injured. Its blood had dripped everywhere. Even its bone lute was in poor condition. He pointed at the instrument and explained to Trix by pointing at his ears and signing, *Bad*.

She frowned at it, but seemed to understand. This was why he'd forced her out of the cavern.

Glossy, acrid liquid drained from the monster's guts toward his boots. He lifted his feet, caught a string of viscous fluid, and curled his lip in disgust. The sticky substance underfoot was the chigumo's poisonous blood.

He pointed to the floor and signed to Trix, *Poison*.

Her eyes widened. *The tree?*

He nodded. This was likely how Kelvhan did it. Now all they needed to figure out was a way to purge the poison.

Water and fire wouldn't be good enough and would likely cause more problems to the growth of this tree. While he was thinking, Trix was too.

She signed rapidly to him, her eyes and emotions lighting up. He couldn't follow her meaning. While he figured it out, she went straight to work and put her hands near the ground. It moved beneath their feet.

He startled. A million ways this could go wrong bounced through his mind. He clutched the scruff of her robe to hold her in case the ground dropped out from beneath them. He'd seen worse happen. Peaches, Haze's mate, could move earth and stone. She had caused quakes with gaping holes. She also had a small affinity with plants, so Aeron's mind went straight to this ending in disaster.

But the ground didn't collapse. The soil churned until roots and vines sprouted, slithered over the top, and then dove deep into the dirt again. This continued for a few minutes until the acidic blood—even the carcass—was gone.

She was burying it all... potentially sending the poisonous substance as far as she could from the reach of this Great Elder Tree's roots.

Still... he kept his grip on her robe all the same. A Guardian who assumed was a dead one. She'd just admitted to him that she could be impulsive without thinking things through, so it was better he stayed vigilant for her sake.

When Trix was done, she rose to meet his eyes as she signed, *The tree is happy.*

Her joy washed into him. The very air felt different. Cleaner. No more chemical burn. He breathed freely again. And if this was how good he felt, he imagined the tree would feel better.

Pride bloomed in Trix, and she made an obscene gesture and then spelled Kelvhan's name. He laughed.

Yeah. That's right. Fuck you, Kelvhan. *We fixed it.*

With his eyes crinkling, he tucked his knuckle under his mate's chin and lowered his lips to hers.

Right now, he couldn't care less about the ritual. All he wanted was to love his mate and never miss that opportunity again.

CHAPTER THIRTY-SEVEN

Trix walked with Aeron through the new tunnels beneath the tree she'd created with her gift. It was hard to slow her galloping heart after what they'd seen, but now that she'd connected with the tree, she felt its happiness and joy. It was strange to think trees could have feelings, but she couldn't deny it. It had responded to her request. It had welcomed them here. Even if Aeron had given her the fright of her life by kicking her away and separating them, now that she had a little distance to process, she knew they'd ended up doing something good.

It also felt good to confess her shortcomings to him. Like always, he'd listened intently to her ramblings and then took it all in with patience. How she found such an incredible partner so perfect for her was hard to fathom.

Unless she accepted that maybe the Well did have a plan and she was where she was meant to be.

When Trix felt Aeron's hand at the back of her collar, gripping her and guiding her in another direction, she realized she had been about to take a wrong turn while her mind wandered. She smiled at him and walked with him down the tunnel leading back the way they'd come initially. He smoothed his palm down her back and tucked her beneath his arm.

In his free hand, his sword glowed softly. He'd rubbed dirt on it to clean the creature's acidic blood off. Trix felt better knowing he had a weapon that had nothing to do with magic. She held the cane.

They arrived at the ritual room, still empty and smelling like beautiful blooms, waiting for them as though nothing had happened. Trix placed her palm on the root wall and thanked the tree for taking them to where the monster lived. She could have sworn she felt a responding purr, and then the doorway closed as though it had never been there.

"Wow," she said, turning back to Aeron.

He'd divested his robe and stained boots and had already begun to raid the supplies the attendants left for the ritual. He unscrewed a jar of water and dipped it in a cloth.

Trix's jaw dropped. Beneath his robe, he wore no shirt. Just breeches with buttons on the placket popped open so he could wash.

Tight, cut slabs of muscle flexed as he moved. He had no idea what he was doing to her by washing himself so brazenly. Or maybe he did, and that's why he cleaned parts of himself that didn't need cleaning. Including those illegal muscles over his hips that angled down to his groin. Illegal because they caused distractions. She might never be able to tear her eyes from them.

A rush of warm attraction rippled through her. Attraction and relief because not that long ago, she'd been afraid she'd never see him again. It had almost broken her. When she was separated from him, a monster was born inside her. One that would tear the world down, the tree down, to get to him. One that cared little for her own safety.

If he hadn't killed that beast, she would have, or died trying. The knowledge had settled in her bones. She would have called on those killing vines of hers and would do so again in a heartbeat—no matter what the monster looked like. If it had eight legs or two.

Aeron had astounded her every step of their relationship. The moody and brooding elf she first met was nowhere in sight. He'd reprimanded her for calling him a bastard, and rightly so! She'd never been so ashamed of her stupid, blurty mouth in all her life. And even when she'd confessed her most vulnerable part of herself, he accepted it. He knew it wasn't her trying to give an excuse but asking for understanding. The old Trix would never have felt comfortable telling him. And the old Aeron would probably never have told her how much that word hurt—

even if it should have been obvious. He would have stuffed his irritation down inside and brooded silently.

He knew where his limitations were, and he worked with them. He took on a monstrous spider for her because it made dangerous music. Thinking back on it, she had become mesmerized by the sounds. If he'd spent any longer getting her out, she might have also walked straight into the web.

Aeron tossed his dirty cloth and lifted his gaze to hers from across the room. A spark shocked her from head to toe at the meeting of their eyes. She couldn't breathe. The heat in his stare, the desire punching her down their bond, it was like he wanted to devour her. Like he'd felt the same crushing sense of fear and panic as she had when he thought she was in danger, and he was done waiting for this to happen.

She had no idea how much time had passed or whether the crowds waited outside to greet them after the deed. No sounds were coming from beyond the external door covered in vines. For now, it was just the two of them.

She took a step toward him. Stopped. Swallowed. He took a step closer. Stopped. Swallowed.

Trix tried not to look at his bronze skin, all dewy with water or sweat. Didn't matter. Both were sexy. Her gaze dropped and roamed all over his body with appreciation.

"What now?" she said, signing.

He inhaled suddenly. Then went to the altar and beckoned her over. Heat clenched down low in her belly. Anticipating what came next was like a drug buzzing along her skin. Realizing she still held the cane, she dropped it.

He hadn't touched her yet, and she was ready for him.

Aeron collected her headdress from the altar and placed it on her head with trembling hands. The heat of his stilted breath brushed her face, adding to the flames already fanning her cheeks. He smelled divine—all manly and spicy. The water must have been fragranced. Trix sent a silent prayer to whoever had set up this room.

He bent and cleaned her feet with another wet cloth before standing to meet her.

Upon closer inspection, the altar had garlands of soft flowers, foliage, pillows, and jars of holy dew and fragrant oil. Trix collected Aeron's headdress. She admired the curved antlers and bouquets surrounding them. His long, free-flowing hair fell forward as he dipped his head toward her, a king bowing before a queen.

The gravity of this moment was not lost on her.

It felt right.

She placed his headdress on his head. As her hands lowered, she tucked his hair behind his ears, and a low growl rumbled in his chest.

When their eyes clashed, his were full of darkness that could mean only one thing. The desire simmering between them was ready to burst. But he swallowed. He breathed hard, and he moved painfully slow.

His fingers slipped beneath her robe's collar, and he gently swiped it from her shoulder. Just enough for him to see the thin strap of the lingerie she wore beneath. His breathing quickened, and he lowered his lips to the strap. When his tongue darted out and traced along the line, she reached for him. But he stopped her, shook his head, and put her hands back to her side.

He was taking too long, and she wanted to start, to touch him all over.

Aeron slid the collar of her robe aside on the other shoulder, revealing the strap there too. Then like a waterfall, the robe fell and pooled at her feet. The hitch of Aeron's breath was audible as he took in her revealing negligee.

Her lips curved on one side as she saw the arousal come over him—the heady lowering of his eyelids. The lick of his lips. The subsequent bite of said lips and blush across his bronze cheeks and nose as he no doubt imagined all the hot, lusty things he would do to her.

When Trix had discovered this outfit in the closet, she was hesitant. It was sexy. She'd never worn anything like it in her life. But seeing Aeron an inch from his undoing straightened her spine.

The outfit was nothing but white ribbons running down her body and held together by sheer silk organza. He glimpsed slices of her naked flesh... including the blush of her erect nipples and the dark spot between her legs. Aeron's nostrils flared as his eyes trailed low. He tensed, then circled her waist with strong hands and hoisted her onto the altar, displacing petals and blooms.

Trix gasped as the coolness pressed into her naked bottom.

Sensing her gasp, his palm landed beneath her throat. His thumb pressed the dip of her décolletage. Then he looked at her with begging eyes. She moaned loudly and reveled in the change coming over him. Wicked carnal, dirty thoughts played behind his eyes as he swiped her delicate skin, chasing the vibrations of her voice.

Satisfied with her sounds of pleasure, he placed a palm on each of her knees and widened her legs. Manabee jars on the ground cast light from below, giving his features an altogether ethereal look. Shadows danced about the antlers on his head. Trix would be forgiven for believing he was the horned god himself—virile and magnificent.

He could have her powerless with a single flick of his powerful wrist. He could choke her out in seconds. Something about knowing he was her savior and protector made this all the more enticing. The trust between them was expanding with each intimate moment they shared.

He licked his lips. His eyes dipped between her naked thighs, and then he signed without taking his gaze from that aching place.

Kiss?

He reluctantly dragged his gaze back up to see her answer. Her lips twitched, curving up one side. She pointed to herself and then signed, *Kiss*, but dug her hands into the waistband of his pants. He'd done up the buttons after cleaning himself.

Her fingers brushed the velvety head of his erection, and his hips jerked forward on an involuntary thrust.

A sharp exhale left his lips, and he fell forward, caging her on the altar with his hands, his face inches from hers. She reached into that private space within his pants, digging deeper to access his wondrous length, hard like a rock. Aeron's breathing quickened with each passing second. His gaze heated her face as he watched her intently.

She hit the jackpot, wrapped her fingers around his girth, and pulled him free of his breeches. She faced him, waiting for instructions, blinking coyly, doing nothing but holding him there. Where was that wicked, dirty-mouthed elf she'd experienced before? For a few glorious moments, they existed in this limbo of tension. And then his lashes lowered, he gripped the altar harder and dipped his chin until his lips met her ear. "Spit on your hand."

His syllables and tone were slightly off, but he knew what his voice did to her because his hand was back at her throat, waiting for her moan. She brought her palm to her mouth, licked, and covered her skin with lubrication.

"Stroke," he all but grunted, his breath shuddering out.

She put her lubricated palm on his cock and stroked, loving how it slipped and slid over the hard surface, enjoying the little gasps she elicited from him. He cupped her face and held her ear to his lips, harsher in his force.

"Other hand too. Then touch my balls."

A bolt of heat hit her between the legs, and she

squirmed, trying to ease the need blooming there. But she did as was told because it made her goddamned hot for him. She wet her other palm and let it join the first, this time roaming all over him from the tip of his cock to the balls beneath.

Aeron's hands slid down her back, tugging her closer until her moving hands and his cock were sandwiched between them. So much friction. So much lubrication.

He pumped his hips gently into her. Pushed himself tight against her slick, naked core. The altar was just the right height, so he didn't have to bend or crouch. He went quiet again, and she whimpered in protest, dragging her hands away briefly to sign to him.

Keep talking. I like it.

He threaded his fingers into her hair and clenched possessively until little sparks of sensation prickled her scalp.

"I didn't say you could stop," he growled into her ear.

"Oh, fuck yes," she whispered. "Say more."

His hand found its way to her lips as she spoke, feeling her words.

"Talk dirty to me, Aeron," she mumbled through his fingers. "I need it."

"You like my voice," he grumbled. "It makes you hot."

She whimpered.

"Nod," he demanded.

She nodded. She was so hot for him that sweat coated her skin.

"Keep stroking," he said. "Harder. Tighter. Make your fist like a pussy."

Her fingers squeezed on him, pumping him hard enough to make him grunt.

"Good girl," he said, his praise turning her liquid. "Wet me with your desire. Show me how much you want this."

She widened her legs and slid his length against her slit, wetting him with her juices. The shuddering groan he gave rattled her chest. But she wanted more. She wanted to taste him. Perhaps he sensed her need because he slid her off the altar, so she landed on her feet, then twisted them so his hips rested against the stone.

His eyes blazed with want, but he held back.

"What do you want?" she asked, signing, biting her lip as she took in all his gloriousness.

He was so full of desire that his muscles were pumped and thickly defined. His cock jutted out, jerking at her attention. She lost her breath looking at it and licked her lips.

"You want to taste it." His hesitant voice was almost a whisper.

"I need it," she replied, signing.

His eyes fluttered. He threw his head back, exposing the column of his thick neck. His Adam's apple bobbed as he swallowed. She was pinned to the spot when he brought his gaze back to hers.

"On your knees," he said gruffly, pointing down.

Oh, fuck yes. Her eyes widened as she realized what was

about to happen. Her clit throbbed at the thought, ratcheting her desire to hopeless heights. But as she lowered, she didn't open her mouth and take him in. She waited, demurely looking up at him for more instructions.

"Talk more," she said, signing. "Talk dirty."

"I'm going to fuck your mouth," he said darkly. "Until your lips swell. Until you feel me in the back of your throat, and I feel your moans with my cock."

Yes yes yes. God, she needed this from him. Loved how he was straight to the point. Loved how he'd found a new way to feel her voice. She wanted more. She darted in, hesitated, and glanced up at him.

"Open," he growled, grabbed the antlers on her headdress, and tugged her to him. Her lips parted, and the head of his erection slipped in. He was thick and smooth. As she licked his salty slit, a long, drawn-out groan vibrated out of her.

"You fucking love it," he breathed, gasping through the sensations she gave him. To answer, she moaned again and kept licking, kept sucking, and kept taking him deeper. "I feel it."

She moaned again as she bobbed on him.

"Yes," he hissed. "Take me deeper."

She opened her throat. He thrust in. This time, his hand wrapped around her throat and tightened. "Take me, my queen. Let me fuck your sweet little mouth."

That he'd completely lost all his inhibitions around his voice made Trix squirm with desire. She couldn't sit still as she worked him, as he thrust into her, hitting her deep. Before long, she had to submit to him, could do nothing but let him use her mouth and try to breathe. Then she grabbed his balls and tugged.

"Vixen," he hissed. "You know..." His breath came out in short gasps. "You know how to... make me come."

His hand tightened around her throat as he climaxed with a thrust and spurt into her mouth. But she didn't stop. She kept pumping him, kept squeezing his shaft until his eyes shut hard, and he wrenched away from her, chest heaving, cock still jetting evidence of his orgasm.

His fever-bright eyes darted to her hands, mouth, to the dirt where more had spilled, and the ground beneath the altar. Trix spat out what was in her mouth and added it to what was already in the dirt, then she rubbed it all in, making sure to fulfill the ritual's needs.

Aeron slotted his hands beneath her arms and hauled her up. He placed her on the altar and spread her legs so he could fit between them. Then he cupped her face and devoured her mouth with his, stealing her breath with the full force of his emotions.

They'd done it. They'd fulfilled the ritual and killed the monstrous beast. There was nothing left to do but chill out until the morning, and then hopefully, the Great Elder Tree would blossom with new life and prove Aeron's destiny was here as Delphinium's new king.

He pulled back from her and held her by the shoulders, searching her eyes.

Are you okay? he signed, then pointed to her knees.

She nodded, grinning. "Oh yeah. Fucking best night of my life."

He didn't seem bothered that he couldn't understand her because his eyes softened, and he washed her dirty hand with water from one of the jars. But she sensed his reservations through their connection. A bashful blush stained his cheeks and ears when she asked him about it.

He pointed at himself and then used the "talking" hand sign. Was he still self-conscious of his voice? She thought he was okay after that demonstration. She took his hand and placed it between her legs as she signed, *Your voice did this.*

She would never forget the wonder in his eyes as he felt her soaked center.

This is what it does to me, she signed and then rocked into his fingers.

"My voice makes you wet," he said, and she nodded.

It's not how you sound but that you trust me to speak. Never stop, she signed. *For me. Promise.*

She had to spell out a few words for him, but his lips curved in a slow smile when her meaning took root.

He signed, *I promise.*

Then he plunged his fingers deep into her core, wrenching a gasp from her lips. She clutched his shoulders, panting at the onslaught of sensation threatening to undo her.

He dropped to his knees—in the dirt, with her sitting

on the altar—and he worshipped her with his tongue. But he went too slow, as though he savored a favorite meal. *Too slow*. She needed this now, just like he'd needed her to go faster when she'd sucked him off. It was a compulsion itching beneath her skin. She wondered if this intensity to mate was part of the bargain or a need to complete the ritual, but realized they already had. This was just them—the insatiable hunger they felt for each other.

Trix took him by the antlers and pulled him closer. She clenched her thighs around his head. Her eyelashes fluttered as he picked up the pace, licking, flicking and probing, and plunging. But then, just as she drew closer to the edge, he stopped and stood. He stared at her, all darkly, with his wicked thoughts clashing behind his eyes. She almost cried out in bereavement, but he took himself in hand, fitted the tip to her needy center, and thrust in.

She sucked in a breath and signed, *That was fast.*

He was hard already. He tapped her between the breasts and said, "You."

"Me?"

He crushed her to him as he drove in, thrusting relentlessly. It didn't take long for her to get to that mindless edge his tongue had brought her to. Soon she was panting, sweating, and scraping her nails down his smooth, muscled back. And when he whispered into her ear in that harsh, guttural way of his, "All of you," she came undone.

CHAPTER
THIRTY-EIGHT

Outside the Great Elder Tree, Kelvhan waited with the steward and three of his most loyal guards. The sun was about to rise, which meant the festival was officially over, and the seeding ritual was done. In the past, the tree bloomed anew under the first rays of dawn.

But that wouldn't happen today.

Anticipation buzzed beneath his skin. This was the moment he'd been waiting for. He'd put his plan into place a century ago. It had almost derailed when the Guardian turned up, but it seemed life had worked out in his favor. Kelvhan almost laughed when he'd discovered the king's plan to convince his people that one of Eulios's ancestors still existed.

Even if, against all odds, the tree started to recover

from the poison he fed it, Kelvhan had a backup plan for getting rid of the human. Being the next Spring Court King was inevitable.

CHAPTER
THIRTY-NINE

Aeron wasn't sure what had woken him, but he rose before his mate. The room was still softly glowing from manabeeze in the jar, but Trix was fast asleep on the pillows they'd dragged down from the altar.

Something was wrong.

He felt it in his soul. He shook Trix to rouse her, then quickly put his pants on. He collected *Honor* from where it lay against the altar. Maybe he was overreacting. Maybe there was nothing wrong.

Trix hadn't roused, so he shook her gently again, this time adding a soft kiss to her still-swollen lips. He almost hardened again as he remembered how they'd become that way. She truly had a gift. And the sense of her moans caught between his cock and hand was something he'd never forget. Love for her burst into his chest. He didn't want to wake her. He didn't want this night to end. But it must.

He grazed his knuckles down her cheek.

With her eyes still closed, she smiled wistfully and stretched. His eyes immediately went to the way her breasts popped against the negligee. He groaned and scrubbed his face with a hand. What he wouldn't give to throw away the day and fall back into the soft place between her thighs.

But that tingle on the back of his neck hadn't gone away. He handed over her robe and then urged her to dress fast. Her brows puckered in the middle as she sensed his wariness.

What's wrong? she signed. *Is it the—*she pointed to the altar.

She thought he was concerned about the ritual. He hadn't thought that far. He'd been too wrapped up in experiencing all his mate had to offer last night. Enjoying her body too much, feeling a strange kind of freedom that he could still be himself, unleash the neediest parts of him, and explore new sensations. But he supposed what came after the ritual could be worrisome if the king's plans didn't work.

If he wasn't who they thought he was.

If he was just the useless bastard son of a dead king.

Aeron shook his head. No, that's not why he was feeling this way. He pointed to the doorway with the vines draping over and then signed the only word he knew that fit—*danger*. Trix quickly covered herself with her robe and tied it around the waist. Seriousness stole over her features, and she gave a curt nod—she was ready for whatever they would face.

Dawn light stretched through the gaps in the thick vines and roots. Trix suddenly clutched his arm and pointed outside, then to her ears.

Was someone talking?

Was there a sound?

Anxiousness riding his system spiked with the unknown. He gripped his sword hard, ready for battle, but then Trix relaxed and smiled at him before shouting something at the door. She signed, but he'd not learned that one. As soon as they returned to their rooms, he would study the rest of her notes.

The vines peeled apart and in hobbled King Tian. The look on his face was grim. Where was his queen? Before Aeron could sign for Trix to tell the king about the spider, three horned guards and Kelvhan pushed into the room, violating the space. Kelvhan's lips moved silently, but his body language threw Aeron off. Smug. Vindictive. Satisfied.

Aeron looked to Trix for translation. She signed something about the tree still being dead. Hadn't the ritual worked? Was that why King Tian looked so glum?

Kelvhan lifted his chin haughtily and motioned for everyone to exit the room. As they walked, Tian grabbed Trix with a desperate look. He questioned something and pointed at the altar. With a glance Aeron's way, Trix nodded her head.

Her words made Tian's shoulders slump further.

What was happening? Was Kelvhan kicking them out?

Aeron reached for Trix and tucked her beneath his arm. In his free hand, he gripped *Honor*. They walked out, facing their fate together. Outside, the fresh air hit him, and he breathed in deeply. Dawn painted pink and purple lines across nature. A few stragglers from the festival walked the lawn. A few crow shifters stood at the cold remnants of the sacred bonfires, dipping their fingers in ash and painting their faces. The ash was said to be magical and lucky.

Aeron glanced up, and his heart sank.

The tree still dropped leaves. Still withered.

So, he wasn't Eulios's descendent. He wasn't part of this world. He was foolish to believe he had a higher purpose, that the Prime's meddling in his life had meaning. He would have to return to the Order with nothing to show for his absence. Nothing except the most valuable thing of all. He met Trix's eyes and held her stare. As long as he had her, he was not worried about the future.

It was an odd realization.

How could he feel so calm facing uncertainty? Never in his life had he enjoyed a mystery. He'd hated those parts in his novels and skipped ahead to the battle, needing to see the hero overcome adversity.

Kelvhan said something that made everyone tense and bewildered. Panic scorched down the bond from Trix.

Aeron went on high alert, his gaze darting between each person, wondering where the threat would come from first.

Trix turned to him and signed a few words he couldn't catch, but they really wanted Aeron to understand because the steward handed him a letter. It had the king's unbroken seal on it. When Aeron glanced to the king to confirm, he appeared resigned and nodded his head—yes, whatever was inside the letter came from him. And he didn't look too happy about having to write it.

Aeron cracked the seal and read the letter.

> D'arn Aeron, your mate is accused of murdering two of my subjects. Because she is human and can lie, we cannot trust her word. She must be taken into royal custody until the matter can be appropriately investigated and an appropriate punishment assigned.
> Signed,
> King Tian of the Spring Court.

Aeron scrunched up the letter. This was preposterous. He shook his head and pointed at himself. There was no need for Trix to take the blame. Technically, she did kill one of those nymphs, but they didn't know that. So long as he kept his voice to himself, the Well wouldn't force him to speak the truth.

He pointed at her and shook his head, then nodded as he pointed at himself.

I did it.

He stabbed *Honor* into the ground and held out his hands for arrest. It didn't matter what they did right now. He would contact Forrest, get to his team and the Prime, and have this matter cleared up in no time.

If a Guardian claimed self-defense, there should be no other words about it. They knew that. This was Kelvhan removing Aeron from the equation while he staged his coup. Trix didn't understand what he was doing. Her panic and fear surged. As she prepared to fight, he caught defiance in her eyes.

He signed, *Stop.*

Wide eyes hit him, so he added, *I will speak with Forrest. Nothing to worry about.*

Some of her panic left. She knew he had a plan. She stepped back and nodded.

But the guards didn't just arrest Aeron as he insisted. They took Trix, too.

CHAPTER
FORTY

Alone, Trix paced the small length of her dirty cell in the Spring Court dungeons. She tried not to freak out, to summon her gift and fuck up all these mother fuckers, but Aeron hadn't been worried. She had to trust that.

At least they'd given her fresh clothes to dress in. She had on pants and a blouse but no shoes.

She placed her palms on the mana-fortified wooden bars and glared outside her cell. Aeron was somewhere in this dungeon, in another cell, out of earshot. Not that he could hear her anyway, but the walk to her cell had been down a vast corridor with prisoner hands grabbing her through wooden bars. Admittedly, the conditions were more habitable than the ones at the Autumn Court. At least the dirt here wasn't covered in shit and piss. They must wash them out. That should count for something. But try as she might, she couldn't get the panic out of her head.

What if Aeron couldn't connect to his brother? Did he have the fae cell phone device thingy? And if not, what if there was no water in his cell? What if his call went the wrong way, and he alerted his wanker side of the family tree. What if—

Stop it, she chided herself. *Stop freaking out. It's not helping anyone.*

Pushing off the bars, she took a few slow breaths. Inhaled. Exhaled. Unless she went all Poison Ivy on their asses, she had to remain put and trust in her mate's plan. Aeron always had a cooler head than her.

She suddenly wished for her old Irish worry stone. Her fingers itched to rub it but, instead, focused on something blue—not green. Her Well-blessed marks. She sensed Aeron's emotions which meant he wasn't far. She must have stared at her glowing marks a hundred times to feel closer to him. Still marveled at how the marks had appeared. Still wanted to study them further.

Wherever Aeron was, he was unworried.

That's good.

Occasionally, when she spiraled with anxiety, she felt his calm press into her. It was almost as though he'd placed his palm on her rabbiting heart and washed her with warm water. Her lips curved briefly at the memory of her arrival in this palace, legs broken, lost, and agitated.

She put her hand on her chest to emulate his touch. It made her feel so much better.

She would give anything to be with him right now. Frustrated, she went to the bars and rattled them.

"Oi!" she shouted. "Someone better start talking soon, or I'll..."

She pushed off, brow furrowing. Then started pacing again and shaking her hands to stop herself from fidgeting. Questions upon questions dropped on her head. Each one heavier than the last. Why hadn't Oleana come yet? Why did Tian backtrack on his decision to dismiss them at fault over the nymph attack?

Trix stopped pacing and threw her mind back to that boozy dinner with the royals. She was sure Oleana knew he'd been poisoning the king, so why hadn't they executed him or sent him to this cold, dirty place? Trix's mind whirled. Oleana had said Kelvhan had denied poisoning Tian, and she had to believe him. She couldn't execute him because fae never lied.

Just because Kelvhan didn't do it personally didn't mean he didn't have a hand in doing it. He probably paid someone else, bribed them, or indirectly poisoned the king. Maybe Oleana had a weak spot for her brother, just like Trix had for Trevor.

A part of Trix had always wondered if Trevor had sold his belongings that time in the hippy commune. She'd always wondered if he'd lied to her to get sympathy and enough money for his next fix. But that same part was willing to be stuffed down and ignored. Because she loved him. Because he used to buy her things like worry stones. He was family.

Trix twisted on her feet, winced at the sharp rocks prickling her bare skin, and paced back to the bars.

She'd opened her mouth to shout when two shadows walked down the corridor. The usual groans, moans, and prisoner spits ensued as they passed each cell. Hands reached through bars. Trix's lip curled when she recognized Kelvhan and a guard.

The High Lord had something in his hand. Was that a folded letter? Trix's heart beat erratically with his every step closer. She started to sweat. The inscription was in Aeron's handwriting: *To my mate*. With a shake of her head, she dismissed it as a trick of the light.

But when Kelvhan stopped at her cell with a sparkle in his eye, he lifted his chin and put his hands behind his back, hiding the letter.

"I came to tell you that your escort back to Crystal City will arrive any minute."

"What?" she blurted, her skin going cold.

He seemed to revel in her horror. "Yes, you see, I just needed a good excuse to plan an extradition. Murdering fae is the perfect reason."

"No," she rattled the bars. "You can't send me back there. I refuse."

He continued speaking as he checked his nails. "You killed two innocent fae. There's no denying it."

"They attacked us," she snarled. "It was self-defense. Do fae have a rule against protecting yourself?"

His eyes narrowed. "Nymphs don't attack. They are peaceful. A little frisky but harmless."

"Someone made them *not* peaceful, yeah?" She wanted to punch him through the bars, to call on her vines and stab him through the heart. But it would cause more trouble. It would not be self-defense but murder, and Aeron said he would call Forrest and handle this. She had to be patient. "I want to see my mate. You can't keep us from each other. He's a Guardian!"

Kelvhan chuckled. "He's indisposed."

"What have you done to him?" she gasped, then her brows slammed down, and she pointed right between his eyes. "If you so much as harmed a hair on his head, I swear to god I'll make you pay."

Aeron had been through enough.

But Aeron wasn't worried. She had to remind herself that she'd feel it otherwise. Kelvhan was goading her. Trying to get a rise out of her, but she wouldn't take the bait. She stepped away from the bars and folded her arms.

Kelvhan snarled, and she sensed that she'd won that round. But then he pulled that letter out and unfolded it. He glanced at her to see if she watched and then returned to the letter and cleared his throat.

"Dear mate," he said. "The Well has chosen for us to be mated, but it doesn't mean we have to be together. I have learned of your arranged marriages from Melody and will not force you to be with me. This mating is a burden. I have urgent plans that take priority over this union. We should go our separate ways."

As Kelvhan folded the letter with a smug look, Trix's mind scrambled to catch up and process.

He tossed the letter in her face and spat, "Keep it to remind yourself that your loyalty is misplaced. At least the humans want you back. Your mate doesn't want you. You are a burden."

He strode away with the guard, leaving Trix feeling alone and afraid. She sat heavily on the dirt and clutched the letter to her chest. Aeron would never leave her. This letter was wrong. He would never call their relationship a burden. He loved her... didn't he? Instantly, her mind went to when she'd called him that horrible word and then her confession that she might always have moments her mouth ran faster than her sense.

But no...

She inspected the letter and took note of the crinkled and handled paper. Yes, this was Aeron's handwriting, but hadn't she seen this letter on the coffee table long before the ritual? This was how he'd felt before meeting her. Tugging her hair, she forced her mind to stop zig-zagging and to focus.

She reread it. The paper was definitely crumpled, as though it had been handled many times. As though he'd held it, wondering if he should give it to her and then deciding against it. He'd been so stand-offish when they'd first met.

The burden he'd described might not be her... but how he'd felt about himself then. So this letter was not new like Kelvhan had tried to insinuate. She was sure of it. It was old and written before they'd met. Before they'd fallen in love.

She should crush it up and forget about it. But her cheeks still prickled. Her heart still palpitated. Her lungs still gasped.

Doesn't matter, she kept telling herself. *Doesn't matter.*

A wash of calm hit her squarely in the chest. It was so sudden and foreign that she knew it came from Aeron. With tears burning in her eyes, she placed her palm on her sternum and conjured Aeron's patient, kind face as he smiled down at her. As he tucked her hair behind her ears. As he tugged her back into line when she wasn't paying attention to where her feet went. As he brought her food and nursed her to health. As he brushed away her tears.

When she opened her eyes again, she was good.

Fuck Kelvhan. He was only trying to get her to give up on her mate.

He's indisposed, Kelvhan had said.

Goosebumps of premonition prickled Trix's skin. If Aeron was in trouble, then she needed to help him. It had been hours since they'd been put in this dungeon. The light at the end of the corridor had darkened long ago, meaning it was well and truly night. Trix couldn't wait another second. She had to see him.

Sitting on the floor, Trix turned over ideas on how to break free from the cell and get to Aeron before President Nero, or worse, Rory and her team of Reapers turned up to drag Trix back. They'd force her to make more gadgets that relied on the death of fae as fuel. Now that her eyes were wide open, she would never create something without knowing its possible uses. She would draw the big picture even if it hurt. Her fingers clawed the ground as her anger deepened, turning the dirt.

The churned dirt reminded her how she'd drained the toxins beneath the Great Elder Tree. Perhaps she could take herself underground. Or maybe she would suffocate. But she had to try something.

CHAPTER

FORTY-ONE

The problem with plans was that they often went awry. For Aeron to escape his dungeon, he needed the use of his hands. But Kelvhan had ordered Aeron beaten until his ribs cracked and tossed him into a cell with his wrists bound behind his back.

He could thank the Well for small mercies—he'd managed to keep his emotions in check throughout his ordeal so his mate wouldn't be concerned. Her increasing panic had fed through their bond to him. He'd tried his best to push calm back to her, and for a few times, he thought it had worked, but she kept triggering anxiousness.

The need to be with her drove him to insanity. He just needed his hands free, then he could find some water, contact Forrest, and the cavalry would arrive. Whether the Prime wanted him for the future of the Twelve didn't matter. He was still a Guardian. For now, he was a part of that jurisdiction.

Forrest wouldn't leave Aeron here to rot.

He wrenched at the bindings on his wrist. They wouldn't budge, so he searched the dark cell under the glow of his Well-blessed marks, looking for anything he could use to cut the restraints. A rock was in the corner. He shuffled across, intending to rub the rope against it, but the ground rumbled beneath him.

He tensed. He focused on the vibrations. Where did it come from? Was it a quake, footsteps, or a battle? The earth turned at his feet. Dirt tumbled. Then a slim, pale hand shot from the ground, reaching for the sky.

What in the Well's name...?

A fist wrapped in vines and roots joined the first, and then a black curly head covered in dirt. *Trix.* His heart leaped into his throat. She'd burrowed beneath the surface like a rabbit, using her vines to dig a path and carry her. He moved back, wincing at the pain in his ribs. Then he wrapped his legs around her underarms, hooked them together, and squeezed his thighs to anchor her out.

She used him to scramble out, covered in dirt and vines but smiling. She launched into his arms and hugged him. His breath hitched at the sudden pain in his ribs, but he refused to tell her to get off. She showered his face with kisses, so much that it brought a chuckle to his chest. And sand. Then she sat back and wiped her face.

What was in her hand?

He nodded to it. Her lips flattened, but she showed it to him with a wry arch of her brow. His heart stopped. It was the letter he'd written before he met her. His eyes lifted to hers, and he shook his head. No. None of that was real. Please see it in his eyes.

Her gaze softened, and she patted his cheek fondly.

"I know," she said, signing. *Kelvhan gave it to me.*

Anger turned his vision red. Kelvhan had been in their rooms, looking through things that didn't concern him. Aeron should have thrown that letter out a long time ago. That Trix's eyes were rimmed with red wasn't lost on him. His anger turned to angst at the thought of her crying over his damned, stupid words.

He exhaled, forcing himself to relax. Trix didn't seem upset now. She'd kissed him. Repetitively. He gave her a tentative smile, but she was already going about the business of cutting the rope from his hands, but the rock wouldn't cut. Thinking of an alternative, she pointed to the transference rune scratch marks on his hand and raised her brows, questioning.

The marks were half healed, but the outline was probably visible. If Trix could scratch them again for him, he could use his mana to call on *Honor*. He nodded. Why didn't he think of that?

Trix attacked his palm with a tiny rock, gouging as gently as possible with haste. Once done, she patted him and signed, *Go.*

Aeron closed his eyes, summoned his mana, and sent it

into the runes. His palm burned as magic gathered. He called on his sword *Honor* and prayed to the Well that the taint wouldn't warp his intentions, but he would keep trying if it did.

Maybe it was his determination not to give up, but *Honor* came as called. Trix jumped out of the way as the long, heavy blade materialized. She tried to take it from his hands to help but dropped it like it was hot coal. Wide eyes met his. Her curse words were so clearly annunciated that he read her lips.

What the fuck?

He grinned wryly. She most likely hadn't experienced touching forbidden substances now that she'd been filled with mana. The sensation of being cut from the Well could be shocking, disorientating, and anguished. But not for a Guardian. He shuffled until he placed his rope along *Honor*'s blade and cut the binding in one swift slice.

Once his hands were free, he went straight for Trix's face, cupped it, and crushed his lips to hers. After a long, hot, hungry kiss, he pulled back and signed, *Need water*.

Thirsty? she signed.

He shook his head. *Forrest*.

She nodded in understanding.

Taking *Honor* in his hand, he clutched his aching ribs and checked up and down the corridor by the dungeon cell. The dark length gave away no secrets. Getting through these bars would cause a stir. He'd prefer not to draw attention until he'd contacted Forrest.

Trix pointed at something in the cell opposite them, across the corridor. He squinted, following her gaze. A bowl of water. Perfect. But how to get it over here? She was already leaping into action, using her gift to conjure a vine, hoping to latch onto it and drag it close.

It wasn't a vine that arrived, but a snake, slithering and hissing. *Well-damned taint.* He grabbed her by the collar and yanked her back. The sooner they fixed it, the better for everyone. He stabbed *Honor*'s point into the snake's head, halting it before it could attack. Trix gaped at him and started apologizing. He clasped her on the shoulder, dipped his chin, and looked into her eyes.

It's okay, he mouthed.

She gave a small smile and signed, *Should I try again?*

He rubbed his jaw and glanced around. There was no other option. The rope he'd cut was frayed and in pieces. It would be of no use. He gave her a nod, readied his sword in case something worse was conjured, and waited.

It took Trix two more goes to get what she wanted. More snakes and then bugs. But he stabbed every one of them before they caused trouble. Once her vine curled around the bowl, she dragged it slowly toward her, careful not to disrupt the water too much.

The instant it arrived outside their cage, Aeron drew blood from his finger and dropped it into the water. *Please go straight to Forrest.* With bated breath, they waited for the blue glow to settle into a reflection.

Forrest.

Aeron exhaled. He nodded for Trix to tell Forrest what had happened. While he waited, his brother's expression turned from happy to see him to a deep, extremely dark scowl. Warmth spread across Aeron's chest. Forrest would come for him, no matter what the Prime ordered. Leaf, too. The uptight team leader didn't precisely have friends, but over the years they'd all worked together, a sense of loyalty had developed between the elves particularly. Now the Well-blessed mates were here, that final barrier between the racial groups within the Twelve was melting.

Even the crows had turned up to the festival. Aeron was sure Forrest had sent them, for however brief they'd attended. He'd not had a proper chance to talk to them before the ritual, but he guessed they were now gone. Otherwise, they'd have noted his absence. And if they were gone, Maebh mustn't be on her way with the Autumn Court army to attack here.

But as the connection cut, Aeron remembered how close Leaf was to the Prime. Fifty years ago, when Rush was manipulated into his curse, and then Jasper was tortured for a decade, Leaf didn't step in to rescue them. No one had asked him if he knew about the Prime's plans.

Perhaps he did.

Perhaps he was as big of a meddler as the Prime. And if he was, if he saw this whole situation as something that had to unfold to fulfill this Well-damned prophecy, then Leaf would go out of his way not to help Aeron. He would stop anyone who tried.

CHAPTER FORTY-TWO

Trix offered to take Aeron down into the dirt to escape the cell, but he preferred not to tempt the taint again. She was lucky she hadn't suffocated and had to admit there were a few touch-and-go moments when she couldn't breathe.

His sword had cut through the wooden bars like they were butter. She'd gaped at its power, and he explained the metal cut the efficacy of the mana used to reinforce the strength of the wood.

That answered her other question—why it had almost hurt her to hold the blade. She'd never experienced such a cold, horrible sense of loss than the moment she'd tried to handle it. Aeron explained it was her being cut from the Well.

The horror of what she'd contributed to at Crystal City dawned on her anew. Shame pushed in at her as they jogged out of the dungeon, but she did her best to push it from her mind and focus on the good. She had Aeron. They were both alive. That was all that mattered.

They could see the light at the tunnel exit. Aeron readied his sword to take on guards when a shaky voice nabbed Trix's attention.

"Trix? Is that you?"

She stopped in her tracks, peering into the last cell they'd passed. It took a moment for her eyes to adjust to the dark, but when they did, alarm hit her.

Queen Oleana was spread eagle, her arms locked in wooden manacles, her dress dirty, her cheeks sunken and sallow. Seeing her stop, Aeron skidded and backtracked. He signed, *No stopping.*

Oleana, she spelled out in sign, then pointed to the cell.

His eyebrows lifted, and, bless his soul, he came back. Trix knew he wouldn't leave a friend in trouble. Oleana's capture must be why Tian had backflipped on his view of the nymph deaths. Kelvhan had done this.

"We'll get you out," Trix whispered. "Don't worry."

Oleana's sobs almost broke Trix's heart. But she didn't let it show on her face—someone needed to remain strong. Aeron had been calm for her. She could do it for Oleana.

Aeron cut through the bars effortlessly. Trix helped him remove the poles as quietly as possible, so the guards weren't alerted. He climbed in over the stubs, scrutinized the manacles, and then did that super brilliant thing he did with Trix but to Oleana. He gripped her shoulders and calmly looked into her eyes.

Oleana's eyes watered, and she said, "Thank you, Aeron and Trix."

A ripple in the atmosphere signaled her debt. Goosebumps erupted over Trix's skin at the unseen energy. Aeron and Trix had earned a future debt paid from the queen.

Aeron signed something for Trix to translate.

"He wants you to look away from the blade," she said to Oleana after reading his gestures.

Oleana nodded, closed her eyes, and Aeron slammed his blade on the manacle. He did the same to the other, and the queen slumped off the wall. He dropped the sword to catch her.

"Are you okay?" Trix asked, getting to her knees to look the elf queen in the eyes. "Can you walk?"

She nodded, sobbing. "I'm so relieved you found me."

"I know." Trix stood and pulled Oleana into a hug. "We've got you now."

"I should have killed my brother decades ago. I should never have believed a single word that came out of his mouth... or... asked better questions earlier... or—"

"Playing the blame game solves nothing," Trix said. "Believe me, I know."

"But I failed."

"There are no failures. Only successes and lessons."

369

After a few moments, Oleana's sobs settled, and she pulled back.

"I was so happy after you both went into the Great Tree to complete the ritual. I felt so sure of our future that I decided to confront Kelvhan once and for all. I wanted him to admit to my face that he'd been poisoning Tian. He manipulated me. He said he would tell me the truth in private. And he did—he admitted to everything. To how he'd ruined our lives. How he'd destroyed the tree with his machinations. And how he planned to take the crown. But while he had me sequestered, he knocked me out. When I woke, I found myself in here. I used all my mana trying to get out, but the taint warped every effort until I ran out."

"You can run out of mana?" Trix asked, signing for Aeron's benefit.

He gave her a look that she could only describe as, *Oh, you sweet, adoring thing, but you don't understand.* The queen also gaped at her.

"What?" Trix said, signing. "It's a valid question."

"Yes, darling. Most fae run out. Even Guardians. Even Kings and Queens."

Aeron gestured at her Well-blessed marks and signed, *You're special.*

"Oh." She still had a lot to learn. Her mind wandered at the excitement of learning something new, but Oleana's voice snapped her back.

"Tian?"

Trix's jaw clenched. "He was there when we were arrested. He didn't stop it."

"Kelvhan must have blackmailed him." She glowered. "But he's alive, and mark my words: My brother will pay for his treason."

"We need to get out of here first." Trix's heart leaped into her throat, and she realized, with all the haste to escape, she'd not told Aeron why they had to leave so fast. She turned to him. "Kelvhan alerted the humans from Crystal City that I'm here. If he invites them into the palace grounds, they won't just take me. They'll raid whatever they can."

She signed as much as she knew for Aeron's benefit. All he needed to know was that humans and danger were coming. She knew he understood from the way a cool, lethal calm stole over him.

Anyone getting in his way would pay.

AERON DISPATCHED the dungeon guards quickly. By the time they'd found their way back to the lawn before Great Elder Tree's trunk, Trix felt like things were finally going their way. They were to meet Forrest out in the open. It was midnight, and the moon shone high.

But Kelvhan and his guards were already there with three Reapers from Crystal City. Each was armed with a rifle and other guns. And where there were three, there would be more waiting somewhere. Probably with snipers and other metal fae-killing weapons hiding in the shadows. Before they were noticed at the edge of the lawn, Aeron blocked Trix from moving forward by a hand to her sternum. She stopped, but Oleana kept going.

"Oleana," Trix hissed, trying to keep her voice low. But the queen had other plans. She'd spotted her mate leaning heavily on the tree trunk, holding his chest, catching his breath.

Trix tried to run after the queen, thinking if she could get to her fast enough, the elf would realize what she was doing and return quietly. But it was too late. Oleana lifted her chin high and shouted at the top of her lungs, "Guards, seize my brother!"

All heads swiveled her way. That movement lured out other dangers lurking in the shadows. Two dark silhouettes crept forward, their guns aimed and pointed at the queen. Spring Court horned guards stepped forward, unsure what to do.

Humans were threatening their queen. But the king and his high lord were working with the humans. Confusion billowed amongst the guards. Their helmeted faces darted between Queen Oleana and Kelvhan. Trix could see them take in her disheveled and dirty state as she drew close.

King Tian's watery eyes flew to his queen. He gasped and reached for her.

"My love." His old voice was weak and shaky. "You're okay."

Trix's throat closed as Oleana ran to him, but the humans saw the sudden movement as an attack. They opened fire. Trix's scream rattled the sky. The queen jerked from hit after hit peppering her torso. Guns and bullets were so foreign here. Oleana hardly knew what had happened until she couldn't take another step and collapsed on the lawn.

Trix's feet were moving before she could stop herself. Aeron tried to hold her back, but she pulled from his grip. All she could think was to get to Oleana and stop the bleeding. King Tian stumbled over and dropped to his knees, his eyes wide, his face pale. His hands trembled as he reached for his mate.

"My love... no no... no my love."

Trix slammed her palms on the blood bubbling out of Oleana's body. But there were too many holes. Too many places.

"No," she whispered.

Oleana's hand lifted to her mate's face. Blood dribbled down her chin as she said, "It's okay, darling. This way, I won't be around so long without you."

Tian squeezed his eyes shut and shook his head. "No. You will not die, my love. Stay with me. For what little time I have left."

"Tian, darling." She patted him weakly on the cheek. Her voice was wet, gurgling. Her eyes drifted unfocused, darted about, and then narrowed on something behind him. "The tree."

He wiped his nose and glanced over his shoulder. Moonbeams peeked through the bare branches of the Great Elder Tree. But there, sprinkled on a few twigs, new buds bloomed.

Tian looked at Aeron with wonder. "It's true. You are my sister's son and the last living descendent of the Horned God himself. You are my heir, D'arn Aeron. The Spring Court will be yours upon my death." His watery eyes dropped to his queen, her eyes now staring lifelessly at nothing. His shoulders deflated and shook silently, but he sucked in a breath, steeled his gaze, and said to Aeron, "Which won't be long. Take care of our people."

Aeron frowned at him, then looked to Trix for translation. With her emotions swirling, she'd forgotten, so she signed Tian's last words as he stood on shaky feet. Trix barely finished her last hand sign when manabeeze started popping from Oleana's body. The ambient glow cast haunting shadows around the lawn, adding to the moonbeams.

Tian walked steadily toward the Reapers who'd murdered his lifelong mate. And he kept walking. One foot before the other.

"Stop, old man!" shouted the Reaper. "Or I shoot."

"No," Trix choked out through the lump in her throat. She couldn't sit by and watch another unnecessary death. She staggered to her feet, but Aeron was already running.

The glyphs on *Honor* glowed a bright blue as he overtook the king and stood between him and the laughing Reapers.

"We can go through you, Guardian. You'll be more fuel for our machine."

It all seemed to happen in slow motion. The Reapers arrogantly trained their guns on Aeron. Trix's heart leaped in her chest, thinking the worst. She called on her gift instinctually, thinking only of saving her mate's life.

But no killer vines shot out of the ground. Not even snakes. Butterflies crawled out of the dirt and took off. Was the Well mocking her? Was this Trix's punishment for inventing something so cruel?

Aghast, Trix's eyes burned with tears. "Not now, Well. Don't do this now."

A spray of gunfire filled the air. Trix ducked on instinct, dropping over the queen's corpse to protect her. Why, she wasn't sure. But she didn't want the elf—her friend—to be defiled in death. She glimpsed Aeron's sword flashing in her periphery as he sliced, deflecting bullets. How he moved so fast boggled her. She crawled to her feet, intending to run toward the king and Aeron, to keep attempting to access her gift.

Someone slapped a wet rag over her mouth. *Chemical burn.* She remembered this scent. It was the same chemical the Captain had used on her before kidnapping her and selling her to the Autumn Court. She refused to breathe in. Instead, she elbowed the person behind her and thrashed at the Reapers dragging her away. She broke free enough to gasp in the fresh air, but it was no use.

They'd dragged her off the lawn and to the darkness of trees where the portal device she'd made waited. Never had she been so ashamed of something she'd created. A Reaper scowled at her through his battle mask. "You better be worth it, Tinker. We're losing good men because of you."

Then he activated the portal and pulled her through.

FORTY-THREE

When Aeron saw the Reaper's trigger finger twitch and the tiny burst of flame from the barrel of their gun, a burn on his shoulder told him a bullet had been fired. He glanced down at the thin tear across his bicep—a welling of blood but no mortal wound. The shot had only grazed him. But the same bullet had sailed past and went straight into King Tian's forehead, killing him instantly.

A sudden rush of power flooded Aeron, heightening his senses. He still couldn't hear, but everything else became ultra-clear. Night was day. Sound was visible. Air had taste. Time didn't exist. Gasping under the new sensations, he blinked slowly, trying to understand what had happened.

Movement from the Reapers drew Aeron's attention. He noted the gun's recoil, the blurring of air around the nozzle, and the bullet sailing toward him. Aeron could *see* the bullet in the air. He lifted *Honor* and swatted it, amazed that he'd been able to move fast enough.

What was happening?

Rumbling beneath his feet was the king landing on the ground. No manabeeze popped out of the king's flesh. He was mortal, so this power now in Aeron's veins had been sitting somewhere, waiting for another king to claim it.

No other confirmation was needed.

This was Aeron's destiny.

He was the new Spring Court King.

Every bullet that came at him, he deflected with *Honor*. Bullets pinged and sparked across the blade. In time, what felt like minutes to him but was probably seconds to them, he learned how to aim the ricochets. He shot those bullets back at the men who dared threaten his mate, who dared come into their territory and murder a king and queen. Who used the mana of Guardians as though they were cattle in an abattoir.

One after the other, Aeron returned fire until no more bullets sprayed his way. Only then did time filter back, and his senses dulled. The night became night again. Sound became invisible. He squinted, adjusting to the new low light, but a strange flickering was everywhere. He needed to get used to this change in his gift. Jasper had reported something similar about a tithe of power when he became the Seelie High King. He'd learned to use his body as a portal upon mating with Ada.

Aeron's powers evolving this way made sense. He was also a king and mated to a Well-blessed human.

Panting from exertion, Aeron kicked the dead humans with his boots—to ensure they were dead. Trix's safety was a priority before anything else. He turned—*No!*

Bright light rippled a hole through space and time. A portal had been made and was now closing. He'd not heard the usual electric rip. Aeron pumped effort into his thighs and ran. He called on this new power and begged it to answer, but time did not slow for him again.

Humans dragged Trix through the portal. It closed before Aeron was halfway across the lawn.

⚖

KELVHAN WAS DEAD. Aeron wished he could take credit for it, but the humans he'd invited into their territory had killed him too. Whether the bullet came from them or Aeron, he'd never know. And he didn't care. All he wanted to do was find Trix.

Aeron was in his rooms, tearing through the destruction Kelvhan had left, looking for anything in her notes that might explain how her device worked. It was a long shot, but it was the first thing his mind latched onto when she'd gone missing. He felt her still through their bond, somewhere in the distance. She was alive.

Forrest, Leaf, and a handful of Guardians arrived to help. Too late, he thought bitterly as they pushed their way into his room. Sucking in his grief, Aeron faced his peers.

Thorne and Indigo glared at the horned guards outside the room. The guards had loitered around Aeron, wanting him to acknowledge that he was their new king. But he couldn't. His mind was a blur of emotion and the need to find his mate.

Aeron vaguely became aware of Leaf trying to talk to him, but he understood not a single word. Frustration welled in his body. Why did it take so long for people to get that? He shoved Leaf against the wall, and the team leader took it with a scowl. Eventually, Leaf shouted something at the others. Forrest came up behind Aeron with a note:

What happened?

Aeron gritted his teeth and released Leaf.

Before Trix came into his life, he thought his cadre understood him. But without her, he was that same floundering person he'd been before. He needed Trix. He missed her. He felt normal around her. Less of a burden. He laughed bitterly at the irony. The very fear he'd had at the start—his excuse for not being with her—was that he didn't want to burden her. But that's what he was without her.

Until he found her, he would have to write his communication like a Well-damned incumbrance. He found a pencil and replied,

Humans came. I killed them, but they kidnapped Trix.

He was about to write that they took her through a portal when he remembered Leaf was a master at creating portals. He was the only fae alive who could create them with his mana—a skill that came with age or a tithe like Aeron had just received. This realization was another small fact that made Aeron distrust Leaf.

The elf had joined the Order only slightly before Aeron and Forrest. He said he wasn't old. But something didn't add up.

Whatever the case, Leaf could trace energy left behind after a portal was closed to reopen it to the original destination. Perhaps they would find Trix.

She belonged with him.

⚖

AERON WROTE TO FORREST.

How much longer?

They were outside on the lawn, watching and waiting as Leaf worked to unfold the signature left behind by the portal the humans had made. It had been less than an hour since Trix had gone missing, but it felt like a lifetime. He was back in Guardian battle gear, *Honor* in hand, ready to face any threat on the other side.

His worst fear was if they'd taken Trix to Crystal City. In there, Aeron would be as powerless as the humans. The chances of getting Trix back were slim—unless he led a full-on assault on the city. But Tian's final words were for Aeron to take care of their people. Forcing them into certain death would not be that.

Forrest read Aeron's note and shrugged. He clapped Aeron on the shoulder and squeezed. He said something, and Aeron scowled at him until Forrest wrote down:

We'll get her back.

I know, Aeron signed back.

Forrest's brows winged up, and he gestured at Aeron's hands. Rather than writing his explanation, Aeron signed *sorry* and *thank you,* the universally understood signs all fae already knew. Forrest put two and two together as he realized Aeron had a language he communicated with now.

Forrest wrote:

You'll have to teach me.

Aeron gave a curt nod, inwardly pleased Forrest was taking an interest. And if Forrest learned, then Melody might. And if she did...

He suddenly realized how much influence one person

could have. Like wildfire, Trix's ideas shone bright and spread. She'd been so down on herself, blaming her short-comings for not seeing how her invention could impact the world. But that same part of her had the potential to make great change. He hated that the rash, misinformed comments of others in her old life had affected her confidence and self-worth. But who else would have thought to burrow beneath the soil to get to him? Who else would have jumped in head first?

Who else would have taken the time to teach him to communicate, even when he told her there was no point because he'd get his hearing back?

He needed to tell her how special she was. He needed to hold her in his arms.

He let his gaze slide over to where Leaf paced the spot the portal had been. Leaf's hands occasionally moved along the air as though touching an invisible wall.

Movement on the lawn caught everyone's attention. Swords and weapons came out, ready to attack. But it was only Shade stepping out of the shadows with his mate Silver, and Violet. Both the females wore leather outfits like the Guardian battle gear but with no metal.

Were they here to help?

Their expressions were a little too panicked to believe so. And when Forrest quickly found space on the paper and wrote, Aeron's blood went cold.

Maebh and the Autumn Court are attacking the Order. The Prime wants us all back.

Aeron's mind returned to when he'd accidentally made the blood connection with his eldest brother in armor. They must have been marching on the Order. And why not? Maebh hated the Order, especially after they'd not fulfilled their bargain to bring Rory back to her. Why not attack now while the taint was still wreaking havoc but hadn't completely taken their ability to use mana. Why not attack now when the humans had been picking off Guardians for their mana? Maebh was using the Autumn Court to do her dirty work.

Forrest wrote:

I'm going to talk with Mother.

No. Aeron couldn't place the exact moment. He couldn't give an exact reason. But he never knew how much space Trix occupied in his heart until she left a gnawing hole of emptiness behind. He would do anything to fill it again. She came first. Always.

And he would tear apart anyone standing in his way. Even his brother.

Forrest saw the solid determination in Aeron's eyes and hesitated. He swallowed. Then wrote—*Or I come with you to find your mate.*

Bright light burst into the clearing. Behind them, Leaf's tracing had worked. He opened a portal, and Aeron held his breath, praying this wouldn't be affected by the debilitating taint like everything else.

When the destination beyond the portal became clear, Aeron couldn't help wondering if this was all part of the Well's plan—it opened to the Order. To where the demogorgon and the Autumn Court army attacked. To where Trix and her small unit of humans were stuck in the middle, fighting for their lives.

FORTY-FOUR

T rix had been dragged into a war zone. They'd landed in a grassy field, surrounded. So many things happened at once. She struggled to gain her bearings. A wild beast screeched in the night sky. Armored soldiers on horses were on one side, their hooves thudding in mud. Guardians in leather were on the other, their weapons out. It took her a good few minutes before her wits returned enough to single out the voices of the Reapers.

"Fuck, where are we?"

"The portal was supposed to take us back to the airship."

"This is not a ship, fuck-face."

"Don't you think I know that?" The Reaper removed his mask. He glared at Trix, "What did you do to your machine?"

The portal didn't work? No. Not the portal. It wasn't her machine that had failed. It was the fuel—the taint. Trix wanted to laugh. They'd arrived at a different destination than initially intended.

"You bloody idiots," she exclaimed. "There's a taint on the Well. It's warping magic."

"Magic?" one of them shouted. "Nero said it's science."

She shrugged. "Science based on a magical substance we still don't understand."

Grim looks passed across the group, but they had no time to devise a plan. A war horn sounded from one side of the field. The galloping of hooves thundered closer and rumbled the ground, turning up grass and mud. Winged Guardians took to the sky. Shifters shredded their clothes and turned into beasts. Riders came toward them on both sides.

The taint, once the bane of Trix's existence, was her savior... maybe. *If* she could use this opportunity to escape.

Wait.

Had that Reaper said, airship... not ship, as in boat on the water? Trix knew they'd been working on prototypes for blimp-style vehicles but hadn't realized they'd moved into production. She scanned the sky but couldn't see past floating manabeeze already leaving bodies of fallen fae around them. It was like trying to see the stars in a city where pollution and lights drowned out everything else.

The battle had begun. Glowing balls popped into the sky like reverse falling stars. Dead fae. Screams. Shouts.

Blood-curdling cries. The back of her neck prickled with warning, and she couldn't place where the danger was coming from. It seemed to come from all sides.

Where was that screech coming from?

She had to get out of there.

Her opportunity came when one of the Reapers was splatted by a rogue manabee in the face. Gunfire sprayed wildly as he became drunk on the energy, as the memory hit from whatever that manabee belonged to. Trix dropped to the ground and put her hands in the dirt, intending to call on her gift. Even if snakes came, she didn't care. At least it would be something to distract them further.

"The war isn't supposed to be here," another of the Reapers barked over the noise. "Nero said it would be—"

His sudden gurgle made Trix look up and gasp. Something sharp and bloody burst out of his neck. His eyes widened in horror. Blood dribbled from his mouth. The sharp thing retreated, and the Reaper slumped on the ground. Aeron stood behind him, his face spattered with sticky dark splotches.

"Aeron!"

She jumped up to run for him, but he signed, *Get down.*

Danger still surrounded her. Her mate, ever the vigilant one, continued to slice into the humans who'd kidnapped her with that cool, calm lethal prowess he bled from his very core. Trix shouldn't be smiling. Death was not something to be happy about. But she couldn't help it. Her body reacted, rejoicing at her mate having found her.

Aeron dispatched them as quickly as he'd taken out the nymphs and the dungeon guards. Then he spun, gripped her hair in his fist, and claimed her mouth in a quick, blistering kiss. There was no war, no sounds, no blood-curdling cries in that tiny moment. When you love someone as intensely as she did, they become your whole world. Trix only had eyes for him.

He signed in her face, *Pain?*

She swallowed. Up until now, missing him had made it a ten. But with him here—she touched her forefinger to her thumb. *Zero.*

His nostrils flared as though he tried to hold back the tidal wave of emotion cascading inside him. But she felt it. She knew he needed her as much as she needed him. He nodded before glancing around them, taking in the battle, shaking his head in disgust at how the fae were fighting each other.

Come, he signed and took her by the arm across the field. He blocked and parried anyone stupid enough to get in their way. If he didn't see someone coming, she tugged on him. He trusted her every time, immediately responding to her news. They eventually hit the wall surrounding the Order.

Further down by the gate, they spotted Melody's platinum blond hair. Forrest stood in front of her, ready to fight. But she wasn't a warrior. What was she doing out here? Aeron pulled her along the wall to them. As they approached, Trix saw Silver's hand on Melody, her face already a paler shade of green.

"She's purging the taint," Trix mumbled, realizing. Silver only had it in her to siphon a small amount. Probably enough for one attack. Shade looked furious, his hand on Silver, ready to yank her back if she got too sick. What was Melody's gift if it was so necessary?

Aeron turned to her as Melody opened her mouth. He slammed his hands on Trix's ears just as an unholy vibration rented the air, drilling into Trix's bones, trying to get through the small block Aeron had made.

Through his hands, she heard Melody's single word, "STOP."

Every cell in Trix's body wanted to halt. To freeze. To listen to its master and do nothing. But Aeron's small protection had somehow blocked the worst of the compulsion. She could still move her lungs. She could breathe.

Seconds later, Aeron dropped his hands. He glanced back and saw what Trix also saw. Every person on the field, whether fae or human, had stopped like they were playing a game of musical statues. Silver's hand dropped from Melody. Her legs buckled, and Shade snapped her into his arms.

Before he moved, Silver started convulsing and vomiting, her eyes rolling back in her head.

He glanced over, caught Aeron's gaze, and shook his head. Then his vampiric wings shot out, and he launched into the sky with his mate. Trix's hand flew to her heart, hoping that Silver would be okay. That was worse than how she'd reacted with Trix. Other Guardians who'd been close pulled out of their ears whatever they'd used to block Melody's power.

A female with white feathered wings, white curly hair, and flawless brown skin dropped from the sky. Her blue dress billowed. Her expression was fierce as she strode toward Leaf.

"Where were you?" she barked.

Leaf glanced at Trix and Aeron, then slid his gaze back to the winged female. Trix guessed she was the Prime of the Order of the Well from the regal, entitled way she carried herself.

"In Delphinium," Leaf replied curtly. "But now I am here. We all are, and we've successfully stopped the attack."

In other words, no need for her to get her knickers in a knot. But he spoke too soon. Three more silhouettes descended from the sky. As they landed and gathered around the Prime, anyone close by took a few steps back as though they would catch a disease from them.

Trix wasn't sure why. They didn't look diseased. But they weren't human. All three were tall and lithe but powerfully built. They'd descended on tattered draconic wings like demons with angelic faces. All wore the same leather uniform as the Guardians, but none looked as worn or used. One with long, silken black hair stepped toward Leaf and the Prime.

FORTY-FIVE

L eaf glared at the field littered with hundreds of frozen fae. They weren't sure how long Melody's controlling word would last or if the compulsion would kill those it had affected, so they had to act fast. He didn't have time for the Prime's disappointment.

She relied too much on him as it was. The female needed to stop. She opened her mouth to speak again, but he held up his palm, then walked away and barked orders at any Guardian who'd been smart enough to cover their ears when Melody had spoken.

"Stop gawking," he bellowed. "Get out there and drive your swords through the enemy. NOW!"

He pretended not to see the feral grins on all three crow shifters in the cadre of Twelve. They liked killing too much. As soon as the crows moved, others leaped into action. Forrest pushed through some and walked to Leaf.

"No! We shouldn't be killing them," Forrest said. Guardians who overheard hesitated. "What if they were forced to do Maebh's bidding."

"Forrest," Leaf chided. "Don't be naive. I know you think because you came to an understanding with your mother that she is innocent. She's not. Need I remind you that they're on *our* doorstep, not the other way around."

He pointed out there as he spoke, but the Prime snapped his wrist between her fingers and glared at him.

"He's right. No killing."

"Why?"

Legion stepped forward, Varen at his side. "Because then we are playing into their plan."

Leaf winced, unsure whether the voice was in his head or aloud. He could never tell with the Sluagh.

"They?" Leaf asked. "Who is they? The humans or Maebh?"

Leaf squinted into the darkness. Was Maebh out there, frozen like the others? What about the demogorgon? He was hard-pressed to believe that the monster had become a statue like everyone else. It seemed to slip every other attack, even metal.

"Have you seen this in your visions?" Leaf asked Varen. The Sluagh's fathomless, nightmarish eyes blinked, and he answered directly into Leaf's mind.

I have seen battles, near and far.

A frustrated growl slipped from Leaf's lips. What in the

Well's name did that mean? He glared at Aleksandra. "And Dawn or Clarke? What have they seen?"

He'd been so busy trying to find ways of clearing the taint, that he'd been out of the loop with the Prime's usual machinations. From the way her jaw clenched as she glared at him, he knew she had no good answer to give him.

The problem was, as with Clarke and any other Seer, events surrounding Nero were often missing. For this reason, Clarke had nicknamed him the Void.

Aeron shoved into the group. He gestured with his hands in that way only his mate understood. The curly-haired woman translated and said, "He thinks the Prime wants to stop you because of a prophecy."

Stop Leaf from killing their attackers? Leaf's gaze snapped to Aleksandra's—the Prime's—in time to see the flare of her white-lashed eyes as though Trix's words rang true.

"Are they right?" Leaf growled. "Is this one of your plots?"

"I don't know," the Prime confessed. "We're coming to the end of what was foretold. This taint is also creating darkness over future visions. Combined with the Void, it's blocking everything or giving us false futures."

"I want to see the original prophecy," Leaf demanded. "In its entirety."

"That's not possible," she said.

"Why not?"

"Because I don't have it."

"Then who does? Where is it?"

"Jackson Crimson locked it away. Only he can bring it back."

"But he's dead."

She paused, considered, then said, "There is a way to experience his memories."

"We don't have time for this," Cloud snarled, flipping his dagger deftly in his fingers. "Can we kill them or not?"

Leaf's gaze darted between the Prime and Varen, then he raised his eyes to the night sky and shook his head. He was surrounded by madness. When he lowered his gaze, he said, "I'll open a portal to the Autumn Court. Every Guardian will carry the soldiers from here and deposit them on their land. Do it quickly before Melody's word loses effect. If they die because they can't breathe, that's on them. If they die because we put a sword through their hearts, that's on us. No killing."

The Prime didn't wait around for him to open the portal. Neither did the Sluagh, which made Leaf's suspicion grow. They were hiding something, meddling as much as the Prime but for their secret gain.

He was done with this shrouded secrecy and blind trust. But he couldn't leave yet. He had to open a portal to Rubrum City.

Cloud was the first to arrive at the portal with an

Autumn Court soldier frozen and slung over his shoulder. A ribbon of blood, however, dribbled from his hand... which still held the dagger and was somehow half plunged into the soldier's thigh. Cloud caught Leaf staring at him and shrugged.

"I slipped," he said, face deadpanning.

River came up behind Cloud with another frozen soldier but grinned like a maniac. "I also slipped."

"I gave orders," Leaf barked. "No killing. Follow them."

"Or did the Prime give orders?"

"Does it matter?"

Cloud's second nonchalant shrug was at odds with his mocking glare. Leaf had to clench down hard to stop himself from knocking the crow shifter clear through the portal. He settled for distraction.

"Council meeting at the temple after this," Leaf grumbled. "I think it's high time we all find out the details of this prophecy."

"Agreed," Cloud said and then walked through the portal to a field outside Rubrum City. It wasn't exactly the destination Leaf had planned, but it was close enough.

He rubbed his temples as the demands of his station pressed in on him. Sometimes he wanted to say fuck it all and disappear. To drop himself again into the ceremonial lake, hoping to surface in another time like all these Well-blessed humans. But he doubted the Well would ever give this world another chance. If they didn't keep the inhabitants of this world from ruining it a second time, life as they knew it was over.

If they failed, there would be no coming back.

A stream of Guardians followed Cloud. Removing every Autumn Court soldier would take time, but the more removed, the more Leaf realized the army wasn't large. This was by no means an attack meant to win. These fae were lambs to the slaughter. Sacrifices. Perhaps that had been Maebh's plan—with all the chaos Elphyne was in, the Order was the only singular entity still fighting for all faekind. She wanted Elphyne divided so she could swoop in and take control. She wanted to break all that the Order stood for.

Either the Order slaughtered these people, and Maebh would somehow twist it to her Unseelie purpose and rally more people to her banner for revenge. Or the small army would seriously deplete the Order, perhaps even taking them out if Melody hadn't used her power. If Silver hadn't sacrificed her health, who was to know what outcome would have come to pass.

When Cloud returned, Leaf asked, "Where is Shade?"

As a Councilor, Shade also needed to attend the meeting.

"Fucked if I know." Cloud glowered at Leaf as if he was stupid for asking. "He's pussy-whipped and probably nursing his human."

"No need to be uncouth, D'arn." But a part of Leaf

agreed. The state of the Twelve was disgusting. If they were all unmated, as initially intended, then they would be operating at one hundred percent. No expectations to mate or pair up was what attracted Leaf to the Order in the first place.

This attack would never have happened.

When Leaf first read Aeron's replacement list, he'd considered turning it into a list for all the mated Guardians in the Twelve. He was sure Cloud would agree. That was two councilors already in favor of the movement.

The more he thought about it, the more appealing it was.

Cloud's lashes lowered in a derogatory way. He sniffed at Leaf, then wiped his nose, scoffed, and continued collecting the Autumn Court army. Leaf knew that look. It was Cloud's silent dig for Leaf standing around and barking orders instead of getting in there and helping.

But as team leader *and* councilor, it was Leaf's duty to ensure this organization ran smoothly. Plus, he had to remain at the portal. If he stopped feeding mana, it would close. Responsibility had shackles. He wanted to be more hands-on and hated that he had to remain still. But he would not give Cloud the satisfaction and let it show on his face.

When Aeron and his new mate strode over, Leaf was grateful for a reprieve, even if he knew what was coming. From the look of bitterness in Aeron's eyes, he'd seen the replacement list. The only difference now was that they both knew why.

Trix said, "Aeron has asked me to tell you something."

"I'm listening."

"He found old journals at the Spring Court that you might find interesting. Journals by..." Trix paused, waiting for her mate to finish his hand language. "Someone called Jackson Crimson."

Leaf's ears pricked up. "What are they doing at the Spring Court?"

"He doesn't know. Only that he thinks Crimson knows how to clean the taint."

Leaf's gaze flicked to Aeron. "You think you can find the answer with time?"

After Trix translated, and Aeron replied in sign, Trix said, "He thinks Crimson knows... and maybe the Prime knows where the answers lie."

"The Prophecy," Leaf said, rubbing his chin. "Aleksandra mentioned she doesn't have it but knows how to experience Crimson's memories to find it. Perhaps there is a place where more journals are stored."

"Agreed," Trix said, her eyes on her mate's hands. "Aeron said he's got a theory that Maebh is at fault for the taint. And there's more in the journal to back that up. He will give the journal to you."

Leaf let his gaze settle on the new Spring Court King. He'd likely found the list Leaf had started for the Prime weeks ago, and yet he'd continued to work at clearing the taint for the Order. Unlike Jasper, who'd wholly neglected his Guardian duties since becoming Seelie High King, Leaf didn't think Aeron would do the same.

"You are a good Guardian," Leaf said to Aeron, knowing Trix would translate. "You will be missed."

LEAF

CHAPTER
FORTY-SIX

It took a full day to clear the Autumn Court soldiers from the fields before the Order. As dusk settled, Leaf strode up the temple steps, his mind a mess and his body aching. Holding his position and keeping the portal open all day had been draining, but this council meeting was long overdue. It was time to get answers from the Prime and even Dawn, the longtime Seer for the Order.

As he crested the open temple floor and walked into the chamber, he wasn't surprised to see most other councilors growing irritated. He was late to a meeting he'd called. The Prime stood at her usual spot near the columns overlooking the Order campus. Storm clouds gathered in the darkening sky behind her, blowing in gusts of cool wind that ruffled her usual pristine white feathers. Dark circles beneath her eyes said she wasn't immune from the day's events.

No one had expected Maebh to attack directly. All intel from their Seers had pointed to a battle among the fae people—Maebh's attempt at capturing power and uniting the land under one banner. That she used the Autumn Court for her attack and that she kept her demogorgon from getting involved apart from fear tactics was intriguing.

Cloud leaned against a pillar, his intolerant eyes tracking Leaf as he walked in. Still in his Guardian leathers like Leaf, Cloud's were noticeably dirtier.

"About fucking time," Cloud muttered, swiping a lock of black hair from his eyes.

Leaf turned to the others in the open room. Colt, the pixie. Barrow, the Mage. Dawn, the Seer. All were present in their usual blue robes, looking calm and collected as if nothing had happened today. As if they hadn't been a hair-line from invasion and possible death. As if they hadn't had their foundations rocked.

The final member of the Council was not here. Shade most likely spent time healing his mate. Leaf winced at the memory of Silver's reaction to the taint. The convulsing. The eye rolls. The vomiting.

"Time to start talking," Leaf said to the Prime before sweeping his gaze to the Seer.

Dawn was a stout satyr with a butterfly clip in her hair. Her eyes were Seer white, which usually meant she was in the throes of a vision. But lately, her eyes were always like that, and she spoke less frequently. That she bothered to turn up to these meetings still perplexed him.

When no one started talking, Leaf prompted them.

"I want to know about the prophecy—" He held up his hand when the Prime's lips opened, shutting her up so he could finish. "The real prophecy. Not the dribs and drabs you've revealed."

Leaf pulled out a leather-bound journal he'd tucked into the back of his breeches. It was the reason he was late. After the cleanup on the field, he'd portaled Aeron and his mate back to the Spring Court. There he'd collected the Jackson Crimson journals Aeron had found and briefly flicked through them. *Interesting indeed.* Cloud's eyes narrowed as Leaf tossed the journal on the floor.

"Jackson Crimson's journals were at the Spring Court Royal Library," Leaf explained. "Why weren't they kept under lock and key here?"

There was no point asking if the Prime knew about them. Of course, she did. Her white-lashed gaze lifted to his and held. Leaf could see her thoughts collide as she probably contemplated how much to reveal. Machinating as usual.

"No," he said. "No more misdirection. We are your trusted Council. What are we doing here if you cannot share it all with us?"

Cloud's leather creaked as he folded his arms and joined Leaf in staring down the Prime. Barrow, the elderly fae frowned at her. Colt's prismatic wings buzzed—a nervous tic for the pixie. Dawn scratched her head with a vacant look in her eyes.

Did Aleksandra not understand what was happening? Perhaps it was time to replace her too. The entire Order needed a shakeup, from how the academics were run to how Guardians were recruited and trained. Times were changing. They needed to evolve as well.

"It is not about sharing," she said eventually. "It is about how many variables we can allow to exist before the future we want is derailed."

"How do we even know we want your future?" Cloud scowled. "I mean, you've never asked us."

"You know what we know," the Prime said, sighing.

"But not all," Leaf pointed out her fae loophole. Lies hid within semantics.

She visibly bristled. "You once told me, Leaf, that you wish to remain ignorant to the worst. You were too tired to do what was necessary. That it weighed you down."

"I don't recall that."

"No, you wouldn't."

"What's that supposed to mean?"

She clamped her lips shut.

It was Dawn who answered. "You'll soon find out."

Frustration welled in Leaf, and he clenched his fists.

Cloud stepped forward, "Enough of this prophecy. I don't give a shit. What I want to know is, what will we do with Maebh? The bargain to return Aurora is wearing thin.

Failure to do this has caused a war. I say we finish what we started, infiltrate Crystal City, and bring Maebh's granddaughter back. Bargain satisfied. No more war."

The cold calculation in Cloud's eyes was not lost on Leaf. Months ago, Leaf might have taken Cloud's words at face value. But now he knew of the long, painful history between Cloud and Aurora—Rory as she was known now. Cloud only wanted to get to her to kill her in revenge.

"You have no intention of delivering her to Maebh alive," Leaf said.

"So? The bargain didn't say she has to be alive, only that she is returned."

Leaf's teeth ground. "Regardless of the bargain, we will still have Maebh's attack on the Order to deal with."

"But is it an attack on the integrity of the Well?" Barrow pointed out. "Or are her moves politically motivated?"

"You know she's illegally warping mana," Colt said. "Why does it matter if this attack is to do with the integrity of the Well?"

"I agree," Leaf stated. "She attacked us. We can postulate for days over the philosophy of this attack, but it can't go unanswered. Whether direct or indirect, it still affects our mission to uphold the integrity of the Well."

"Her illegal warping of mana is a separate issue," Barrow said.

"You're making no sense."

"Silence." The Prime's wings snapped out, then folded

again. "Maebh is not our immediate concern. Nero is. And the taint is. We must clear it before becoming as blind and weak as everyone else."

That's what Leaf had thought, too, until Maebh ended up on their doorstep. Until they'd almost died. Until Aeron had pointed out that the Prime was keeping secrets, that every Guardian had been a pawn in her plan... and Leaf was probably next.

He glanced behind the Prime to the stormy sky outside. The sun was now well below the horizon. Good. For what came next, he needed Legion here.

Any time Legion, Leaf sent in his mind, hoping the Sluagh leader would hear.

While waiting, he shoved the journal with his boot and said, "You say Maebh isn't our concern, but here's the thing. In that journal, Jackson Crimson states he knew you and Maebh when you were newly mutated from human thousands of years ago." He looked the Prime directly in the eyes. "You and Maebh share a special bond. That wouldn't have anything to do with your reluctance to see her as a threat, now would it?"

"Special bond?" Cloud snarled, his gaze cutting to the Prime.

"It's all in the journal." Leaf pointed to it, even though he knew Cloud would not read it.

"That was a long time ago," the Prime said. "Maebh is a different person now. I am different."

"The journal also says she was changing. That she'd

learned to bargain with the Well."

"That's not news," the Prime said. "We already know that's how she created the Sluagh."

"See, that's the part I'm confused about," Leaf said.

Buzzing outside grew to thunderous proportions as Legion, and the rest of his Cadre of Six descended on the temple like dark wraiths. Tattered draconic wings flapped so fast they blurred.

Every breath in the room held. Even Leaf's. When he'd asked for Legion to attend this meeting, he'd been surprised that the Sluagh had agreed. Leaf had always sensed they had a purpose bordering the Order's but not a part of it. They seemed to inject themselves into missions when it suited them, and they'd stayed out of sight for the rest. Leaf had begun to doubt they'd even existed until they started coming out of the woodworks when the Well-blessed women had thawed.

This was the first time Leaf had seen all six Sluagh in one place.

Legion stood tall and center, his long dark hair and widow's peak a standout. Next to him was Varen, their Seer. Pale, with a haircut like Indigo's—shaved on the sides and long on the top. Fox had close-cropped dark hair. Emrys was a contrast of white hair, dark brows, and pale skin but dark power-enhancing tattoos. The final two Leaf had never met before.

The fifth Sluagh was tall, broad-shouldered, and with brown skin. His hair was shaved above the ears, and the rest was made of dark dreadlocks pulled neatly into a knot. The sixth Sluagh was the most frightening. His dusky skin held a bluish tint. Short spikes decorated his brows and knuckles. Two satyr-like curved horns emerged from his head, but unlike a satyr, this Sluagh had a long flicking tail glimpsed between his wings.

His gaze tracked back across the Six, and he also noted Fox had short horns and an impish tail. He'd not noticed those before and wondered if they had been glamoured to appear less different than the average fae.

All were beautiful nightmares. All were strong. All were lethal, frightening, and unnatural.

I didn't expect you all to come, Leaf sent Legion.

His dark, galaxy-filled eyes tilted Leaf's way. *You wanted proof. We are all proof.*

"Why are you all here, Legion?" the Prime asked, her spine straight.

Leaf had to give her credit. She never cowed in fear. And, even though he was furious at having been kept increasingly in the dark, everything she'd done could be explained as preparation for their final battle against Nero. To once and for all take control of the land, to eradicate forbidden items, and for the Well and life on this planet to prosper long into the future.

Legion replied, "Aeron has theories about the origin of the taint. Coupled with what Leaf learned in this journal and what we know about Maebh bargaining with the Well and her new pet, we believe she caused the taint. She drew too much from the inky side when she created her creature. It left a gaping hole that leaks continuously into the cosmic power source. We are here, Aleksandra, to prove that Maebh did not make us. She bargained for us. She summoned us from a long deep slumber."

Like all fae, the Sluagh could not lie. Leaf had requested this proof, but he had not expected this confession of their origin.

They'd been summoned? They'd existed long ago? They'd been asleep? If so, where? How long ago? Why? He supposed it didn't matter. It was none of his business as long as the Prime understood who was at fault for the taint.

"I thought she was your queen," the Prime said, her eyes narrowing. "That she controlled you with her blooded link to you."

"She used her blood to make the bargain, to tie us to her, but as you can see—we are free from her influence. But our existence in Elphyne will forever be linked to her because she summoned us from the darkness."

"Speak fucking English, Sluagh," Cloud snapped. "What are you getting at?"

A growl slipped out of the Sluagh with dreadlocks. Next to him, the blue-tinged and spiked Sluagh also snarled. Fangs flashed in their mouths. That buzzing sound Leaf had always associated with their draconic wings filled the air again. But he saw no wings move.

Legion's head cocked their way, and he warned with authority in his voice, "Bodin. Spike."

He could have said that to them mind to mind. They had a hive mentality. That Legion spoke the words aloud meant the names were meant for all to hear. This was their introduction into fae society, as it were.

The buzzing sound died as Bodin and Spike turned to look at the night. But the danger was not gone. Leaf tensed as he glimpsed the white flash of their skull beneath their skin. Their invisible wraith forms had just left their bodies. His eyes darted about. They could now be anywhere in this room.

Legion returned his attention to the Council. "We were not creatures made by Maebh but summoned. Her demogorgon, however, is something else."

"It was made," the Prime said, the understanding dawning in her eyes.

"It was made but can be unmade if its maker is too," Varen said, his prophetic voice a smooth dark drawl.

"So we kill Maebh." Cloud threw his hands in the air. "Great. Finally, we have an answer. Just tell me when and where."

"No," the Prime held up her hand, staying Cloud. "Varen said, *unmade*. Maebh must be unmade. What does that mean?"

Before the Six could answer, Legion waved his hand, and they spread their demonic wings. Leaf blinked, and they were gone.

"That buzzing sound," Cloud murmured, his eyes warily on the night, "Isn't their wings. It's the souls of the unforgiven dead they've trapped, crying for the release of the Wild Hunt."

No one spoke as they all realized how perilously close they'd come to seeing the Wild Hunt firsthand. Leaf shuddered and shook off the thought. The Sluagh were not his concern. The Prime's secrets were.

"Did you know?" he asked the Prime. "That Maebh was at fault?"

Had she let Leaf go on a wild wolpertinger chase to clear the taint so she could protect an old lover?

Dawn said, "Since the taint has arrived, our visions are not to be trusted."

Voices raised in a heated argument. Cloud barked demands for clarity. The Prime retorted in her usual vague responses. Barrow was stuck debating what "unmade" meant. Colt asked questions like, are the Sluagh even fae? Leaf's lips parted, intending to bellow above them all and demand attention—his need to see the original prophecy hadn't changed. Everything else was a distraction. But dark shadows gathered in the center of the room, drawing caution from everyone until Shade materialized with murder on his face as he stalked toward the Prime.

He stopped mere inches from the white-winged female leader of theirs.

The air around Shade vibrated with menace. His

expression was tense and full of bottled emotion. Bleak, dark eyes glimmered with hate.

Silver? Had the worst happened?

Shade pointed at the Prime. "If anyone asks my mate again to siphon the taint, I'll kill them. Do you understand? Even the mention of it in her presence, or to me, will result in instant death."

"Understood. Is she well?" the Prime braved to ask.

"She is alive." He swallowed hard. "Barely."

And then Shade was gone, his shadows swallowing him whole.

Leaf pinched the bridge of his nose and squeezed his burning, sleepy eyes before collecting the dropped journal and meeting the Prime's gaze. Without Silver to cleanse the power source, it mattered not how powerful any of their connections to the Well were. He knew he should be joining them in figuring out how to unmake Maebh, but he only desired to find out what this original prophecy was.

He couldn't explain the itch, only that it felt like self-preservation. He needed the unknown to be uncovered.

"I want Jackson Crimson's last known location," he said to the Prime. "I want all your material on him to be delivered to my room. And I want to know where to find this place you said I could experience his memories."

The Prime gaped at him. "D'arn Leaf, you do not give orders to me. You have already avoided finding your mate as Clarke has bidden, and time is running out."

"I don't care," he replied. "I am not a pawn in your

game like the others. And in case you missed it—" He gestured to Cloud. "The only worthwhile Guardians left are the unmated ones. The mated of the Twelve are incompetent, distracted, and useless."

Leaf continued. "Give me what I asked for, or I find it myself... no matter how long it takes."

FORTY-SEVEN

Shivering from her balcony terrace, Maebh heaved in a labored breath and dashed the tears from her eyes. How could she feel like this after centuries of life? How could rejection still feel so cruel as the day it first hit?

When Maebh had directed the Autumn Court to attack the Order, she'd been riding on her demogorgon's back. Until she was at the gates, Maebh had thought she was there to make Aleksandra pay.

But when Aleksandra had come to her gate, Maebh and her beast circled above.

And circled.

And circled.

She didn't realize she was waiting for a parlay, hoping for Aleksandra to fly up and join her until the sting of rejection reminded her why she'd come.

So long as there's breath in her body and blood in her veins.

What a cruel lie.

Now Maebh knew there was indeed nothing worth saving between them. There was nothing worth saving in this world.

FORTY-EIGHT

When Leaf returned Trix and Aeron to the Spring Court, they found it in chaos. The portal dropped them on the lawn before the Great Elder Tree. While they'd been gone, no one had cleaned up the dead bodies.

The queen and her king were still out in the open. The humans who'd raided were strewn about dead.

Soldiers and palace staff ran over.

"Thank Eulios, you're back," said one soldier, his voice muffled behind his antlered helmet. "We didn't know what to do. The king is dead. The queen is gone. The High Lord..."

He kept talking, but Aeron held up his hand, stopping him.

He signed to Trix, *Tell them I will be back soon to help.* He pointed his thumb at Leaf. *He wants the books. I'll be back.*

Trix smiled as Aeron gave her a quick kiss on the head, and then he gestured for Leaf to follow him into the palace. She faced the waiting soldier and a female palace staffer of high rank. A few more fae stood further back but within earshot. They looked at her nervously, but Trix also caught the hopeful need in their eyes. They wanted direction. They wanted someone to take charge.

"Okay," she said, clapping her hands. "Your new king will return. He's just helping his..." *Grumpy blond elf Guardian?* "Uh... friend out with something, but he'll be right back. In the meantime, perhaps I can clarify some things for you. The queen's brother betrayed her. He poisoned your king, made him mortal, and then tried to sabotage your tree by poisoning it too. He made a deal with some bad humans who wanted to take me back to Crystal City without my consent. They attacked and... well, you can see what happened. Before he died, the king announced Aeron as his heir, and the tree is healthy again."

She pointed at the tree in case they needed a reminder of who was responsible for bringing it back to life and what it meant.

Relief shone in many eyes. A few murmurs rippled around.

"Yes, Aeron," someone murmured.

"What do we do with the bodies?" asked the soldier.

"I'm sure Aeron will have an idea, but let's respectfully cover the king and queen."

The female staffer stepped forward.

She bowed briefly and said, "Your Highness, I am Lolo. I'm your new steward. It is my duty to see to the day-to-day running of your palace, including preparing the royal chambers for you and our new king."

Trix flinched. It felt so wrong to take the chambers of someone else so soon after their untimely deaths.

"I think you should take your time with that," she said. "Aeron—ahem—the king and I will remain in the guest suite until we can hold a proper burial for King Tian and Queen Oleana."

"As you wish."

"What happened to the old steward?" Trix asked. She hadn't trusted that elf as far as she could throw him.

The steward clasped her hands. "He was found dead in his chambers. We suspect it was from self-inflicted wounds. From what you've revealed about High Lord Kelvhan, we believe he must have been involved. They were close."

Those fae lingering at the back came forward and asked questions, each one braver than the last. When Aeron and Leaf returned a few minutes later, Trix's voice was dry and tight from all the talking.

They said goodbye to Leaf, and then Aeron directed soldiers and staff on how he wanted the bodies disposed of. They might have been there all night had Aeron not stopped all the questions. He told them to convene tomorrow in the Great Hall to prepare a fitting funeral ceremony for Tian and Oleana.

The setting sun was a sight to see beyond the Great Elder Tree's renewed foliage. Trix glimpsed shades of purple, magenta, and even blue in the moving leaves. The white buds had bloomed into flowers in record time. It brought tears to Trix's eyes to think of all the sacrifices and pain the king and queen must have suffered. Or how they might have handled the treason differently if they hadn't believed the fae inability to lie was the be-all-and-end-all. There had to be other ways of uncovering the truth.

As Aeron took her hand and walked her back to their rooms, she thought she had a chance to make changes now that she was queen. She had a supportive, empathetic partner who loved ideas and new things as much as she did. She slid him a fond look, admired his handsome profile, and he smiled as though he'd sensed her flux of emotion.

A wave of affection returned to her down their bond.

He'd trusted her to take control of things here when he'd gone to deal with Leaf.

Trix couldn't believe they'd almost been separated for good. They were safe. He'd come for her.

When they made it to their room, the need to be close to her mate overwhelmed her. They'd barely set foot inside the door, and she leaped into his arms. Aeron gripped her bottom as her legs hooked around him. She peppered his face with kisses—not even caring about the dirt, grime, and maybe some other remnants of battle she didn't want to think of. He reeled, fielding her kisses while holding her steady, locking the door, and then taking her to the bathroom.

Clean first, he signed, his eyes heating as he took in her already half-naked body.

She'd removed her clothes before his fingers had formed signs. She was already undressing him as he turned on the bath faucet. The instant they were naked, they climbed into the tub and faced each other as the water filled.

"I love you," she said, signing.

Aeron captured her hand and brought her knuckles to his lips. His smile faltered, and she sensed a stab of fear down their bond before he swallowed hard and squeezed his eyes shut. His broad, powerful shoulders shuddered. For a moment, Trix thought he was in tears. But it must be the day's events finally catching up with him. It was relief. When his long, dark lashes parted, and she was rewarded with his coppery gaze, she shuffled closer and signed, *Pain is zero*.

She had no regrets. Nothing was hurting now that she was here with him. They had a future together.

Trix pointed at him and shrugged.

Pain? he signed. *For me?*

She nodded, her brows knitting. After everything, was he okay?

His gaze softened on her as he touched his forefinger to his thumb and made a zero shape. She grinned and leaned into him, running her hands up his defined torso. She washed away the grime, went extra careful around the bruises still healing, and eventually found herself sitting in his lap, where he let her unravel his braids.

Aeron pressed her back to his front and swiped his hands over every inch of her body, washing her with rose-scented soap and kneading her aching muscles with his fingers. What started as soft, reverent cleaning of each other soon became a tactile need to be close. Their loving actions turned hot, rough, and demanding. He squeezed her breasts, pinched her nipples, and slid his hand to her throat to feel her moans. He had her writhing and squirming in his lap, grinding against his growing erection, trying to use it to ease the tension between her thighs.

Impatient, Trix tried to fit his cock where she needed it, but he captured both her wrists and placed her hands on the tub's edge.

"Don't let go." His demand was a harsh guttural sound behind her. "I want to make you come first. And then I'm going to bend you over the tub and show you how afraid I was to lose you. How happy I am to have found you."

She moaned and gripped the tub as his hand returned to the back of her neck. His other slid down her stomach to settle beneath the water and land between her thighs. He wasted no time bringing her to climax, grunting dirty words of encouragement. Even as the blinding pulses of bliss were clenching her inner walls, he lifted her by the hips out of the water, pushed her forward on her knees, and then fit his cock at her sensitive entrance.

Aeron's slow and shuddering groan echoed in the tiled room as he filled her inch by torturous inch. Kneeling behind her, heedless of the water overflowing, he thrust into her relentlessly. Each hit sent her rocking forward, gripping the tub hard. He took the fear he'd spoken about earlier and turned it into something glorious. She felt his fear prickle down their bond and knew he was reliving the same moments that had frightened her, but then he owned his fear. He wore it like a crown. He let her feel it so she could see how much he loved her and needed her. He turned it into love.

THE FOLLOWING EVENING, Trix stood with Aeron before the Great Elder Tree on the same dais they'd been on during the festival. Only this time, the headdress of antlers and flowers on her head was a formal crown, and it wasn't the king giving the speech to a crowd—but her.

Aeron stood proudly by her side, looking suave in a green and brown embroidered suit. His hair was no longer braided. He'd decided he didn't need to conform to the old customs of the Autumn Court. He had nothing to prove to anyone. He'd also allowed her to trim it—something she wasn't sure he'd ever done.

He caught her looking and raised his brows questioningly.

Nice hair, she signed with a wink.

He glanced at her rear end and returned, *Nice butt.*

She almost burst out laughing. Her butt was covered with the volumes of fabric of a formal dress. He could barely see it, but she knew he'd started to embrace the beauty of using a language no one else understood. With the tension well and truly broken, Trix dared to focus on the letter in her hands. Aeron had spent all morning writing it, scratching it out, and starting again.

When they'd asked the palace staff what a fitting farewell would be for their previous king and queen, no one had a simple answer. It had been decades, if not centuries, since they'd had a change of power. So Trix had come up with this—a sort of Viking funeral. Tian and Oleana were wrapped in gauze and floating on a wooden platform on the holy well. Beneath them in the water, sacrificed jewels sparkled amongst the reflections of the Great Elder Tree's foliage and the dying sun.

Already tearing up, she cleared her throat and unfolded the paper. *Better get this done before I lose focus.* Aeron placed a comforting hand on her shoulder. She sensed his nerves, just like her own, but he did that calm thing. He pushed aside his worry for her sake. He made all her jitters float away.

Stepping up to the railing on the dais, the crowd hushed. Trix let her gaze sweep over them, noting familiar faces. Melody and Forrest were here, as were some of the crow shifters in the Twelve. They weren't the only crows.

Perched in the branches of the tree were more, just like they had on the day of the festival.

It seemed many wanted to pay their respects.

"People of Delphinium," she started. "As you know, King Aeron lost his hearing while protecting Elphyne as a Guardian. He has asked me to read this letter to you all in his stead. It is with great sorrow that we gather here today to say farewell to King Tian and Queen Oleana. We knew them for a short time, but their impact was significant. Their love was great. For their people, for each other, and for Elphyne.

"No others would have taken in a broken, bastard elf and a human. But Tian and Oleana did. They patiently waited for us to heal. They invited us to their table. And they put their faith in us to restore your sacred tree to its former glory. The last thing Tian said to me before he died was to take care of our people. Not *his* people, but *ours*. Even with his last breath, he accepted and welcomed me as I was."

Trix swallowed the lump in her throat. Gosh, this was hard. She was going to bawl her eyes out soon. Aeron squeezed her shoulder again, but this time he held up the cane she'd made for Tian, which led her back to the letter.

"This cane symbolizes Tian's failing health and yet his and his queen's enduring devotion to their people. It symbolizes that the people accepted him as he was, despite his frail physical appearance. Tian sacrificed this to the holy well, but it found its way back when we fought the chigumo beneath your tree. It was as though it wanted to stay in the fight with us. We will place it forever here on this dais as a reminder of Tian's and Oleana's legacy: Greatness is not measured by physical perfection, but by the integrity of the heart."

Aeron used his sword to chip out grooves on the wooden railing of the dais. She could see he intended to carve out a holding space, but her eyes widened as each hack chipped off more wood. She quickly stepped in and placed her hand on the rail. She called on her power and felt it answer from deep beneath the soil. Moments later, vines crept up from the ground, wove through the gaps in the wooden dais, and stretched up to embrace the cane. She guided them around the railing until the cane was securely in place.

Onlookers were both awed and humbled by her power. Some looked at the Great Tree, others looked at her, and then, while she had their attention, she turned her power to growing more vines beneath the floating king and queen. They all watched as Trix's vines floated up over the funeral raft.

The Well, or Eulios, or someone great must have been looking out for them. Because when the taint showed up to warp her intention, it didn't throw out snakes or bugs. It caused the imperfections in her vines to blossom into strange, warped flowers. She'd never seen the likes of them before. They sank with the raft as vines took the queen and king underwater and beneath the ground to their final resting place.

Bubbles were all that was left.

Reverent silence covered the people like a blanket. And then the strangest thing happened. Those imperfect flowers floated from the depths, unfurled on the surface, and released beautiful glowing butterflies from their warped hearts. Gasps and sighs rippled over the crowd. Tears stung Trix's eyes. Aeron tucked her under his arm.

The first soldier Aeron had coached at the barracks turned and touched his fingers to his lips, then pushed them down and out toward Aeron. One by one, more people joined in—each showing their appreciation to their new king in a language he understood. The tears finally fell from Trix's eyes when she realized they were also looking at her.

EPILOGUE

"Did your aunty see you?" Nero asked Willow as she walked into his private garden.

"Nope," she replied quietly. She'd done as he'd asked. She'd snuck out of their rooms while Aunty Rory was sleeping and made sure no one saw her on the way down.

Willow was good like that. She'd always been able to sneak up on her father or Thorne when they weren't looking.

"Good," Nero said and patted the stone bench beside him. "It's time to continue your lessons."

"Yes, Nero."

"Willow," he admonished. "We've talked about this. If Rory is your aunty, then what does that make me?"

"Uncle?"

He nodded.

An unsettled feeling churned in Willow's stomach, and she wasn't sure why. It felt like she should know but couldn't grasp the memory. Her brain hurt. It was as though clouds stuffed her head like cotton wool. She stumbled to the bench and sat beside Uncle Nero, facing the fountain.

Some time ago, the center of this maze had changed. Willow was sure a statue used to live here but couldn't remember what it had looked like. Echoes of a female voice entered her head, reminding her there was another woman she'd spent time in here with.

But what was her name?

A little bird flew down and landed on the water fountain's stone edge.

Dread filled Willow as Nero stood up, walked over to the bird, and wrapped his big hand around its tiny body.

Close your eyes, her secret friend's voice cut through the wool in her mind. *You don't need to see this part.*

When she opened her eyes, Nero placed the limp bird's body on the grass before the fountain and returned to sit next to her. Tears burned Willow's eyes as she suddenly remembered why she hated these lessons. How could she have forgotten?

"Now?" she whispered, already on the edge of her seat.

"Not yet." His hand hovered before her chest, stopping her from leaping forward. "Wait."

Little balls of light popped from the bird's body and

floated into the night sky like stars. Only when the last ball escaped did Nero drop his hand and say, "Now."

With heartache burning in her blood, Willow lurched forward and ran to the dead bird. She gathered its still-warm body and cried over its needless death.

"Please, little bird. Don't die. Please come back."

A taloned foot twitched. Then a wing. Then the bird exploded from her hand and squawked. It pecked her on the finger, drawing blood. It came at her again. And again, like a mindless thing.

"Ow!" she shouted, "Naughty bird. *Stop*."

The bird suddenly tucked in its wings and landed on the grass. But it wasn't dead. It rolled to show her its feathered belly and red eyes and waited. She scowled at it until she was sure it wouldn't peck her again. Then she stroked its belly.

"That's better, birdy. You shouldn't hurt me."

"Good girl," Nero said behind her, jolting her from her concentration. "Now, do it again."

"But..." Willow turned to him, her heart thudding. Her sudden lapse in concentration lost her hold on the bird, and it became feral and wild. It came at her with sharp claws and a savage beak.

Nero calmly walked over while she was attacked and plucked the undead animal from the air. With one flick of his wrist, it became silent again.

"Patience and obedience," Nero said as he placed the bird on the grass. "People keep forgetting we have time on our side. You'll need to pay attention and listen if you're to raise an army of the dead. Now, do it again."

Willow wasn't sure how long she stayed in the garden or how many birds she woke from death, but she returned to her bed tired and drained with Nero's last words cutting through her wooly brain.

"Remember, don't tell Aunty Rory. Or it will be her dead body you wake next."

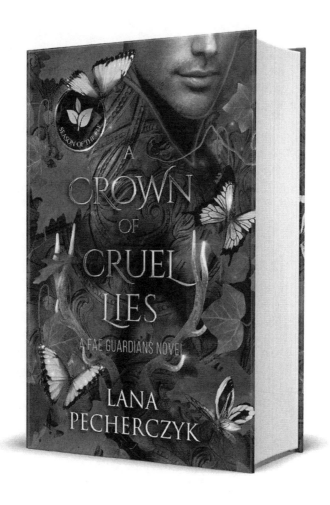

A Crown of Cruel Lies also comes in a hardcover

AFTERWORD

Thank you for reading Aeron's and Trix's story.

As recently diagnosed with ADHD, I wanted to represent by having Trix with the same neurodiverse condition. Sometimes she can be flighty, chaotic, but that's how we roll. To everyone struggling, I wish you all the best in finding peace and understanding.

Acknowledgments

Thank you to my amazing Arc Angels who graciously receive my last-minute manuscript and hunt for the typos that always elude me.

Thank you to the Patrons who support me on Patreon. You all give me an extra layer of confidence and I'm forever grateful.

Thank you to my editor Ann Harth. You always bring the pop to my stories

Thanks to my family and friends who support me. It's been a tough year, but we made it!

NEED TO TALK TO OTHER READERS?

Join Lana's Angels Facebook Group for fun chats, giveaways, and exclusive content. https://www.facebook. com/groups/lanasangels

ALSO BY LANA PECHERCZYK

The Deadly Seven

(Paranormal/Sci-Fi Romance)

The Deadly Seven Box Set Books 1-3

Sinner

Envy

Greed

Wrath

Sloth

Gluttony

Lust

Pride

Despair

Fae Guardians

(Fantasy/Paranormal Romance)

Season of the Wolf Trilogy

The Longing of Lone Wolves

The Solace of Sharp Claws

Of Kisses & Wishes Novella (free for subscribers)

The Dreams of Broken Kings

ABOUT THE AUTHOR

OMG! How do you say my name?

Lana (straight forward enough - Lah-nah) **Pecherczyk** (this is where it gets tricky - Pe-her-chick).

I've been called Lana Price-Check, Lana Pera-Chick-ywack, Lana Pressed-Chicken, Lana Pech...*that girl!* You name it, they said it. So if it's so hard to spell, why on earth would I use this name instead of an easy pen name?

To put it simply, it belonged to my mother. And she was my dream champion.

For most of my life, I've been good at one thing – art. The world around me saw my work, and said I should do more of it, so I did.

But, when at the age of eight, I said I wanted to write stories, and even though we were poor, my mother came home with a blank notebook and a pencil saying I should follow my dreams, no matter where they take me for they will make me happy. I wasn't very good at it, but it didn't matter because I had her support and I liked it.

She died when I was thirteen, and left her four daughters orphaned. Suddenly, I had lost my dream champion, I was split from my youngest two sisters and had no one to talk to about the challenge of life.

So, I wrote in secret. I poured my heart out daily to a diary and sometimes imagined that she would listen. At the end of the day, even if she couldn't hear, writing kept that dream alive.

Eventually, after having my own children (two firecrackers in the guise of little boys) and ignoring my inner voice for too long, I decided to lead by example. How could I teach my children to follow their dreams if I wasn't? I became my own dream champion and the rest is history, here I am.

When I'm not writing the next great action-packed romantic novel, or wrangling the rug rats, or rescuing GI

Joe from the jaws of my Kelpie, I fight evil by moonlight, win love by daylight and never run from a real fight.

I live in Australia, but I'm up for a chat anytime online. Come and find me.

Subscribe & Follow
subscribe.lanapecherczyk.com
lp@lanapecherczyk.com

facebook.com/lanapecherczykauthor

instagram.com/lana_p_author

amazon.com/-/e/B00V2TP0HG

bookbub.com/profile/lana-pecherczyk

tiktok.com/@lanapauthor

goodreads.com/lana_p_author

Made in the USA
Columbia, SC
11 January 2023

10013598R00274